HAVENWOOD

HAVENWOOD

A NOVEL

ERIC SLADE

COPYRIGHT

Eric Slade
eric-slade.com

Publisher's Note: This is a work of fiction. Names, characters, places, and incidents are a product of the author's imagination or are used fictitiously. Locales and public names are used for atmospheric purposes. Any resemblance to actual persons, living or dead, or to businesses, establishments, events, institutions, or locales is completely coincidental.

cover design by Andrei Bat

Havenwood/ Eric Slade. — 1st ed.
ISBN 978-0-9916523-3-4 (pbk)

For my mother, Sharon

And for Seth, who helped me find the Seaming

ONE

1

November 29, 1913
Chattanooga, Tennessee

On the Saturday after Thanksgiving, Tanna Cravens saw a creature from another world bleed to death in the snow.

Her companions, in either their drunkenness or their shock, saw only a dark-skinned child of some vaguely exotic origin. They kept calling it an "Indian."

But it clearly wasn't human.

A large group of them had gone quail hunting up at the Crenshaws' house on Stringer's Ridge. Tanna, Ford Eldridge—the man she believed at the time she was going to marry—his brother Buck, and a dozen or so of their less temperate friends, the ones still in town after the holiday and game to drink their way through New Year's.

The term *quail hunting* was a ridiculous pretense. A more accurate description of their sport would have been *stumbling around loudly with guns.* The young men bellowed collegiate fight songs, their boots crunched across the frozen crust of grass, while hostess Maisie Crenshaw brayed and cackled. Their commotion gave quite an advantage to their prey. Every living thing with wings within a quarter of a mile took flight, shattering the tops of the trees against the sky.

In an affectation of the gilded times, Maisie's servants had set a dining table against a dead honeysuckle hedge. Champagne flutes on silver trays pulled in most of the group, while a few of them settled on shooting empty whiskey bottles off the fence posts nearby.

Ford stood at the head of the table gnawing a cold turkey leg and studying the winter clouds over the city. Maisie steadied herself with a gloved hand on his arm and refilled his glass from a green bottle. With the drumstick, he pointed out a column of dark smoke smudged against the background of lighter gray clouds.

As Tanna walked over toward them, she heard Maisie exclaim softly. "What do you think it is?"

"Well." Ford tossed the bone underhanded, as if skipping a stone across a pond, and sucked grease off his fingers. "Looks to be coming from right down on the river. This side. Straight across from Ross's Landing. A warehouse fire, maybe?"

Maisie gasped in polite feminine shock.

When Ford turned back to the meat platter he saw Tanna standing there behind them. Pomade made his ginger hair dark-gold in all the cold gray surroundings.

"Tanna!" he cried, as if delighted to have only just discovered her presence for the first time that day. He'd either been hanging back, walking far ahead, talking to someone else, or generally allowing himself to be monopolized by Maisie. He smiled for anyone who might witness it, but she saw him glance coolly at the rifle crooked across her arm.

"Oh, Tanna," Maisie gushed, lip rouge on her horsey front teeth. "Did I tell you how *mad* I am for you in this big fur hat? With your cheeks all rosy from the cold, you look like a Russian princess from a fairy tale."

Tanna acknowledged the compliment with a tightening of the lips unlikely to pass for a smile. She mouthed the words "thank you" over a smattering of gunshots and looked off into the distance, waiting for Maisie to grow uncomfortable enough to walk away and leave her alone with the man who was still almost her fiancé.

Over near the brush line along the fence one of the men bellowed, "Hold fire!"

The thunderclap of the last rifle shot. The dropped icicle tinkling of exploding glass. A silence followed. Someone lost his hat jumping the barbed wire fence. There were urgent calls of indeterminate command, and everyone moved on instinct toward a huddle forming near the woods.

Maisie used the disturbance to cut a smooth exit without need for further conversation. Ford wiped his hands and made to follow, frowning in either feigned distraction or concern, trying on the posture of rescue that men like him with money and no meaningful heroic purpose are so eager to assume.

Tanna stopped him by the elbow. "You said you were coming up the mountain for Thanksgiving."

He winced with unconvincing regret. "It was certainly my intention. But something came up." He spread his hands and clasped them back together, illustrating the helpless finality of it all. "How was it?" he asked cheerfully, rocking on his heels.

Her fury at his grin and the empty politeness of the question so consumed her that, for a moment, her face lost all expression. Cheeks flushed, nostrils flared, she spoke in the urgent whisper reserved for rage. "My mother held the dinner for you for *three hours*."

She tossed the rifle over her shoulder, pivoted, and stalked away.

"Tanna, wait!" He came after her, but more slowly than she stomped toward the others.

She pushed into the loose outer knot of the hunting party, now a strangely silent and still tableau. Joshua Alberts, the man who had jumped the fence, crouched over a sprawled body. At first glance it seemed to be a child.

An almost naked child, lying there in the cold, dirty snow.

A small "Indian"—she heard someone use that word—of indeterminate sex, wearing nothing but a loincloth twisted around the tops of its thighs. Its skin was dusky, appearing at once both shiny and powdered. Tanna thought of the inside of a scale of bark broken from a pine tree—brown and gray and rust-colored, all at once. Its limbs were stained with leaf shadows. Its feet had long raised tendons and tocs with claws like a dog. The kneecaps, the elbows, and the clavicles were all knobs and twigs poking out against the fabric of its skin.

The open, staring eyes were solid black, like the eyes of a mouse or a squirrel. The only whites were the glints of light reflecting off the curve of the orbs. Unusually tall ears ended in sharp points with softly serrated edges like flint arrowheads. It was the heavy fringe of black hair in a straight line across the brow that made one think of the haunted faces of Indians in daguerreotypes.

Black fluid leaked from an obvious bullet hole in the creature's chest and spread in an oily pool across the snow. It took a moment for Tanna to process that the blood was not red.

A moment of seizure violently reanimated the lifeless mannequin. They all yelped and fell back, clutching at one another. There was a gurgling sound in the creature's throat, followed by a dark tongue of sludge slipping from its mouth.

Everyone started to murmur, gasp, or speak again all at once. One of the women choked on a horrified sob. The men began to argue.

"Christ. We killed it."

"*You* killed it."

"I didn't kill nothing. I was reloading—"

Tanna was pulled from behind, away from the huddle of observers, and turned by the shoulders.

It was Buck Eldridge, Ford's brother.

She resisted, drawn back to the disturbing sight of the body.

"Come away with me," he said, firmly and softly, his face close to hers. "Let's go. Now."

—

"It could have been either Alberts or Lovejoy that hit it," Buck said, dragging her by the elbow across the frozen field, back in the direction of the Crenshaws' house. "They were both up to take a shot. I saw them. Poor idiots. I'm not sure Alberts has ever killed anything bigger than a squirrel."

Their breath huffed in bright white clouds in time to the brisk march of their feet.

"They called it an *Indian*," Tanna said. "Did you hear that? Every one of them."

Buck shrugged. "They're afraid to say it. Some people just can't bring themselves to talk about elves with a straight face." He certainly didn't sound particularly surprised or troubled—or even sarcastic—about elves.

"Anyone can see with their own eyes what it is. Or what it *isn't*," Tanna said. "And an Indian is still a human being. Did they think that would make it less of a murder?"

Buck released her elbow so he could speak with his hands. "Now, I doubt very seriously either one of them would have shot it on purpose. You can't see the damned things. They blend right in. They have tattoos like twigs and tree branches."

They crunched along without speaking for a few paces. At the field's edge, Buck steered her onto a flagstone path that led toward a copse of trees with a small pond at its center. Whenever they came for gatherings at the Crenshaws' it was a favorite spot to slip off to for some privacy.

"Where do you think it came from?" Tanna asked, her voice quiet with emotion, her gaze trained on the uneven icy steps in front of them.

"No telling. Probably just wandered over. There are openings all over the place around here. A bunch of places on Lookout Mountain. Rock City. Ruby Falls. Cloudland Canyon. Falling Water, too. Chickamauga Creek." He glanced at her sideways. "You've seen one before, haven't you? A fae?"

She met his eyes briefly. "A few times. You know, down at the bottom of the garden." She shifted into the special tone her friends and family had come to recognize as her storytelling voice. There was a smile in it and a sudden rush of secrecy and confession. "When I was nine, my cousin Gayla and I practically lived outside one summer looking for flower fairies. Daddy put up a tent for us over by the roses close to the house and let us sleep out there a few nights. We saw a cloud of sylphs in the moonlight. It looked like a ghost made out of flower petals moving under water. But never anything with a human face. *God.*" She stopped on the path, a pang of delayed despair hitting her. She put her face in her hands, cupping her cheeks and looking out at him between them. "What are they going to do with it? Shouldn't we—I don't know—report it to someone?"

"I don't see that happening. And I'm not sure you'll want to know what they end up doing with it." Buck took her by the shoulders. "Listen. I didn't pull you away because of the dead elf. I was already on my way over. I saw you talking to my brother. I figured you needed to be rescued."

"That bastard," she hissed through clenched teeth.

Buck sighed, grabbed her hand, and led her over to a wooden bench that someone had carved from the side of a fallen tree.

"Oh, Tanna," he chided her. "You didn't really believe he was *finally* going to give you a ring for Christmas this year, did you?"

"I had to believe it." She was insistent, stubborn. "It was my last chance at having any kind of life of my own."

He shook his head at the drama of this statement. "That ain't true."

"No, it is true. My first mistake was not being born a man. And now I'm twenty-eight years old and I've failed to land a husband. It's the plot of a thousand common novels." She stared off into the middle distance, as if able to see some future vision. "The nightmare is that you can see it coming—how common you're about to become—but you can't stop it. And those Jane Austen girls who get their happy endings are still young and pretty and ... *virtuous.*"

"Oh, come now. You're not ... *bad*-looking." He giggled and dodged the fistful of snow she scraped off the tree and flung at him. But at least he'd been successful in breaking the spell of her dark scene before she'd gone too far into it. He composed his features into an expression of sincerity and leaned close to her, forcing her to make eye contact. His blue eyes were like jewels in the winter setting with all its grays and browns. He was every bit as handsome as his brother, but where Ford looked haughty, Buck had a mischievous twinkle. "You could certainly have a profession," he said.

"Ha." She knew he was teasing her about her looks, but the rest of it wasn't a joke. "They won't let me do anything useful. Not of my own choosing. What? Do you see me as a nurse?" She watched him struggle to suppress a grin. She stared at him until he started to squirm. "So, a schoolteacher I guess it is, then?"

"Well, you are charming when you read out loud. And those little spectacles I've seen you wear at your writing desk ... You do look the part. You could be a writer. You could write those silly novels with the happy endings. People love them."

She couldn't sit still. She stood, gloved hands clasped in front of her mouth. "Oh, Buck. I've run out of time. It's too late to make anything out of this life. Here, anyway, with these rules. I just want to go somewhere else and start over."

"Where would you go? Out West?"

"I could go anywhere." She looked around wildly as if there might be signs with possible destinations hung on the bare trees. "Africa. Australia. Into the Bush. Into the Outback. I could go to Alaska." She paused and made eye contact. "You could marry me and we could go into the Green."

His expression was wary. "You can't be serious." He reached into his breast pocket and pulled out an engraved silver flask.

"You said it yourself—there are openings everywhere. Right here. All around us. Gateways into another world." Her brown eyes flashed. "Fairyland."

"I meant the other thing." He took a swig from the flask and grimaced. "The part where I marry you."

"Well, for the money, of course." She tilted her head and pursed her lips at him. "Oh, please, don't look shocked." She snatched the flask from him, tasted the warm bourbon, and, with a moue of disappointment, thrust it back at him. "It's probably not as much as you've already gambled away. And you won't be touching it, if I can help it. But I can share it with you. Thanks to my mother, it's a dowry. I can't have it at all without a husband."

He looked genuinely shocked. "You're serious." His fair cheeks were flushed in a way that made her think of the porcelain Bavarian boy figurine in her mother's curio cabinet.

She sat down on the rough bench again, closer beside him. "Buck, listen to me. You're out of time as well. Everyone knows you've run through every penny that's come your way. Your parents won't have anything to do with you anymore. And Ford's been saying he has no intention of supporting you. No family of means is going to let you anywhere near their daughters. Not with this growing string of servant girls and—"

He held up a finger. "Willing temptresses, I assure you, every one of them."

"Yes, and a calculated distraction from those willing stable boys and rich people's sons," she said, arching an eyebrow.

"I can't believe you even listen to that kind of slander." He straightened his back and smoothed his lapels in a prideful gesture.

"Honestly, I think you're probably every bit as heartless as your brother." She sighed. "But I don't care about your love affairs."

"Why would you ever stoop so low as to align yourself with the likes of me, let alone marry me?"

"Because there's one very important difference between you and Ford." She paused, waiting for him to catch her gaze. "You're actually my friend."

He studied her, obviously skeptical. "You've really been thinking about this," he said. "This is a plan."

Her brown eyes narrowed. "I know you're going to run away. What other option do you have? It's just a matter of weeks—maybe a month or two at best—before I hear that you're gone." She shifted from bullying to pleading. "I can't bear to be left behind. Don't you dare do that to me. All I'm asking is that you take me—and my money—with you." She watched him expectantly. "At least we would've been somewhere. Seen something other than this. Something unusual. Something worth writing about."

He leaned back on the bench, arms crossed, watching the low gray sky with a faraway expression. He pouted for a few moments in silence, and then, as if repeating the sweetest piece of gossip, he whispered, "I've heard they travel by airships there."

—

When they returned to the fork in the flagstone path they saw a splash of bright-orange fire across the gray field. The pillar of smoke hung low and billowed in unusually dark, greasy swells. Tanna thought of the oily look of the elf's green-black blood.

"So, they're just going to burn the body." All her energy and chatter about their future schemes crumpled in sudden despair. "Like it never happened."

"I didn't expect them to send for the sheriff," Buck said. "Or ask the coroner to open an investigation. Not for the likes of that lost, wretched little thing."

"No. It doesn't matter." Tanna sighed. "In the scheme of things, some lives don't matter as much as others. But who decides that? When does it all get decided? I want to have a say."

2

Tanna bought her own emerald engagement ring. She wore it to her mother's Christmas Eve dinner at Blackwood, their home on Lookout Mountain, where she announced to assembled family and friends that she would indeed be marrying an Eldridge after all. Without acknowledging that she had replaced the man who had courted her for three years with his younger brother, she simply introduced her future husband with a toast. Buck half-stood and made a happy little bow to everyone present. Combined with the now-glaring absence of Ford Eldridge, this bold but simple act confirmed Buck's identity as the lucky groom.

Unprepared to respond to such a profound substitution, the guests retreated to basic good manners, out of habit more than sincere intention. They chuckled good-naturedly—maybe uncomfortably—and murmured cheers to the couple. Everyone spent the remainder of the meal trying to not stare at Tanna and Buck, while hoping to surreptitiously catch one another's eye for some crumb of wordless communication. They prayed for a cue as to how they might behave in the aftermath of such a quiet, but potentially scandalous, revelation.

The gossip went more smoothly once they retired to the parlor for coffee and cordials in front of the tree.

Tanna's mother, Dorothy Black Cravens, gave a convincing performance of having known all along that her daughter was engaged to the notorious younger brother of her presumed fiancé, and being just thrilled about it. She did contrive to pull Tanna aside by pretending she needed help finding a gift she'd hidden too well in the study.

Dorothy pulled Tanna into the room behind the door, leaving it open for the sake of appearances. Her perfect hostess's smile dissolved into a face frozen by hushed tones and clenched teeth.

"What has possessed you to choose *that* one?" Her mother's face was pale and her eyes darted in panic.

By *that one*, of course, Dorothy meant the Eldridge brother about whom everyone whispered and implied, with only an arched eyebrow, unspeakable things.

"I've decided at last to release Ford. He has despised and humiliated me for years. I've thrown him back in favor of the one I can stand to be around."

"That one will make you a laughingstock—"

"Ford has already made me look like a fool a hundred times over. I'll never be able to completely control Buck, I know that. But at least, with a little effort on my part, Buck does bend to my will. Because he's happy to do it. He's easier to manage, and he's certainly easier to bear." She frowned. "What do you care? How do the details matter to you?"

"What do you mean? It's not like your choice of a china pattern we're talking about here."

"Isn't it? I think it actually *is* sort of like that."

"What am I supposed to say when people ask me?"

"The only thing you've ever seemed interested in is the Eldridge name and being able to say I've married into that family. So, it's simple, really. Focus on that, and polish the rest up with whatever embellishments you want."

"Well, I certainly don't want my story to contradict what you're going around town telling everyone."

"It won't. I'm not going to be going around town talking to anyone about anything. We won't be here for anyone to scrutinize. We're leaving as soon as we can arrange it. So you can tell it however you want."

They were interrupted by Tanna's Aunt Mona, who came clomping down the hall, calling out and threatening to come find them.

Dorothy smoothed a stray hair back into her bun, worked her smile back up, and went back out to assume her role as mother of the bride.

—

During the Christmas carols, accompanied by Tanna's niece Gracie on piano, Buck turned the singalong into a rousing solo performance. He'd had enough wine and brandy to bring out the roses in his cheeks and his surprisingly big baritone. At some point, all parties were the same for Buck. He wasn't any less inhibited at a family holiday than he would be at a saloon, a church revival, or a brothel. Buck was always himself, in full bloom. It was a quality Tanna had always adored in him as a friend. Now, she did hate to admit what a mortifying feature it might prove to be for a respectable husband.

But Buck was here, at her side, happy and proud to be so. That was more than his brother had ever offered her. Or, for that matter, any other suitor.

When she was still waiting on Ford to propose, her two older sisters, Greer and Larissa, had constantly asked about him with patronizing concern. She'd always hated those little pitying frowns, sitting right on top of the smirks and glances they'd share the minute her back was turned. They'd felt sorry for her, just enough to outweigh the contempt they felt for Ford Eldridge and the way he had strung her along. They thought she didn't have the sense to pick a man she could control.

But now they thought this choice was beyond willful. She'd somehow managed to do what they'd been advising her to do all along, yet in true, stubborn Tanna fashion, she'd taken it too far. Her mother was a willing servant to public opinion, but her sisters no longer seemed bound by society or family loyalty or sisterly affection. Tanna caught them looking at her with open amusement and a faint trace of disgust.

Fortunately, they were distracted by their own broods of wild offspring and the dull husbands they had to drag and direct through every social minute of their lives. The energy required by their matronly authority was the only thing that saved Tanna from open confrontation. She could see withering comments buzzing about their skulls like tiny swarms of insects. She spent the evening always finding the other side of the room and someone else with whom to talk.

Tanna's younger brother, Teddy, slipped up beside her during Buck's intense "O Holy Night" and offered his own protests.

"This one's a bit of an ass, Tanna. There's no getting around it." He sipped a tumbler of whiskey as if he'd been doing so for years.

"Who said you could have that?" Tanna hissed, making an unsuccessful grab at the glass.

"There's whiskey in the eggnog," he whined, showing his age. "What difference does it make?" He self-consciously lowered his voice. "You can't marry this ... *vaudeville* performer."

Teddy was thirteen years old and already speaking to her like every other drunken, arrogant man who assumed his opinion was law over hers. Was it an instinct? Their own father would never have treated her this way, and he'd been dead since soon after Teddy was born. She had to wonder who could have possibly taught him to act like this.

"He's going to reflect poorly on your character," Teddy said, assuming she could be swayed.

Tanna sighed. She turned around and faced him with her back to the room, so it was at least slightly less obvious she was speaking during her fiancé's singing. "I don't expect you to understand this yet. It's taken me long enough to come to the sense of it. I'm no longer basing decisions on love. Especially not decisions about my money. I can't afford to make choices clouded by romantic notions. Or fantasies. I can't afford to wait on fate or Cupid or the gods. Whoever it is that's supposed to have power over my life. I don't think I can afford to believe in any of that anymore. People of real character *make* their lives the way they want them to be. They demand the world show up for them in the form they require. They go out and take it as they want to. They hack it out of the wilderness, prune away the thorns, and stand it in a vase for everyone to see, regardless of who approves. It's all a matter of will. If the gods try to bully you, you shake your fist at them. You simply refuse them. Of course, you can't have everything the way you want it. So you have to give some things up. If you make the hard choices, then they can't be made for you."

"So, you don't love him." Teddy sounded satisfied. "That's not what this is at all."

"That's not why I'm marrying him, no." She glanced over at Buck, wincing a little as he bellowed out a big note. "But I do love him, in a way. A little bit. Enough to marry him."

"Then I give you my blessing," Teddy said, haughtily lifting his chin. "And I will walk you down the aisle."

"Thank you, Teddy," Tanna said, smiling but trying to match his serious tone. "Your blessing means a lot to me."

—

Buck had offered to take away the ring, wrap it up in a velvet box, and bring it back on bended knee. "For the tradition, for the *theater* of the thing," he said.

Tanna didn't trust him not to pawn it or lose it in a card game.

When she told him so, she layered the cruel truth of it with a frosty smile and a twinkle. This kind of banter had long been their private language. In the presence of less capable intellects such honesty would have resulted in war, but there was no romantic passion between them to fuel any real anger.

Her words launched with initial humor and music, fluttered with cleverness, but now they settled around her in a veil of power. With the irony of independence that the engagement afforded her, Tanna's quips were quickly elevated to commands.

Buck restricted his pithy retorts to one token volley—for show, for sport, for the honor of their old game—and then he simply complied with whatever she wished. Her intentions mastered the will of not only house servants and young nieces, but grown men. Strangers. Even, for the first time in her life, her own mother, Dorothy Black Cravens.

Suddenly, as if by some magic or secret prior arrangement, everyone did as Tanna ordered. Because she was a bride-to-be.

She acted with a sense of urgency. She wanted to be sure she changed her life before this spell wore off. A younger version of herself might have been seduced into reconsidering her emigration, now that she seemed to have all that she'd been missing. But she knew this grace was temporary; it would evaporate, and what remained would congeal into a matronly mantle she would wear for the rest of her mortal days. It was the same moth-eaten cloak she'd seen around the shoulders of her mother and her sisters.

The preparations for the wedding were secondary to her. She spent the bulk of her fleeting influence on plotting her escape, which was the primary feature of the *rest of her life*. She did enjoy this ability to manifest her will, but she planned to use it constructively, to build a life where she might rule indefinitely.

The federal government of the United States did not openly acknowledge the existence of another world overlapping their sovereign territory. Neither did the fallen aristocracy of the former Confederacy nor any other element of polite society. Tanna and Buck were engaged in an, if not illegal, then unsanctioned enterprise—the colonizing of their own piece of Fairyland.

Given the secrecy surrounding their intentions, the clandestine arrangements, back-room introductions, inquiries laced with innuendo— not to mention the secondary characters who populated the shadows of questionable commerce and inter-world travel—Buck too found himself, at last, uniquely positioned in the best light of his influence.

Buck revealed himself to be quite good at spending other people's money—especially when it came with an intention. Far from constraining him, Tanna's guidelines and instructions refined him—it focused his inherent abilities; it elevated his less desirable qualities. He was used to employing all his cleverness with an aspect of shame, and now he no longer had to apologize.

Every day, he reported back to her about their progress with unflagging enthusiasm. As happy as she was that Buck excelled at managing a purse with a purpose, it was a hungry one. Those daily meetings always ended with a request for money.

"Darlin, I don't know what else we can do." Buck paced up and down the length of the bookcases in her father's study. Tanna sat behind the desk making notes in her ledger. After her father's death when she was thirteen, she left the formal parlor to her mother and took to using the study as her own day room. Buck usually came in the morning to go over their plans and once again in the early evening. "These people are operating in the shadows, you realize," he continued. "It's not like they're going to give us a line of credit."

"But *that* much? In cash?" She realized she was shouting and lowered her voice. "Who keeps an amount of money like that lying around?"

"Well, if you can think of another option ..." He gestured at the futility of it. "But we're talking about a land purchase here. This is the down payment for our farm."

"We're starting an apothecary," she reminded him. "An apothecary. Not a farm. We've talked about this. It's decided."

"Yes, you decided," he murmured.

"What did you say?" She froze with her pen in the air, staring at him until he looked up. "I decided because it's my money."

He gave a false laugh and bounded across the room, chuckling. "I was only teasing. We talked about it so much, of course it was decided. I was just making light. It was a bad joke. Don't look at me like that."

She sighed, releasing some of the anger. "Then why do you keep calling it a farm? We need a house, a small factory or distillery, which we will likely have to build a few years into—"

"They have chunks of land parceled out," Buck interrupted. "Homesteads. Already existing estates. All of them have vast acreage for cultivating crops. And we will be growing medicinal plants, so we'll need *some* land."

"We need a very small patch to grow those specialized ingredients we can't cheaply source. But is that going to require a farm? How many acres are these estates?"

"A couple thousand," he said, shoving his fists in his pockets.

"A few *thousand*? That's a plantation. We'll have to hire someone to manage it."

"There are a lot of overseers for hire."

She made a disgusted sound. "Are we going back in time?"

He shrugged with his hands still in his pockets, looking like an uncomfortable little boy. "Look. If you go to the bakery and buy a loaf of bread, you might point to the one you want. But you don't ask for them to slice off two-thirds and keep the rest and charge you a different price. We put the money down, upfront, and when we get there, they'll show us an option of several properties and we pick one."

"Well," she finally said. "Obviously, I'm going to have to go to the bank to get it out." He looked relieved to have convinced her. "That's a sackful of bills. We're going to look like a couple of bank robbers from a picture show."

This was all currently coming out of her personal account. She wasn't sure how much she had left in there, if she could cover the purchase of their estate and still have enough left over to hold them until the wedding. As much as she loathed the thought of it, she needed to ask her mother about releasing the dowry money early.

—

"No, I will not," said Dorothy Black Cravens, blowing primly on a spoonful of soup.

Tanna had sent Buck away before dinner so she could ask her mother without him there. Since the engagement, he had taken to staying for meals after their meetings. Her mother despised having him there, but she felt obligated to extend an invitation to her future son-in-law.

Tanna's mouth hung open in shock. She looked for solidarity in the only other person in the room, her brother Teddy, but he was intently slurping potato and cream and pretending not to pay attention.

"No?" Tanna repeated. "Just no?"

Dorothy ignored her. "Teddy, stop making so much noise while you're eating."

"What difference is a few weeks going to make?" Tanna asked. "It's for the purchase of our home as a married couple."

"But you're not married yet," Dorothy said with infuriating politeness, reaching for her iced tea.

"It's mine," Tanna said. All attempts to ingratiate herself and to choose her words carefully were gone. "It's my money. It's Daddy's money that he left for me. And he never would have attached these stipulations—this dowry—without your talking him into it."

"No, I doubt he would have ever accomplished anything so practical," Dorothy said dryly. "But I don't know why you think being hateful to me is going to do anyone a bit of good. There's nothing we can do about it now. Even if I wanted to, I can't change wills and laws. Now, I will happily go to the lawyer's or the bank—or wherever I need to go—the first business day after your wedding, and I will release those funds into a joint account in both your names. Until then," she paused and lifted her spoon again, "you will have to wait. Because it's not yours. Not yet."

Tanna stood, clenched her teeth to keep from screaming, and threw her napkin on the table. She glared at the top of her mother's head, who continued eating as if she were alone at the table. Teddy paused, wiped his mouth, and glanced up at her with a stricken expression.

Tanna shook her head for her little brother's benefit and then left the dining room without a word.

—

When Tanna emptied her personal account the following day, she requested that she be allowed to complete the transaction in the bank manager's office. An acquaintance of her late father, he was happy to oblige. She left Buck waiting in the lobby.

She was right; they did hand her a conspicuous canvas bag filled with bound stacks of bills. She asked for a piece of plain paper, wrapped up half the money, put it in the bottom of her carpetbag, and covered the lump with a scarf. The remainder she folded in on itself to make the bag as small as possible and tucked it under her arm.

Buck took it from her and squeezed it, a puckish gleam in his eye.

"I have a stipulation," Tanna said. "You're taking me with you to make these big purchases. I want to be there for the final negotiations for the property and for the crossing voyage. I want to learn as much as I can about what we're getting into."

"You may not like everything you're going to find out."

"Now you've only convinced me that I have to attend."

"Promise me you'll let me do the talking," Buck whined.

"We'll see," she said, patting his face, "maybe some of it."

3

Buck brought Tanna along on one of his last meetings with Major Calvin Gray, also known as the Graycoat, the guide they had hired to transport them and their belongings through a portal into the Green.

Tanna could tell from Buck's obvious excitement that whatever petty thrills he had found in cards and horse races paled in comparison to a game with stakes this high. As he progressed through the list of information he had been dispatched to find, and the sometimes unusual resources he had been requested to acquire for their venture, some of the realities that emerged were not only mortally dangerous but also philosophically disturbing.

With each new discovery he reported to her, she saw a boyish, feral flash in his eyes. The more deliciously uncivilized the details were to him, the more he felt he should filter them for her.

She grew weary of trying to convince him she did not need nor desire this kind of protection from the truth. At the foot of Lookout Mountain, once Buck had negotiated the last of the curves and steered the horses onto the relatively straight shot of Broad Street headed toward downtown, she confronted him about whatever it was he was keeping from her.

"I'm not going to faint if you confess some petty illegal procurement to me. What exactly is it you think I'm going to be so afraid of?"

"I'm afraid—" Buck started, and then stopped with a sigh. He glanced over at her, then stared straight ahead at the street, preparing himself to say it out loud. "The only thing I truly fear is that you might change your mind. That I'll cross some line or introduce some unsavory character to you—like this Graycoat individual we're going to see—or you'll get wind of some of the harsh truths about this place we're going to and you'll say, *No more.* You'll back out. And I have come to really want this. The further we go into it, the more excited I become. When you first mentioned it, I wasn't sure if you were just talking. Trying out something provocative. But you were right. The more I discover about this place, the more it feels like a new life. Like it's meant to be." He finished with an uncomfortable chuckle. "Destiny, I suppose."

She turned toward him on the seat of the wagon. "But I feel the same. Of course I do. Nothing's changed for me. I'm not going to back out. My excitement has only grown as well. This is a great adventure. The opportunity to start over, to shed our failures, to free ourselves of this stupid, suffocating society." She let her contempt hang in the air for a moment. "Are you trying to be careful with me because I'm a woman? That's the very thing I most want to escape."

"It's not that you're a woman, Tanna. It's that you're a ... snob. You're a *lady*." He kept one hand on the reins and held up the other to stop her before she exploded in protests. "I know, I know. That's not how you see yourself. That's not who you want to be or how you want to live your life. And I think you're going to get the chance to change all that. Once we're there. But up to this point, you've been a rich girl of privilege. This is hardly a honeymoon tour of Europe we're planning."

She chose to let that comment pass. She didn't want the conversation to get sidetracked; she wanted an answer. "What is it exactly you think I'll find so objectionable that I'll want to back out? Just tell me."

"Well, it's inevitable that you're going to find out. And it's better that you have an opportunity to make the decision with your eyes open ..."

Her voice became shrill with impatience. "What is it?"

He pulled up the reins and they stopped at an intersection; a line of wagons rolled by, piled high with lumber. He took the opportunity to face her and to lean in close in that earnest way he only did in the most serious of circumstances. She was struck by how much his eyes were like his brother's, how inhumanly pale blue they were.

In the low, steady voice reserved for the worst news, he said, "Time runs differently there. There's a lag."

"A what?" she asked. She really did simply need it repeated.

"A lapse in time. A time difference. Between this world and that one." He watched her face so closely that, to a bystander, it would have looked like he was going to kiss her, but in that moment he was trying to read her mind.

"What does that mean?" Tanna asked, pulling back a bit and looking at him sideways.

"Time runs more slowly there than it does here."

"And?"

He tossed his hands up in exasperation. "It's Rip Van Winkle, Tanna."

"Buck, what are you babbling—?"

"When we come back—if we ever return—everybody we know and love will be old. Maybe even dead and gone."

The traffic passed. He flicked the reins and they were moving again.

Tanna stared at the dirty edge of the curb, at the scattered blades of grass that had managed to take root in that inhospitable place. If she allowed her eyes to blur, it looked like a tiny river of green light streaming past.

"By how much?" she finally asked. "How much more slowly does time pass there?"

Buck shrugged. "Nobody will give me an exact ratio. They say it depends on the total duration of time spent—"

"But generally," Tanna interrupted. "One year here is roughly ...?"

"Roughly, they tell me it's about nine years." He winced. "Maybe ten."

"Why are you looking at me as if I'm supposed to be distressed about this?"

"Tanna. If we go into the Green for, let's say, two years, and then we decide we want to return, twenty years will have passed here in this world."

He waited, watching for the comprehension to shift her gaze.

"It means," he continued, "that if we go away for any significant amount of time, say ten years, and then decide to come back, a century could have passed. People that we know and love—our families—will be gone. Our friends will all have gotten old, while we're still young."

She chuckled. "That doesn't seem so terrible. When I'm thirty-five years old and Maisie Crenshaw will be a ninety-five-year-old crone."

He held up a warning finger. "Ah, yes, a genie's wish. It doesn't sound so bad when you first consider it. But everybody I talk to, everybody who's been there and come back, is haunted by this. They say it's like coming back as a ghost. A lot of the people who emigrate are presumed dead. They return to find their own tombstones worn by decades of rain. Of course, there are no bodies in the grave. But imagine that. They all say it—*imagine it*. That it really is like your past life is gone."

"Which is exactly what we want."

"Is it? If you're OK with it. I just needed to make sure you understood. That you've thought deeply about this aspect of leaving and what it might mean. It could mean forever."

"You do realize," Tanna said, looking pointedly at him, "that the marriage part is supposed to be forever."

Buck let the comment pass. "We might not be able to come back."

She shrugged. "Then we just won't come back."

—

They didn't speak for a while, but as they approached the warehouses along the river Tanna said, "So, this soldier, the one they call the Confederate ..."

"The Graycoat," he corrected her.

"He's the one who's been talking to you about this lost time?"

"He's one of them. But everybody who's been into the Green has mentioned it."

"It's true, then. It's not just a myth. About the Graycoat, I mean. He's still young?"

"Well, he's not exactly young. And I wouldn't doubt if his stories were a bit exaggerated in a few areas. But, yes, the part about his age certainly seems to be true. Assuming he hasn't concocted the entire thing. He just doesn't strike me as much of a storyteller."

Buck repeated the tales she had heard her entire life. In November 1863, while hiding in a cave above Cravens House during the battle for Lookout Mountain—the Battle Above the Clouds—Sergeant Calvin Gray became separated from his men. He was declared missing in action and presumed dead. He was thirty-three years old.

He claimed he followed an underground stream through a tunnel of rock and emerged in an unfamiliar territory. Another world, where he stayed for what he understood to be a little over three years. He emerged twenty miles north of his last known position and thirty-seven years later.

In 1900, a man walked out of the woods beside Chickamauga Creek at the foot of Mowbray Mountain, wearing a faded Confederate cap and tattered coat, skin sun-browned darker than an Indian. He appeared to be in his late thirties, maybe early forties, but with the old-fashioned mutton chops and mustache of an older generation. He approached a group of young people picnicking on the boulders above the swimming holes. He introduced himself as Major Calvin Gray, announced that he'd been away with fairies, and asked if he could get a ride into town.

"Major?" Tanna said. "I thought you said he was a sergeant?"

"Apparently, with no one around to protest, he decided to promote himself," Buck said.

After several turns through a maze of gravel streets and mud puddles, between soot-stained brick buildings that all looked alike, Buck pulled the wagon up to a stop in front of a building with no windows and a double set of barn doors large enough to drive the wagon through.

"He knew what had happened to him, though?" Tanna asked, when Buck came to help her down from the bench. "Where he'd been?"

"Oh, absolutely. He wasted no time turning it into a business enterprise, guiding people into what he calls 'New California, the Last Great American Frontier.' Here, give me that—" Buck yanked the rolled-up canvas sack of money from under her arm, and before she could protest he opened her carpetbag, shoved the money in, and closed it. "I don't want you walking around down here with your life savings out for everybody to see." He barely glanced inside, and certainly didn't seem to notice what else was in there.

Buck gave the bag back to her and took her elbow to help her navigate the mud. "He's been doing this for almost fifteen years," he said, continuing his story in a low voice. "And no matter who you ask in this town, all rumors about the other world lead to him."

Buck pulled the barn door back enough to let her slip through, but she stopped and turned to him.

"You believe him, though?" she whispered. "You trust him?"

"Well." Buck's mouth twisted. "Those are two different things. I do believe he's been where he says he's been and he knows the way. If he's not delivering these people into the Green then he's taking them out into the woods and killing them. No bodies have turned up so far."

He had not been able to provoke a reaction from her about the time difference, but now he grinned in satisfaction at the quick trace of shock on her face.

"I'm teasing you," he said. "If anybody will get us there, the Graycoat will. You'll understand when you meet him."

4

The Graycoat reminded Tanna of her grandfather on her father's side, a tobacco farmer from North Carolina. She thought also of her great-uncle Caleb, a forty-niner, who loved to tell stories of his journey out West during the Gold Rush. Something about the Graycoat's voice, his inflection, the antiquated expressions that seemed to roll so genuinely off his tongue. It all did immediately connect with the ancient men she had known from that era. It was a bit like traveling back in time. Surely this is what they had looked like in their prime. The Graycoat was a living tintype, flushed with color and noise, animated with brash movement and life.

She despised him on sight.

He was the roughest sort of character—sly-looking and villainous, somewhere between a beggar and a petty crook, the type of man one crossed the street to avoid. He reminded Tanna of an evil leprechaun—he was small in stature, with wiry limbs, bent over with a crooked spine that only enhanced the feeling that he was inhumanly small. His gray-streaked red hair hung in long, greasy tendrils, and a wild beard the color of new pennies exploded from his face and obscured his cheeks, mouth, chin, and neck. He seemed to be wearing the very coat for which he was named—a shabby old Confederate dress overcoat of heavy wool, moth-eaten, ragged, stained, bald at its edges. He smelled exactly as one would expect him to by looking at him—soured clothes, unwashed skin, tobacco, whiskey, and something Tanna could only, unfortunately, identify as the scent of urine.

She could find nothing remotely redeeming about this individual. She couldn't imagine that this—this dirty, mean little man—was the fairy godfather of her new life.

The Graycoat was hard to understand when he spoke. He muttered or mumbled everything, without making eye contact or directly facing the person to whom he was speaking. Tanna could barely see his lips moving because of his beard, and his accent was so thick she understood barely half of what he said. With the permanent scowl he wore, reading his facial expressions was useless.

The Graycoat merely grunted when Buck introduced Tanna as his fiancée and then turned and stalked off, clearly intending for them to follow.

He led them through his operation, essentially a cavernous warehouse down on the banks of the Tennessee River, west of where it curved past town. Buck had been coming down here for weeks, amassing their provisions, managing deliveries of the household items Tanna had been purchasing from mail-order catalogues. Everything had to end up at this location, where Buck oversaw the organization and packing. The workmen who crawled through the maze of trunks obviously knew Buck and liked him. They waved and called out to him. He slapped a few of them on the back and cracked jokes in their ears as they pushed past.

These were sweaty laborers who reeked of liquor and spat tobacco. Tanna tried to maintain an impassive, pleasant facial expression while keeping the hem of her skirt lifted a few inches off the floor. One worker was shoveling sawdust into the full crates before the lids were nailed down. When the Graycoat passed by, trailing Tanna and Buck, he dropped the shovel with a clang and began to follow them.

Tanna kept discretely glancing back at him while appearing to be taking in their surroundings. He was different than the others, a slender boy in a newsy cap, overalls, and boots. He had big brown eyes and a frightened expression. He seemed to be awaiting orders from the Graycoat.

When they stopped walking, Tanna turned and smiled at the boy. He stared at her in open adoration.

"See the way these here have been wrapped?" the Graycoat was asking Buck. He pointed to a pyramid of crates. Each wooden box, regardless of size or shape, had been bound with wire, like gift packages tied with twine. "You've gotta go through every single thing and make sure it's got the wards on it."

"Wards?" Tanna asked.

The Graycoat ignored her, but paused for Buck to explain.

"Warding spells," Buck said. "It's just the presence of iron."

Tanna frowned, prompting him to explain further.

"The iron is poisonous to them. They don't like it. It smells bad. It makes them sick. It keeps them away from our belongings."

"Most of the crates just need some simple wire," the Graycoat continued, "but the more valuable stuff, in the leather steamer trunks—see those right there?—those need the iron chains."

"Do they not need locks on them?" Buck asked.

"Nah," the Graycoat drawled. "The chains are the locks. And you—" He suddenly jabbed a finger in Tanna's direction. "Got to fix all the lady's clothes."

Tanna realized he was pointing past her, speaking to the boy.

Again, Buck jumped in to explain. "All your personal luggage will have to be gone over in a similar fashion. Your clothes, too. Eyelets, buttons, hooks. The nails in the soles of your boots. Anything. Jewelry, hatpins. Anywhere you can put the iron wards on your clothing."

Tanna scowled. "So, I'm going to go waltzing into Fairyland studded with the stench of metal and dripping poisonous ear bobs?"

The Graycoat gave a contemptuous snort and spat a nasty brown stream of tobacco on the floor.

"It's for your protection," Buck insisted. "Without it, they might swarm you. Tear you to pieces or spirit you off into the underbrush before anybody looked up and realized where you'd gone. Humans, women in particular, disappear into the Green all the time, without a trace. Even from this world."

"It sounds ... *vulgar* to me for some reason." Tanna folded her arms and hugged her elbows. "I don't want all my clothes manhandled. No offense to your boy, but things do tear easily, especially around the closures. And you could have told me sooner. It'll take hours—no, probably days—to make all those alterations."

"This here's my girl Holly." The Graycoat was pointing at the boy. "She knows all the spells. She sews. She'll get it done."

Tanna's eyes widened as she looked at him—at *her*—at Holly. On closer examination, the slim features and soft skin were indeed revealed to be decidedly feminine, although her skinny body was well-disguised by the baggy work shirt and overalls.

"Ma'am," Holly mumbled, and dipped in an awkward partial curtsy that only a girl would have attempted—a young, untrained servant girl, or a farmhand's daughter who had no exposure to etiquette.

Holly's gracelessness embarrassed Tanna—she was mortified for this poor thing, working here among all these crude men—but she managed to quickly mask her agony with dignity, for both their sakes.

"Miss Gray," she said, inclining her head and smiling warmly at the wretched creature.

Holly had a hard time holding her direct gaze, but Tanna noticed, out of the corner of her eye, that the girl continued to study her with an open-mouthed expression of wonder.

"Well, what about jewelry made from precious metals?" Tanna asked, addressing Holly directly, wanting to draw her out. "What about gold or silver?"

Holly took a breath and opened her mouth to answer, but the Graycoat spoke over her. "Gold, now that's a whole damn other story. Silver, too. Valuable to the brownies, to the wild folk, same as anybody. Maybe more so. They don't even care if it's real. They like anything that sparkles or shines. Seems they like the fake stuff even better. Glass is good. Tinsel. Mirrors. Broken mirrors, even. They don't care. If it sparkles, you bring it."

Tanna insisted on Holly's having an opportunity to speak. She began to mimic the Graycoat, in a way, by ignoring him as he did her and addressing only those whom she wished to acknowledge. "I'm sure you're every bit as knowledgeable about these details as your father," she said to Holly. "I hope you'll advise me about what I should pack. I'd hate to get there and realize I'd left something important at home. I'm sure your help will save me a lot of grief. I'll be depending on you."

"She better make herself useful," the Graycoat groused.

"You can count on me, ma'am," Holly stammered, but she did manage to smile. Tanna was glad to see she had a lovely smile, full lips, dimples. The girl just needed someone to bring it out and give her a bit of confidence to share her virtues more freely.

"Well, I figure, if nothing else, it'll be better for your wife to have another female with her in the dirigible," the Graycoat said to Buck.

Buck nodded thoughtfully.

Tanna put her hand on Buck's arm to get his attention. "Dirigible?" she asked in a low voice.

"That's the airship," Buck said, as if only just realizing he'd forgotten to tell her one of the most delightful parts. "Isn't that fantastic? It's easier for them to drag the larger cargo across. It's safer for the passengers too. Won't that be a grand way to start this adventure? It'll be like you're sailing on a cloud."

"What about Ginger? How am I supposed to take her?"

Buck winced with regret, obviously unwilling to say what she was thinking.

Tanna's voice became shrill. "I can't leave her, Buck. She's my baby."

He placed his hands on her shoulders, closed his eyes slowly, and sighed. "I think, just for now, this first trip in, getting settled and everything, you may have to consider—"

"No," Tanna wailed. "I can't abandon my baby."

"Don't matter none to me," the Graycoat muttered, annoyed with Tanna's display of emotion. "She and Holly are the only ones that'll have to listen to a kid bawling."

"Wait a minute," Tanna said to Buck. "Holly and I are the only ones on the airship? Where will you be?"

"I'd planned to discuss all the details with you at home," Buck said in a low voice. "We'll need me to go on ahead, by a separate route. It's faster on foot."

"Oh," Tanna exhaled, relieved. "I suppose you can take Ginger with you, then."

"Well, now, I will need to stay at a hotel for a few days once I'm there," Buck explained. "I don't know that it's practical for me to try to care for her in temporary lodgings. They may not even allow it."

"Aw," the Graycoat grumbled. "Let her take the baby."

"No no no no, sir," Buck turned to address him. "She's not talking about a real child. She's talking about her dog."

"Oh, then, hell no," the Graycoat said immediately, shaking his head. "Absolutely not. You ain't taking no dog on my balloon. That's days up in there, without touching the ground. It'll be pissing and shitting all over the cabin."

"I don't understand why you won't take her with you," Tanna continued. "You'd really force me to leave her behind? How could you even suggest that?"

"You're right, you're right," Buck said, trying to end the conversation. "I wasn't thinking. We'll discuss all this later. Between *us*." He clenched his teeth and growled slightly on the last word, begging her to let it be for the moment.

"Fine," Tanna said, lips tight. "We'll discuss it at home."

The Graycoat scowled at both of them and jabbed a finger back the way they'd come. "We'll go settle the payment in my office."

The Graycoat's office was a tiny box fitted into the front corner of the building near the oversized doors. There were walls of normal height, but the ceiling was open to the cavernous interior of the warehouse. One wall had paned windows, allowing the Graycoat to oversee all the activity taking place inside his domain. A large cluttered desk took up most of the space, with cubbyholes and shelves on all sides bursting with what appeared to be untidy stacks of invoices, rolls of blueprints, and anonymous brown paper sacks.

The space was too small to admit them all—there was just enough room for a wooden swivel chair, into which the Graycoat lowered himself with a grunt. Buck followed him inside but remained standing, the only other chair in the room piled high with a teetering tower of cardboard boxes.

Tanna was left outside the door. Buck looked back at her and shrugged apologetically. Holly Gray stood nearby, still watching her, sipping from a canteen.

Tanna pushed Buck to the side a few inches and called out over his shoulder to the Graycoat. "You'll bring all our things up the mountain, then?" He didn't seem to have heard her, so she repeated her question, more loudly, allowing some of her annoyance to show. "You'll bring our things up the mountain to Blackwood, to my mother's home? Once the packing is complete? Major Gray?"

The Graycoat did not answer. It was obvious he was willfully ignoring her. She could see his beard move as he muttered to himself, but she couldn't hear what he was saying under his breath. Probably cursing her, no doubt.

"I don't think you could, um, hear her," Buck said, diplomatically. "My fiancée was asking about our possessions being transported to the crossing site. She—we—actually were under the impression that we'd be embarking from one of the locations up on Lookout Mountain. Possibly Cloudland?"

"Up the mountain?" The Graycoat blew out his lips in disgust. "My boys are about to ferry all this across the river and haul it up to the launch at Chickamauga Creek."

"I thought there were caves close to Blackwood," Tanna said. "Caves up above Cravens House?" She hissed in Buck's ear. "Isn't he the one who discovered those caves?"

The Graycoat took a pouch of tobacco from his desk drawer and unfolded it. "Big hauls have got to come and go up past the Blue Holes." He proffered the tobacco to Buck, who declined with a polite hand gesture. "Through the gorge right up there about twenty miles north of town, between Falling Water and Mowbray Mountain. Not only is it the only passage big enough for the balloons, but the geography ain't as simple as you think. Twenty miles over here ain't twenty miles over there. It could be a hunnerd. And the land ain't even recognizable. You want to get to the colony around Treebridge, don't you?"

"Yes," Buck said. "I'll need to stay at Treebridge while I look at available properties."

"Well, the quickest—and safest—way is through Chickamauga Gorge. I can take you right to it. As soon as you pay me."

Buck turned to Tanna and silently mouthed, *Let me handle this.*

She started to say something, but he glared at her and furiously shook his head. "Darlin, can I get our payment, please?" he asked with showy false brightness.

Tanna dug the canvas sack from the top of her bag and shoved it at him.

"Why don't you wait over there and get to know Miss Gray while we men settle up?" Buck said, all but shooing her from the office door.

"What—" Tanna started, but he cut her off.

"I won't be but a minute," he said in his loud stage voice.

Staring daggers, Tanna backed away a few steps from the door. She stood close to Holly, but watched Buck through the office windows.

Buck placed the canvas sack on the desk. The Graycoat peered inside, then stuck his hand in and seemed to be counting the stacks. Satisfied, he stashed the money somewhere behind his desk that Tanna couldn't see. He produced a small, rolled brown paper parcel, similar in size and shape to his tobacco pouch. Buck quickly took the package and, without looking at it, slipped it into the breast pocket of his jacket.

Buck emerged and motioned to her they were leaving. He turned back to the office and asked the Graycoat, "When do we need to meet you up at the gorge, then?"

"The lady needs to be up there and ready to go in three days. Tuesday. And you better get there early. We leave at daybreak."

—

Holly Gray followed them to the wagon, and, to Tanna's surprise, she climbed into the back.

As Buck helped her up onto the bench, Tanna pitched her voice low. "She's coming with us *now*?"

"You heard the list of what we need to bring. She can help you prepare, pack all your personal things. Not to mention she can add the iron wards to your clothing."

"I suppose these magic spells she knows will also make it all happen in record time," Tanna muttered. Buck settled beside her and picked up the reins. "Three days, Buck?"

"The Graycoat doesn't like to stay here any longer than he has to. He wants to get back in the Green. He's not going to wait for us."

"Then find someone else who can take us on our own timetable."

"There is no one else. Not anybody who can get us to Treebridge in one piece, with all that cargo, without getting us lost or killed. We're lucky we approached him when we did. It could be at least a year before he makes another trip."

"This means we need to get married in two days. And on a Monday. That's an awfully odd day for a wedding, don't you think?"

Buck winced. "I've spoken to Pastor Robert and he's agreed to conduct the ceremony at the end of the Sunday services tomorrow."

Tanna's head snapped around, her mouth open in objection, but too caught off guard to form words.

Buck rushed on. "You said you didn't care about all that perfect wedding stuff. The ceremony, the theater, the big spectacle of it all."

Tanna crossed her arms and looked away, watching the maze of dirty warehouses and gravel paths give way to the proper streets around the Read House Hotel.

Buck waited for her to say something on her own. "You said you didn't care about all that," he repeated.

She shrugged. "It's not as though I ever expected any romance here."

"We talked about the practicality of simply getting it done so we can access our funds."

"Exactly," Tanna smiled. "Purely practical. Anything more is unnecessary."

"Well, that's what I thought we'd talked about all along. But now you look disappointed. Like you're in a huff, but trying to hide it."

"I guess I just wasn't prepared to hear that it was going to be *tomorrow*."

"It has to be tomorrow, Tanna. You're leaving in three days. And I'm leaving in two."

She looked over her shoulder in the direction of Holly Gray at the back of the wagon. She imagined that, to an observer, the girl in the shabby boy's clothes must look like a laborer they had hired in town and were now driving home. In a way, it was almost true.

"Why do you need to go before me?" Tanna asked. "I'm not convinced."

"Besides the fact that I need to find a place for us to live? Do you want to be wandering about for days with nowhere to stow your possessions? We have no idea what passes for a hotel over there. I could end up camping under a canvas tarp beside a tree somewhere. I'm sorry, but I can't see you, Tanna, sleepless and trembling beside the embers of a dying campfire, beneath a damp, scratchy horse blanket, clutching your valuables to your breast. There you are, under a naked sky, with only the smell of iron in your skirt hems and your blood to hold off the evil fairy hoards darting and swooping overhead."

"All right, all right." She shuddered. "God, Buck."

He cackled at the effect of his cruel humor.

"But what difference is one day going to make?"

"The time gap, Tanna!" His voice became shrill, needling. "You're leaving only a day after me. With the length of time you'll be en route on the dirigible, I may only have a day or two there on my own as a head start. If I'm lucky. I'm not certain how much time will have past."

She shook her head, annoyed. "I wasn't thinking about that. But I don't know how I could have forgotten it. It's one of the most far-fetched things I've ever heard."

"The Graycoat's men, the haul teams that work for him, going back and forth, dragging the dirigibles through. The airships. As I understand it, they have three dirigibles, but only two of them can handle weighted freight, the other is simply for passengers and not used as often. They'll need to take two teams through the crossing, both freight dirigibles, just for our cargo. I've proposed to go early, with all the provisions necessary for the farm and any heavier items for the house, and to go on foot, camping with the first haul team. That will leave another team behind to pull a big passenger blimp with you, riding in stately comfort, and all the household items you're bringing bumping along behind it under a little caboose balloon. And you and I both know you'll want to keep an eye on all your things."

She sighed. "True. You know me well. But why didn't you tell me any of this? Why can't you ever warn me?"

"I didn't want to worry you with details. I was taking care of it. I was just trying to spare your feelings."

"Then you're doing a terrible job of it. You're not sparing me any kind of feelings at all. If anything, you're making it worse because you wait and then I either find out about it last minute, or you spring it on me and it feels like an ugly surprise."

"I'm sorry. I'm not good at delivering bad news."

"It's just news, Buck. It's not good or bad. But it's my news as much as it's yours. I'm not a child. I'm not weak. I'm fully capable of responding to whatever comes up."

"I promise you, I've never thought of you as weak."

"Then stop taking away my choices. Usurping my power." She regretted the overly dramatic choice of words, even as she heard them coming out of her mouth. "I don't want you to reveal another decision you've made that I've had no chance to veto or reverse or even append, let alone weigh in on. Give me some warning to work with so I at least feel like I have a say in what's happening to me. And to my money." She muttered the last few words and turned to watch the broken edge of the road.

Buck had an infuriating way of diffusing her ire by never getting the slightest bit angry himself. At some point, he would apologize, ingratiate himself, and eventually wear her down. He always managed it.

After passing the Incline Station at the foot of the mountain, he urged the horses onto the last few switchback miles. They rode in silence for a while, until Tanna broached another subject. "So, what was it he gave you?"

"Excuse me?" Buck said, frowning.

"The Graycoat. In his office, just before we left. He handed you some packet of tobacco or something."

"Oh that!" Buck laughed. "It's just a sample. A medicinal flower that's native to the Green. Very profitable. I've been advised we might want to plant some for use in our apothecary."

"What is it? Like a poppy?"

"Something like that. More like some kind of coneflower, by the looks of it. It's called haint. The colonists call it shine. They make a tonic with it called tarwater."

"Why was the Graycoat giving it to you now?"

"I expressed an interest in obtaining some, partly for seeds, of course, considering our business venture. I was warned that a new colonist, just arrived in the Green, asking for shine, would be easily exploited. Some snake oil salesman on the street would likely charge me a small fortune, give me an inferior specimen or a minuscule amount. I'd be none the wiser, and the crook would be laughing behind my back."

Tanna arched an eyebrow. "How do you know the Graycoat's not laughing at you right now?"

"You met him, darlin. Can you honestly imagine him laughing about anything?" He glanced over his shoulder, as if wary Holly might overhear him. "I don't think that man has smiled since Buchanan was president."

She brought up the issue of Ginger again. She couldn't understand why, if he was crossing on foot, he couldn't take the dog with him.

"First of all, she doesn't care for me much, and you know it. But the bigger issue is I have no idea where I'll be staying. Probably a hotel, but you never know, some of the other plantation owners might invite me to stay once I've been introduced around. I just don't want to be dragging along a dog the size of a small horse who wants to get away from me and go looking for you. I know how much she means to you, so I can't take the chance on being the one who loses her. Can you imagine if she breaks away from me and goes running off into some foreign land? You wouldn't be able to look at me again without bursting into tears, and I'd never be able to forgive myself for losing something so dear to you. Please don't ask me to do that. Don't put me in that position. We can always come back for her once we're settled. Or send for her and have somebody bring her."

"What, a stranger? Or have her put in a crate and dragged over in a hot air balloon?"

"For now, let her stay with Teddy and your mama. He loves her, he knows her, she'll be cared for."

Tanna wasn't convinced. She let the subject drop, for the moment, but she continued silently considering some option or strategy. She thought she'd ask Holly Gray about it later; maybe she would think of something.

By the time they rolled into the circular drive in front of Blackwood, she was exhausted from Buck's convincing her his opinions were all justified. She dropped her head back and sighed. "I understand why you need to go first. Of course I do. And I know I'll have to accept other arrangements regarding Ginger. I just didn't want to be traveling alone."

"You won't be alone," Buck said. "You'll have the Graycoat's daughter."

As if on cue, Holly sprang down from the wagon and landed on the gravel with a crunch.

5

Sometime during the past weeks of planning and preparations, Buck had been overheard mentioning that the couple was bound for the Graycoat's "New California." He had probably originally said it in irony to someone who knew the legend. Whatever the rumor's origin, others repeated just "California" back to Tanna. She let the presumption stand uncorrected. The misinformation saved them from defending a radical emigration story in which, quite frankly, most people would not have believed.

Dorothy Black Cravens—who over the past month had absorbed a nearly constant stream of plans in the form of her daughter's thinking out loud—shared just "California" to anyone who asked. Whether she mistakenly heard her daughter was moving there or she had willfully chosen to ignore the truth, Tanna couldn't say. The pretense—if that's what it was—seemed to be the easiest escape from questions and potential resistance.

Over the years, Dorothy's aggravation with her willful daughter had increased by not-so-subtle increments. With every passing season, Tanna had failed to find an acceptable husband. The struggle between them had existed since Tanna was sixteen years old; in twelve long years, it had grown into a weary burden for both of them. This hurried engagement had produced a brief but bright respite. For a few weeks in and around the holidays, Dorothy Black Cravens had acknowledged Tanna's entrances and exits with warm exchanges, almost entirely free of unspoken disappointments. Dorothy chattered eagerly to friends and family of Tanna's engagement to "an Eldridge," and throughout the day, her usual put-upon instructions and martyred demands were now peppered with terms of endearment, like *child* or *dear*.

For a while it seemed that God had switched Dorothy's script with one intended for the kind of mother Tanna had dreamed of having as a young girl. More than anything, the uniqueness of Dorothy's parcels of affection and approval was faintly disturbing to Tanna—as if her mother were suddenly recovered from a near-fatal fit or fevered illness, or she had been kidnapped by devils in the night and replaced with an impostor only Tanna could detect.

A changeling mother. This time, for some mysterious reason, instead of an infant, the fairies had stolen an old woman and replaced her with one of their enchanted substitutes.

Tanna shuddered at the thought of it.

Dorothy never questioned the presence of Holly Gray in her daughter's bedroom at Blackwood. She was a servant, and servants were invisible. One afternoon after retrieving a book from upstairs, Dorothy had stopped in Tanna's door to remark on the chaos of the trunks and suitcases and clothes draped everywhere.

"My goodness, Tanna, this is a job." She cast her gaze around the room but never so much as acknowledged Holly. "I don't know how you're ever going to finish in time to leave on Monday."

It reminded Tanna of how everyone had seen an "Indian" that day on Stringer's Ridge. She thought there must be people, human or fae, all over this world, with a special magic for blending into the background, going unseen by those who simply didn't want to see things that challenged their reality.

Holly certainly wasn't offended by it. She was mortally shy. She froze in place and gaped in terror until Dorothy Black Cravens left the room in a swirl of faint disapproval.

Although her hair was chopped like a boy's and she wore men's work shirts, pants, and boots, Holly soon revealed herself to be more similar to other girls her age than not. Once they were alone together in Tanna's bedroom and she became more comfortable, Holly revealed herself to be every bit as talkative as Tanna's nieces Gracie and Shannon.

As she worked on the alterations to Tanna's clothes—sewing tiny iron fishing line weights into the hems—she twittered away, tentatively at first and soon giving way to bolder, open conversation. Like Gracie and Shannon, she was curious about boys, men, and romance.

"I know I'm supposed to like them," Holly said, looking visibly pained. "I'm supposed to want to let them ... *catch* me, I guess. But I just don't want to. Those men down at the warehouse, and the ones on the haul team, try to grope me. I just haul off and punch them. They laugh about it, but they leave me alone."

"Is that why you wear boy's clothes?" Tanna asked.

"Nah." Holly made a face like she smelled something foul. "I can't stand dresses. And I don't how you can wear ... *this.*" She picked up a brassiere, shuddered, and let it drop back onto a pile of undergarments.

"So, if I were to offer you one of my skirts ..." Tanna prompted.

"No, thank you," Holly blurted. "Ma'am," she added when she realized she might have sounded rude. "It's nice of you to offer."

But some of Holly's questions were blunt, inappropriate, and physically graphic.

Tanna found herself blushing, trying to honestly answer questions about male anatomy. Exasperated, she finally said, "Aren't these the kinds of things you should be asking your mother?"

Tanna regretted it as soon as it came out of her mouth. Holly grew quiet, withdrawn, obviously uncomfortable.

"I'm so sorry—" Tanna began.

"No, it's OK." Holly shrugged. "I don't have one."

Tanna waited for the girl to say more.

"Anyway," Holly said, carefully ripping apart a seam. "Did you ever really want to ask *her* these kinds of questions?" She inclined her head toward the door, where Dorothy had stood a few minutes before.

Tanna laughed. A single bark of sound. "No. Most certainly not."

"I'd rather ask somebody like you," Holly said. "You're different from other women."

"Oh," Tanna said. "In what way?"

"I can ask you whatever and you never look shocked."

Tanna rolled her eyes a little, but she was privately pleased by the compliment.

—

Unlike their mother, Teddy was immediately curious about Holly Gray.

He had knocked on Tanna's door a few hours after she and Buck had returned with Holly. "Who is that?"

The girl was kneeling on the floor beside Tanna's bed, allowing Ginger to lick her in the face. The large, shaggy deerhound had never warmed to Buck, only grudgingly allowing him to pet her for the sake of Tanna's feelings. But she immediately loved Holly.

Tanna moved out into the hall with her brother, shutting the door on Holly and Ginger and leaning against it. "It's a girl."

"I know it's a girl," Teddy said. "I saw her."

Tanna was a little surprised he hadn't mistaken Holly for a boy. "What business is it of yours?"

"I'm the man of this house," he said, lifting his chin. "Who is she, and what's she doing here?"

"Her name is Holly Gray. *Miss* Gray." Tanna put her hands on her hips and brought her face toward his, so close he had to lean back uncomfortably. "She works for me."

"Doing what?"

Tanna had already prepared an explanation in the hours since Holly arrived. "Miss Gray is acting as my lady's companion for the journey."

Teddy sneered and made a rude noise. "She's dressed like a field hand."

"Yes, well, she could probably clobber you with one hand. So you can either be nice to her or leave her alone."

"I just asked who she was," he said, looking chastened and offended.

Before he walked off, Tanna stopped him with a change in tone. "Teddy, wait. I need to ask a favor. It's important."

She explained to him—vaguely—about being unable to take Ginger with her. She made up a story about a first-class sleeper car on the train and restrictions about traveling with live animals. Teddy never quite let on whether or not he believed the misinformation about where she and Buck were headed.

"Why can't *he* take her?" Teddy rarely spoke Buck's name.

Tanna told him, more truthfully, she didn't trust Buck not to lose Ginger.

"Will you take care of her for me? Just until I can come back for her?" Her pleading was entirely genuine. "The servants will feed her and Mama will take her on walks, but there's nobody else I can rely on to love her. Hey! Maybe if it works out with your break from school, you could even bring her to me yourself."

"If Mama'll let me," Teddy said. The flash of excitement in his eyes betrayed his knowledge of where they were really going. His own future adventures in the Green became part of the negotiation.

"I'll write to her when the time comes and insist you be allowed to visit," Tanna promised.

"OK," Teddy said.

"Just promise me we won't have to talk about it anymore. I'm afraid I'll collapse at the last moment if she tries to follow me or barks as I'm climbing into the wagon. When I go, you quietly hold her by the collar and comfort her. I need to be able to walk away quickly."

Teddy nodded, turning away as his own big brown eyes welled up with tears.

"And the same goes for you," she called to his back as he fled down the hall. "You know I'm terrible at goodbyes."

—

January 4, 1914

That Sunday, after morning services at St. Paul's Episcopal Church, Tanna Sophia Cravens became Mrs. Buck Elliott Eldridge.

Teddy walked Tanna down the aisle, almost comically solemn in his role. There were murmurs in the pews—the bittersweet image touched those in the congregation who had known their father. Dorothy Black Cravens stood erect and dignified, pressing the pointed corner of a handkerchief to either side of her nose. Out of the corner of her eye, Tanna saw this pantomime of tears. With a flash of bitterness, she wondered if her mother teared up because the role traditionally demanded it of her, or if she grieved for her daughter's choice of husbands and the imminent, unconventional future toward which she was headed.

Ford was there—Tanna had noted the back of his head next to Maisie Crenshaw's ostentatious hat. She imagined his pompous smirk. She had been relieved to know that Joshua Alberts was going to stand up for Buck as best man. Her niece Shannon had been thrilled by the last-minute nomination to be her maid of honor. She took Tanna's bouquet from her as if it were a live bird. When Tanna caught Buck's eye, she saw he was suppressing a grin. It was the kind of moment they would dissect later over a few glasses of bourbon, cigarettes, and a fit of giggles. She looked away immediately, focusing on Pastor Robert's calm, benevolent authority.

Anyone who saw Tanna and Buck together would have mistaken their camaraderie for love. They were together in a way that made others feel excluded in their presence. They seemed to be always tittering over some private joke or communicating volumes of meaning by sending pointed looks and silly facial expressions over the heads of everyone else. If they had more physically resembled one another at all, a stranger passing them on the sidewalk or dining at a nearby table in a restaurant might have assumed they were brother and sister. But they were clearly some other type of enigmatic pair. Tanna was willow-thin, with brown hair that tended to curl in humid weather. She had the pointed angular features and fashionable slouch of a young, glamorous witch. Buck was short, muscular, with flushed skin, ice-blue eyes, and floppy blond hair. It was their superior cruel wit and arrogant sense of humor that most truly bound them together.

When Pastor Robert presented them to the congregation as husband and wife, the look of affection that passed between them was genuine enough. The kiss was sweet and familiar enough. The women in the pews sighed. Both the unattached and the married saw a woman who now had not only a husband, but a husband who was her friend.

Tanna was, at last, sufficiently envied.

There was a time—all those years ago when she was about the age of Holly Gray or her nieces—when she would have wanted other women to look at her as the bride of Ford Eldridge and to envy her. But now that this moment had finally arrived, it was only a small part of a nearly ungraspable, absurd reality, one more item on a long list of requirements she had to complete in her race to leave this world behind.

As Tanna and Buck left the church, nodding to well-wishers on either side of the aisle, no one could have guessed the thought that most consumed her in that moment, the thing about her new life and the new world to which she was headed that she could not wait to implement.

Chafing in her lace, she silently vowed that when she got to her farm in the Green, she was going to wear pants. Every day.

—

There was no reception in the fellowship hall. No dinner. No party.

Those who attended church that day specifically for Tanna and Buck's wedding understood the couple had an upcoming journey and tight train schedules to consider. Of course, this was a common-enough lie—one they had not initiated, but allowed to spread.

When they left the church, Buck immediately drove her home to Blackwood.

"Do you want me to carry you over this threshold?" He helped her down out of the buggy. "Or should we wait until we have the other?"

Tanna waved it away as unnecessary, silly. "This isn't our home, anyway."

The moment of their goodbye was awkward. Unsure of how best to fill it, they both hurried it along. They played it down. There was a peck, at first meant for the cheek, but then settled on the lips. The kiss was a little long, or maybe not long enough. Regardless of the swift legal shift in their titles, the reality of their relationship was the same—they were friends, and they would meet again soon.

Tanna had nagged him all the way up the mountain, going over last-minute instructions. There was nothing left to say, nothing they hadn't argued about for hours.

Buck took up the reins and gave her a final jaunty little wave.

But in that moment of his leaving, she could not shake the feeling she might possibly be looking at his face for the last time. It crossed her mind she should commit this moment to memory in case it was to be elevated in the near future to the Last Time I Saw My Husband Before He Disappeared into Fairyland.

She looked up at the eaves and gables of Blackwood, the house where she had lived her whole life. She breathed a near-silent goodbye, in case when the time came and she was rushing to leave, she didn't get another chance to do it properly. Not to mention, in the moment, she would instinctively protect herself by hurrying it along, by turning and leaving with a final jaunty little wave of her own.

Over the next few days, she found herself repeating the ritual in different rooms. Saying goodbye to the view from her bedroom window; to a portrait of her father over the mantel in the study; to the garden, falling steeply away down the mountain ... She would not be here to see it bloom again.

These waves of sentimentality had taken her completely by surprise. She had never been one to enjoy grief or to romanticize mourning. If anything, she put it away for what it was, with an emotionless efficiency that made her feel unshakeable. Tanna did not like to cry at the sad endings of novels or plays. It made her faintly angry at the authors who could so easily manipulate her, either with an irrepressible streak of cruelty or creativity or both.

These authors inspired her to work this emotional magic on others. She could make her nieces weep with after-dinner stories of lost and loyal family dogs. Their bodies would be clenched in agony for an hour as she dragged them through forests of missing children; into towers with kidnapped princesses, unrequited in love, awaiting rescue. Until, finally, she released them with the dog's happy bark as it came bounding from the underbrush to be reunited with its master; incarcerated maidens discovered by princes; enchanted beauties awakened by kisses; or, more darkly, every once in a while, the ghost of a lover who died tragically before the wedding and returned with a message from the beyond.

She realized in these final hours that the voice—the tale spinner—was with her, watching these scenes as if she were a character in one of her own dark romances. She was conscious that her own life might become material for future fireside tales in the Green. If she made the kind of friends who would want to hear them.

She shook herself and packed the moments away with all her other possessions.

—

Upstairs, Holly helped her out of the wedding dress.

"Are you nervous?" Holly asked. "You know, about the wedding night?"

Tanna's brow creased in confusion. "Why would I be?"

"You know ...," Holly said, wagging her eyebrows.

"Oh," Tanna said, belting a silk dressing gown around her waist. "No. Hardly. He's gone." She began to move about the room, closing up her suitcases and trunks. "This—" she inclined her head toward the still-unfinished packing, "*this* is my wedding night."

"Do you want me to bring this with us?" Holly said, holding up the wedding dress. "I could fix it up later, add some of the wards while we're in the dirigible."

"No," Tanna said, reaching to take the dress from Holly. "I think we'll leave it." She hung it in the empty cedar-lined wardrobe, said another of her silent goodbyes, and shut the door.

6

January 6, 1914

It looked like they were headed for a place where clouds were stored until they were released into the sky.

A heavy fog rolled out of the gorge and crept down the wide, tumbled rock bed of Chickamauga Creek. Holly pointed it out as their final destination. They had watched the shredded mist from miles away as the wagon carried them north and out of town.

High up on their left above Red Bank, a few miles to the west, Signal Mountain rose out of the mist like a gargantuan wave of stone, perpetually frozen before it could crest and roll. Along the brow of the mountain's cliff face, the glass windows of houses winked with the rising sun. This mountain was really the edge of the Cumberland Plateau, a ridge of rock stretching from northern Alabama all the way to Pennsylvania. Here in the valley of the Tennessee River it appeared as a solid wall parallel to their journey north, as far as the eye could see. The wall was broken only by the cleft of the gorge and its great, white, smoky bank of clouds.

—

In her mind's eye, Tanna kept seeing flashes of Ginger's long face, her lolling tongue, seeming to smile, excited by the infectious bustle of leaving. Only Teddy and a few of the servants had been up at that early hour—her mother was still in bed, having said her farewell the night before when she had gone up after dinner. Teddy had done his best to soothe Ginger, but he couldn't muzzle the barks. Tanna had turned away quickly, as she had promised she would, motioning for Holly to hurry and jump on the wagon as well.

"Let's go," Tanna kept saying to the driver. "Let's go."

But it still took interminable seconds for the laden wagon to gain enough momentum to finally pull away from Blackwood. All the while, Ginger barked with rising hysteria. She knew she was being left behind.

And although Tanna had accepted leaving her for now, she refused to act out a scene of goodbye. Even in her own mind.

Now, every time the thought occurred, she shook the feeling away, swallowed past the tightness in her throat, and gazed at the mountains northwest of the city, lighting up with the rising sun.

—

Tanna had been eager to see the dirigible since the moment it was first mentioned to her. Until she could at least lay eyes on this mysterious vessel, she couldn't fully accept the reality of traveling by airship into Fairyland. She expected to see something like an enormous Fabergé egg nestled in the pillow of fog along the creek, slowly fed by loud, intermittent rushes of dragon's breath. She'd seen hot air balloons at fairs, like ornaments from a giant's Christmas tree, caged by a net of ropes, anchored to the ground with a basket, weighted with burlap bags of sand.

The wagon turned west, then north, and finally west again onto the final stretch of Montlake Road running along the north side of the creek. It looked as if they were driving straight into the deep cleft cut into the mountain wall. As soon as the frothing waters cleared the steep, wooded walls of the gorge, the creek bed spread out wide, broad, and flat, shallow enough to ford. Here beside the level part of the road, before it began its steep climb up Mowbray Mountain, it was mostly a river of stones and small, spindly trees. The water rushed beneath the layer of rocks, visible only as winks in the morning light, or a sparkle of icy crust.

The wagon pulled off and stopped at the last flat stretch of shallows. As they climbed down from the wagon, Tanna could hear the hiss of the white water spilling out of the gorge. She still saw no sign of an airship, a balloon, a blimp ...

On the opposite side of the creek were cliffs of sandstone and granite boulders, most of them the size of wagons, some as big as small houses. The rocks were covered in splotches of green and gray lichen, like the spotted shoulders or flanks of some enormous stone leopards diving and wrestling in the crust of the earth. They broke and tumbled across time so slowly that the motion was imperceptible to the human eye. At the top of the boulders, the ground flattened out into a shelf of dirt carpeted with copper-brown needles. Behind a line of pine trees were a small team of mules and a dozen lanky, scraggly men standing along a path leading up the south side of the gorge.

A crude wooden watchtower had been built among the trees. At first glance, from their angle on the ground, the spindly boards of the tower were almost hidden among the branches. It wasn't clear if this was a scaffold meant to hold up the thin, gnarled forms of the pines or if the rickety, man-made structure was supported by the trees. Each floor of the tower was a simple horizontal plank, with a dozen feet of ladder inclined steeply to the next level. The rough boards and ladders switchbacked up the center like the hooks and laces of a boot. The tower terminated in a flat platform of graying planks, a simple decking with no railing, curled at the edges by years of weather and sun. It only just cleared the topmost branches, which stretched out like giant, spindly hands as if to lift the platform from below or catch it should it collapse.

"This is where Papa first came back through," Holly said, as if to explain something at which Tanna might be staring. It didn't answer even one of the questions trying to form in her mind.

"I don't understand. Where's the balloon? Or the dirigible or whatever it is?"

Holly pointed a few hundred yards downstream of the tower, to an area they had driven past on their approach. The morning fog had risen from the creek bed in a snake of mist and hovered as a low cloud bank along the treetops. Through a break in the clouds, Tanna saw a strangely colored patch of sky. As she stared, her sense of proportion, depth, and distance adjusted to the vision. The low discolored bit of sky was merely a glimpse of what must be a giant object hovering above the creek. Along with the bleached color of its material, the scale of the airship's balloon envelope had rendered it almost invisible.

At first, Tanna couldn't see it because it resembled nothing she'd ever seen before. She didn't know how to look for it. It was exotic to any frame of reference, to any human vehicle she had ever encountered, even in books, photographs, or illustrations. Even if there had been no mist steaming from the icy creek, no low-hanging clouds, the airship was large enough to block out the sky.

As she watched, she noticed it was drifting, slowly emerging from the mist. The curved edge peeking out of the fog suggested a lozenge-shaped craft whose width spanned the entire creek bed. The belly of the balloon fit the size and shape of the gorge.

Looking up at the dirigible was like standing underwater on the bottom of a narrow canal and seeing the hull of a boat passing overhead. There were striped graphic lines, perpendicular to a central ridge, like the rib cage of a dinosaur, or ... as she stared, the form resolved itself into something more like a colossal leaf, dried and curled in on itself to form a seamless pod. The envelope was faintly translucent, as most leaves tend to be, darkly veined and bleached a non-color. It could have been canvas, raw silk, or a skin like vellum or parchment, but more than anything the material resembled paper. Plant material that had once been verdant, now dead and bleached by the sun to the color of dried grass, stone, or bone.

In a field of dead wheat or tall winter grass, the balloon's color might have allowed it to disappear, but against the gray sky, it glowed like a golden oriental lamp.

—

Looking back up at the tower, Tanna watched the silhouettes of two men unfold from the crisscross lines of ladders lacing up the center of the structure, crawl through an opening in the platform, and walk toward its edge. They leaned out toward the dirigible, then rocked back onto the platform, like fishermen hauling in nets. She could just make out the thin cables they used to pull the craft toward the tower platform. They wrapped the ropes around a wheel of some sort and were now reeling in the craft at considerable speed. Its yellowed hulk slid farther out of the fog and soundlessly slipped over them, casting a long shadow on the ground.

"We have to climb up there to board that thing," Tanna muttered. It was a defeated realization more than a question, but Holly answered her anyway.

"Yes, ma'am." The girl smiled at her with an apologetic wince. "You afraid of heights?"

"I'm not afraid of heights," Tanna said. "But I hate ladders."

"That's as low as they can bring her to keep her clear of all the branches."

Tanna shielded her eyes, scanning the rickety contraption and the sad winter trees. She finally gave a bark of mirthless laughter. Shaking her head, she looked down and lifted the sides of her full skirt, heavy with the iron wards Holly had sewn inside the hem. She spread it wide across her lap and then let it drop.

"I wonder if you might have an extra pair of pants I can borrow?"

—

She changed in the bushes as they unloaded the wagon, transferring the boxes and trunks onto a wooden pallet elevated a few inches above the water on a bed of stones in the middle of the creek. She wondered how they would ever maneuver that load up to the level of the tower, and she was grateful it wasn't her job.

Holly waited with Tanna's personal luggage piled at her feet—a train case, a suitcase, a picnic basket, and a canvas duffel bag stuffed to the size and weight of a small child. "If you can handle your case, I think I can get the other two and then come back down for the suitcase."

"Climbing that with both of those? And two trips? Are you sure?"

Holly shrugged. "I've been up and down those ladders more times than I can count." She watched Tanna staring up at the tower. "You know, you don't have to carry anything. I can go up and down multiple times. The men can help."

"No, no. I can surely do the small case."

—

She followed Holly across the creek from stepping-stone to stone. The girl went in front of her with the duffel bag slung down her back, the picnic basket over one elbow, the suitcase in the other hand. They scrambled up the small bluff between the larger boulders, grabbing on to laurel branches and pine tree roots. It was a good climbing test, and she felt liberated by the pants. She would have been a blundering fool stumbling over her own skirts. Tanna found she could grasp the handle of the relatively lightweight case with her left hand and still wrap a few fingers around a handhold, leaving her dominant right hand free to pull the majority of her weight.

Even still, nothing could have prepared her for the ladders.

"You don't have to carry anything," Holly reminded her.

Tanna insisted she could manage.

Holly suggested Tanna go first and she would follow. "If you need to rest or use both hands, lay against the ladders with the case between your body and the rungs. If you have to, drop it. Let it fall. It's all clothes, there's nothing inside that can break. I'll come back for it."

Tanna was sickened by the way the rungs bounced. She closed her eyes once and was sure she could detect the entire tower swaying. The sensation did not seem noticeable with her eyes open. She hesitated before navigating the plank between the first ladder and the second, which required her to change direction and swing out into space.

Her heart started hammering so hard she could feel her pulse in her temples. She looked up to count how many more times she had to perform that maneuver—was it five or six?—but this proved almost worse than looking down.

She put her right hand on the rung just above eye level and placed the handle of her bag against it with her left. She could still comfortably grip with both hands, as long as she remembered to lead with her right. She focused on the rung itself, studying the grain of the wood, the worn edge where hundreds of hands and feet had gone before her. She counted silently to slow and steady her breathing.

She went up the next expanse of ladder fairly quickly, then paused to negotiate the turn, resting each time, breathing, talking to herself. When she started up the third ladder, she felt vibrations in the structure as Holly followed.

She did well until she reached the final ladder—the sixth—and briefly glanced up, anticipating what was to happen when she reached the platform. Two male faces watched her, peering down through the square frame of the opening in the deck. One motioned for her to come up; he said something she couldn't quite catch, but the tone was one of encouragement. Watching the men, she again detected the faint side-to-side rocking motion of the entire tower.

And that's when she froze.

Her right thigh started to shake violently, thumping against a rung. Her teeth chattered. She vibrated all over. The thought of moving any part of her body an inch in any direction ... It was impossible. She knew if she moved she would fall.

She managed to look up briefly at the men and shake her head the tiniest bit. There was a lurch, and the ladder shuddered as a pair of boots came toward her. First, he took hold of her train case and told her to let it go. He went back up a few rungs, handed it through to his companion, and then came back down, partially crawling over her.

She could smell his sweat and feel his breath on the back of her neck. She would have been mortified by the intimate contact if she hadn't been so frightened. Considering the circumstances, she didn't want him to move; he was anchoring her to the ladder.

He positioned his arms beneath hers so they supported her. Softly, as if quieting a panicked horse, he explained to her that he wanted her to climb, right hand, then left.

"I got you. I'm right here. You move first, I'll follow. You can't fall."

She nodded, unable to speak. But she did as he said, and within seconds he had her at the top. The ladder did not extend beyond the platform; it just ended. She gripped the decking with both hands and wondered how she was going to pull herself through the opening. The man behind her shouted something unintelligible to his companion at the top. Before she could ask what she should do, she felt a strain in both shoulders as she was grasped under the arms from above and hauled up like a child. She was simultaneously pushed from below, sitting on her rescuer's shoulder.

There was a nauseating moment of weightlessness, like at the top of a swing, and she was set on the platform. She collapsed at once into a sitting position, breathing hard, grabbing the handle of her case as if it would save her from falling. The golden balloon of the dirigible occupied the entire sky.

"Oh my God. Oh my God," she muttered. She wanted to say thank you, but the only thing that came out of her mouth were prayers and curses.

"You all right?" One of the men grinned down at her—she wasn't sure which one. "Don't like heights?"

"I don't like *ladders*," she snapped.

—

The men took the other pieces of luggage from Holly, and the girl pushed herself up like a swimmer climbing out of a pool. She had managed it all in one trip. The men returned to the ropes, turned the wheel a few times, and the floating behemoth nudged a few feet closer. Something resembling a small train car was bearing down on the platform, threatening to scrape them all off the tower.

Holly squatted low and grabbed hold of an iron rail on the near end of the car. "Here!" she yelled over her shoulder. "Help me anchor the gondola." When she stopped the front of the vessel, the momentum of its tail caused it to angle sharply, briefly presenting one side to them. Tanna saw the word *Queen* painted in flaking gold script on its side. The name continued in a few other words she didn't catch before Holly and the men brought it back in alignment with the tower platform. They tied it off like a boat to a dock, where it rocked slowly with the motion of the wind, knocking and faintly scraping against the wood of the tower platform.

"Come on," Holly said, grabbing up the duffel bag and extending her hand to Tanna. "No sense waiting. Get on." She unlatched a gate in the car's railing and swung it open.

Tanna grabbed her case and, half-crouching on wobbly legs, lurched to the railing and grabbed it. The dirigible jumped under her hands like a whale threatening to pull her into the sea. Holly pushed her from behind, and with two quick steps and a duck of the head to clear the low doorway, they were across the car's small porch and standing inside. There was a moment or two of sickening bouncing as the floating craft adjusted to their weight.

The interior of the "gondola"—the word Holly used for the passenger car attached to the underside of the dirigible's balloon—had been designed in an attempt at opulence. The richness of the décor might have been convincing thirty or forty years ago, but now it evinced the shabby antique quality of antebellum parlors in old downtown hotels like the Read House or the Grand.

Tanna remembered a gypsy car at a carnival where a woman with kohl-rimmed eyes, a head scarf, and a thick (although questionably authentic) Russian accent had read her cousin Gayla's palm for a nickel. (The babushka had predicted that Gayla would marry for love and have seven children. She did not mention the weight that Gayla would gain with each pregnancy or the great quantities of moonshine her husband would be known to consume.) The gondola recalled a stateroom on a steamboat or a first-class sleeper car on a train. The walls were paneled in an old-fashioned cherry-stained wood. The window shades were the same yellowed parchment color as the dirigible's fabric, trimmed in gold tassels and fringe. The green floral carpet runner was worn to a soft lichen gray in a strip down the car's center. The cushions were upholstered in cranberry and gold brocade. The ceiling was covered in a button-tufted sky-blue silk, drooping in one corner around a browning water stain.

Crinkling her nose at the musty smell, Tanna put her case down on a built-in couch along the wall beneath the windows. She pulled back a shade and peeked outside. The cloud bank was still low and thick; the entire world had disappeared into blinding whiteness. She saw winks and sparkles in the fog, which she assumed were the result of a faint lightheadedness from either the altitude or the floating motion. After she walked up and down the car a few times, the sensation became pleasant. The tension of all the weeks of preparation, packing, traveling—not to mention that harrowing climb up the tower—began to melt away.

She sat on the couch and sighed. She thought it might be the single-

largest exhalation of breath in her lifetime. She was finally here, on an
airship bound for Fairyland.

7

When the fog lifted, she watched the team on the ground affix a smaller cargo dirigible to the pallet laden with her possessions. This simple craft was inflated much like a hot air balloon and raised to the level of the dirigible. It was attached to both a long cable from the ground and to a short line at the end of the larger dirigible.

Airship was an appropriate term for the vessel—the creaking of ropes, the soft swaying, the gentle up-and-down motion when one of them walked. The speed was no greater than the rate of mules on any steep unpaved track, but the ride was the smoothest form of travel she could imagine.

Some of the windows had no glass, only wooden shutters with louvered panels. It seemed the choice was either a freezing view, less windy but hardly less cold, or closed and dark. There really wasn't much to see beyond the persistent fog. Above and out toward the middle distance there were only layers of grays and a variety of vapors created by the intersection of sky and water—cloud, mist, fog.

The smaller cargo vessel followed behind like a baby elephant holding its mother's tail in its trunk, occasionally bumping against the main craft with a hollow thump. Below, there was nothing but the thick ropes slanting away and the occasional taller treetop poking up out of the fog. The tips of leafless branches scratched the bottom of the cabin like bony fingers, while the pines and cedars brushed by with a slithery caress. From even farther below and ahead were the faint shuffling sounds of the mules' hooves over the rocky path, the jingle of metal chain, the hardware on harnesses. Every now and then a snatch of human voices reached them.

"Isn't there some kind of brazier that might keep us from freezing to death?" Tanna asked through clenched teeth.

"No, ma'am." Holly huddled closer to her on the bench, heaping furs and blankets around them both. "Any kind of flame's too dangerous. With the gas in the balloon and all. But it'll only be cold for a few more hours."

"How can you predict that?"

"It should be spring when we cross into the Green. Spring at least. They time the trips as best they can, based on the seasons when they last came back."

"It will just go from winter to spring, all at once?"

"Probably. When we cross over."

"How long is the journey before we reach the crossing?"

"A few hours. Most of the day. Starting in the morning like this, we should cross as the sun's going down."

"Will we ... feel anything? Is it noticeable?"

Holly scrunched her nose in a regretful smile. "Some folks do get pretty dizzy. Especially on a first journey. It always storms really hard. You hear people talk about feeling mazy. I've never been on the ocean, but I've heard Papa say it's like being seasick. It passes, though."

Hard as it was to fathom, Tanna chose to believe there was unseasonable warmth on the horizon. It allowed her to sit up from the cocoon of blankets. "So, what can we do to amuse ourselves? Other than sewing metal pellets into the rest of my clothes."

Holly suggested cards. She said card games were serious business in the clubs at Treebridge.

"Wonderful," Tanna muttered. "Buck will feel right at home."

By the time she arrived in Treebridge, Buck would have been on his own in Cumberland Colony for a few days. He would happily sleep on the floor of a drinking companion's room and put the money saved down on a card table instead. She hoped the stacks of bills she'd given him had already been safely invested in their house, with as little left over as possible. She reached into her train case and squeezed the second secret bundle of cash.

Holly produced a worn, faintly damp deck of cards from a cabinet in the wall. She spent fifteen minutes showing Tanna how to play a childish game called "Wipple" and then the better part of the morning on something a bit more complex, along the lines of bridge, called "Pass and Parry."

At midday, Holly pulled the picnic basket from a storage compartment beneath the bench cushions. They lunched on the food Geneva had packed for them that morning in the kitchen at Blackwood—cold fried chicken, biscuits, and a jar of sweet tea. There were additional provisions for later in the journey—hard salami, apples, cheese, honey, and even a few bottles of wine. Holly's eyes widened when she sniffed the jar of moonshine.

"Don't look shocked," Tanna said. "Geneva has a brother whose stills are legendary. There are several cases packed in sawdust and straw in a trunk back there with the household belongings. I hope they survive the trip. I thought they might serve us as a form of currency."

The gondola—Holly said it was also called a *nacelle*—was just long enough to allow a person to stretch her legs. Tanna could pace up and down from a sort of bay window seat in the rounded triangular prow of the cabin, with its booth benches on either side of a small table. The surface folded down from the wall and hung from a ceiling cable by a hook and an eyelet bored in its edge. As she moved toward the back of the car, she squeezed through a narrow hallway defined by two sleeping berths on either side, each with two bunks stacked on top of each other; past a water closet on the left, which was balanced by a sort of wardrobe or storage pantry on the right; and finally to the door that opened onto the small, iron-railed platform. Once they had boarded and the gate had been closed and latched in place, it became a sort of tiny widow's walk, like the caboose of a train.

Turning around, she briefly investigated the interior of the water closet. It contained a simple removable porcelain chamber pot dropped into a hole cut into a wooden bench. It was held in place by its own rim. The tiny space also featured a hanging rubber bladder with a clamp that released a stream of water into a smaller basin mounted on the wall.

"*Queen* of what?" Tanna asked, sitting back down beside Holly.

"Ma'am?" Holly looked confused.

"This airship is called the *Queen* of something. I saw it painted on the side. What's its name?"

"*Queen of Clouds*." Holly smiled.

"Of course." Tanna pulled aside the closest shade to look out the window again.

A quick peek toward the south on the port side of the craft revealed the same near-endless vacuum of white fog. It was disappointing to be up this high with so little view. They were traveling directly west, dragged on slowly by the men and mules several hundred yards farther up the gorge trail that paralleled the creek. A gentle breeze pushed them out to the end of their tether, and they drifted toward the southern rim of the gorge. Tanna could just make out the dark silhouettes of tall pines. Sometimes a branch appeared out of the mists, close enough to brush against the *Queen of Clouds*.

The lower end of Chickamauga Creek Gorge, an area of deep pools of water called the Blue Holes, was a popular spot for swimmers. Tanna had been up the gorge as a day-tripper on dozens of occasions. Having peered up into this gorge many times from a distance, she thought the way forward should be narrowing. They had traveled for hours upstream; at this point, the walls of rock and forest should be closing in around them. But each time she looked out to orient herself and ponder their progress, the cliff edges—which had been close enough to reach out and touch at lunchtime—were now incomprehensibly farther away.

For a moment, she had a fleeting sense that the gorge hadn't grown at all but their vessel had shrunk to the size of a toy.

She shared this vision with Holly, who nodded as if she'd heard something similar before or felt it herself. "We're getting close to the crossing." The girl looked out at the evaporating fog, pointing out the shreds of higher clouds blushed pink and gold by the setting sun. "It won't be long now. The men want to be through by nightfall."

"Why is that?"

"They don't want to camp outside in winter when they can sleep out under the stars. They time it. It's easier to predict the time difference when it's only a few days or weeks. The longer the time spent, like a year or more, the harder it is to nail it down. Anyway, that's why they were so rushed to get going this morning."

Tanna got up to pace again. They had taken out some sewing, but it was already growing too dark to see in the cabin.

"There's something I don't understand," Tanna said, turning around with a frown on her face.

"Ma'am?"

"Why isn't there an engine? I thought dirigibles—or blimps or whatever you want to call them—had some way of being propelled. You know, so they could actually fly. We're just being dragged along with ropes."

Holly shook her head. "Engines don't work for very long in the Green. They're just impossible to keep going. All those iron parts ... They rust, and the little gears grind to a halt. Just like that." She snapped her fingers.

Tanna shrugged with a bewildered expression. "But they can be oiled."

"Nah." Holly shook her head again, more emphatically this time. "I mean, yes, they *can* be oiled. It's just never enough. Iron rusts really fast over here. In a matter of hours."

Tanna frowned. "So, what about trains?"

"There aren't any trains in the Green."

"Steamboats?"

"They would definitely rust. There are some airships like the *Queen* that did have engines at some point. Originally. They've usually been removed, though, to save the weight."

Holly got up to address the failing light. She grabbed a box of matches from a drawer in the wall, went down the length of the car to the pantry, and pulled out a pair of rusted lanterns. She moved around with obvious knowledge of where everything was kept.

"How many times have you made this trip ... across?" Tanna asked, standing aside to let her pass.

"A half a dozen times, I guess. About once a year, over the last five years or so. Since I started to stay with Papa all the time."

"Where were you before staying with him?"

"With my mama."

"They weren't together?"

"Well, no. Papa's always traveling back and forth to here, you know."

"I guess it's like being married to a sailor," Tanna smiled. "But wouldn't she rather you be with her?"

Holly didn't answer. For a moment Tanna thought she hadn't heard her.

"My mama's dead," the girl finally said.

"I'm sorry. Yes, you mentioned something ... about not having one." Tanna hesitated, knowing it wasn't pity she wanted. "You don't have to talk about it."

"It's OK. Papa said I'm better off. Mama was lost to the haint."

Tanna grimaced apologetically. "I'm not sure I know what that means."

"Smoking haint. Drinking the tarwater in a pinch when she couldn't afford to smoke. She couldn't live without it. She spent all her time in the dens with other people like her."

"Like an opium den?"

"They put glamours on it so it looks like you're in some kind of real nice hotel. But if you're not shining with the haint, you can see it's really just a cave."

"That sounds awful. Maybe your father's right, you know. About you being better off."

Holly nodded but didn't say anything further. She struck a match and blew it out, watching the ghost of the flame twist away in the air.

—

Tanna must have dozed off. The sound of the first few raindrops woke her. Holly was up, moving along the cabin, checking the latches of the window shutters. Within seconds the downpour was deafening. The balloon above them amplified the sound of the rain like an enormous drum, sending vibrations through the entire craft.

Tanna bolted upright, intending to jump up and help secure the other windows, but her head felt too large and heavy for her body. She collapsed back into a sitting position on the bench. Holly rushed forward, taking her by the hands and dragging her into one of the sleeping berths. She insisted Tanna lie down.

"Trust me, the maziness is only going to get worse if you try to stand up or walk around. You'll end up hurting yourself."

Once she lay still and closed her eyes, Tanna didn't feel quite so dizzy, but the sensation became much more than a matter of physical nausea. She experienced a wave of something like ... powerful emotion. Like regret. Nostalgia. Like *deja vu*, only overwhelmingly physical in its manifestation. It wasn't just a state of the mind but an energy throughout the body. A clutching of the heart. She kept waiting for the feelings to fade away and leave her clinging to the evaporating threads of its meaning—as usually happened with this kind of phenomenon—but it did not pass this time. It lingered, a spasm locking into place and sustaining itself within her. She couldn't catch her breath. And then she was sobbing. Uncontrollable hiccups. Her nose ran, her chest heaved, and her body was wracked with tremors. Her muscles clenched and her teeth chattered, as if against the worst chill or fever she'd ever known.

Holly seemed entirely—impossibly—unaffected. She tutted and fussed over Tanna, clearly helpless to do more than stroke the hair away from her face.

"It'll pass," Holly whispered, offering her a sip of water from a canteen. "You're all right. I promise it will pass."

Tanna desperately wanted to ask how it was that Holly seemed to feel so normal. Was it just that the girl had experienced this so many times she had become used to it? Or was this thing only happening to Tanna? She felt drunk, overcome—almost poisoned with emotion. She couldn't stop thinking about Ford. She had thought of him often on the day of the wedding, but then she'd completely put him out of her mind. Now, she was reliving every moment he had humiliated her over the past few years of their courtship. It was all coming at her, a procession of bad memories. She had never cried like this in the moment, even when some of the worst of it was happening. She'd been angry. She'd raged at him in the mirror, alone in her bedroom. She'd thrown things, broken things, ground her teeth. But she'd never wept like this—about anything in her life—with such shame and grief. Not even thirteen years ago when her father had killed himself.

In that moment on the *Queen of Clouds*, it felt like all the tragedy and pain in her life had only happened yesterday.

—

It did pass. It must have been hours later. It was dark around the windows and the cabin was dim with the gold, quavering glow of the frosted lanterns. Holly slept on the opposite bunk, lightly snoring. Tanna lay still for a while longer, studying her slack and youthful face. You could see the little girl within Holly's features, the prettiness usually covered by her gruff, self-conscious, boyish mannerisms. The short, chopped haircut and the men's work clothes blended in with the bedding, revealing Holly's aristocratic nose, high cheekbones, long baby goat lashes, and full lips.

When Tanna sat up, she realized the ship was not moving in the same way it had been. The motion was so subtle it could have been the aftereffects of the spell. The memory of the emotions gripped her senses and pulled at her heart like water spinning down a drain.

The sky had grown quiet too. The lightest wind thrummed as it skidded around the balloon above. Ropes creaked with the sound of slow, old souls in rocking chairs. She couldn't have told anyone how, but somehow she knew the airship was no longer moving.

She felt wrung out and hollow, but when she finally stood to test her legs, to feel for any residual dizziness, she realized she felt better than just well. She felt elated. She tried a few tentative steps and felt like she was floating, softly bouncing.

Maybe it was just the sensation caused by walking through the *Queen of Clouds* when she was moored and drifting in place.

When Tanna looked out the window she saw a bright silver moon in a clear sky. The fog was gone. The streaks of color from the sunset clung tightly to the western horizon like the faint edge of a burning page. There was nothing but a dome of sky and treetops stretching to the horizon in every direction. The airship floated on a sea of green. A breeze raced across the silvery leaves, rippling in a convincing imitation of moonlight on an enormous, quiet lake.

Peering down between the green fluttering waves, Tanna could see the orange globe of the haul team's campfire. She thought of the men sleeping on the ground like that, how cold they must be ... But then she realized she wasn't cold at all. She stepped to the cabin door and out onto the widow's walk. The breeze on her cheeks was like an early evening summer wind, flowing back from the sunset lands and into the cool eastern night they had left behind.

Winter was gone. The downpour had washed it away.

How much distance could they have possibly traveled during her fever to produce such a total change in environment? It simply was not possible. Yet it was true. Every cell in her body knew it.

She had been transported to another world.

8

It had taken an entire day to reach the Sea of Trees. Holly said it would take three more to cross it.

The most obvious difference about this new world was the scale of things. The trees were as consistent as blades of grass in a lawn, but they were giants. The boles were at least four hundred feet tall, with few lateral branches and scant foliage below the crowns. The leafy tops spread in flat, heart-shaped, horizontal planes of dark-green. Each treetop resembled a giant lily pad composed of overlapping shingles of leaves. The individual leaves were the size of carpets. The *Queen of Clouds* moved across them with a faint slithering sound, curling back the edges of the leaves to expose their silvery, velvet undersides.

They traveled now with all the gondola's shutters held open by a series of metal hooks and eyelets installed just for this purpose. The unyielding view of green and the susurrus of the *Queen*'s movement through it were hypnotic. Tanna found she was content to gaze for hours without need for conversation or employment. She'd never been one to take naps in the past, but she couldn't help dozing off in the middle of the day. At the sun's highest point in its glide across the sky, the balloon's shadow draped perfectly over the gondola beneath it. Although it was the hottest part of the day, the shade, the dimming of the light and color inside, had a powerful sleep-inducing effect.

Holly busied herself with chores around the cabin. She tidied up the bedclothes, brushed crumbs off the little table, and turned out the chamber pot and rinsed it carefully over the railing of the gondola.

"There's nobody down there," she said when she saw Tanna's stricken look. "The haul team's a few hundred yards up ahead of us. As long as we're moving, there's nobody right below the dirigible."

Holly was constantly opening storage compartments Tanna would never have known existed—cabinets cleverly recessed into the walls, drawers that appeared with the tug of a decorative piece of wooden trim. She seemed to be making an inventory of what she found or failed to find, writing with the nub of a crude pencil in a hard little accordion of a book.

Long after Geneva's fried chicken and biscuits ran out, Holly continued to produce the rest of the food from thin-sided boxes and burlap bags—apples, nuts, dried berries, salami, round loaves of bread, and wedges of cheese. Tanna had no appetite and would not have pursued food on her own, but it tasted good when Holly put it in her hands and ordered her to eat it. Once the awful spell had passed, she didn't feel nauseous or dizzy, but the floating lightness in her limbs and the sense of moving more slowly than normal persisted. It wasn't unpleasant, though. Even breathing felt incredibly satisfying, like she'd just discovered it.

"You're still a touch mazed," Holly explained, and offered her another spoonful of honey infused with ginger, peppermint, and an herb Tanna could not identify.

—

During the day, the only wildlife they saw were birds, many of which dove beneath the tree canopy to escape the approach of the airship. They spotted other flocks in the distance, traveling on much higher streams of air. Most of the species seemed familiar, such as the unmistakable V formation of a passing flock of geese, while others bore the colorful markings or gaudy head plumes Tanna had seen in illustrations of tropical, exotic species.

At dusk, she saw the first unmistakably fairy life forms. Drifting schools of jellyfish-like creatures with a lozenge of inflated tissue the size of a melon. They were chartreuse in color, with the shiny texture of a new spring leaf, and darker ribs and veins. A cluster of tendrils hung from their undersides, some of them trailing three or four feet long.

"They look like toy versions of this airship," Tanna observed out loud.

"They're called delfin or delfs. I bet we built the airships after them. Even you all's zeppelins and blimps."

"Are they some kind of sylph?"

"Not really. They're just animals, kind of like fish, I guess? Some of the fae eat them. You'll see nets strung up between the trees."

—

At night, a significantly greater amount of noises came from far beneath the canopy. Tanna could identify the hooting and screeching of birds, the unmistakable heart-wrenching bay of a wolf, and the screams of either monkeys or some kind of cat.

A small lizard like the blue-tailed skinks one saw flashing into cracks between stones in the garden appeared on the windowsill. Skinks were well-known to children in Tennessee because they could lose their tails and survive. It was rumored they could grow them back. She wondered where this one had come from, how it made it to the window of an airship hundreds of feet above the ground. Surely it must have stowed away.

When she moved a step closer toward it, something shivered along its back; a part of its body seemed to peel away. A pair of wings unfurled, like a folded umbrella when it first began to unhinge and open. The creature's wingspan was surprisingly large in proportion to its body. It looked at Tanna, hissed once, and darted off so quickly it seemed to disappear. She saw its small shadow racing away like an arrow over the treetops.

Holly noticed her standing frozen at the window, her mouth open, a faraway look in her eye. "What is it?"

"I think I just saw a dragon."

"Yeah?" Curiously, Holly scanned the ground instead of the sky. "Where? How big?"

"No, it was a tiny little thing." Tanna brought her hands together, about six inches apart.

Holly laughed. "That's not a dragon! Little black and blue thing? Just a lizzie."

"But it had *wings*."

Holly shrugged. "For every critter in your Gray world there's probably one here in the Green with wings."

—

The second night after the crossing—the third since the beginning of the journey—the haul team stopped and went through their usual evening preparations. They winched in the cable attached to the airship so it would not drift so far away from their camp on the ground. Tanna watched as their campfire winked into existence with a bright flare and then steadily bloomed. She had grown more comfortable with the height, particularly at night. She felt less dizzy looking over the side of the suddenly rust-covered railing into the featureless sea of darkness.

It was customary for a few smaller fires to appear on the ground, not far from the center of the camp, but tonight another flame caught her eye, too far to the south to be one of their own. It was hard for her to judge distances from the new perspective of this height, but it had to be at least a few miles away. The fire was small and steadily moving toward the camp.

Tanna called Holly over to watch with her. "Someone on foot," she murmured, "carrying a torch. Looks like they're running."

Just before the runner reached the camp, they heard the mournful sound of a horn. Three small flames broke away from the campfire and sped out to greet the visitor.

"Listen," Tanna hissed.

They heard a few shouts, and then all the smaller torches, including the new arrival, returned to the center of camp and went out.

Careful not to get the abundant rust all over her arms, Tanna leaned over the railing, wondering out loud about whom it might be.

Holly shrugged. "May have just been a scout they sent ahead earlier in the day."

After neither hearing nor seeing anything further, they went back inside the cabin, ate dinner, and went to bed.

—

Tanna didn't sleep well. She kept waking throughout the night, thinking she heard human voices shouting from a distance.

The gray light of morning finally came, but the dirigible remained strangely still. The haul team usually began moving at first light. Tanna was used to waking up with the airship already in motion.

"Why aren't we moving?" Tanna asked Holly.

The girl frowned and shook her head.

"What do you suppose that is?" Tanna pointed south, in the direction they were heading. Far off near the horizon a black column of smoke rose from beneath the leaves, bent in a current of wind, and stretched toward the east like a single angry thundercloud.

Holly squinted and stared, glancing at Tanna and then away, not meeting her eyes.

A steady, rhythmic, tapping vibration shuddered through the craft. It was so faint at first Tanna thought she was imagining it, but it grew until she could visually detect a slight bouncing tremble in the whole of the ship. Holly was looking at her now, but her eyes appeared a bit glazed, head cocked. She was listening.

"What is that?" Tanna asked, adding it to a list of irritating unknowns.

Holly darted down the length of the gondola, twisted open the door, and leaned far over the railing.

"Come away from there, you're making me nervous." Tanna had followed her as far as the doorway. "You really could fall leaning over that much."

Holly righted herself. "Somebody's coming up."

"Coming up *what*?" Tanna went to her side and peered over tentatively.

"There's a rope. One of the men from the haul team."

Tanna was horrified. "He's climbing a rope dangling from the bottom of this ship?" The sheer height involved was unimaginable to her. Holly had mentioned it was probably close to four hundred feet.

It was twenty minutes before a hat appeared, followed by a bearded face, red with exertion.

"Hey, Emmet," Holly said.

He scowled.

Holly introduced Tanna to him as Mrs. Eldridge, their passenger.

"It's chivalrous of you to risk your life and come all this way up to check on us, Mr. Brown," Tanna said. "And probably not at all necessary. Do you need us to help pull you up?"

Emmet Brown grunted, offended at the suggestion. "Hell no. It's just a lot harder coming back over that damn railing."

Tanna stiffened at his tone. "I see. You won't mind telling us why you're up here, then."

He chuckled rudely. "To attach these, if it's all the same to you." He held up a brass hook on the end of a rope coiled about his neck. He fed it through the railing, in and out between a few of the iron bars, then anchored the hook in a matching eyelet screwed into the stern of the gondola. He produced another connector of some kind from the bib of his overalls and a pair of rusty, squeaking metal wheels wrapped in an oily cloth. "We're blowing up another balloon. Just a small cargo raft, but we've gotta pick up a few passengers this afternoon. Last stop."

"Passengers?" Tanna asked.

"Some genies," he spat over his elbow. "Or some ferals out here wanting to hitch a ride into Treebridge." Emmet tested the rope with a tug and mockingly tipped his hat. "Now, here's the fun part." He dropped away so quickly Tanna cried out and involuntarily reached for him. She leaned out over the railing as far as she dared and searched for him falling through the still-dark woods below.

"It's all right. It's all right!" Holly pulled her away from the edge and back toward the door of the gondola. "He didn't fall. He slid down."

It took a moment to sink in. Tanna's face was pale, and even though her mouth was open she seemed to be holding her breath. With her hand to her throat she listened for cries of alarm from below. She heard only the faint, distant sound of men laughing.

Once she'd caught her breath and drank a sip of water from the canteen, she asked Holly about the genies. "Are spirits going to emerge from lamps to grant us wishes now?" Tanna chuckled uncomfortably. "Surely that can't be."

"No, ma'am, that word—*genie*—it's short for something else. I hear people say it sometimes, I just can't remember it. It's a long word, out of a schoolbook, you know? Papa could tell you." Holly's voice became low. "Anyway, genies are the ones who have always been here. At least, they're the ones who were here before any of us."

—

A half-hour later, with the dawn sky turning red on the port horizon, another smaller balloon rose up behind their cargo raft, another baby elephant following its mother and sibling. It wasn't a flat pallet of boxes and crates. This was a long, rustic vessel. It resembled a wooden rowboat or oversized canoe, open to the elements, with high sides that curved in slightly at the top. It was empty, its lightness allowing it to swing about in the wind.

"There's no one in it," Tanna said. "Or are these genies invisible?"

"No one in it *yet*," Holly said.

—

They were moving at a steady pace, the sun finally rising over the treetops to their left. For the first time since the crossing, Tanna could see a break in the endless sea of trees, like a dark crack or fault running in a line from east to west. Her first thought was that they must be approaching a river.

Against the background of the orange glow, a man stood in the top of a tree. What looked like a man from this distance, anyway—he had an enormous pair of wings silhouetted on his back. Like a bat or a much larger dragon than the one Tanna had seen the day before. He was impossible to miss, the only thing above the treetop canopy for hundreds of miles in all directions, like a man standing in the middle of an ocean.

9

Tanna was transfixed. He looked like an angel who had fallen from heaven, hovered briefly, and then alighted on the top of a four-hundred-foot tree. Or, she realized, as the initial jolt of the spell passed, like a devil in a cowboy hat.

Distances here in this world could be so illusory; they seemed to have drawn up alongside him too quickly. She made eye contact through an open window, only then fully waking to the fact that she was still in her nightgown, her hair a mess of tangles at the back of her neck. He grinned with a lopsided smirk, but when his lips parted his teeth were beautifully even and straight.

He tipped his hat to her as he slid past the window. She blushed.

He wore a brown suede hat with a wider brim than a cowboy's. His skin was reddish brown, the tan of a fair man who had spent too much time in the sun. He had probably been burned and peeled and tanned again many times over, but he wasn't haggard or leathered like a laborer. He was handsome. He had a comfortable aura, sky-blue eyes, and a long, strong, aristocratic nose. His startling white smile was a privileged contrast to the sweat-stained shirt and the pants mud-caked up to his knees.

Tanna lurched to the door of the gondola to follow him, hurriedly pulling on a light silk dressing gown. She almost stumbled as the vessel was yanked back to a stop by the tow team far below. Thankfully, the momentum tripped her back toward the cabin and not over the rail.

Holly was hanging from the side of the gondola, tying a short line to anchor the airship to a small platform in the tree. The man had already removed the wings from his back, swinging them around and beneath his arms. The hard bones of the wings were a blackish-green. The thin membrane stretched between the bones was translucent, pallid white, marbled with gray veins. The spindly crossbones of the wings ended in digits like fingertips with curved talons. Stretched open to their fullest potential, the wings would probably span more than twenty-five feet from tip to tip. As Tanna watched from the widow's walk, he struggled to close them in front of him like a large broken umbrella. He wrestled them flat on the boards at his feet and started binding them with twine.

"I really ought to tie these up with leather straps or something," he muttered, sensing he had an observer. "I'm afraid this hemp is liable to shred them." He tipped the bundle carefully into the rowboat-shaped craft that had been added to their caravan that morning.

Tanna struggled to compose herself with some dignity. She helplessly smoothed her hair and tied the robe closed with its sash. "You could use nylon stockings," she suggested, her morning voice sounding rough. "Old ones."

"Yes!" He clapped his large hands together and pointed at her. The direct gaze of his light eyes startled her. "Old nylon stockings. That would be perfect. Do you have any?"

Awkwardly, she looked behind her and around her feet, as if she might have left some old nylons lying on the floor. Which of course she had not—other than a nightgown when she slept, she'd been wearing men's pants ever since Holly gave them to her.

"No, sorry. I don't," she said with a tight wince. "I just meant it might be a good idea for next time."

He didn't seem to hear her. He was speaking in low, unfamiliar words to a dark, impossibly thin person who had appeared on the platform and leapt onto the cargo craft with soundless feline grace. Other, smaller beings followed, climbing off a spiral staircase onto the platform. Tanna thought the spiral staircase winding up from the tree was a much more elegant solution than the damned laddered watchtower she'd been made to climb. The aborigines streamed without hesitation into the new craft, crawling over one another like insects.

She recognized them. In many ways, they were duplicates of the creature her friends had shot the day they'd gone quail hunting. The day she'd decided to come to this place. They all had the same heavy fringe of dark hair like an Indian and the faintly iridescent rusty skin, almost powdered like the wings of a moth. These beings were a bit taller, though; she feared it may have been a child after all she'd seen on that day back in November, leaking its dark oily blood onto the snow.

She felt increasingly unnerved as more and more of them looked at her. Their black eyes—with no colored irises or whites in them—made something lurch in her chest. There were dozens of them now, swarming up the spiral staircase and into the boat like an army of ants. They seemed to fountain up from beneath the feet of the handsome human man, so identical in appearance that, at first, Tanna could not make out their sex.

But then she noticed a few of them had larger bared breasts—pointed, flaccid, small but still pendulous folds of gray-brown flesh. They all wore either some type of loincloth or a longer piece of woven fabric wrapped around the tops of their legs and snaking over one shoulder like a toga.

They were packed on top of one another in the boat-shaped craft. Several of them clung to the ropes running down from the balloon, with nowhere even to place their feet. This new passenger craft and its smaller balloon had dipped precariously and steadily dropped beneath the level of the gondola and the cargo raft.

As the *Queen of Clouds* jerked and bobbed, Tanna gripped the railing, wondering if there were too many of them, if it were possible for their mass to drag her own ship out of the sky.

The human man—the dragon hunter, as she'd already come to think of him—was now leaning over, handing down parcels and small crates. He seemed to be pulling packets of goods from the leaves beneath him. Holly had jumped onto the platform and was helping him. Tanna saw a glimpse of long silver-brown fingers pushing the cargo up from below the level of the treetops. Some of the creatures in the small craft stowed the bundles beneath them, using them like cushions; others balanced them on their heads with one hand to keep them in place.

Tanna finally found her voice and called to the man. "Is there something we can do for you, sir?"

"You've already done it," he said, flashing his smile.

Tanna squinted out across the vast emptiness of sky and trees, the dark smoke still drifting in the distance. "Have you had some trouble?"

"Oh, many times in my life," he said, as if acknowledging a good-natured joke at his expense.

"You're not ... stranded?" Tanna asked, somehow feeling it was a foolish question even as she asked it.

"No, I'm quite well. I do thank you for stopping."

"Are you famous, then?"

"I'm not sure if I deserve to be called famous," he said.

"Well, important enough that they would stop all this for you, out here in the middle of nowhere."

"I'm not sure this place deserves to be called nowhere."

He seemed to be toying with her, enjoying a banter he could keep going without actually going anywhere.

Wondering if he might not be some person of prominence, she almost asked him *Who are you?* But she stopped herself, realizing at the last moment it would sound rude, like an interrogation. She opted for a more straightforward approach, going back to a simple beginning.

"I'm Tanna Eldridge."

"Ah, yes. Bucky's wife."

"You've met my husband." She was delighted to be able to ask about Buck.

"I have."

"Is he all right?"

"The last time I saw him, he was. We've been out on safari for a few days now."

The first tall aboriginal man, the one with whom he had been speaking, crawled back out of the boat and stood with him on the platform in the treetop. His appearance was different from the others'; she couldn't put her finger on what it was about him. He was much taller, comparable in height to many human men. His eyes were striking, like amber jewels. He put a horn to his lips and blew it. It was the sad sound she'd heard earlier. A shudder went through the gondola and the ropes groaned against the balloon. After a few moments, they started to drift away, but the hunter and his dark companion made no movement to leap into the raft and join the creatures who transported his things.

Tanna worried they were about to leave him behind.

"They say it will be at least another day until we reach Treebridge."

"Yes, you're almost there," he called out cheerfully. "Welcome!"

"But. Well. Aren't you coming?" she yelled.

"Not just yet, no. Oh!" He held up a hand. "You could do me a favor."

"Yes, anything, I'll try. Hurry though!"

"Tell Cole Mathers to get my things. Make sure he knows about the wings."

"Cole Mathers," she repeated, cupping her hands around her mouth so her voice would carry.

"Yes, thank you!" He waved goodbye, as if to a departing train of loved ones. His companion had already disappeared down the spiral staircase.

"Who *are* you?" Tanna finally bellowed, abandoning all etiquette.

He cupped his own hands and called out something, but she couldn't catch what he said.

"What did he say?" she whispered, mostly to herself.

"Gallagher, ma'am." Holly had been standing right behind her, quietly watching the exchange. "That's Jackson Gallagher."

"Do you know him?"

"Everybody does." Holly shrugged. "You were right. He's famous."

"Really? Who is he?"

"An explorer, as far as I know."

Tanna looked back at the lone figure, wingless now, but still standing atop the sea of trees. Even from the growing distance she could swear she saw the white flash of his smile. His blue eyes lingered in her mind, fading slower than the rest of him, like the Cheshire Cat.

"Jackson Gallagher," she said softly, trying out the name like a spell.

10

The dirigible caravan followed the great rift in the trees Tanna had spotted earlier, a large stream. There must have been a straight, even trail parallel to the watercourse because the airship noticeably picked up speed. The normal heave and pull, the swinging glide they had plodded along with up until that point, gave way to a steadier pace. The gondola rode directly over the wide streambed. Tanna glimpsed the flash of the sun on the water as it passed between the shadows of the *Queen of Clouds* and the crude floating crafts trailing in her wake.

The dark aboriginal passengers were silent and watchful. They didn't even speak to one another, as far as she could see. A few of them shifted and rotated according to some unannounced schedule, taking turns clinging precariously to the ropes. They made it look effortless, but she shuddered when she dwelled on the way they leaned out over the air, one small, thin hand curled in a fist around the line holding them over a drop of at least three hundred feet, if not more.

These were the *genies*—that's how Holly referred to them.

"I don't like the way they stare at me," Tanna whispered to her. "Those black eyes look right through you."

"They're Seelie, ma'am," Holly said. "They would never hurt you."

Tanna turned to look at her. "Seelie?" she asked.

"The Seelie are friends with humans. They're the good fairies."

Tanna looked doubtful. "I thought the good fairies would be pretty."

"The members of this tribe are known to be very peaceful," Holly said, trying to convince her further.

"So, there *are* tribes of these creatures that are dangerous, then," Tanna said petulantly.

"You shouldn't worry," Holly insisted. "Really."

"What are these people, then—these genies?"

"Ma'am?"

"Who are they? To what tribe do they belong?"

"These are the Ti'waga. The People of the Red Maple. They're one of the largest elf tribes from just north and east of here," Holly spoke softly without moving her lips so it wouldn't be obvious she was talking about them. "You can tell who they are by their colors—by the paste in their hair and the stain on their lips and fingertips."

The wine-colored sheen to their black hair was like the henna Tanna had sometimes seen on stage performers. The elves, men and women alike, were also painted or possibly tattooed with colored markings. It was hard to know if the designs were permanent or not—they mostly resembled the unmistakable shape of maple leaves in overlapping patterns. The effect was subtle, like dappled sunlight and shade on the skin of someone crouching in the underbrush. No doubt they would be virtually invisible in their silent frozen poses, clinging to their namesake trees.

"You know," Holly said, "they're probably just staring at us for the same reasons we're staring at them."

Tanna flushed, tore her eyes away, and ducked back inside the cabin.

"I should probably pack up all your things," Holly said. She began stripping the bedclothes from the sleeping berth. "We're close."

"Do I have time to change?"

Holly frowned, not understanding her question.

"I wasn't planning to wear a nightgown," Tanna explained. "Or pants."

"Oh. Then yeah. I'd go ahead, if I were you."

—

The cleft of the stream in the trees narrowed and the rock banks rose abruptly, becoming sheer walls on either side. They were traveling deeper upstream into a gorge. The streambed also narrowed, and the tall pine trees along the banks pressed close on either side of the airship. They began to hear the faint scratching hiss of branches, needles, and leaves rubbing the underbelly of the dirigible's balloon.

Tanna heard calls from the haul team below, and the airship ricocheted in a slow stop. She had learned by now to anticipate the jerk in the opposite direction and braced herself. She had only a few seconds to regain her balance and catch her breath before she felt the airship start to rise. The trees dropped away beneath them with considerable speed. It was like a balloon string slipping from a child's fingers. As the ship rose straight up into the sky, the force made her body heavy and drove her toward the floor.

"What's happening now?"

"The haul team's letting out the slack," Holly said, nonchalantly braced between the sleeping berths. "The cliff faces are real tall at this point. We've got to be a lot higher if we're going to line up with the dock at Treebridge."

"Do they have to do it all at once?"

"Well, this is the last point where it's relatively easy to stop and raise the ship. The gorge gets pretty narrow. They'll transfer the lines too. The rest of the way, they'll use a little tugboat down there."

A strong vibration ran through the vessel, the outside air grew cooler, and a soft, glittering mist enveloped the gondola, frosting the few windows that still had glass. Tanna thought this had to be much closer to what traveling in a hot air balloon felt like. The elves clung tighter to their open craft as the *Queen of Clouds* dragged them higher. She saw the southern side of the gorge on their left. The gondola continued to rise until it was fifty or sixty feet above the top of the cliff.

Tanna felt dizzy and the back of her mouth began to water. Holly must have been watching her; the girl shoved the porcelain basin from the water closet into Tanna's arms and pointed straight out the window. "Just look toward the horizon," she said in a commanding tone. "Don't look up or down."

With the lines played out so long and slack, the airship drifted farther from side to side, like a kite sailing into low, scudding clouds. The long ropes from opposite ends of the dirigible's balloon began to cross one another. The entire airship rotated, slinging the smaller crafts out behind them. The elves all leaned into the turn, anticipating the change in position. Tanna squeezed her eyes shut, unable to look out into the spinning white distance anymore.

"They have to swing us around so we can come onto the dock sideways," Holly explained. "You know, kinda like a train pulling into a station. That way the stevedores can get to the cargo, but we can go ahead and get off. The genies too."

—

Tanna wasn't sure what a colony center would look like in this place. She'd been picturing a large clearing in the forest, some shantytown of cabins with a mud street near a common stream. She'd been scanning the cliff tops for a man-made structure jutting up, dreading the climb back down another rickety wooden tower. She was hoping for one of those spiral staircases. Even still, on the edge of a gorge ... The thought of being out, exposed, climbing down anything in this vast open space made her teeth start to chatter.

A thousand feet below, the creek lay like a narrow silver ribbon dropped in a deep ditch. Up ahead was the largest tree she could have ever imagined, toppled and lying on its side across the gorge, spanning the gulf of empty air between the opposing cliffs. It was something like a massive redwood, an ancestor of the trees they had been sailing over these past few days. The Tree had to be well over a hundred feet in diameter. She couldn't see either end of it—given its size, it probably stretched beyond the edges of the gorge for miles in both directions.

As they slid in sideways closer to the enormous Tree, she saw flashing rows of glass windows along its side. She counted five or six stories of balconies embedded in the deep grooves between the scales of bark. A steady breeze rising from the cool gorge beneath them forced the many flags that were flying to flutter upward.

From the view afforded by the airship's approach, the people on the balconies and along the top of this amazing structure were still far enough away that they resembled ants. Maybe it was giddiness from the altitude that gave Tanna the unnerving sense of having been shrunk to the size of an ant herself. It was hard to grasp the true size and scale—not to mention the material—of this city. If she covered one eye and squinted just so, she could see it as a normal-size tree lying across a stream. It was almost easier for her to imagine that she and the *Queen of Clouds* and Holly and everyone around them had been struck by some magic that made them small.

Other than the sprawling cities of human civilization, there was nothing so large in the Gray world from which she came. Certainly nothing that began as a living thing. Now she truly appreciated the web of secrecy and disinformation protecting the reality of the Green. At no time, among even the tallest tales, had anyone hinted at anything as miraculous as the sight before her.

All along the Tree's side—or what had become its top since it had been lain or fallen across the gorge—as far as she could see in both directions was a ridge of traffic like the main street of any town: people walking on foot; riding on horseback; driving traps and buggies, laden carts, even bicycles and rickshaws. Above them all was an elevated boardwalk studded every fifty feet or so with mooring masts.

There were hundreds of these masts, all along the spine of Treebridge—spires like the top of the Empire State Building—and, curling tightly around each spire, a spiral staircase.

Closer to the southern end of Treebridge and the nearby cliffs, in line with the *Queen of Clouds*'s trajectory, dozens of vessels were currently docked. They resembled all manner of ships, both sky and sea. Some levitated by an obvious mechanism, like the hot air balloons, blimps, and dirigibles; and others were floating clipper ships with bulbous, horizontal sails fat with gas. But there were other vessels that remained aloft through some mysterious magical means—rowboats, rafts, and flat-topped barges that simply seemed to hover in midair.

As in any busy harbor, this long, linear port and its supporting structures swarmed with activity. Thousands of beings scurried about— she couldn't quite call them *people*. They certainly couldn't all be human. No doubt many of them were people of alternate species she had yet to encounter. The throngs moved in a bustle of intentional commotion that rivaled the train stations and ports in even the largest cities to which she'd traveled. The crowd here was larger than the train station in Atlanta, larger than the boardwalks of Charleston or Savannah.

The *Queen of Clouds* slowed as it approached its imminent dock with an empty mooring mast. Just before it disappeared beneath them, Tanna stuck her head out an open window to view the sides of Treebridge. She took in all the windows stretched along the cracks in the bark—literally miles of windows, end to end. She could only imagine that the interior must teem with life, like termites in a log. How many tunnels and warrens, caves and rooms could be honeycombed inside a structure of this size? Quite simply, this was an exotic metropolis.

"My God. It's enormous," she breathed. "Have you been here before? Inside this place?" She was almost angry that Holly had not thought this was worth describing to her.

The girl shrugged. "Sure. Whenever Papa's business brings us here. We're usually just in and out on top, or along the highway up here. Coming and going, as folks demand. Mostly wander around or wait in saloons."

"It's extraordinary." Tanna's initial wonder was rapidly giving way to anticipation. And more than a bit of fear.

As the nose of the dirigible's balloon passed the mooring mast, dock workers reached out with long crooked poles, grabbing loops of rope and yanking the airship to a stop. Tanna felt the *Queen* shudder, grabbed a handhold, and braced for the forward momentum to knock her off balance. Stevedores tied off the ropes as the airship swayed back and forth. The platform at the top of the tiny spiral staircase had a protective copper railing, blue-green with age, but it was hardly large enough for more than one person to come and go at a time.

The ship was barely docked before the elves began leaping off their craft, some of them jumping over ten or twelve feet of empty space. They carried Jackson Gallagher's parcels down, deposited them in a growing heap, and then they melted away into the crowds. Tanna noted that two of the dark beings stayed behind, standing at attention, guarding Gallagher's wings between them.

She followed Holly out the back door of the gondola, but she hesitated before stepping onto the platform. The intensity of the wind rising up through the gorge was shocking. If she'd had a parasol in her hand, she feared she would've been ripped out of her boots. Holly shouldered one of Tanna's travel cases and reached back to help her across.

"Only a few feet, ma'am. Don't look down if you don't want to."

But of course it was too late. As quickly as she'd been advised against it, she had already looked. Holly skipped down a few steps to make way for her, and shaking, Tanna lurched forward, practically wrapping her arms around the mooring mast.

Her voice failed her when she first tried to speak. She took a deep breath, licked her lips, and formed the words again. It was like blowing into a reedy instrument, and she hated that she sounded so shaken.

"I hope you know where I'm supposed to go?"

The girl smiled kindly. "Just follow me."

When they reached the bottom of the stairs—certainly more treacherous in the long skirts she'd changed into—Tanna put her hand on Holly's shoulder. "Please stay close."

—

Before Holly could answer, a tall person in a silver-green turban stepped forward and bowed to Tanna. He definitely appeared to be male, but his features were pretty, effeminate, and vaguely Oriental. His eyes were almond-shaped, hooded, almost closed to slits as he quietly stared at her. His skin was darker than any colored person she'd ever seen, almost cherry-black. Her instincts told her his slow, feline movements were not human, and when he blinked she realized that his eyes were exceptionally different. They weren't the black orbs she had so far encountered in most of the other races. Like Jackson Gallagher's tall fairy companion, they were like a cat's—around the small, dark slit of a pupil, the eye was entirely composed of shimmering amber.

He wore more clothing than the genies who had stowed away on the cargo raft behind the *Queen of Clouds*. He was dressed formally in a long coat of storm-colored felt that reached his ankles. He wore oiled black leather boots that appeared too large for his feet and soft with use. They were missing their laces and their tongues lolled out in great curls over his toes.

"I am here for you," he said. His voice was barely more than a whisper, yet it vibrated with a beautiful low musical quality, like a purr.

"Thank you," Tanna spluttered, not knowing what to say. She had no idea who he was, but her intuition told her it would be rude to demand he identify himself.

She was right to hesitate, as Holly said, "Mr. Eldridge probably sent him."

"Still," he said, with a recognizable tone of introduction.

"Still?" Tanna repeated the name uncertainly.

The creature held her gaze, bowing again in response to his name, more deeply and slowly than before. "*So'onah*," he said.

"I'm anxious to be reunited with my husband."

"I will take you to him now."

Tanna was no stranger to communicating with servants. This Still emanated respect and esteem that rivaled any butler she had ever encountered. She responded graciously, as she had been trained, comforted that familiar social exchanges seemed to have common meaning here.

"That would be very kind of you."

Still extended his hand toward her. For a moment she was horrified that he intended her to shake his hand—the nails on the end of his twig-like fingers were long, sharp, and thick. They were both shiny and chalky, like horn. When she hesitated, he gestured toward her bag.

"Oh! Yes, thank you," she said, allowing him to take her carpetbag from her.

Still turned with a stately grace and began to glide away. The hem of his coat seemed to hover a few inches above the ground, and as he floated into the crowd, it parted around him.

Holly inclined her head to indicate that Tanna should follow him.

"You *are* coming?" Tanna asked. "We're not parting ..."

"No, ma'am. I'm right behind you," Holly said. "I'm supposed to stay with you, you know. Come to your house and everything. If you want me to."

Tanna exhaled with relief. "Yes, I'd like you to stay with me as long as you can. But I have a condition going forward."

Holly raised her eyebrows, looking a little worried.

"You have to stop calling me *ma'am*."

"Oh. OK," she mumbled. "What do you want me to call you? Mrs. Eldridge?"

Tanna's nose wrinkled in distaste. "God, no. I'll get tired of that too in no time. Just call me Tanna." She tried to smile warmly at the girl, to encourage her.

Holly returned a shy hint of a smile.

—

The crowds allowed them through, but many people stopped to openly stare. Tanna was unnerved by some of the strange faces passing so close. She hid her discomfort and revulsion by lifting her chin and focusing on the back of Still's turban.

She possessed no vocabulary for the variety of people she saw. She was unable to name even the characteristics that distinguished them. There was every kind of human being she'd ever encountered or merely heard of—white, brown, young, old. Most were a bit wretched, covered in the sweat of labor and the filth of a life lived entirely outdoors, maybe on top of this Tree in the sun and wind. Moving among them were wealthy Americans of European descent like herself, overdressed, haughty with fear, scented handkerchiefs held to their faces to offset the closeness and stench of so many bodies.

In addition to colored humans, women were also generally underrepresented here. Once or twice in a hundred, a servant girl darted past, plainly dressed, usually intent on some errand. Tanna sensed these women moved quickly to run a never-ending gauntlet of lecherous jeers and grabbing hands. Their faces were emotionless and determined, no doubt intended to hide their anxiety. Holly's simple hardness and expressionless manner made more sense to her now.

The human men were more overtly dangerous than these exotic races. For the most part, even though these indigenous peoples outnumbered her kind three to one, they seemed at least unaggressive, if not actually gentle. The ones who most resembled humans were stoic and seemed to move as if through molasses. They did not jostle one another or speak; they flowed with and around one another like schools of fish or flocks of birds, as if they were attuned to one mind.

But when they looked at her, the intensity of their black bottomless gazes, or their golden stares, was terrifying. A cunning awareness like birds or cats stalking prey. And yet there was a haunted sadness about many of them, too.

Once Tanna became accustomed to the initial shock of these alien faces, she was able to look around and notice more detail. She became aware of a constant presence of butterflies. No, not just butterflies, slow and fluttering like flower petals on a breeze—there were also dragonflies, quick, darting flashes of color that whizzed by her head. There were swarms of insects everywhere, clouds of pastel colors and glittering metallic wings, some so small they were fluff on the air, others five times the size of bumblebees, all contributing to an audible hum.

There was a background slithering hiss like an infinite bag of rice being poured. Tanna caught herself looking up for the sight of rain on a metal roof. It muffled the cries and shouts of the human voices in the crowd—her ears rang from the constant susurrus.

A dragonfly whizzed by, close enough to her face to make her flinch. It alighted on a fold of Still's turban in front of her. A tiny blue face like a china doll's looked at her. The top half of its body was diminutively human—bare blue breasts, arms, and hands. Instead of legs, its trunk ended in a lizard's tail.

Tanna gasped. The creature flapped its veined, lacy wings and disappeared.

A trio of small naked females passed on her left, just slightly overhead, hovering approximately seven feet off the ground with no discernible movement or effort. They were six inches tall, emanating the greenish-yellow light of fireflies, and faintly humming.

When they caught the corner of Still's eye, he turned to look at them with casual interest.

There was a flash of light. The luminous creatures scattered in a flurry of shrieks. Tanna's hand flew up instinctively to protect her face. She felt the slap of a wooden switch on the back of her hand. Still's hand shot out and grabbed a small pole with a net at the end, attached to a struggling urchin—a human boy. Cursing, he tried to wrestle his net away from Still. Holly moved in front of her and grabbed the dirty collar of the boy's shirt. He spat in Holly's face and she slapped him, hard. Still snapped the net between his fingers and threw it at the boy. Holly raised her arm to strike him again and he melted into the stream of bodies moving south along the main street.

"Little monsters," Holly fumed, the apples of her cheeks bright red.

"Did that boy hurt them?" Tanna asked, bewildered. "The fairies."

"No, but he would have if he'd gotten ahold of them."

"What did he want with them?"

Holly snorted with disgust. "Some of the feral believe their magic can ... be used for stuff."

"Like what?" Tanna asked.

"Spells. Making things." Holly's features settled back into a mask. "He'd catch them and sell them and it'd be a sad ending for them, that's what."

Tanna realized they had stopped and the crowd was flowing around them like water around boulders. Still waited patiently, but his hand hovered near her elbow, ready to take it and steer her along.

"So'onah," he urged her gently.

"We're going to meet my husband, right?" Tanna asked him, trying to catch her breath and not reveal how shaken she was. "Mr. Buck Eldridge. I want you to take me to him. Now."

"Yes, so'onah." He bowed briefly and then physically pulled her by the sleeve.

11

A dozen yards ahead, an elaborate archway rose above the crowd. Everyone seemed to be streaming toward it and disappearing down a flight of stairs. As they passed beneath the arch, Tanna looked up in wonder at the scrollwork detail. She was unable to decide if the structure was man-made or ... *grown*. There was a pattern of intertwining vines and leaves, like a tangle of stylized rose bushes. She had seen impressive topiaries and garden mazes carved from hedges, but surely nothing cultivated—nothing alive—could be this perfect and regular.

The long, curling stems were woven into a large awning above the staircase, which disappeared into the darkness of a tunnel. As they descended and her eyes adjusted, Tanna saw lines of tiny amber lanterns embedded in the walls. One row of lights ran along at a height of six feet, while another followed the apex of the tunnel's slightly pointed arch in a groove directly above their heads. Each individual lantern looked like a dried bubble of sap, as one might see running down the bark of a pine tree. There was liquid motion inside, drifting bubbles, as if the light shone from molten fluid.

"Stay between us," Holly whispered, pressing close as they passed deeper into the tunnel.

Tanna pinched a fold of fabric along the back of Still's jacket and allowed him to pull her along. The stairs descended in a switchback that must have taken them down two or three stories. They emerged into a cavernous interior, as large as a train station or a cathedral. Tanna's senses were bombarded by opulent materials, patterned surfaces, jewel-bright colors, and light dancing from hundreds of directions.

Lamps resembling antique gas fixtures hung in space, lit with a ghost-green firefly light. They appeared to be made of rough glass, organic and irregular, perhaps even quartz crystal. There were thousands of them hanging in the empty air, by either magical means or some kind of invisible wires. When she looked down Tanna glimpsed a floor of cobblestones, bright and colorful in a mosaic design. The thought of the effort it would have taken to set each and every gem in these intricate spirals, into a floor of this size, in a room this big ... It boggled the mind.

The artistry. The obsession. The wealth of labor, not to mention materials.

This was a glimpse of the fairy palaces she'd imagined as a girl. This was the promise of the other world she'd hoped they might discover on this adventure.

Still pulled her sharply to the right, and they began to ascend a grand staircase of low, broad, shallow steps. It swept up the sidewall of this great hall, the balustrade carved again to resemble a stylized rose vine, thorns turned inward to become balusters. It was made to look as if it had once been a real living thing, grown, then bewitched, frozen into this form. Maybe it still lived and was growing even now. When Tanna allowed her hand to trail across its gold-brown skin she could have sworn she sensed a faint vibration.

As they gained the height of the first gallery overlooking the throng below, she slowed and took in the sight spread out beneath her: a sea of heads—human, indigenous, feral, and fae. And there were almost as many forms in the air of the great hall as there were on the floor. Tanna thought of pigeons in train stations, bats in caves, butterflies in her Aunt Lida's greenhouse.

As she gawked at their surroundings, Still stopped and waited patiently behind her, blocking the flow of foot traffic speeding by. Holly tried to provide a similar protective screen at her side, but she was small and continually buffeted, almost knocked off her feet.

Seeing the anxiety in the young girl's face, Tanna suggested they move on.

Still led them away from the balustrade at the gallery's edge and along the interior wall of the cavernous space. Tanna put up a hand to steady herself and realized the wall was not solid. It was an enormous hedge of leaves, vines, and thorns, so closely packed together its surface was almost as flat as paneling. There were no signs of cutting or split leaves. From a distance, the walls appeared to be papered in an intricate floral pattern, more sumptuous than any velvet-flocked design one would find in the grandest old Victorian homes. Those were representations, simple illustrations that attempted to capture something of this nature. Here, this—*this*—was the original. She saw now where it all came from—all the botanical flourishes and turned wood carvings of the craftsmen in the world back home. This is what they all hoped to capture, to reference even a little bit.

As Tanna focused on other surfaces she saw that almost nothing was solid or closed. Even the carpet under her feet seemed to be a living surface, not unlike moss or lichen. It was spongy and scattered with diamond droplets of moisture, like a lawn in the morning before the sun had risen to burn away the dew. She looked up, wondering where the rain could fall from. The carpet was not solid green or the mottled green-grays one saw splashed in circular bursts across exposed boulders; it was as colorful as a Persian rug. The background threads were mostly the gold of fresh hay, with runners of tiny plum-red flowers peeking from the empty spaces in the woven cords.

Still stopped in front of a large pair of double doors made from the interwoven branches of a plant that resembled crape myrtle, trained like banzai to conform to a particular shape and size. They too produced a flawlessly flat plane. From a distance, their bright fuchsia flowers, clustered in the regular spaces between the branches, resembled the leaded red glass windows of a church or saloon.

A small elaborate plaque, the typeface so decorative it was almost illegible, announced this to be the entrance to *The Fairchild*.

"So'onah." Still pulled open the door with a branch that curled outward in a scrolling knob.

Tanna inclined her head in thanks. Still brought out an impulse within her to behave in a formal way. She normally would have found such affectations pretentious and ridiculous, but in Still's presence, to not do so would have made her feel more uncomfortable.

She stepped through the door, chin raised.

—

The interior of The Fairchild club was significantly darker. The only sources of light were dim tangerine crystal globes hovering together in a grape-like cluster at the center of the ceiling. They appeared to be standing in some sort of small, round foyer. There was a gaudy circular velvet couch in the middle of the room, rust-orange in color and dripping with fringe. The carpet resembled a scattered crush of overlapping red rose petals.

A counter was set into the wall at chest height with a window opening into an alcove behind it, like the front desks found in small hotels. A human man stood behind the desk, scribbling on something out of sight. His hair was slicked back along his skull with pomade so thick the teeth of his comb had left permanent rows. A large mustache covered his entire mouth and chin. He glanced up at them, raised a disdainful eyebrow, tapped a quill pen on an inkwell with a flourish, and then promptly returned to ignoring them.

"Is Mr. Eldridge staying here, then?" Tanna asked Still, loudly enough that the desk clerk could overhear and ascertain who she was. She anticipated a change in his demeanor, but he only scowled at her, as a librarian might glare at someone for speaking above a whisper.

"Where's Buck?" Tanna said, lowering her voice in spite of herself.

"You will wait, so'onah," Still announced gravely, and strode away from her through an arched doorway beneath a sign that said *Members Only*.

Holly collapsed onto the sofa with a sigh, dropping the bags she carried onto the floor beside her. She looked around with patient disinterest.

Tanna peered discreetly after Still, but he had already been absorbed by the inner gloom. She thought she glimpsed his turban through a haze of smoke. She could hear the murmur of low conversation; the clink of glassware, sliver, and china.

Several minutes passed. Holly dozed off. The desk clerk retreated into some deeper interior office. Tanna leaned around the doorway into the members area, but all she saw was blood-red carpet disappearing into a cave of a room that reeked of pipe tobacco and cigars.

She had not seen Buck in four days. It annoyed her to think she had traveled all this way to now stand in the same building he was in and wait. She felt certain she would recognize her husband in a dim room faster than Still ever could. And if Buck was composing himself after a long night of drinking and playing cards ... Well, it couldn't possibly be as bad as some of the states in which she'd found him over the years.

Tanna exhaled in an impatient huff. She craned her neck once more to see if the snooty clerk would reappear, but he did not. Holly had begun to snore softly with her chin on her chest. Tanna squared her shoulders, lifted the hem of her skirts, and swept into the members area. Her Aunt Mona had taught her to seize confidence by entering a room quickly, as if she owned it. She'd practiced the tactic here and there over the years in various circumstances—it disarmed people. It also had the added benefit of causing everyone to collectively turn and look in one's direction.

Tanna crossed a long dining room crowded with small tables draped in crisp white cloths. Oxblood wingback chairs and Chesterfield sofas were grouped on either side of a great stone hearth. The room was filled with men smoking, drinking, eating, and talking.

A bar with a copper foot rail ran along the far wall. A turbaned creature who could have been Still's brother was polishing and stacking a pyramid of glassware.

Still himself stood at attention near the bar, like the most reserved of footmen, not speaking, eyes focused on something unseen in the middle distance. He did not seem to see Tanna until she had walked up right beside him. He turned his head slowly, and when his catlike eyes focused on her, his mouth dropped open. He pressed his lips together, as if suppressing an outburst of rage.

Tanna was unsure how to read Still's expressions, so she addressed the creature behind the bar. "I'm meeting my husband, Buck Eldridge," she declared grandly, and turned to survey the room. At any moment, she expected to easily spot Buck's bright blond hair in the gloom.

At the sound of her voice, all the faces in the room turned toward her. Conversations puttered away into tense silence. Several of the men began to push back their chairs and stand, looking to one another as if waiting to see who would do something first.

An elderly man reading a newspaper near the bar looked over his shoulder, and seeing that he was closest to her, set his jaw, heaved himself out of his chair, and stepped to her side.

He took her elbow. "We have to ask you to leave, miss," he said. He spoke in a low voice that nevertheless carried in the silence.

She shook her arm free of his hand, offended that he would touch her without hesitation. "It's *missus*," she said. "Mrs. Buck Eldridge. I'm here to meet my—"

"Not here, ma'am," the man said, looking embarrassed. "I'm afraid this room is for members only."

"Well, if you could just go get my husband—"

"I'm afraid we must insist," the man said, lowering his eyebrows and looking to the creature behind the bar for assistance.

Like Still, the creature's face remained an expressionless mask of stone, but his deep voice reverberated throughout the room. For one second, Tanna thought he had ridiculously burst into song. She stifled a laugh. But he pointed at her, an ominous, accusatory gesture, and began to move around the bar. He proceeded toward her, pointing, reciting some kind of rhyming verse, louder and louder, over and over and over again.

Still stepped forward, grabbed the wrist of the elderly man who had approached Tanna, and pushed him away from her. It was done so slowly it could hardly have been called a *shove*, but the man did have to take a few steps backward to keep his balance.

"Is he casting a spell on me?" Tanna asked Still in a furious whisper. She was focused on the genie who continued to stalk toward her, chanting.

"So'onah," Still said, gallantly wrapping her arm in his elbow. "We must go now."

Tanna was thankful Still forced her to match his intentional grace instead of fearfully fleeing from the room, as was her impulse. All eyes remained on them. Not one man looked away or intervened; they simply watched, some with curiosity or amusement—or, stranger still, anger—as Still led Tanna from the room.

As they neared the door to the foyer and the front desk area where she'd left Holly, Tanna was calming down enough from fright to wind back up toward rage.

"Did that creature really just *curse* me? I have never in my life—"

"Tanna!" Buck said, striding up and grabbing her in a bear hug. "Here you are at last."

—

She melted with the relief of being reunited with Buck. She didn't realize how much nervous energy alone had been sustaining her. She couldn't help but smile at how excited he seemed to be that she was here. He peppered her with questions about her trip, which he didn't really allow her to answer. He was manic with all that he wanted to tell her and show her. He seemed a bit drunk, really. He could not hide his high color. He was one of those blond men whose flushed cheeks always betrayed him.

"So glad you found Still. Isn't he something? I couldn't have survived here so far without him ..."

Buck had taken Tanna's carpetbag in one hand, threw the train case that Holly had been carrying over his shoulder, and left the club with both Tanna and Holly struggling to keep up. Still somehow managed to stay close behind them with his effortless glide.

Buck dodged the crowds flowing along the gallery.

"Where are we going?" Tanna cried out.

"To the reception," Buck said, turning without stopping, incredulous that she should ask. "We're already late."

"You're not taking me to see our house?" Tanna asked.

"The house?" Buck frowned and then laughed at her. "It's awfully far from here. I don't expect we'll make it there before lunchtime tomorrow, if we leave in the morning. But not to worry, Lord Daughtry and his wife—his fairy wife, by the way, gorgeous, captivating creature—they'll likely extend an invitation to stay the night with them in South End after our reception. I'll just drop a few expert hints, ever so casually. Don't forget who you're with, I'm a master of these things."

"A lord?" Tanna asked.

"Oh yes, the aristocracy here is grand and entrenched beyond anything you've seen before. I was quite surprised by it. Wait until you see the way they live. The way we could live. They've managed to preserve something of the Old South here."

"And the reception?" Tanna prompted him.

"Our wedding reception," Buck said, as if she should know this. "Well, it's partly a literal reception, our being received into society here. Presented to the leaders of the community. It's certainly important for new colonists to be acknowledged. It legitimizes us. And besides, we never had much of a party to celebrate after our hasty church ritual. We were so consumed with preparing to leave at that time—"

"Wait!" Tanna cried angrily, and stopped by a fountain with a face carved to look like it was made of leaves. Holly ran into her. She patted her hair self-consciously, arms out, imploring Buck to look at the condition of her clothes. "I've just come off that—" she wanted to say *damned* but only just restrained herself "—awful floating train car less than an hour ago. I'm exhausted. We haven't eaten a hot meal in days. You could at least offer me something to drink, Buck. Not to mention you expect me to be received by some fairy lord and lady looking completely frightening."

"They're throwing us a lavish feast—for you, it's all for you! The spread they put out is sure to be amazing, they always are. Every meal is like a Thanksgiving dinner here. Just so you know, Daughtry's not a fairy, just the wife." Buck lifted both of her cases with a shrug. "You have something appropriate in here to change into, no?"

Tanna struggled to think what clothes were in her cases, which were packed away in the trunks, and, most importantly, on which of them Holly had managed to install the iron wards.

"We can find something suitable," Holly said, giving her a reassuring smile.

"You can take a moment to freshen up," Buck said. "But the sooner we get there, the more time you'll have."

Tanna sighed, dropped her shoulders in defeat, and groaned.

"You know what you need?" Buck wagged his finger at her. "A glass of champagne. The food here is beyond description and the drink is like nothing you've ever experienced before. We'll demand champagne be sent to you while you're getting dressed. The minute we arrive. Now, come on."

—

Buck led them along the second-floor gallery for what must have been the equivalent of ten city blocks. They passed a few more of the cavernous rooms within the Tree, which were like the city squares in Savannah. Eventually, he took a left turn into a high-arched tunnel much like the one they'd taken down from the mooring masts into the interior of Treebridge. The same lines of jeweled lanterns were embedded in the walls. They emerged onto a large exterior plaza, a curving triangular balcony nestled in the space where the bottom curve of the massive Tree met the edge of the southern cliff.

The view over the gorge was breathtaking.

Tanna was able to study the course they had taken when they arrived. There were several other vessels making a similar approach, like Chinese lanterns sliding overhead to snag on the spine of spires high above. Few ships seemed to be leaving in the other direction.

A lightheadedness accompanied this sight—not unpleasant, like vertigo or the maziness of the crossing, but the soaring lift she'd felt on the last leg of their journey, when their ship had risen so high and fast up the face of the cliff. There was a direction from which the sun obviously shone, a brightness to the sky, but it was just over the horizon, as it might appear at sunset or dawn. It created an uncommon blue twilight that was impossible to describe.

Tanna had never fainted in her life, but in that moment she felt truly overcome.

Buck squeezed her hand and grinned like a devil. "It's amazing, isn't it?"

Tanna shook her head. "I don't have words. I had no idea it would be like this. That anyplace like this even existed on earth."

"It's more than I'd ever imagined." Buck sounded emotional. "More than the wildest rumors I overheard at home. I realize now it was all disinformation, purposefully downplayed to protect the truth about this place. It's more than a new start here, Tanna. A new life, yes, but a new life in a whole new *world*. Who could've known? How did you know? Was it some intuition that drove you?"

"It seems a joke that they called America the New World when *this* existed. Did I have an intuition of this? How could I? How could I have ever imagined this? I'm not exactly convinced I'm not dreaming the whole thing, right now."

"If you dreamed it, then it's a dream come true." He caught her eye and beamed at her. "We will be happy here, Tanna. And rich. I can feel it. I can feel fate smiling at us."

"Hush," she said. "Don't you dare say such a thing."

12

Buck gave Tanna back one of her bags, took her free hand, and pulled her across the plaza, up tight switchback stairs cut directly into the rock of the cliff face. He stopped short of the grand portico up ahead, squeezed through a tight cleft behind a boulder, and knocked at a small round wooden door.

"I take it you'd prefer no one see you just yet. Until you've had time to fix all this," he whispered, motioning at her hair, her dress. "I'll pass you off with Holly. She can take you through the servants' area down here and to whatever room is suitable for you to change in. I'll take Still on with me. We can meet inside."

"How will I find you?" Tanna asked.

"It's a party, darlin, and we're the guests of honor." He beamed his charming smile, excited as a little boy. "We'll see each other at the center of it all."

The door was opened by a small inhuman person about three feet tall dressed in the formal black-and-white uniform of a European maid. She wore a starched crinoline, full skirts, a crisp apron, and a smart little white cap on her head. She resembled a mouse with solid bead-black eyes and an impossibly long, thin nose. Her top front teeth stuck out above her lower lip. Her skin was more gray than brown, shiny, almost the purple color of a bruise. Her hand on the doorframe was composed of a long, multiple-jointed thumb and exactly three fingers, like a bundle of kindling twigs.

She curtsied.

Buck smiled at her sweetly enough. "Take Mrs. Eldridge through the kitchens and up the back stairs to somewhere she can change before anybody sees her. She just arrived after a long journey and she's not ready to be received quite yet."

She curtsied again and stepped back to allow Tanna and Holly to join her in the passageway. Buck heaved the remaining bag he'd been carrying into the little maid's arms, waved brightly, and disappeared with Still. Before the door closed, Tanna heard him calling out a greeting to someone he must know. There was an answer she couldn't make out, and then an explosion of raucous laughter.

—

Tanna followed the little maid through a passage so low she had to duck. Holly struggled to manage all the luggage she was carrying.

Tanna stopped. "Give me that."

Holly put up a mild protest, but Tanna wrenched the heaviest traveling case from her, leaving her only a few bags with which to contend. They passed an arched entrance that led into a big room with an enormous hearth and a raging fire. They were enveloped by warmth and the smell of baking bread. Tanna glimpsed what looked like an army of emaciated children, naked and barefoot except for white aprons and caps.

Elves. It was the only word her mind would return. What else could they be? Elves doing domestic tasks, just as one hears about in fairy tales.

Their little maid led them up a steep flight of stairs, passing a few other servants identical in stature, appearance, and dress. Only—bless her, Tanna thought—their guide was the only one with such enormous teeth. The servants were visibly startled to find tall human women in their domain, but they eyed Tanna and Holly discreetly and did not linger.

They emerged into a long paneled hallway, carpeted in perfectly formed and overlapping leaves made of some felt-like material. The individual forms were the browns and reds of autumn, arranged in a fish scale pattern. Sconces carved in the shape of enormous bees glowed with that liquid amber substance Tanna had seen in use in so many places since their arrival. There were identical doors up and down the hall, all of them closed.

The little maid opened one on the left and motioned them inside. It was a well-appointed bedroom, similar to guest rooms in all the homes of the wealthy Tanna had ever visited. These people loved pattern and texture, but the color palette was subdued—soft minty greens and the golds and browns of dried leaves and hay. The room smelled of chamomile and lavender. Tanna took one look at the soft lumpy bed and longed for a stolen hour's nap.

She peered at herself in an old looking glass, mottled like tarnished silver. She sighed at what she saw there—a bird's nest of hair, puffy eyes, pasty skin. The little maid was watching her from the door, a frown of concern on her face. She looked like she felt deep pity for Tanna, like she was almost about to cry. She held up a long twig of a finger, a universal sign that meant *wait one moment*, and then she disappeared, closing the door behind her.

Tanna turned to Holly, who was unfastening her bags and pulling out rumpled bundles of clothing, smoothing the dresses across the bed. "Maybe this light gray jacket, with the pearls. That seems like a wedding outfit to me."

"I'm not getting married," Tanna snapped, more harshly than she intended. "The gray makes me look pale as a ghost. The midnight blue won't show wrinkles as badly. It's the only thing in there that remotely flatters me."

"I don't think I put too many wards in it," Holly muttered, pinching the hem between her thumb and forefinger.

"Do you need to add more?" Tanna asked.

"No, not *more!*" Holly yelped. "I'll need to take them back out."

Tanna threw up her hands, exasperated. She shook her head in confusion, her mouth open, but the right question wouldn't form.

"There's a lot of fae here," Holly tried to explain. "The lady of this house is fae."

"I thought the wards were meant to protect me from fae."

"While traveling, yes. On the crossing. In random company. But you don't want to offend the hostess."

"Why would she be offended? How would she even know?"

Holly looked at the floor, reluctant to say. "The wards ... give off an odor."

"They can *smell* me?" Tanna was mortified.

"It's more than just a smell. But yes, to them, it does stink."

"Oh my God. So, right now, I'm walking around stinking? What exactly does it smell like to them?"

"Blood."

Tanna slapped a hand over her eyes and collapsed into an armchair.

Holly rifled through a bag and produced a sewing kit. "It won't take me long to take them out."

"Just fix it," Tanna growled.

She jumped up to pace around, afraid to sit down in the chair again. It was so comfortable and she was so tired she might not be able to get back up. She discovered an adjoining bathroom, well-appointed and surprisingly modern. There was a sink, linen towels, and black soap that looked like tar but smelled like rose petals.

There was a tap at the door and the little bucktooth maid reappeared, elbowing in with a large tray.

"Is that tea?" Tanna said. "Oh, thank you, thank you, you darling creature!"

She immediately regretted using the word *creature*—it had always been a term of endearment to her, but one she realized she might need to censor here. But the little maid's eyes twinkled; she nodded and smiled shyly.

"How thoughtful of you," Tanna felt herself tearing up over this small gesture of empathy. She must be ridiculously tired.

There was the faint rattle of china as the maid set the tray on a low bench at the foot of the bed. She poured the cups and passed them on saucers to first Tanna and then Holly.

The tea was dark as oil but smelled strongly of citrus and honey. When Tanna held the cup to her face the steam seemed to invigorate her skin. She had the impulse to bathe in a tub full of the stuff.

She sipped carefully, fearing she might burn her tongue, and the tiniest sip traveled through her mouth and across her face in a blush. Her eyes watered, her nostrils flared, and she felt her scalp begin to crawl at her hairline.

She blew softly and took a slightly larger sip, feeling the tingling sensation pass down her throat and seep out toward her shoulders. Only the strongest moonshine could move through one's body with such speed and stimulation. There was an aftertaste like pine or rosemary.

"This tea is amazing. I've never had anything like it," Tanna said to the elven maid. "What is your name?"

She went from looking very pleased with herself to slightly terrified. Her voice was reedy, like a tiny oboe. "Giselle, so'onah."

Tanna held out her hand to Giselle. Giselle stared at it, unsure what she was meant to do, but finally slipped her small hand around Tanna's index and middle finger, as a baby would.

Tanna softly pressed Giselle's long, dry fingers and looked into her black, bottomless eyes. "Someday you should come work in my house."

—

She found Buck where he said she would, at the center of a ballroom, in a circle of people hanging on to every word of a story he was taking too many words to tell. She checked to see that Holly was still with her. Giselle was already scurrying back along the darkness of the passageway by which she'd brought them. Holly's eyes were wide in the light of the ballroom.

"Stay with me," Tanna said.

"I don't know that I'm allowed—I can't—" She looked stricken, motioning at her workman's clothes.

"Please," Tanna said. But realizing how desperate she sounded, she altered her tone. "Whether you like it or not, you are now my closest friend and the only person I can trust in this world."

"What about your husband?"

Tanna scoffed. "I assure you I've never trusted him in my life. Don't look so scandalized. I do adore him, but surely you can see he's a bit of a rogue."

"People always seem to take to him very quickly," Holly said.

"You're quite the diplomat, Holly."

"I never know the right thing to say," Holly said, as if to warn her.

"You don't have to say anything. Just stay close to me and follow my lead. Pretend you're mortally shy."

"I don't have to pretend," Holly murmured.

"You're one of the bravest girls I've ever met. No, correction. You're one of the bravest *people* I've ever known, period. I don't know many men with half your gumption."

Holly flushed with pride. "You really think so?"

"Yes. But there is a price to pay for that, you know. It will take a very rare type of man to marry someone like you."

"I don't think I want to marry any type of man."

"I wonder if, in this world, you'll even have to."

—

Tanna set her shoulders, raised her chin, and swept across the room toward Buck. It was a predominately human crowd, at most a hundred or so, nearly all of them men dressed in jackets and ties, like a dinner party at home. She was less startled now by those few faces who turned to look at her with their cat's eyes. Those eyes must belong to the more civilized among the indigenous peoples here.

The knot of men holding court around Buck reminded her of a drunken fraternity of students—loud, laughing, quick to burst into limericks, cheers, and chants. Little differentiated them from the crowd at home with which Buck was most accustomed to socializing.

They did part as Tanna approached, making a path for her, but it was also a gauntlet of scrutiny. She was momentarily distracted by the floor itself—an elaborate mosaic with mother-of-pearl and glittering black micah. Remembering she was in a foreign land, clearly one of unsurpassed opulence, she looked up at the domed ceiling overhead. Beyond a chandelier of delicate crystal was a realistically painted twilight sky of midnight-blue, with stars that appeared to twinkle. The clouds were masterfully painted—they seemed to shift and move across one another. The illusion was uncanny; it threatened to topple her. She regained her senses by returning her focus to Buck's golden head and ruddy, smiling cheeks. He still had not seen her approaching.

When she finally caught his eye he roared, "Tanna!" He thrust a crystal glass into the air, sloshing drink on his companions, most of whom did not seem to mind any more than he seemed to notice.

Everyone in the room turned to look at her as he clasped her hand and raised it together with his in some unwarranted gesture of victory.

"Buck, really!" Tanna said, hissing through the mask of a perfect smile.

"It's a party, darlin!" He smelled as drunk as he acted. "You've got to meet everybody. These are all your new friends here. This is our new set."

He rattled off a series of names, turning in a circle and pointing to anyone he recognized. She caught almost none of them, but nodded politely and shook hands with a few.

One man seized her by the shoulders and kissed her wetly, his mouth reeking of some alcoholic spirit that smelled like perfume.

"Oh!" She tried her best to giggle and pass herself off as lighthearted, impossible to offend. But this opulent palace was really no different than a saloon full of rowdy drunks. Where were this lord and lady? What kind of hosts inspired this type of behavior in their guests?

One of Buck's companions had offered to get Tanna a drink, and Buck took it up as a singular purpose. "You won't believe what they have to drink here!" He yanked her toward the far side of the room, nearly dragging her off her feet. Holly clasped her arm and followed, as she'd promised.

There was a table set with crystal punch bowls, pyramids of little iced pastries, glowing candelabras, silver platters of some kind of roasted fowl decorated with its own impossibly colorful plumage. A tall, turbaned indigenous male, one of those who resembled Still, offered her a glass of effervescent, golden liquid.

It tickled her nose like champagne, but tasted more like gin and roses. Like the tea Giselle has served her earlier, the effects of this drink were drug-like in their intensity, almost airborne, like smelling salts. She inhaled, and it set the front of her forehead tingling from the inside.

She politely thanked the servant, and at Buck's enthusiastic cries to drink, she took the smallest sip. A chill flashed through her body, all the way down her legs to her toes. She felt instantly lighter. It took her breath away. She coughed, and then sighed loudly. She couldn't help but close her eyes in pleasure.

"Aha!" Buck wagged his finger in her face. "You see what I mean? Have you ever drunk anything like that in your life?"

"No, I can safely say I haven't." She was hesitant about drinking any more, or too much of it too quickly. But she found herself suddenly incredibly thirsty. She slurped from the glass, the liquid sloshing past her cheek and running down her throat. It pooled in her clavicle, and Buck pulled her to him, sucking the liquid from the side of her neck.

"Buck!" she yelled, and slapped at him with her free hand.

He cackled and hooted, his eyes glittering with that mad joy he always found at parties.

Tanna lurched around to see what had happened to Holly and found the girl faithfully beside her, guzzling from a horn. Holly planted the drained cup on the table and snatched what looked like a fried chicken leg. She gnawed at it ravenously and, seeing Tanna watching her, offered her a bite.

"Holly, I can hardly understand you. You shouldn't speak with food in your mouth like that, it's disgusting. And you're going to get grease all over my dress," Tanna said, batting her hand away.

Holly grabbed a large stuffed mushroom and shoved it at Tanna's lips. "Taste this. These are so good!"

Realizing she still had not eaten anything but biscuits and tea for hours, no matter how magically restorative it may have been, Tanna took the mushroom primly between thumb and index finger. She nibbled at the melted cheese oozing from the morsel. She swooned at the taste of it, groaning with pleasure.

"My God," Tanna said to Holly. "Get me another one of those."

"You should eat something," Buck roared drunkenly in her ear. "Didn't you want to eat something? The food is wonderful. Eat, eat!"

"What does it look like I'm doing?" Tanna mumbled around a mouthful, rolling her eyes. "You're an idiot."

Buck only roared with laughter. "You married an idiot, darlin. Are you only just figuring this out, or did you suspect it already? Do tell. What was your first clue?"

Tanna shoved Buck away. He put his hand on the back of her head, forced her face to his, and kissed her with his mouth open, shoving his tongue between her lips.

She slapped him.

He laughed again.

The men around them cheered.

—

It was the most gorgeous peach she'd ever seen or tasted in her life. She feared the juice was all over her face, but she couldn't take it away from her mouth. Her slurping grew loud in her own ears, and she realized the room had gone silent. She looked up to find everyone staring at her, clearing their throats uncomfortably and looking toward the center of the ballroom floor.

There in front of Tanna was an astonishingly beautiful woman, watching her with an expression of haughty bemusement.

She had the same tall, regal bearing as Still, and those golden cat's eyes. But she was fair in every way that he was dark. Her skin was porcelain-white; her hair was like silvery cornsilk that defied gravity. It was styled to look as if a strong wind were blowing directly in her face. It swept back at the temples, up at the crown in the shape of a tornado. The wispy ends moved on their own, as if dancing in a light breeze. The trailing edges of her pearl-colored gown drifted around her, away from her body, soft and slow-moving as a cloud. The entire effect of her appearance was a water nymph suspended in liquid. Tanna thought of Ophelia and the paintings of the Pre-Raphaelite Brotherhood.

The lady was entirely alien. No, preternaturally *of* this world in a way that only seemed exotic. Her beauty alluded to the deeper grace of nature that humans often observed in fleeting moments, but never seemed to dwell in for long. They weren't capable of sustaining such divinity.

The little man by her side, supporting her elbow, was entirely, unflatteringly human. He was in his fifties if he was a day, barely more than five feet tall, with a bald head, the enormous mutton chops of a bygone generation, and a gut overhanging his belt. He wore the immaculate full dress uniform of a Confederate officer.

He smiled at Tanna, with a kind twinkle in his eyes.

She froze beneath their gazes, her jaw in mid-chew. She forced herself to swallow the mouthful as discreetly as possible. Since it was obvious from the behavior of everyone in the room that this pair must be the illustrious hosts to whom she was to be formally presented—and because she wasn't sure what else she could do—she curtsied. Ridiculously. Like an eighteen-year-old debutante.

The lady's head tilted to the side as she peered at Tanna. Her golden irises pulsed with a black slit at the center, deepened momentarily to amber, then flashed white before returning to gold. A whistling sound, both the trill of a bird and the purr of a cat, rose and fell in time to the bewitching spectacle of her eyes.

Tanna's mouth hung open in dumb shock. The little man was speaking to her, but she could not tear her attention away from his lady. "I'm sorry," she managed.

"My wife finds you charming," he said, clearly repeating himself. The lady also repeated her fragment of song. "She welcomes you to our home."

Tanna shook herself, realizing the peculiar musical sounds were the lady's way of speaking, and her husband was translating.

She opened her mouth and swallowed, trying to think of something thoughtful and redeeming to say in response. But before she could speak, Buck appeared at her side, slipping his arm around her waist and lifting her ever so slightly. Had she been wobbling? Buck was certainly intoxicated enough to topple himself and drag her to the floor with him.

"Your lordship," Buck said, making a magnanimous sweeping arm gesture. "Allow me to introduce my wife, Tanna Cravens Eldridge. Tanna, this is our host, Lord Daughtry."

"How do you do," Tanna mumbled, bobbing in another awkward half-curtsy.

"Ah, Mrs. Eldridge, dear old girl. So glad you're finally here. Bucky's been counting down the hours," said Daughtry. "Allow me to introduce my wife, the Lady Glare."

The fairy lady's eyes focused even more intently upon her. Tanna found it challenging to hold her gaze. Even though it wasn't the bottomless black orbs of the elves, the fairy's eyes were somehow soulless. Piercing, yet indirect. Disconnected. Predatory.

This time when she spoke, a few seconds of the trilling purr preceded heavily accented English. "Madame Eldridge. You are most welcome in my home."

Tanna nodded and smiled, unwilling to trust her voice in the glare of the lady's attention.

"You're from Chattanooga also, I assume?" Daughtry asked.

"Yes," Tanna said, relieved for an excuse to make eye contact with a human. "Lookout Mountain, actually."

"Of course. You're a Cravens," Daughtry beamed. He was assuming

Tanna belonged to that historical family everyone knew, but this wasn't the time to correct him. "It will be good to have another household we can count on when the war comes this way."

Tanna looked to Buck, confused as to how she should respond. She hadn't heard anything about a war. She wished Buck had taken some time with her before thrusting her into this elaborate social situation where she knew nothing of what was going on around her.

Buck winked at her. "Now, don't go scaring the hell out of my wife, Daughtry. She's barely two hours off the damned airship."

Tanna was a little worried Buck's intoxication was fueling blatant disrespect, but Daughtry didn't seem offended.

"Crossing the Seaming does addle the mind a bit," he said to Tanna in a stage whisper. "And then you've got to get accustomed to this intoxicating drink. We won't press you into politics tonight, old girl."

"I look forward to learning your concerns," Tanna promised diplomatically, "and the intricacies of your local customs. In the very near future."

Buck laughed out loud, hugging Tanna to him and shaking her. "Don't let your guard down, Daughtry! This one was raised to rule."

Tanna struggled to maintain a polite, dignified smile.

"Well, old boy, the fae actual prefer female leaders," Daughtry said. "The sooner we all accept it, the better, I reckon."

Daughtry and his lady were quickly pulled away by the attentions of others, the music played again, and the circle of guests who had stopped to witness the exchange had moved on with their revelry.

"Buck, what war is he talking about?" Tanna asked, pulling him toward an empty corner. "Should I be worried?"

Buck waved away her questions as if they were petty concerns. "War's good for business."

"Daughtry's wife, Glare," she said, changing the subject. "What's her lineage?"

"You mean, what the hell is she?" Buck smiled at her shock and discomfort.

She hissed for him to keep his voice down. "She's clearly a different type of person than some of these others. She has eyes like Still."

Buck frowned and became suddenly, miraculously sober. "As near as I can figure it, Still's some kind of half-breed. His kind are usually close to the rich. They seem to be an elevated class of servants. I know Lady Glare's a Seelie. I've also heard them called Troopers, and the Shee—spelled S-I-D-

H-E—or something like that. They're the pretty ones. They look the most like us. They're rich, they're powerful, and—I'll tell you what—I think they might be a little dangerous. They have some kind of magic power over the others. All the little brown genies are docile as can be, scared to even look you in the eye. And if one of her kind gives them a command, they don't even question it. I'll bet the brown ones would kill for them."

"*Genies*," she repeated, the term obviously distasteful to her. "What does that mean? Holly said it's short for some other word."

"Aborigines. The indigenous people. They're the ones who've been here as far back as anybody knows."

She silently divided the room into groups—predominantly white human men with a few of their colorful ladies; small brown fae servants, androgynous in appearance were it not for their uniforms. There were a few of the tall, elogant fae like Lady Glare or even Still's kind. There were even fewer dark-skinned humans. She hadn't seen many black people since she'd arrived.

Crushed in a hot ballroom outnumbered by drunken men ... It was just like a party at home on Lookout Mountain.

She grabbed Buck by the elbow before he could slip away. "Can we go soon?"

"Go? This party is for us, for *you*. We can't leave yet. It'd be rude."

"I don't mean to be ungrateful, but I'm exhausted. And this drink has gone straight to my head," she looked at her empty glass suspiciously. "I just need to lie down. At least sit still for a minute."

"Listen," Buck said, taking her hands in both of his, his tone patronizing. "It's important for our future prospects that I talk to the people here tonight. I need to shake a few more hands, kiss a few more cheeks, raise a few more glasses. You know what I mean. Once we're out at the farm, we won't have the opportunity to be around our kind this much. If you're going to make any friends in this world, you better find them here."

She scanned the crowd, again hoping to catch sight of Holly.

"Tell you what," Buck said. "Just one more hour and then we'll go. How's that? Why don't you walk outside and get some air? It's a nice night. You should see the view of Treebridge from here on the cliff. All the lights. It's beautiful."

"Why can't you take me out and show me?" Tanna pouted.

Something—or someone—caught his eye. He held up a finger that he was on his way. "I'll come find you in a bit," he said, barely looking at her. He kissed her on the cheek and waded back into the crowd at the center of the room.

She watched Buck put his arm around a woman's waist. Tanna had noticed her several times during the evening; she was small, with kohl-blackened eyes and dark-red lip rouge. There was a man who must be her companion always at her side. He leaned in close to Buck's ear. Whatever he said made Buck grin like a devil. It looked for a moment as if the two men might kiss. Buck's hand had strayed down to the top of the woman's hip; she placed her hand over his, guiding, affirming. At that moment, she stared right at Tanna.

Tanna looked down at the bottom of her champagne glass and pretended she hadn't seen.

13

Tanna put some effort into her search for Holly. She made a circuit of the ballroom, looking behind curtains into alcoves where furniture had been arranged for more intimate conversations. Unable to find the girl, she wandered through a set of doors onto a balcony under the cloudy night sky. She drifted out toward the lights. The breeze was heavenly after the feverish closeness of all those bodies in fine clothes, pressed together, dancing and shouting into one another's faces.

A few couples stood at the chest-high balustrade, captivated by the great Tree dominating the left-hand view. Tanna saw a woman's leg wrapped around the thigh of a man who pressed her against the stone banister, leaning her dangerously backward into space. Tanna moved away from their soft grunts and sighs.

She couldn't look away from the amazing bulk of Treebridge, this great skyscraper lying on its side across the vast emptiness of the gorge. Shreds of fog drifted around the vessels coming and going from the mooring masts, as if they either sailed on clouds or towed them across the sky. There were mists of small glittering lights, as if the fireflies here could mimic schools of fish or flocks of starling birds wheeling over a city square.

She recognized moonlit sylphs, like those she and her cousin had seen in the garden that night. *Did* see. Here was the evidence, the proof of their existence. They had called out to her across time to this moment and place. So much of the swimming motion of the air fairies was slow, dreamlike, a speed that one would normally believe incapable of defying gravity.

Something much faster, relatively large, and unrecognizable swooped by low enough to make her duck. When she ignored the music and the murmur of the partygoers inside, she could discern unfamiliar sounds. From deep below in the gorge were faint and distant shrieks, the cries of nocturnal birds of prey.

The skies here were as full of life as the oceans.

She saw an airship rising in bumping lurches as its lines were let out. Her stomach flipped with the recollection. That had been her, only hours before, unaware of this world. Her entire impression of reality had changed in the course of an afternoon. The world was not just the world anymore.

Her eyes welled up with tears. She didn't know if she was drunk, tired, or slightly euphoric. She felt covered in raw nerves, emotional and fragile, just wanting to slip away where no one could see her and perhaps have a good private cry in a hot bath.

Farther along the balustrade, in the protected corner where the Tree met the neighborhood of grand vertical mansions stacked on the cliff, there was a large wicker birdcage filled with small round forms. They made soft cooing, hooting noises and shuffled around on their perches as she approached. At first, she was unsure of what she was seeing—they appeared to be large gray bumblebees. The ones flying around inside the cage hovered. Hummingbirds, maybe. Finches? Certainly birds of some kind, tiny things, and a great number of them. One of the brown and silver creatures rotated its head and blinked at her with shockingly round eyes. The entire bodies of the little things were dominated by these enormous eyes and flat stumps of heads. They were some kind of impossibly diminutive owls. Not baby owls—fully grown, but still small.

"You should see them take down a cocker spaniel. Wicked, efficient creatures."

Tanna jumped at the voice. It belonged to the silhouette of a man, seated on a bench, legs crossed, smoking a cigarette.

"I'm sorry," he said. "You don't have a dog, do you?"

"I do," Tanna said. "But not here. I had to leave her at home."

"Oh, good. I think those women who bring their little dogs to parties like this are insufferable."

"Well, she's not a little dog. And I didn't just leave her at home for the party. I had to leave her behind when I emigrated. She's still back in Chattanooga. In ... the Gray."

"Ah," he said. "You must be Mrs. Eldridge."

Tanna hesitated. She smiled awkwardly, but prepared to turn and leave.

He leapt up, launched the butt of his cigarette over the balustrade into the gulf of air, and bowed low, his arm sweeping through his own cloud of smoke. The effect was both elegant and humorous. "Forgive me, Mrs. Eldridge. Please don't let my drunken lack of manners run you off." He had the chiseled features and dark hair of a moving picture star. "I'm Cole Mathers."

"Oh!" She pointed her finger at him, suddenly remembering. "Mathers. I'm supposed to give you a message. You're a friend of that man with the wings."

"Um," Cole frowned, which actually made him more handsome. "You have no idea how many different people you have just described."

"Gallagher."

Cole closed his eyes and nodded. "Jackson."

"That's him!"

"What does he want from me now?"

"I beg your pardon?" Tanna asked, uncertainly.

"A message. I believe you said ..."

"Oh, yes. You must think I'm drunk. I'm not, I assure you." She rolled her eyes. "Well, I don't think I am ... But it seems a bit like everything I've tasted has gone to my head."

Cole Mathers blinked slowly above an unwavering, patient smile.

"He said to tell you to collect his things. His *wings*." She swept her arms behind her in a wide gesture. "He had an enormous pair of wings I brought them with me on my dirigible. We ran across him out in the Sea of Trees. When I first spotted him, I thought he was a fallen angel."

Mathers rolled his eyes with mock exasperation. "Oh God, he's an angel now, is he? Well, I assure you, he is definitely *fallen*. But, of course, you wouldn't be the only one to fall under his spell at first sight."

Tanna tried to remember the details of her arrival and worried that she may have failed in her errand. "Come to think of it, I'm not sure where they would have taken his things. Do you know? I don't even know where my own cargo has ended up. We just left it up there. I did see the genies unload Mr. Gallagher's things when we disembarked. My husband had a servant named Still there to meet us. Maybe he knows where everything was taken."

"Still, did you say? I wouldn't worry, then. He's a capable person. Behind the scenes, the members of his tribe—the Alleegee—run most of our lives around here. No doubt why your husband hired him. Still will have directed a team to take care of your things. They were most likely sent on to your husband's room at The Fairchild."

"Yes, that was where we met him after I arrived."

"Jackson keeps an apartment there too. Which he mostly uses as a warehouse. It's piled high with his treasures. You should see it. The proverbial dragon's lair. Trunks and crates full of curiosities. Skins, furs, gems, and rare plants. Weapons. You could spend hours going through it all. It's like a bazaar. I'm sure they've most likely dumped everything there."

"I hope they didn't break my china."

Cole looked amused. "You brought china?"

"Oh yes. My wedding china."

"But not your dog."

Tanna's face fell. "She couldn't travel in the dirigible, so I had to leave her. I apologize if I start to cry now. I'm sick with guilt."

"What's her name?"

"Ginger," she said, as her eyes filled with tears.

Cole Mathers produced a handkerchief from the inside breast pocket of his jacket and offered the wilted cloth to her.

She pressed the corners of the silk beneath her eyes and dabbed at her dripping nose. "My God, I don't know what's come over me. You must think I'm ridiculous, crying over a dog. I think I'm just exhausted. Honestly, I just want to go home."

"Already? You would turn around and go back?"

"No, no. We have a farm here now. I think. I want to go to my new house there."

"Buck doesn't seem like the kind of man to leave a party early. Especially not his own."

Tanna sighed. "I just hope he'll come and find me later, and not leave me. I may end up out here sleeping on this bench."

"Well, that's not going to happen as long as I can help it. I have a proposal. Why don't we go and find him together? And if we can't, I'll escort you back to his room at The Fairchild. I can check and see that Jackson's wings are there."

"I don't know whether or not I'm supposed to go back there," Tanna said.

"I'm pretty sure you're sleeping there tonight." Cole squinted at her, regretful he had to bear the bad news. "Brynmor is a few hours' drive from here. It's awfully late. Surely Buck intended for you to rest at the club first."

"They threw me out of there!" Tanna said, her unmanageable emotions shifting to anger. "I'm apparently not allowed."

Cole frowned. "Who told you such a thing?"

"They threw me out. They cast a ... *spell* of some kind to drive me from the dining room."

"Oh, I see. You tried to go in the members area. Yes, women are not allowed. But just in that one room. It's an inn too, you know. A hotel. All the floors above are rooms. You should be welcome there."

"Buck said something about maybe staying here." Tanna had little hope of finding her husband anytime soon. Through the windows, she watched the dancers inside. Remembering something Cole had said she turned to him. "What is Brim More?"

"Brynmor," he enunciated, and spelled it. "I think it means *big hill* in Welsh, or something like that. Your farm sits on top of Brynmor."

"Brynmor." She tried the name out on her tongue. She loved the way it felt to say it. "I'm Tanna," she said to him.

His eyes crinkled at the corners when he smiled at her. "Tanna," he repeated, inclining his head in the slightest bow.

—

They had spent a good quarter of an hour scanning the thinning dance floor and peering into all the alcoves. No one knew where Buck was, although everyone seemed to have talked to him at some point, and most remembered seeing him last in the presence of a couple named Jed and Cookie Blevins.

"He'll have to return to the club at some point," Cole said. "Even if he stays out all night and wakes up in a gutter tomorrow, he'll still have to change his clothes and splash some water on his face. Why don't I walk you and make sure you get back to his room safe and sound?"

"That'd be very kind of you," Tanna said. "I don't know what's happened to Holly either. We weren't supposed to become separated."

"Is there someone here with whom you could leave word for her?"

"There's an elven maid named Giselle."

Cole pulled aside a silver-turbaned Alleegee with molten eyes, one of the genies who looked like Still, and asked if he could bring Giselle to speak with them.

They sent the elven maid to check the room and see if Holly might have found her way back there. She reappeared faster than Tanna would have anticipated, shaking her head and looking a little fearful to have to use the word *no* with Tanna in any context.

"I hope she remembered my bags," Tanna said. "Did she take them?"

Giselle nodded.

An hour ago, it would have made Tanna anxious to be left behind by both Buck and Holly, but Cole was superior company. He led her back through the tunnel into the Tree and along the main promenade. The crowds Buck had dragged her through earlier had dwindled considerably, but even at this late hour, Treebridge was alive with lights and people, and not-quite human beings glimpsed from the corner of the eye.

It was easier to study the architectural detail of the interior caverns. All the surfaces mimicked an outdoor park. The carpets were moss, flowers, or leaves. The roof overhead was a curve of blue crystal, like the inside of an enormous geode. The facets gave the impression of twinkling stars. There were few hard geometric edges or corners anywhere—every doorway was arched; every wall was curved. Even the most permanent materials, such as the banisters on the galleries overlooking the main promenade, seemed to have been grown into their present form. At the same time, every natural element seemed too perfect to be a living thing.

Tanna didn't see a single clock anywhere. It had to be well into the wee hours of morning, but inside the great Tree it could be any time. There was an energy among the people and the fae who were still out and about, a collective mood that reminded Tanna of a holiday parade or the aftermath of a sporting event. She thought of Mardi Gras in New Orleans, Times Square on New Year's Eve. Intoxication in this world was certainly pervasive and public. While most of the genies were expressionless and impossible for her to read, there was a level of madness in nearly every human face they passed.

Cole was the opposite—lighthearted yet calm. He was the antithesis of Buck in every way: tall, lanky, dark-haired. He carried himself with dignity.

Tanna grew quiet. The sustaining effects of the elixirs she had consumed earlier in the evening had finally worn off. Yet, here she was walking through a waking dream. She was grateful to Cole for escorting her back to The Fairchild, but she was privately humiliated. It was her first day in a new country, and she was a newlywed ... He should have been her husband.

"You know what the worst part is?" she asked.

"The worst part of having me walk you home?" Cole clutched his chest as if wounded. "I thought I was at least a half-decent substitute."

"No, I'm sure you're the *best* part," she said, feeling the blush burning her cheeks. She hesitated, weighing the consequences of saying it out loud. "This is supposed to be my honeymoon."

Cole was clearly unsure of the appropriate response. "Congratulations?" he said, with the hint of a question mark. "Were you just married today?"

"No. We were married several days ago. Well, it was several days ago in Chattanooga. I'm not sure how long Buck has been here. But we didn't have a reception after our ceremony. He left that night to come ahead and establish a place for us here so I'd have somewhere to come to. And today was the first time I'd seen him since he dropped me off after we left the church."

"I'm sure he's had a lot to contend with and wanted to get everything taken care of before you arrived."

"That's what I'd like to tell myself."

Cole smiled, silently acknowledging the implication.

"I'm sorry," Tanna murmured. "I shouldn't be complaining. I've barely known you for an hour."

Without stopping, she did a slow turn, taking in the beautiful fairy architecture. It renewed her to know that she would be living in a world where buildings looked like this. "So, what can you tell me about Brynmor?" she asked. "Is that the name of the farm? Or does the house itself have a name?"

"As far as I know, everyone just calls that part of the country Brynmor," Cole said. "It's a beautiful area, south of here. Mostly rolling meadows as far as the eye can see. Except for this enormous round knoll rising up out of the landscape. A hill so big it splits Wavy Creek, and the Big South Road has to bend and go around it. There's a tribe of hill-dwelling fae called the Nunnahee who've lived there for centuries. Possibly thousands of years."

"They're still there?"

"Oh yes. They've been living in peaceful cohabitation with the colonists since they started arriving. I'm sure many of them will be working for you. The property spreads in terraces down the southeastern side of the knoll, and the house itself sits on a nice level patch at the top in a copse of blue atzeenah trees, with a view of the Hawnee Hills."

"*Blue* trees?" Tanna asked.

"You know, that dusty color you find in spruces, hemlocks, and the skins of blueberries. But the atzeenah aren't evergreens. They look a little bit like tulip poplars. The leaves have that distinctive shape. They also happen to be blue."

Tanna smiled and shook her head. "I can't wait to see this. It's hard to even imagine it."

"You'll see all kinds of interesting plants here."

"You sound like quite the botanist."

"I suppose I'm something more of a naturalist. Being raised here brings that out in some of us."

"Not everyone?"

"You see all this?" He swept his hand through the air before him, indicating the spectacle they walked through. "This is hardly what I'd call *natural* anymore."

"I would think it's impossible not to appreciate nature, especially here, on this scale."

"You would think so."

"But not everyone does."

"No." He looked suddenly serious and a little bit sad. "Unfortunately not."

"I don't think I could bear to disappoint you by being one of those people."

He smiled at her. "I don't think you could."

—

Cole guided her up one of the grand flights of stairs, which brought them close to the entrance to The Fairchild. In no hurry for their walk to be over, Tanna asked if he would sit with her on a stone bench overlooking the promenade. She talked about her plans to start an apothecary. He made appropriate noises of encouragement and asked polite questions, but he gave no indication whether he judged her ideas to be brilliant or terrible.

"So, tell me about your family," she said.

"Well, we're known for our orchard. It's where I grew up. We've been in the house there for five generations. I'm more feral than most people realize. I've only been into the Gray twice. Long enough to turn around and come back."

"Is it far?" she asked. "Your orchard?"

"The foot of the Hawnee Hills. It's definitely not close to here, twice as far as Brynmor. But you can actually see my house from yours. The atzeenah trees around your house grow in a sort of horseshoe shape with a gap. When you go out into the garden behind your kitchen and you look straight out, due south, through the gap you'll see a set of hills to your right, in the southwest. They look like the knuckles of a fist. My home is on an eastern slope of those hills. It's in shade from midday through the afternoon, but when the sun rises, you can see a flash of orange. That's the copper roof of my stables."

"You must have been at my house in the morning, then?"

"I have." He paused mysteriously. "I've spent the night there a few times."

She knew it would be rude to ask him why, so instead she asked him if his house had a name.

Cole chuckled. "You like a house with a name, don't you?"

Her eyes flashed. "I do."

"Most people just call it the orchard. But, no, our house has never really had an official name. Maybe you can think of one."

She studied her hands in her lap. "Well, I'd need to be invited out to see it first."

"Then you must be especially anxious to see your own home. What would you call it if you could name it anything you wanted? You must have a few favorites you're considering."

"I've been daydreaming about having my own home since I was a little girl. In my family, house names always have the word *wood* in them. My mother's house, where I grew up, is called Blackwood. I've always thought Havenwood would be a beautiful name for a great house."

"Havenwood," he said, trying it out. "It sounds like something we're all seeking. I like it."

She was pleased by his response, but her smile fell into a frown. "The only thing is, do these blue trees around the house even qualify as a wood? Everyone keeps calling it a *farm*. The word *farm* makes me think of open, grassy spaces, with lots of fenced-in paddocks and fields of crops."

"It's more like a little crown of trees, really. You'll have to decide. But Havenwood is a good name."

"Well, if it doesn't suit my farm, I'll let you know and you can have it. Somewhere in the Green there should be a place called Havenwood, don't you think?"

"You've certainly convinced me."

—

Her ears started to ring the moment she and Cole entered the foyer of The Fairchild. Her body had not forgotten the spell that had been thrown at her earlier in the day. She felt uncomfortable in her clothes; the topmost pearl button on her collar restricted her breathing. Holly had helped her into this dress; there was a stab of panic at the thought she might not be able to take it off on her own. So far, she hadn't seen any female staff in The Fairchild, and she was loath to draw attention to herself by making requests. The same arrogant young man sneered at her from behind the front desk. She didn't know where Buck's room was, either, and she was afraid he might refuse to tell her if she asked.

Thankfully, Cole spoke to the clerk on her behalf and was given a key.

The clerk nodded to her, curtly but respectfully, as Cole steered her through an arched opening and onto a staircase. He held her elbow and pushed her up ahead of him. Several times on the long walk back, it had occurred to Tanna that she and Cole Mathers might appear to be a couple. It felt different from being on Buck's arm. She was always fearful Buck would embarrass her with his loud voice, his free laugh, or the reputation that preceded him. When she had been engaged to Buck's brother Ford, she had felt judged by others—by other women especially. Many thought her a fool for being so attentive to a man who did not return her love and did not respect her enough to say so.

She wished she could have met Cole Mathers six months ago. She felt a connection with him, a warmth, a safety, and a sense of being valued she had never felt with Ford and likely never would with Buck, either.

She had thought she was making a strategic decision by marrying Buck, one that would allow her to make her own way, with her own money, and claim her own power. And by choosing to marry a friend, she was free to be her own person, supported by her husband in ways few women could hope to be. It never occurred to her there was any part of her still left that believed in some prince, some fairy tale notion of romance. She'd never really bought into the motivation that drove the fantasies of young girls. Some part of her instinctively dismissed the idea of love, of one day meeting a mate who would treasure her.

And now, just as this man made her consider all those things again, it was too late. She had been right about one thing, though—the kind of man she might have daydreamed about never existed in her world. Cole Mathers, if he was indeed such a man, had been in another world the whole time. There was nothing she could have done differently. Until she had made these irreversible choices, there had been no opportunity to discover him.

"Buck's staying a few rooms down from Jackson," Cole said, leading her along a wood-paneled hall. "We've had a few nightcaps and smokes together over the last few days."

"Oh really?" she asked casually.

"We all like your husband, Tanna. And he speaks very highly of you."

"Thank you for saying so."

"That's Buck's door right there. But, if you want ..." He tapped the door closest to them with his key. "I wouldn't mind showing you the famous dragon's lair."

"I wouldn't want to intrude on Mr. Gallagher."

"Oh, I doubt he's actually here," Cole said, his grin appearing slightly suggestive in the context.

She felt a blush threaten her cheeks as she imagined going into this empty room alone with a charming man she'd only just met at a party. "Even more reason for me not to be snooping," she demurred.

Cole waved away her objection. "Jackson's my business partner, and he's also like a brother to me. I have a key. And I'm inviting you. Besides, he entrusted you with the wings and whatever else he's collected on this last safari. I was going to check and make sure it all made it here. Wouldn't you like to know?"

She nodded, finding it a reasonably decent proposal. "I would like to know I managed to keep my word."

Cole unlocked the door but leaned into it with his shoulder, shoving it open. "It sticks a little bit," he mumbled.

He crossed the dark room quickly and lit a lantern from the embers of the fire in the hearth. Tanna lingered in the hallway, but when the contents of the room emerged from the shadows, she was pulled in without further hesitation. Here was Jackson's collection of treasure, a mad, unorganized emporium—skins, furs, tusks hung on the walls. Trunks, crates, boxes dumped in heaps in the middle of the room. Bundles of herbs dried on hooks, potted plants sat on the floor, and cut flowers stood in a crystal vase on a table. The wall above the fireplace was covered in weapons—rifles, spears, bows. Rocks and crystals lined the mantel. Every other wall was crammed from floor to ceiling with books—every inch of space, between the tops of the spines and the shelves above them. In a few places, the books spilled onto the floor in piles. Even more volumes had been stacked near an armchair as a makeshift end table. An overflowing glass ashtray perched on top.

Tanna turned her head sideways and ran a fingertip lovingly across the spines. "I was so anxious that I hadn't brought enough books of my own. Now, seeing all these, I don't know why I thought no one else in this whole world would read but me. Does he lend them?"

"Not nearly as much as he should. These books leave little space for all the other things we sell. He's had to move his rooms here three times over the years. This is as large a set of rooms as they have."

"So they're for sale?"

"He'll never read them all, but no, he insists the books aren't for sale. Everything else, even the shirt off his back."

"I hope I'll have the proper space in my new house to devote to a library." She looked at Cole, hoping he might offer an opinion.

"There's space in your main living room I think you'll find suitable."

"Wonderful," she said over her shoulder, going back to browsing the titles. "Please tell Mr. Gallagher when his collection outgrows his rooms again, I'd be happy to let some of them stay with me."

Cole chuckled. "I will tell him."

Movement in the corner drew her eye. "Oh God. More of those little things." Another elaborate matchstick cage stood tall in the corner with a dozen or more finch owls. "Are they popular here as pets?"

"No. They're not pets. They're trophies." His voice changed, tight with a trace of suppressed anger. "Evidence of wealth. To humans, anyway."

Tanna scowled. "Really?"

"Some consider them symbols of underestimated power." The bitter tone was still there.

"And you sell them to these people?" She turned away from the cage. "For what?"

"Jackson's known for being one of the few humans who can capture the things alive. But, between you and me, he has help. He has a way with the fae. He gets them to do all kinds of things for him and he takes the credit." He pursed his lips, but playfully irritable this time. "Anyway, I'm not sure how much he's motivated to sell them. He always keeps the damned things around. I think the finch owl has become his personal totem."

"But didn't you say they were dangerous and cruel?"

Cole shrugged. "All part of their charm."

"What do they represent to him?"

"The cumulative might of the small." The bitter tone in his voice had returned.

There was an awkward silence.

"Would you like to sit by the fire?" Cole asked.

"It's really late. If I sit down there, I'll be done for." She started backing toward the door. "I'm afraid I can't keep my eyes open much longer."

"Of course."

She winced. "I don't see the wings anywhere here, though."

"No," Cole said, nonchalantly looking around. "It doesn't look like they've made it up here yet."

"I hope they haven't been misplaced. Or stolen, God forbid. I'm sure they're unbelievably rare and valuable—"

He shook his head and held up a hand to stop her. "Please. Don't worry—"

"But I feel responsible. I told Mr. Gallagher I would deliver them to you—"

"The elves are very superstitious about things that don't belong to them.

They make excellent couriers. When you ask them to carry something of yours, they feel a mortal curse has been placed on them that can only be remedied by fulfilling your wishes. None of the fae who travel with Jackson would steal from him. You weren't responsible for delivering Jackson's cargo—no matter what he said—you were transporting his servants. And it's their job."

"I see. So they probably still have all his things with them?"

"I'm sure. They're not allowed on these premises. Jackson will have to retrieve them and bring them here tomorrow himself. Or else I will."

Cole left the door to Gallagher's rooms opened, walked her a few steps farther down the hall, opened another door for her, and handed her the key.

Tanna peered into the room and saw that there was someone in the bed. She crept a few feet inside, saw the dark head, and heard the familiar snore. Holly. Buck's fair hair would have shone like moonlight, even in the dark room

"She's here," Tanna pointed and whispered. She moved back to join Cole in the hallway for a moment, pulling the door shut behind her. "I'm relieved. But I do wonder how on earth she knew which rooms were Buck's. And how she got in here ..."

"She's a resourceful girl," Cole smiled. "You'll find that most of the feral can be quite cunning."

"Is she considered feral?"

"Well, yes," Cole spluttered. "She's the Graycoat's daughter. He's famously feral, in your world as well as this one. They are also unique in the way they travel between the two worlds so much more frequently than most of our kind. But don't look so concerned. It's not like she's a thief or a murderess or even uncivilized. The feral are simply those who have chosen the danger and beauty of this world over the materialism and industry of the culture that produced us all."

The remark felt loaded, political.

She wasn't sure how to respond. "Well, thank you, again, for everything. You saved me tonight, in more ways than you may ever know."

His smile was genuinely soft and warm. "I'm happy I could." She felt guilty for ever doubting his intentions.

"Will you be staying here tonight, then?" she asked.

"I'll think I'll get a few hours' sleep in Jackson's favorite chair by the fire. Head out in the morning."

"Maybe I will see you again tomorrow."

"If not tomorrow, then soon."

She had a bold thought, and she remembered Buck telling her if she were going to make any friends, she'd better do it here, tonight. "Give me some time to unpack my china, and then come for dinner. Bring Mr. Gallagher if you like."

"I'll bring a bottle of something," he said. "And a book or two."

—

Tanna considered waking Holly to help her undress, but the girl's snores ceased only temporarily. She turned toward the wall, pulling the blanket reflexively over her head. Tanna sighed, unfastened the buttons on the collar around her throat, pulled the pins out of her hair, and took off her boots. Fully dressed, she stretched out beside Holly on top of the covers. She lay awake for a few moments, thinking of the grandeur of Lady Glare's home, the surprising opulence of Treebridge in general. She couldn't wait to see her house. She imagined a grand lodge with exposed timber beams and shining wood banisters that curved like living vines.

She wondered how late into the day Buck would have to sleep before they could start the journey to Brynmor. She hoped he would at least be here in the morning when she woke up.

14

Tanna awoke to banging on the door. Holly sat up beside her and looked around, disoriented. Tanna was thankful, as she crossed the room, that she was still dressed.

"Thank God you're here!" Buck stumbled into the room, his wispy pale hair waving on top of his head, cheeks flushed, tie and collar unfastened. He had his shoes in one hand, a key in the other. He reeked of alcohol and his eyes were unfocused and wild. "I can't get the damn key to work."

Buck dove onto the bed, twisting in midair to land on his back beside Holly. "Ah! Good morning, my dear," he said, patting her elbow affectionately through the coverlet.

Holly's face was expressionless with sleepiness and shock.

Tanna looked up and down the hall before closing the door. She imagined Cole Mathers's blue eyes peering in to witness this unconventional scene. The doors to Jackson Gallagher's rooms were shut.

She wanted to know where Buck had been, but she was hesitant to demand the details in front of Holly. She was afraid of what candid information might come out of his mouth in this state. The girl climbed off the bed and padded sleepily into the adjoining bathroom.

"Buck, surely you're not going to sleep this day away."

"No, no, of course not," he groaned, throwing his legs over the side of the bed and sitting up. "I know you want to see the house." He shot her one of his puckish grins. "But I'm warning you now, I am going to nap on the road."

Tanna glared at him. "When you finally leave me for good," she said, pitching her voice low so Holly wouldn't overhear, "at least I'll be free to marry Cole Mathers."

—

Since the women weren't allowed in the dining room, they ate a hasty breakfast of dry toast brought to the room by a servant. Tanna muttered a few complaints about the way women were treated at The Fairchild, but she mostly wanted to get going. Buck sent Holly on a mystical errand with a single grunted word Tanna didn't quite catch. Holly returned five minutes later with small steaming cups of what looked like strong black tea. They were little more than thimbles; both Buck and Holly tossed the contents back in a single swallow.

Tanna sipped hers first, experimentally. It had a strong resiny smell, like rosemary or pine. It tasted like hot gin—Tanna coughed—but from even that small taste, she experienced the same restorative tingling sensation as she did with the tea Giselle had served them the evening before. This was a less appealing brew, but the outcome was the same. To taste as little of it as possible, she finished it off with a large swallow. For a few seconds, she feared it might come back up, but then a sense of energy and euphoria suffused her limbs.

She felt like she was dancing when she moved about the room. Buck was skipping around humming a jaunty tune while hunting for a change of clothes. Holly was repacking Tanna's bags with lightning speed.

Buck disappeared into the bathroom and returned dressed in his hunting clothes.

"Let's go!" he cried, already out in the hall.

"Aren't you taking any of your things?" Tanna asked.

"Nah, I'll leave them here."

"You're ... keeping this room?"

"Yes. It's quite useful. I'll still have some business here in town."

"It's not expensive?"

"No." He made a rude dismissive noise and waved the thought away. "Besides, we're practically aristocrats here, darlin. Wasn't that the point of coming?"

She couldn't help but smile at the thought. She had no reason to doubt him, given the surprising display of taste and wealth she'd seen here so far. Maybe her money was worth more here than they'd anticipated. After seeing the Daughtrys' mansion, built into the side of a cliff, she couldn't wait to see what a house with property looked like. She hoped the linens were as nice as the Daughtrys'. She had the sudden inspiration of a lilac-colored bedroom—restful, feminine yet dignified. Given the extended growing season here, it should be easy to keep fresh-cut flowers throughout the year. No doubt there were exotic blooms here she could not even imagine.

—

Upon leaving the inn this time, Buck led them back up to the top of Treebridge through a different sloping tunnel. Sunny, green natural light poured through a ceiling of translucent veined panels like enormous leaves. The overall effect was walking through a greenhouse made entirely of natural materials.

They emerged onto a sidewalk of cobblestones beside the busy highway that ran along the top of the great Tree. Horses, mules, wagons, and foot traffic streamed in both directions. The mooring masts were farther along toward the middle of the Tree. They were closer to the end where Treebridge met the southern cliffside.

Still was waiting for them beside an ancient horse-drawn carriage. The vehicles here had something of the same quality as the cabin on the dirigible—old-fashioned designs from previous centuries that looked like they had been executed with rustic, native materials. The curves, the shapes, the lines were similar, but the attention to sanding and painting and gilding and lacquer was virtually nonexistent. Buck handed her up, and she felt like she was climbing into the carriage on a dilapidated carousel. The red velvet upholstery had seen better days.

Still took the driver's seat in his statuesque manner. Buck collapsed beside her, and Holly climbed up on the bench beside Still. Buck turned to her and grinned, his eyes squinting in the sun. "It's just a rented coach," he said. "I thought I'd wait and let you choose something newer we can purchase for the long term."

"It's hard to tell what's *newer* here," Tanna said, looking around at the other pony traps, buggies, and wagons. "The designs are perplexing. Everything is either rustic or antique or some strange combination of both. Even the most luxurious coaches look like they were made when my grandmother was a little girl."

"Yes, they do have some deceptively novel, forward-thinking inventions here, but nothing *looks* new. I think it's because of the lack of iron and steel we're used to seeing in manufactured items."

"Everything seems handcrafted," Tanna observed.

"Very," Buck said, wrinkling his nose at how distastefully quaint it all was. This was typical of their past friendship, to critique the taste of those around them and find their own a bit superior. It made Tanna like him again. Just a little bit.

It took them several minutes, creeping through the dense traffic along the top edge of the Tree, to reach a sloping ramp to level ground. They traveled another quarter of a mile before reaching what was clearly the rootball of the Tree. When it had been toppled, the knees at the base had torn away from the ground, like a giant shovel lifting a mountain of earth and moss-covered boulders. Over the centuries it had been weathered into a vague pyramid shape, covered with shelf lichen, houses, and parks. There were small cottages, fountains, and statues clustered among steep switchback walkways.

"I thought it was a huge hollow log, fallen on its side," Tanna said, "purposefully brought to this spot and lain across the gorge."

"No, it grew here," Buck said, suddenly shedding his bleary-eyed fatigue. "And from what I understand, it's still very much alive. It's been like this so long, its origins are mostly legend. It either blew down on its own or it was purposefully felled, and then the engineers hollowed it out and cultivated the rest of its modifications through some kind of fairy magic. There's no other tree of its kind anywhere up on this plateau. The closest *wawona* specimens are down in the Sea of Trees, which you crossed on your way in. But nothing there really compares in size or age. One old man told me most of the Tree—the center, the part that spans the gorge— has petrified." He realized he was rattling on, although Tanna didn't mind. He was clearly intrigued by the topic. "Anyway, it's a popular thing for drunks to argue about here in the saloons."

The gentle bumping of the carriage on the smooth, hard-packed road out of Treebridge soon lulled them all into quiet introspection. Holly was already dozing while sitting upright. Tanna felt the effects of the restorative tea evaporating, and Buck's gaze was starting to soften into the far distance.

"So, which one of them were you with last night?" Tanna asked, before he could nod off.

"Hmm?" Buck asked, rousing. "What?"

"When I asked where you had gone last night, I was told you left with that young woman and the man that was with her."

He didn't answer.

"I know the ones," she said. "I saw you with them myself."

"Jed and Cookie," he said, as if mentioning old friends. "They're a couple."

"You left with them?"

"I'd arranged to meet them there," he said. "Beforehand."

"You left our wedding reception with them? To go where?"

He paused for the longest time, clearly trying to get up the courage to say something.

"I have a confession to make," he finally said. "I wasn't at all sure you would come."

The turn in the conversation surprised her. "Wouldn't come? I wouldn't make the journey into the Green, at the last minute, after weeks of preparation? After all the money I gave you?"

Buck exhaled through his nose, irritated to have to explain it to her. "I honestly thought when you saw that dirigible—when you realized you had to climb that tower ... Yes, I did think it was entirely possible you'd say to hell with me and this marriage and head straight back to Lookout Mountain."

She was more incredulous than angry. "And what? Just let you have the money as a gift? So you could buy a nice farm here for yourself?"

Buck squeezed his eyes shut and pinched the bridge of his nose between his thumb and forefinger. "Tanna, can we have this conversation another time?"

"Of course. How rude of me." She pursed her lips and looked out at the hundreds of quaint cottages hunkered along the road. "You need to have your little snooze and sleep away the dregs of it, don't you?"

Now, with both Buck and Holly asleep, Tanna wished she'd sat up front on the driver's bench with Still. He could have at least told her about the countryside through which they traveled.

—

Traffic thinned considerably only a few miles outside of Treebridge. The road was broad, packed with long red pine needles that dulled the clatter of the wheels and made the ride soft and pleasant. The vegetation became a thick solid hedge on either side, and the branches of the taller trees arched to meet directly overhead. The effect was like driving through a cross between a tunnel and a cathedral.

Every so often, there would be a large gap in the hedgerow with a gated avenue leading off the main road and back into the forest. Tanna glimpsed what appeared to be plantation houses. Some of them looked like the Georgian antebellum mansions of the South she was used to seeing; others had thatched roofs like houses in drawings of medieval folklore and European fairy tales.

These properties encouraged her, shifting her away from the sour mood she'd been in after the exchange with Buck. It was all starting to look even better than she'd originally thought. This was what she hoped to find when they reached the farm at Brynmor. She had a vision of herself as the mistress of a plantation.

Now that she was here, witnessing the fantastic architecture, the rich detail found in every object and surface, the exquisite textiles from which the fairy people made their clothes, she saw the evidence of a long human history in the Green. There had clearly been an American presence in this new world for at least as long as they had been settling North America. There were also bits and pieces of a European culture, possibly dating back centuries. She wondered when this was all discovered—was it in the age of Christopher Columbus, or had the European explorers wandered into the Green long before that and emerged in the Indian lands by an entirely different route?

How much of the history she'd been taught was truly *known*, and who knew it? Even if she had been educated at a university, which had always been her wish, she still might never have been exposed to this greater truth. Her father had done his best, teaching her from his own library, sharing his stories and philosophies, alluding to his suspicions that folklore was based in fact.

Her father would have been so excited to see all this. She realized he may have been the one person in her life who suspected this place existed. How close had he come to knowing? She tried to remember all the little things he'd mentioned from time to time. He had made odd comments. There were mysterious sketches in his journals.

She had to wonder.

—

Holly awoke before they were really close enough to see anything. The burning smell must have roused her. She stood up on the front bench of the carriage, sniffing the air. Both she and Tanna craned their necks and shielded their eyes from the sun.

The tree trunks to either side of the road were scorched. The smaller limbs and foliage had been blasted away. One of the largest trees directly beside the road had fallen, its roots ripping the surface of the road in an eruption of earth and gravel.

"Buck," Tanna hissed, shaking his arm. "Buck!"

"Why are we stopping?" Buck said, shaking his jowls like a dog and blinking painfully.

"There's been some kind of explosion in the road," Tanna said.

"Rippers," Holly said over her shoulder.

"Here? On this road? That can't be," Buck said, coming immediately awake. "Still! What's going on?" He motioned for Holly to trade places with him, and he climbed up and sat on the bench next to Still. Their heads were close together, obviously conferring, but Tanna couldn't hear what they said.

The urgency with which Buck had stirred alarmed her. He was not one to be fearful, or even respond to danger in a timely manner. He usually chose to wave away even the most obvious disaster. He was the last to leave a card table, placing a bet with his single remaining chip, sure that his luck could still turn around and he'd win back everything he'd lost. That had never happened, not once, but this was the kind of expectation with which he viewed the world.

Once when they had all been picnicking in a large party at the lake, a sudden summer thunderstorm had come up out of nowhere. The skies opened and they were drenched to the skin before anyone could run for shelter. "It'll probably blow over," Buck had continued to insist. A bolt of lightning had split a pine tree less than a hundred yards away and it had burned to cinders. "Oh, well. The chances of that happening again anywhere in this vicinity are virtually impossible now," he had said.

For Buck to leap up from a nap meant something was truly, terribly wrong.

Tanna grabbed Holly's arm. "Are we in danger?"

Holly frowned and shook her head, as if to silence Tanna so she could listen. She was as alert as a hunting dog. Tanna watched the girl's face for some cue about how she should respond.

Still climbed down from the driver's seat. Tanna leaned sideways out of the carriage to watch him walk up the road in his slow, purposeful march. She couldn't see where he went or what was going on up ahead.

Buck turned around, saw her hanging out the side of the carriage, and furiously waved her back in. "Get back inside!" he hissed.

"What is going on here?" Tanna demanded in her most imperious tone.

"For the love of God, Tanna," he said, exasperated. "Keep your head down and be quiet."

There were shouts and the sound of a rifle shot, close enough to make Tanna and Holly drop to their knees in the middle of the carriage floor.

Still came back, moving more quickly than Tanna had ever seen him. He swung himself up into the driver's seat and snapped the reins. Tanna and Holly were flung back together against the seat. They held on to one another as the carriage gained speed.

"Hang on," Buck called back to them, unhelpfully.

The carriage lurched to the left, leaning dangerously as it went off the road. Tanna yelped, bracing herself with her left arm against the tilt, clutching Holly with her right hand.

They rumbled along the sloped shoulder of the road, over rocks and underbrush. Tanna's teeth rattled and she couldn't see anything beyond the tree trunks speeding by.

The burning smell became oppressive. There were streamers of black smoke hanging between the trees. The ground leveled off but remained rough. They were moving much too fast and the ground was too rutted for the wheels. On their right, where the dense, dark trails of smoke seemed to converge, they passed a crater in the ground large enough to swallow their carriage whole. There were broken parts of other vehicles spread through the woods. There were people everywhere, many of them dragging limp forms away from the carnage and laying them carefully on the ground.

A man pointed a rifle up into the trees. Two more shots rang out in quick succession, and Tanna heard screams coming from the lowest branches. A naked, gray body erupted with a spray of black oil and fell onto the road with a thud. Their carriage missed it by inches.

Tanna looked back up at the branch from which it had fallen and saw two or three others of its kind, hissing and spitting, slinging rocks at the rifleman below. A pair of black eyes made contact with Tanna, its gaze followed her as they sped past, its face wrinkled with anger, its mouth parted in a scream. It raised a skinny arm into the air, shaking a fist at the departing carriage.

—

Tanna struggled to catch her breath. "*What* just happened?"

Still had turned the carriage back onto the road and continued to drive fast for a half-mile or so before allowing the horses to slow down on their own. He eventually pulled back on the reins and stopped in the middle of the road.

Buck jumped down from the driver's seat and walked around the carriage, apparently checking for damage. Tanna caught him staring at Holly, looking grim. The girl returned his look, but neither of them said anything.

"What *was* that?" Tanna was stirring to anger, incredulous that no one would answer her. "Some kind of bandits on the road?"

"Something like that," Buck said. "It doesn't usually happen this close to Treebridge, does it?" he asked Holly.

She shook her head. "Never inside the colony. It's usually the crossing points in the Seaming. They go after the haul teams."

Buck nodded. "There was a minor disturbance when I came through several days ago. But nothing when y'all came through on the *Queen of Clouds*, right?"

"Nothing," Holly shook her head. "She got pretty mazy, but really the crossing wasn't bad at all this trip."

Tanna interrupted. "Is this the war Daughtry was talking about?"

Buck and Holly looked at one another meaningfully, but neither of them spoke.

"Buck," Tanna said. "Are we in the middle of some kind of war?"

Buck held up his hand in a placating manner. "It's just a few isolated incidents. Small groups, making noise, trying to terrorize the rest of us."

"Small groups of who? Why?"

"Some of the fae don't want us here," Holly said. "Never have, But it's been going on for hundreds of years."

"Should we go back to Treebridge? Wouldn't we be safer there?"

"No, no. We're not that far from the farm. It's only about another ten miles."

"Wait," Tanna said. "Our house is only ten miles away from the place where the road has just been blown to bits by angry elves? Our new home is ten miles away from a war zone?"

"Now, don't get worked up about this. This is an isolated incident. Nothing like this has happened before, I assure you. Holly, tell her," Buck pleaded.

"Your farm's in the middle of a big area that has belonged to the Nunnahee for as long as anybody can remember," Holly said. "And they've always been friends with humans. Rippers don't bother the Nunnahee. You should be safe at Brynmor."

"Should be?" Tanna scoffed. "But if the road to Treebridge has been compromised to this degree ... What's to keep us from being cut off, isolated on the farm?"

"Let's just get going again," Buck said. "We can talk about all this more when we get home. We're practically there."

Buck got back up on the bench and rode beside Still the rest of the way. Tanna couldn't help but feel he did so to avoid having to answer any more of her questions.

Holly watched the woods pass, silently alert, but she didn't seem particularly anxious. Tanna imagined she saw angry faces in the bark of trees. She felt eyes watching her from the undergrowth.

—

Everyone was silent, as if Still's ability to drive them to their destination quickly and safely depended on his concentration. Tanna found herself willing the wheels of the wagon and the hooves of the horses forward.

She watched Holly scanning the woods. A few times the girl glanced over, saw her looking, and avoided eye contact.

"What are Rippers?" Tanna asked her. "Are they one of the tribes?"

Holly shook her head. "It's a name for the ones who don't want us to keep coming here. They're from a lot of different tribes."

"So there are a lot of fae who hold anti-human sentiments?"

"Well. There are a lot of Rippers that are human too." Holly said. "Rippers want the crossing points closed down. The worlds have been naturally drifting apart for hundreds of years. But we've been keeping the doors open, keeping the worlds connected. That's the Seaming. It's like the seam between two fabrics that are sewn together. They can fray in some places, get ripped apart, patched back together."

"And this is something everyone here knows about?" Tanna asked.

"Some say if we just stop trying to keep the worlds connected, they'll come apart on their own. But there are lots of people working to keep the seams strong, the crossing points clear, to even add others wherever possible."

"How do they make more connections?" Tanna asked.

The girl shrugged. "Spells."

"But obviously the Rippers want to hasten this drifting apart," Tanna said. "Violently."

Holly pressed her lips together in a small rueful smile and nodded.

Tanna released a sigh and stared a hole through the back of Buck's head. "God help us. I swear, that man has a talent for wandering right into the thick of something, every time."

Holly shrugged again. "It's been going on forever. You always hear about them destroying things, here and there. But it's usually never anywhere near the colony."

Tanna pursed her lips sourly. "Until today."

15

Tanna spotted the hill at Brynmor long before she could see the farm or the house. The great rounded knoll rose out of the woods in a perfect mound, situated in the fork of a stream, with meadows sloping down its sides and, as Cole Mathers had described, a crown of startling blue trees.

Still turned the carriage off onto a drive marked by two columns of stacked flat stones. Tanna couldn't imagine how they managed to stay upright—many of the stones touched in only the tiniest spot, balancing on a point or sharp edge. They looked as if she could walk up to them, give them a good shove, and they would collapse in heaps. They had obviously been standing in this precarious formation for a long time because moss covered them, a carpet of flowers flowed over their sides, and the column to the right sported a small sapling tree that had taken root in a cleft on the topmost rock. It was close to three feet tall and its branches dripped with clusters of red berries.

The drive went up the knoll in a long clockwise spiral, with barely any grade or steepness. They rose slowly higher and higher as they went around. They had been driving for five minutes and still not come back around on the side where they had begun. Already Tanna could see out above most of the surrounding countryside. By the time she looked down and saw the gate beneath them, they were a little more than halfway up the hill and much higher than she would have imagined. Brynmor was deceptively large. It had no cliffs or steep backbone edge, but it was the size of a small mountain.

Once they reached the trees crowning the summit, the road started to level off and curve toward the center of the hilltop. The flattened top was large enough to appear mostly level to the eye.

"Are those people?" Tanna muttered, seeing motion and color on either side of the road ahead of them.

"The Nunnahee," Holly said. "The ones who live on your farm."

Now there were genies lining the drive—children were barely two feet tall; full-grown adults were willowy at three and a half feet; the elderly were shrunken and stooped. They were nearly identical in feature and dress—red-stained hair, all wearing nothing more than the red cloths draped across their bodies.

"They look like the ones who came with us on the dirigible. The People of the Red Maple."

"The same elven race," Holly confirmed. "Just a different tribe."

"I wonder why they don't wear the blue of the atzeenah trees."

Holly shrugged.

"So none of the ones we picked up with Jackson Gallagher's cargo are here among this crowd?" Tanna asked.

"Not likely," Holly said. "There are a lot of elven tribes around these parts. Not just on your property. All over."

Unlike the black-eyed stares and stoic expressions Tanna had seen on most of the indigenous people, these diminutive creatures greeted her with a chanting song, their faces wrinkled with grins. Most of them held their hands above their heads and shuffled from one foot to the other in unison.

Buck stood up in the carriage, waving to them and calling out. He turned around to wink at Tanna. "These are our workers!"

The crowd of Nunnahee was thickest in the front of the house, but they parted to let the carriage approach. Tanna strained to get her first glimpse of the grand plantation house that would be her new home.

She saw only a long, rambling, one-story structure made of stacked, mortar-less gray stone. The weeds in front were almost as tall as the house itself. The shrubs were too close and untrimmed, threatening to lift off the porch roof and topple the walls. A vine curved up the main post of the front entryway, branching to run along the roofline in both directions and up over the top of the house like the veins on the back of a hand. The roof was tiled in wafers of rough black slate. Some of the tiles had slid through a hole at the west corner of the porch. The roof overhung a deep patio that ran the full length of the house in front and turned the corner onto a side veranda with shutters.

This was nothing like the manor houses on the plantations they had passed along the road out of Treebridge. This building was in worse shape than a stable; it wasn't even tall enough to be a barn.

The carriage rolled to a stop in front of a few elves dressed in human clothes.

"Here we are!" Buck sang out brightly, jumping onto the gravel and crunching around to help Tanna down. He extended his arm up to her as she stood and faced the house. "Welcome home, darlin," he said, beaming up at her.

Tanna did not move to take his hand or climb out of the carriage. She glared at him, clenching and unclenching her jaw, feeling the color rise in her cheeks.

Buck's grin faltered. "Come on, Tanna," he said softly, as if calming a nervous horse. "Let me introduce you to your servants."

Still watched her from behind his expressionless mask.

Holly was now standing beside her in the carriage, looking at her fearfully, wondering whether she should get out or stay. "Can I help you down?" she asked, tentatively reaching to take Tanna's elbow.

"I'm perfectly capable of getting out on my own," Tanna snapped. Seeing Holly flinch as if she had been slapped, she added, "But thank you."

Buck continued to pose for an uncomfortably long time as if her glare had turned him to stone, one foot up on the running board, one hand held out to Tanna.

Tanna looked out at the sea of brown faces and black eyes, all of them now quiet, expectant, staring at her. At last, she lifted her chin, took Buck's hand, and squeezed his fingers as hard as she could, until he pressed his lips together silently in pain.

She dropped onto the gravel beside him, noting in that moment for the thousandth time how much taller she was.

"Well," she said quietly, her face close to his. "Let's see what you've done with my money."

Still had taken a place in front of the elves in human clothes. He gestured silently to a pair of them and they stepped forward.

"So'onah," Still said, bowing formally to her. "These are the ones who will be working inside the house."

They were dressed in long white shirts with no pants and human boots that were ridiculously too big for them, with curling tongues and no laces. Small stature aside, they both appeared to be male, no older than children, and completely terrified.

Still introduced them. "Navvee is your cook. And Joona will serve you at table and greet your guests."

Tanna shook hands with each of them in a daze, remembering the little maid Giselle, and tried to mask her fascination with their hands. Like clutching small leather gloves full of twigs. They seemed shocked she was touching them at all, but knew enough of the custom to respond more or less correctly. Their handshakes were passive and limp, with less instinct to grip than a human infant.

Tanna climbed the three broad, shallow steps up to the veranda and turned slowly to look out over the crowd assembled to greet her.

She projected her voice and put as much of a smile into it as she could, unsure how much they could understand of her words but hoping they would hear the tone and sense the intended warmth. "Thank you for welcoming me. I look forward to learning all your names and all about this wonderful place."

The sea of waiting faces erupted in squinty grins. They waved their hands above their heads, hopping up and down in place. Some of them cried out with a haunting, ululating, wordless vocalization.

She continued to smile at them, cutting her eyes at Buck with a flash of fury only he was close enough to see.

He chose to ignore it. "Come inside and see your house, Tanna."

She tried to suppress her disappointment—her shock, actually—at the state of the interior. After the architecture at Treebridge, particularly the Daughtry mansion, and the plantation houses she'd glimpsed on their journey out to Brynmor ... She was unprepared for this reality.

She hid the dull, throbbing panic behind constructive declarations of what repairs were needed. "... a good carpenter ought to be able to shore that up ... Not too bad in here. A happy paint color will work wonders ..." She commanded Holly to begin a list for her. The girl looked desperately at Buck and asked him in a whisper where she might find a paper and pencil. Buck assured Tanna a list had already been made.

"As a matter of fact, the builder will be here tomorrow," Buck said. "I assumed you would want to make repairs to your specifications and with the placement of your furniture in mind. It's my understanding that whatever you brought with you on the airship will be following us out here shortly. Maybe this afternoon or tomorrow at the latest."

Tanna stared at him coldly, without expression. "I hope my china and crystal will survive that madness on the highway."

—

An excruciating, bristling silence accompanied them as they toured the rest of the house. Tanna stopped in the main bedroom, calculating how far her bed could be placed from the water stain on the ceiling.

Buck rattled on about the room's best ephemeral qualities. "Wait until you experience the light in the morning. The dappled shadows on those French windows ... I know you're going to love it."

Holly muttered something about grabbing the bags from the carriage and fled.

As soon as they were alone, Tanna pinned Buck with another glare.

He took a cigarette case from his jacket pocket, popped it open, and offered her one. She took it, angry with him for knowing she would want it.

She allowed him to light it for her, took an enormous pull, closed her eyes, and exhaled a cloud into the room. "When were you going to tell me about the war?"

He was visibly surprised, prepared to defend the purchase of the dilapidated house, not explain the political unrest. "I'm shocked. Everybody is," he spluttered. "From what I understand, that's not normal. You can ask Holly or Still, but I'm pretty sure that was just some random violence by a small, rogue criminal element. Highway robbery, outlaws, that kind of thing. We knew this was going to be a bit like the Wild West."

"They're called *Rippers*, Buck. Because they want to tear the world apart. If that isn't a war, what is?"

"Nobody's using the word *war*."

"Daughtry did. As I recall, it was one of the first things out of his mouth upon meeting me."

Buck rolled his eyes. "That old bastard was already drunk by the time you got there. Daughtry's parties are a big spread and a big draw, but that means a lot of politics and hot air."

"Politics and hot air? Bands of fiendish elves setting off explosions in the streets—"

He held up a hand to silence her. "You're talking about things that haven't even happened—probably never even will happen. Fantasies. Dark, paranoid flights of the imagination."

"Fine," she said, biting off the word. "Let's talk about the reality of this crumbling hovel."

—

Dinner was a strained event on a table of wooden crates covered with a drop cloth and a mixed set of tin plates and cups. Buck continued to pretend the rustic elements were charming. He was no doubt thankful Holly was there so he didn't have to face conversation with Tanna alone.

But Tanna was distracted by Holly's appalling lack of manners. The girl ate with her hands, talked with her mouth full of food, and noisily slurped her cup of beer. Holly sensed she was being observed and looked miserably uncomfortable. As irritated as Tanna felt toward Buck, she bit her tongue and tried not to say anything critical to the girl. Lessons in etiquette could wait until they were alone and Tanna could be more constructive.

Navvee the cook had prepared cold cuts of some kind of poultry, a large salad of unusually bitter greens, and loaves of round black bread. The bread was shockingly good. It produced that near drug-like effect Tanna had already experienced with some of the other fairy food and drink. The bread invoked a sense of warmth and a purring contentment. She was disturbed to find she had to consciously resist the impulse to moan as she chewed.

Buck attempted to fill the silences with lively chatter about plans for the house and farm. In keeping with the late afternoon ritual they'd established at Blackwood in the weeks preceding their emigration, he briefed her on the ongoing state of tasks, projects, and timelines. Tanna nodded while she chewed, reserved and civil in front of Holly.

When Buck mentioned that the overseer should be arriving in the next few days to direct the planting of the haint, Tanna interrupted him. "Wait. Haint?"

"Six hundred acres," Buck beamed proudly.

She set down her mug with a thud. "We never talked about devoting so much land to a crop. It was supposed to be a small garden of diverse plants that would specifically support an apothecary. The products—the medicinal mixtures—are supposed to be the primary focus of our business."

"But, darlin," Buck said in a placating tone. "Once I was here and able to really engage the locals in choosing some of the plants, I realized the potential money to be made from the haint industry. All the different products that can be made, not to mention the raw, unprocessed material—"

She blinked in disbelief. "You didn't think you should discuss any of this with me before you started making these kinds of fundamental changes?"

"You weren't here. I had to act on your behalf. Decisions needed to be made. There were opportunities that required an immediate response."

"Well, now that I've arrived, we can review the decisions you've made and I'll decide if they need to be changed back."

"Tanna, the land's already being cleared. The plants are en route, due to arrive by the thousands over the next few days. The overseer will be here tomorrow, expecting to organize the hundreds of elves you saw out there on your front lawn—"

She threw her napkin across her plate and stood, overturning the wooden crate that was her stool with a loud scraping noise. "The next time you decide to make any changes, you do it with your own money."

Buck opened his mouth to say something else, but she had already stalked out of the room. Her boot heels echoed loudly in the empty hall, and she sent menacing shadows up the walls.

Before she reached the bedroom, she overheard Buck picking up a casual conversation with Holly, pretending nothing had happened.

She paused in the doorway and yelled for the girl to come help her.

"What?" Holly asked.

"I want you to take every single one of those iron wards out of my clothes."

Holly blanched. "Now?"

"Immediately." Tanna regretted snapping at her. "I know it's a lot. I'll help you myself. But I can't walk around here stinking, repelling the very people I'm trying to lead."

—

They spent the rest of the evening working, until Tanna felt they'd done enough for one sitting. She asked Holly if she'd mind staying with her for the night. She knew Holly could fall asleep anywhere, and she'd already come to rely on the girl's soft, familiar snore.

Holly didn't ask the unspoken question about where Buck would be sleeping. Tanna's request was an explanation in itself.

There was only an old wooden bed in the middle of the room. The mattress was bare and there were only a few thin blankets. No real sheets or even a pillow. Tanna lay awake, trying to acclimate herself to the new environment, thinking about how this room could one day seem familiar and restful. This patch of ceiling would see her off to sleep for hundreds, maybe thousands, of nights. But she found it hard to imagine. She listened to the distant birdlike calls and the cicadas' grinding wall of sound. She wasn't sure if there might be crickets too, or something else entirely, but the volume of the night noises here was near deafening.

She missed Ginger's presence. She could almost feel the dog lying on the floor beside her bed. The thought produced a physical ache. She clutched her fist to her stomach and forced herself to breathe.

The lack of furnishings in the room depressed her. She contemplated the journey of her possessions with more than a little anxiety. She imagined the wagon blown off the road by angry, pinched faces hiding in the trees. She could hear the crack of her china, see the black smoke of her furniture broken into sticks and piled onto a pyre by the side of the road, mad little figures cavorting around it in celebration.

Her own imagination disturbed her. The drastic shift in the vision for her life sent her mind spinning. It had all changed so completely, in less than one day. At some point, along the Big South Road from Treebridge, she had passed from a paradise into a hostile frontier.

Fortunately, she was so tired from the day's journey and the lingering intoxicating effects of the fairy food that she fell asleep quickly. She was blessed with no dreams, no sense of time passing.

—

She awoke with the sun in her face, the windows in her bedroom having no curtains. She laid a hand across her eyes and bitterly recalled Buck's promise of dappled morning light.

Holly had already gotten up. She'd thoughtfully left Tanna's dressing robe draped over the footboard. Tanna wrapped herself in it and put on her boots without lacing them. She went clomping through the empty, echoey house, looking for signs of Holly or Buck. She caught a glimpse of her own hair, wild as a nest, in a smoky glass on the wall. She looked like a patient who had escaped from a mental ward in a gothic novel.

She found Holly in the kitchen, a small separate building behind the house, preparing a pot of tea.

"Where's Buck?"

Navvee and Holly looked at each other, but neither of them answered her.

"What is it?" Tanna asked. "Have you seen him this morning?"

"He left early, so'onah," said Still, surprising her by appearing soundlessly in the kitchen door behind her.

Tanna jumped, arranging the lapels of her dressing robe closer across her chest. "Did he say when he'd be back?"

Still said nothing. He stood, motionless, staring through her for some moments. He did not seem to have heard her question.

"Where has he gone?" Tanna asked, trying another.

"He has gone on safari, so'onah," Still said. "He will return in a month."

TWO

16

She didn't tell Still, but she was relieved he had stayed behind. From the moment she stepped off the dirigible, she had felt safe in his presence. She didn't want to feel grateful to Buck for anything at the moment, so it annoyed her that he might have shown consideration by leaving his servant for her again. It made the story of his having abandoned her seem less complete. It would have been simpler, emotionally, if Buck's behavior and character were consistently despicable.

Still quickly became an extension of Tanna's person—he was her butler, bodyguard, driver, and translator. Without him to exercise her will, she would have had no true authority. No voice, even. She was surprised the Nunnahee showed her any deference at all—she was a strange human woman who had appeared out of nowhere, taken up residence in a house on land they had occupied for centuries, and then proceeded to order everyone around.

Maybe they were afraid of Still; maybe it was his authority to which they responded. She wasn't entirely sure why he bestowed the grace of his influence onto her. What was stopping him from taking over this property himself? Why wasn't he motivated to lead these people, who obeyed him in all things, in some uprising against the relatively small population of humans who were merely acting as if they were in control? She'd always wondered why the African slaves hadn't risen up against the plantation owners and taken over the South, and how the Indians had been systematically duped out of their homelands.

As much as she fantasized about her place among some quaint aristocracy, she was anxious about the fragility of it all. How did they not see it for what it was, this assumed power of the white human landowner? It was all a bluff.

Dorothy Black Cravens had always told her the only way to maintain control over servants was to never let them know you knew about the bluff. If they caught scent of your fear, it was all over. If you apologized for your position, you could never rule. You couldn't lead them, and they needed a leader.

And so, remembering her mother's tutoring, she behaved more coldly toward Still than she wanted. He was so proud and terrifyingly graceful she felt she had to err on the side of distance and superiority.

The sad truth was, other than Holly, Still was the closest thing she had to a friend. He was the only person remotely her moral equal. He was someone whom, under different circumstances, she might have openly admired. He was superior in manner and authority to all of them—human and fae.

Holly was young. She was immature, graceless, uneducated. She wore her weaknesses on her face, plain as day. But she was also earnest and humorous without trying. Tanna was comforted by her presence, but at best, Holly was a pupil, a little sister, a niece. She did feel compelled to raise Holly's status so that at least she, Tanna, could feel more comfortable having the girl sit at her own table.

With Still, that could never happen.

—

The farm overseer, Carl Gentry, was a human immigrant as well. He was knowledgeable about dirt and weather and growing things, but he was illiterate and mean. He kept using the word *brownies* to refer to the Nunnahee, and the contempt with which he said it told Tanna it must be a disparaging term. He growled about the monks at Old Rath Abbey, for whom he had last worked. He sidestepped her question about why he'd left that position with gloomy predictions about this new one. Apparently, the monks were the only ones who had successfully grown haint at an elevation higher than Brynmor's, but no one had ever grown the plants on terraces, as Buck had proposed.

"My husband has a great deal of confidence in you," Tanna murmured, but the overseer only scowled at the flattery.

Gentry had a rarely clothed little son named Davis who must have been about six years old. He ran around dirty, barefoot, and naked, more savage than the genies in their loincloths and red mud. Davis was loud and wild as a monkey. Tanna was concerned that he should be in school; he was unlikely to ever learn to read.

She observed Davis carrying wood to the kitchen and performing other small tasks for Navvee in exchange for morsels of food. She knelt down in front of the boy as he gnawed a chunk of hard cheese and told him that if he would let her give him a bath, he could work for her as a servant in the house and eat only the best meals. Davis promptly ran off through the atzeenah trees, in the direction of the overseer's cabin down the hill, and would carefully avoid her for weeks to come.

She let him go for the time being and focused on those who already occupied positions in her household. If she intended to survive a month, she had to find a way to impart instruction to her employees. The kitchen looked more like a stable than a place for preparing food.

Navvee stared at her in silent horror when she demanded all kitchen surfaces be swept and cleaned at the beginning and end of each day. Everyone who touched her food must also wash his hands and face. She waited patiently as Still translated her directions, but it was impossible to tell what anyone truly understood. Navvee and Joona were both too scared of Tanna to do anything in her presence, including the tasks she had just requested. Throwing up her hands in frustration, she tied a towel around her waist as an apron to protect her dress, rolled up her sleeves, and started cleaning in front of them.

Still conveyed the orders she barked, sending Joona to fetch what she required—a bucket, a broom, a brush, a hard cake of black soap. Holly was quick to work alongside her, and after watching the women in shock for several minutes, the elves eventually began to imitate them.

Navvee gestured, as if drawing quick symbols in the air with his fingers. He muttered a rhyming chant, like a limerick. Dust from all corners of the room rolled toward the center and gathered as if moved by a breeze. With a swipe of his hand, he sent the pile of it through the door into the garden.

It was Tanna's turn to be shocked. She recovered her composure by commanding him to continue with this magic. "Yes, well ... every day." She enunciated both words in a threat, looming over the little elves. "Tell them, Still. I don't care what means they use to accomplish the tasks, as long as they're done daily."

"So'onah," he said, and repeated her words in the elvish tongue.

Navvee smiled shyly, bobbing his head up and down.

—

Buck had been wrong about the movers and the builder—it was almost a week before the wagons with her possessions pulled up the drive. She found it difficult to instruct the genies about where to put her things. It was hard to get any of them to make eye contact with her. With Still at her side, she pointed and fussed, but regardless of her specific instructions, they mostly ignored her, bringing the items into the house and depositing them either in one large heap in the middle of the room or sticking them in odd, inappropriate corners.

They dropped a crate of Tanna's china with a minor crash and then scampered out of the house when she came running, screaming at them about the price of Limoges.

The carpenter Curtis was human as well, although barely so. Tanna thought the term *feral* must have been invented for the likes of him. He looked like he hadn't bathed in weeks and he smoked a corncob pipe full of something that reeked of rotting flowers. Curtis loved to tell tales of his burdensome personal history, how he had run away into the Green as a boy of twelve after his mother's death to escape an abusive drunk of a father. The cloying, sickly sweet substance he smoked seemed to addle his thoughts because he repeated the same story without seeming to realize he'd already told her. He cried at the same part where he mentioned his mother. Whether the sob story were true or not, the telling of it was well-rehearsed and delivered like a scene from a play.

Tanna walked Curtis through the house, pointing out a half-dozen most pressing projects—the corner of the main living room ceiling sagged and dripped with rainwater; the vine that was taking over the roof had sent a slender runner in through a crack in the windowsill and would soon attach itself to the stone wall. Few of the windows had all their panes intact. Curtis said he'd have to order glass next time he was in Treebridge. Ignoring the priorities of the repairs, which Tanna was very clear and redundant in stating, she came back through after working in the kitchen to find Curtis building recessed bookshelves on either side of the hearth. Tanna, exasperated, pointing again at the hole in the ceiling, wound up to protest, but she was so surprised by the progress he'd made on the shelves that she let the tongue-lashing go. Not only had a week's worth of custom carpentry manifested within an hour, the craftsmanship was impeccable. The trim on the cabinetry doors had the same beautiful, organic *beaux arts* curves that she'd admired about the interiors at Treebridge. The corners looked like they might bud in the night and she would come in to find flowers and shoots of tiny green leaves growing out of her walls.

"Curtis," she said, with a sudden, sweet shift in her tone.

"Ma'am?" he asked around his pipe, turning drunkenly on his stepladder and trying with some difficulty to focus on her.

"How would you like to build me some furniture?"

—

After supper that evening, she saw Curtis wander across the lawn. He climbed into the low, broad branches of a magnolia tree, strung up a bright-orange hammock, tied the laces of his boots together, draped them over a branch, and promptly went to sleep.

She had told him he could set up the side veranda as a workshop, and when she looked around the corner of the house, she discovered a completed four-poster bed, carved with a pattern of stylized wisteria vines. She ran her hands across the lines of the wood. It felt like green wood, velvety cool to the touch. It was more than finely sanded; it was slick, as if it had been lacquered and buffed a thousand times.

Tanna looked across the lawn at Curtis, hanging from the tree in his pumpkin-colored cocoon. A trail of blue smoke drifted away into the dusk, stinking of overripe flowers.

—

The next morning, soon after leaving Curtis with instructions to begin work on a dining table and six chairs, Gentry showed up at the front door in response to her summons.

"These weeds need to be cut back, obviously," she said. "But what can we do about these vines?" Frowning, Gentry followed the curving branches, seeing where each part split, examining how much the plant had invaded the architectural structure of the house.

"The vines are mostly just wrapping around the porch roof pillars. With the exception of this bit going in by the window. I'd have to get a ladder and look at it more closely. I'd say you just need a bunch of hands pulling them off and following them backward to the root. Could probably cut them in a few sections, but they have to be unwound. If they're yanked too hard, they're liable to pull the supports out. The whole porch roof could come down."

"Could you and Davis do that?"

"Me and Davis? Do all that? By ourselves? Mrs. Eldridge, I have crops to plant. That's what your husband hired me for."

"Well, can you at least send over some of the Nunnahee workers and tell them what needs to be done?"

"I'm not planting the crops by myself. Nature has a schedule, and it's already almost too late in the spring to be starting. Those plants have to get in the ground on time or there won't be any reason for anybody to live at this farm at all. Let the vines wait until the planting's done. At least until the next rains start."

Tanna sighed in frustration. "Rain is exactly what I want to avoid. I need the vines pulled out so the holes in the roof can be repaired."

Gentry spat off the porch and shrugged dismissively. "Hire some more brownies. A team of five or six ought to do it. But I'm gonna have to go ahead and warn you, every able-bodied, fully grown elf on this property, male and female, is already working in the fields."

"Then whom do you suggest I hire for the yardwork?"

"Some of the *yolos*, I guess."

"Yolos?"

"That's what the brownies call their little ones, the youngest kids."

"Wonderful. Send them up here." Tanna smiled tightly and turned to go back in the house. "We'll bake something special for them and make a game of it."

"You better get permission from the queen."

Tanna blinked. "The queen?"

"The queen of the *brugh*." He shook his head at her blank expression, disgusted. "There's a whole city under this hill. She don't speak any English, though, so be sure you take somebody to talk for you."

"This queen lives here, on my land?"

"Your land," Gentry chuckled rudely. "Her people have been living in this hill forever. There are caves all inside Brynmor, like Swiss cheese. It's a big rabbit warren. You can't dig a root cellar for fear of breaking through into one of their rooms. She don't like the idea of her people working for us, let alone cultivating haint plants for humans. These brownies don't hate it as much as some of the other tribes. The poor biddy thinks she's holding on to some kind of control by only letting her people work the plants. They'd like it better if our kind didn't actually touch the plants at all. Fine by me. I'm called the overseer, so that's all I'll do. She's a stubborn old bat. Scary as hell, if you ask me. Daughtry's the one who convinced your husband it's time we controlled our own supply of haint. Whoever makes that happen is going to make a fortune, and that's the only thing keeping me here. It's a risk, but hopefully with a big payoff. And just so you know, your husband offered me a profit share when it's all done. But I'll tell you the same thing I told him. We start drawing any kind of heat from the other tribes, you'll have to pay me a lot more to stay."

"Are you worried the Nunnahee will rise up against us?"

"Nah. I'm not worried about these ones here. We pretty much own them. Your husband's got gumption. It took him ten hours of negotiating to convince Queen Anna What's-her-name to let us hire her people, in exchange for them not getting thrown off their own land."

"Buck didn't threaten them, did he?" It wasn't difficult for Tanna to believe Buck had connived, lied, manipulated, and twisted the facts to benefit himself, but she couldn't imagine him being warlike.

"Nah, he sugared it up real good. Concentrated on how they could stay on the land. But you and me both know the alternative of getting kicked off was implied. We've done the same thing here as we did with the damn Injuns back home. This queen is rolling over because she thinks she's protecting her people and her land. Anyway, good luck getting her to bless you taking the yolos too."

"It's just yardwork. I can't imagine these children are in any kind of school. What harm could it do?"

"I think she's just being stubborn because when you get right down to it, no matter what, she's offended about the haint."

"Why?"

"The plant's religious to some of the genies. They don't like human beings consuming their magic."

She was uncomfortable speaking to Gentry, but she couldn't turn away from the information he so bluntly supplied. "Are a lot of humans consuming it?"

"You came through Treebridge, didn't you? It's in everything—tea, cake, liquor. And then, of course, smoking it by the bushel like your little vine trainer boy over there." He nodded toward the corner of the veranda, where Curtis was crouched on his haunches, arranging something in a careful line across the patio tiles, exhaling a steady fog of that sickly sweet, blue-white smoke.

"Is that what he's smoking?"

"Smell the rotten flowers? That's how you tell."

She was tempted to ask him about the invigorating tea the maid

Giselle had given her at Daughtry's house, but the realization that she had partaken in some kind of intoxicating drug was not something she wanted to share with the likes of Gentry. Only that morning she had asked Navvee about where they might acquire the tea. She hoped she had not offended his religion.

"Gotta get back to it." Gentry turned on his heels and left.

Tanna walked around to the side veranda. Curtis didn't hear her coming; he was lost in his work. He had arranged what looked like four root bulbs in a rectangle and was unwinding a spool of hemp twine between them, connecting them.

Gentry had called him a *vine trainer*. Not a carpenter. Come to think of it, she'd seen some wooden pegs, shims, and splinters, but she hadn't once heard the sound of a banging hammer.

Before she could ask Curtis what he was doing, Still spoke at her side. "Did you want to see the queen, so'onah?"

"God, you startled me," Tanna said, clutching her heart. "You heard our conversation, then, about putting some of the little ones to work pulling weeds and vines?"

"You must ask the queen," Still said in his irrepressibly grave tone.

"That's fine. I feel it's only proper etiquette that I receive her anyway. Can you send a messenger and tell her to come this afternoon?"

Still's frown was faint but stern. "You do not summon a fae queen away from her own brugh."

"Fine," Tanna said, turning away to cover her blush. "You can take me to her, then. I assume you will translate for me. Let me go and change my boots."

17

"I just don't think you understand what you're doing," Holly said. Having failed to convince Tanna to wait, she and Still followed their mistress across the lawn toward the woods.

"What could possibly be wrong with my going to ask their queen for her blessing so the little ones can do yardwork for me?" Tanna asked.

She pushed through a gap in the tall ferns where she had observed the genies disappearing in the evenings. She had seen a village of huts on her walks around the farm, but she had not wanted to intrude upon their private domain.

"It's a gesture of respect, and I have no problem paying it," Tanna continued, Holly falling into step beside her. "She sees herself as a queen, and all my workers recognize her as such." She frowned over her shoulder at Still. "I do wonder why she wasn't there to greet me the day I arrived. No one has even mentioned introducing me to her. It seems like an awful breach of etiquette. I hope she's not offended. At least this provides a meaningful context for me to meet her and show her that I acknowledge and deeply value the rights of her people."

"It's just that we don't usually go alone into the presence of fairy royalty," Holly said, trying to keep up with Tanna's longer strides. "Especially not into a brugh."

Tanna had a tendency to walk quickly and purposefully whenever she needed to convince herself to be brave. Something about the physical momentum managed to elevate her spirits.

"Well, I'm not alone, am I?" Tanna said, huffing more from exertion than annoyance. "You're both with me. Still's going to speak on my behalf. And they all obey him."

"But," Holly said in a small, worried voice, "the queen doesn't answer to Still."

The path curled into a trench of sorts, and eventually they were walking down a ramp into the earth, rock walls rising on either side. The narrowing passage forced them to continue in single file. Still went in front of her, with Holly bringing up the rear.

Tanna looked up at the top of the walls, where the slope of the external ground would be, and there, fifteen feet above her, were guards on both sides. There were like crape myrtle saplings lining an avenue, with their dark gray-brown skin, papery togas, and aprons; their spears, some decorated with pennants and standards, towering over them. There were no other signs or gates or official-looking entrances of any kind. The trench transitioned into an underground tunnel that immediately began to turn in sharp corners, switchbacking on itself. An obvious defensive element designed to slow a direct invasion.

There were none of the rows of tiny lanterns embedded in the walls, as there had been at Treebridge, but even still it was not pitch-black. The walls themselves seemed to glint with a faint light like moonlight on frost, although it was comfortably warm. Quite suddenly, the tunnel emerged into a dimly lit cave. The only discernible feature of the place was the reek of rotting flowers.

As Tanna's eyes adjusted, she turned slowly and surveyed her environment. She found herself surrounded by more of the willowy males, tall for Nunnahee at four feet, all holding their five-foot spears in an upright position pointed toward the cave ceiling.

Tanna's heart beat high in her chest; she could feel it in the bottom of her throat. Other than the hush of her own breathing, the cavern was oppressively quiet, with only the slithering papery sounds of the genies' scant clothing rustling in the darkness. Their bone- and stone-beaded necklaces and body decorations clicked with a sound like pebbles tumbling down steep hills.

When they were all massed together in a crowd like this, it made Tanna think of insects. They were too tall and appeared always to be moving too slowly, with a preternatural grace like the praying mantis or the stick bug. It felt a bit like they were animated by clockwork, like ants or bees, passive, controlled en masse by a singular thought or motivation. There was definitely a hint of predatory alertness about them.

Surrounded by these inhuman creatures in such great numbers, in darkness, Tanna fidgeted with tortured impatience. She could make out Still by the faint silhouette of his turban. She leaned close to his shoulder and said in the lowest voice possible, "I don't know if they have better eyesight than we do, but could you request that someone light a lamp for my sake?"

Still pressed her wrist with his long, cool fingers in a clear gesture of suppression. "Do not speak, so'onah." In any other circumstance, she would have been furious that he shushed her as if she were a misbehaving child. Given her discomfort and the nerve-wracking situation in which she found herself at present, she bit her tongue and regretted her request.

A glow appeared on the far side of the cave. At first, a glittery effect on the high cavern walls and the ceiling intensified, tinting the blue moonlight color of the rock with a bit of the firefly glow Tanna associated with fairy illumination. A bright flash of gold appeared on the floor of the cavern opposite where they stood. An orb of light crept upward, like a torch carried out of a pit, throwing shadows and bars of slanting yellow light in all directions. The glare became too bright to continue watching directly.

Tanna resisted the urge to shield her eyes and peer at the phenomenon. It was like a small sun, both rising out of the floor and drawing closer. Maybe it was the same pathway she'd taken into the hill, picking up on the other side of the cavern and continuing farther and deeper at a similar gradient into the heart of the brugh.

There was something—someone—within the radiance, coming to meet them.

Holly squinted at the ground, her face screwed up from the discomfort of the light, but Still and the elves in the room bowed their heads or closed their eyes in a stoic, passive reverence.

Tanna tried to peek discreetly through her brows. Careful not to look directly at the glare, she could make out a tall, dark figure, shaped in the fae's characteristically unusual thinness, its height exaggerated by a headdress that extended the crown of the skull. The being approached, surrounded by attendants, all of them silhouetted by the mysterious light. Tanna could not determine the source of the illumination; it stopped moving at one point, while the figures continued to advance.

The queen of the Nunnahee was a heavenly body, the light of majestic power and glaring truth that drives darkness from its presence. Once the pageantry of the rising sun was complete, more normal lighting flared into existence in recesses along the walls. A single strong column shone down from the ceiling to the floor with the exact effect of a theater spotlight. The queen of the Nunnahee stepped into the light, her breasts naked, her legs obscured by a voluminous red skirt made from the same swath of fabric all her people wore. Her skull was wrapped in a matching turban; her red-stained fringe of hair accentuated her eyes. Here, underground, in a cavern of dark-red earth, Tanna realized why the Nunnahee wore red instead of the blue of the atzeenah trees above.

The queen leaned on a beautiful bright-fuchsia parasol as if it were a cane. It looked a bit ragged and threadbare, an old Victorian piece. Tanna thought it might have been a gift from one of her predecessors, a former human master of the farm. She regretted not having thought enough to bring the queen some small token. She had been told the fae coveted human things, especially if they were gaudy.

But even with her naked chest and her chintzy, store-bought parasol, there could be no doubt they were in the presence of royalty.

If these creatures did indeed move in a hive like ants or bees, in unison to the singular direction of one mind, then that consciousness resided in their queen. Most of the elves' black eyes appeared to Tanna as either timid or vacant. The queen, with the same featureless, liquid black orbs with their pinprick spark of reflected light, looked straight into Tanna. She felt the queen's eyes pushing at her own thoughts, prodding the soft tissue of the mind, examining her. She had never felt so unable to meet someone's gaze, but she was terrified that if she looked away, she would not see what was coming and the creature might strike, lash out at her with insect speed.

The queen opened her mouth, as if she were tasting the air and tracking her prey.

This was not the vapid Lady Glare of the Seelie Tanna had encountered at Treebridge, a vain Marie Antoinette-like creature presiding over intoxicated parties. This being was a female who led in darkness, who bent the power of the wilderness to her will, who ruled with fear and animal power.

Tanna felt a small pang of jealousy meeting both women. She coveted the beauty and the style of the Lady Glare. But she truly envied this woman's power. The creature's appearance, her scent, the way she moved were predatory—threatening, and faintly vile—and Tanna both admired and feared her. There was something this queen possessed that few women would ever wield—even the female monarchs of the Gray world and the wives of the wealthy.

In the presence of women who made her feel inferior, Tanna's defense was usually a haughty bluff, a condescending manner of speech, and an affected commanding vocabulary. A weaker woman, even a petty or stupid one, would become flustered, offended, or unsettled.

Tanna lifted her chin and clenched her teeth, but when she opened her mouth to speak, there was no breath to fill her words. They died on her trembling lips, without volume or enunciation. She tried to speak; she opened her mouth to speak ... She managed nothing. With the desperate, clawing panic of needing to fill her lungs, she discovered her nose and throat whistled like an old, broken clarinet. It was like being unable to scream in a dream.

This was a hundred times worse than the Alleegee who cursed her and threw her out of the dining room at The Fairchild. Her cheeks grew hot with shame and fury. She clutched for Still's arm in desperation and found he was already there, propping her up, supporting her with one hand at her waist and the other at her elbow, as if they were partners in a dance.

He squeezed her arm, a silent command to let him take the lead. He didn't look away from the queen to see if Tanna was following along; when he bowed low he simply bent her into a half-curtsy along with him, like an enormous doll. She caught on and was able to complete the move with something that resembled grace and intention.

In the Nunnahee tongue, Still introduced Tanna. His tone and accented pronunciation made her name sound important.

"Your highness ...," Tanna stammered, realizing too late she had been so singularly determined to force this visit that she had not asked about the most basic protocol of addressing a fae of this position. She didn't know the queen's name or even her proper title. She had thought of her as some Indian squaw, lording over a band of savages.

"The queen will wish to hear you speak her name," Still whispered. "Ananjooee."

"... Queen Ananjooee," Tanna finished with salvaged confidence. She mimicked Still, trying to give the name a musical flourish. She felt the hard part was over, and she could trust Still to reshape her words as he translated them, so she allowed her natural oratory skill to take over. "It is an honor to be received by you. I want to express my deep appreciation for the hospitality, kindness, and generosity with which your people have embraced me." As she warmed to it, her voice became reedy like her Aunt Lida reciting poetry after a few glasses of sherry—all trilled r's, careful enunciation, and locked jaws. "I hope you will come to see me as a faithful steward of our shared lands, an ally against our common enemies—"

Still interrupted her by clearing his throat, mimicking a human affectation that would have amused her greatly at another time and place. He spoke succinctly, in his dry, deadpan version of the Nunnahee tongue. The brevity belied the obvious edits he chose to impose with his own good judgment. Tanna understood nothing but the occasional "Eld-a-rich," which, in his exotic pronunciation of the name, made it hard to associate with herself. She concentrated on keeping her body language open and pleasant, her hands folded in front of her lap, a frozen, unvaried smile that quickly started to feel like an insincere grimace under the queen's gaze. Ananjooee stared mostly at Tanna, glancing over slowly at Still every few moments when he paused. She ever so slightly inclined her head in a gesture that obviously gave him permission to continue.

Tanna felt it was going well. When Still stopped speaking, she looked down deferentially and bowed a little.

And then the queen lurched toward them with a menacing hiss.

Tanna barely suppressed the urge to back away.

Ananjooee made no other noise that could have been mistaken for speech. She brought her face close to Still, as if smelling his breath. She turned her head directly toward Tanna for a moment, but did not come near her. She spun on her heel and stalked away, rattling the parasol.

Tanna thought Ananjooee was leaving the room in a royal huff, but she began to pace a circle around the center of the room, counterclockwise, encompassing her personal attendants, Still, Tanna, Holly, and a few of the Nunnahee guards who stood closest to them.

Tanna followed the queen's circumlocutions with her eyes but resisted the urge to turn around when she walked behind her. Tanna could feel the air move and hear the rustling hiss of the queen's voluminous papery skirt as she passed directly behind her. It was a menacing act, a simple and effective intimidation. The hair on the back of Tanna's neck stood up, and she prayed silently that the queen was not winding herself up for some royal tantrum or display of rage.

It was clear the queen was unhappy, agitated, possibly ready to explode.

"Good God, Still," Tanna muttered, "what did you *say* to her?"

He did not answer but silenced her with a look.

After three revolutions around the room, the queen stopped, returned to her formal position in the center of the spotlight, thrust her parasol at an attendant, and clasped her forearms, hand to opposite elbow. Apparently having made some decision, she began to speak. Her voice was louder and projected further than any other Nunnahee Tanna had heard, but it was a low, mumbling speech by human standards.

Ananjooee twittered on, with reedy whistles and occasional tiny punctuations of sound like the squawk of an oboe on a missed note. She looked directly at Tanna the entire time she spoke. It was unnerving to hold that gaze and maintain an expression of receptivity, not knowing what was being said. At the end of her long speech, the queen took back her parasol and held it out in a horizontal line above the floor. She planted it back onto the stones with a crack, looked briefly at Still, and turned her back on them.

This time she clearly intended to leave the room.

"What did she say?" Tanna mouthed desperately.

"Only the littlest ones may work for you. The yolos no taller than her parasol. The older children must stay here in attendance of their queen."

Tanna was surprised. "The littlest ones? I would have thought it would have been the older ones she would prefer to work in my home ..."

"She will keep the youths with her and educate them before she allows them to work in the fields as adults."

The spotlight went out and the cave was plunged into gloom. Tanna called out her thanks to the queen's back as her silhouette descended the ramp into the hill with her accompaniment of golden light. "I am most grateful to you, Queen Ananjooee," but her voice faded as she realized that, even if the queen could hear her, she could not understand her. Not to mention she clearly did not care what Tanna had to say in response to her decree, and there was no cause for translation or further conversation.

Tanna had been dismissed.

As they walked back toward the maze of tunnels leading out of the hill and into the daylight, Tanna saw an incongruous sight. A small, pale human face looked up at her. The copper curls were tangled and disheveled, although not stained in the henna of the Nunnahee red. In a sea of dark faces and black eyes, her green eyes were alien and shocking. The girl was four or five years old, naked, with some type of shoes tied around her feet that looked like slippers made from dried cane leaves.

Tanna stopped near her, but Still took her elbow gently but firmly, telling her they could not stay. "You must leave this place."

"Who is that child?" Tanna asked as Still dragged her away. "There was a human child back there, did you not see her?"

"Yes," Still said, but offered nothing else. He pushed her before him through the switchback tunnel.

"Who's taking care of her? I want to go back and talk to her. Make sure she's all right."

"We are not welcome to return at this time, and that child is none of your concern."

"It's a human child on my property. I have a right to know who she is and to whom she belongs."

"She belongs to the queen."

"A changeling," Holly said regretfully, like the way one spoke of an orphan begging on the street.

"What does that mean, exactly?"

"She's been traded for one of theirs. She works for the Nunnahee, probably as a special servant to the queen."

"Works? That child's not old enough to work for anyone. She should be with her mother."

"She's the same age as the Nunnahee children who will now come work for you," Still said.

Tanna wanted to protest further, but there was no meaningful defense. The reality dawned on her that she had just bargained for child laborers. She was filled with shame at the injustice that resulted from her careless, willful attempt at courage.

"Well, at my house, they will be valued and treated with kindness," Tanna vowed. "They will be given license to play and to learn."

Holly nodded. "Of course."

Still said nothing.

18

The next morning, she and Holly found four little elves on the front steps, staring up at the topis vine covering the house. They were naked except for the slippers bound to their feet, like the human child Tanna had seen in the brugh. They were accompanied by an older Nunnahee girl and shadowed by various creatures they kept as pets.

"Their familiars," Holly explained, squinting skyward at a slowly rotating cone of tiny, nearly invisible white-and-silver sylphs, gray finch owls, blue-and-green flying lizards, and one intimidating brown hawk. "You want them to start cutting down the vines?"

"Well, we can hardly give them scythes and clippers," Tanna said. "You and I will cut the plants down, and the little ones can pull them free. We'll drag the cuttings around to the woodshed behind the kitchen. We'll make a game of it."

"So, we're just gonna watch these yolos all day long?" Holly asked.

"It wasn't quite what I had in mind. But maybe this is an opportunity for me to educate my Nunnahee, teach them to speak properly. These yolos may grow up to occupy more distinguished positions in human society, such as our Still. Or the Daughtrys' little maid, the one we liked."

"Giselle."

"Yes, Giselle. She speaks the language, she wears lovely clothes, and she works in a fine house in town."

"She's a house elf."

Tanna ignored the blunt adolescent sarcasm. "Can you speak to them at all?" She handed her a pair of leather gloves. "Do you know enough of their language to at least tell them what we're doing?"

Holly shrugged. "Most of the yolos usually understand. If not," here she pointed with her eyes at the older Nunnahee girl, "she can tell them. But I think if we just start doing it, they'll mimic us."

"I bet you're right," Tanna pulled out a curved copper gardening machete. "It would be too hard to explain what I want the vines to look like anyway. I'll start chopping and shaping. You pull them down and haul them around the house."

Tanna went over to the children and asked the older girl her name.

"Aliata," she said quietly.

Tanna sat cross-legged in the grass and pulled one of the yolos onto her lap. The others encircled her, investigating her pockets, climbing onto her back, and touching her hair. Although the elf children were hardly toddlers, they were so small it was hard not to think of them as infants, dolls, much younger than they actually were. Tanna explained to Aliata that if the children helped them carry the vines off, she would have Navvee make cookies for them to have when they were done. Their little faces all burst into smiles—Holly was right; they didn't require translation. Aliata said a few words of encouragement, maybe commands in their own language to be on good behavior, but the yolos were already eager to participate.

An hour later, Tanna was covered in sweat, her face and arms scratched by the topis she had stripped away from the house. Their tips were fine as wire. If she had not been wearing gloves they would have shredded her hands. The smell from the flowers on the vines choked her. As she chopped and pulled and yanked, they released a kind of dust into the air, either pollen or spores; it got into her mouth and nose and lungs, and produced a coughing fit. Either the cough or the overpowering scent eventually made her feel lightheaded. She had to tie a handkerchief over her face in order to continue.

Holly was right about the little elves imitating them. After a few trips, they quickly caught on and continued hauling away the torn vines. Holly was able to help Tanna with the cutting. The yolos stayed focused for about an hour before they began to wander off. Their work devolved into a true game of chasing one another around the lawn, in and out and all through the house.

It seemed like the four little heads were multiplying before Tanna's eyes. She called a break for refreshments. She sent Holly to the kitchen to bring out the cookies while she attempted, with Aliata's help, to corral the wee elves. They were only able to keep them all in one place for the two minutes it took them to devour a plate of oatmeal cookies. They ran around squealing again until Tanna thought she was going to scream herself. Then, they all became quiet. Concerned that something had happened to them, Tanna ran inside and found them all asleep on the rug in her sitting room.

Aliata tried to rouse a few of them with no success, but Tanna told her to leave them alone. "Let them sleep. The peace is a gift." She invited the girl to have iced tea with her and Holly on the veranda while the yolos slept. She attempted to engage her in conversation, and the girl answered politely enough, in good English, but she was mortally shy.

The elven children didn't sleep for long. As soon as they started to stir from their naps, Aliata rounded them up and led them out of the house. Exhausted, Tanna and Holly stood on the front porch and watched as they left for the brugh. Before they stepped onto the path between the tall ferns, Aliata turned and waved. Most of the little elves turned and waved too, jumping up and down, and then they were gone, disappearing into the underbrush like a litter of puppies.

The next morning, the vines had returned. All of them. They had grown back in the night, replacing all that they had worked to cut down.

"What?" Tanna cried with so much anguish it was little more than a whisper. "How is this even possible?"

Holly gave her a small pitying smile and an apologetic shrug.

"Things like this just happen here, don't they?"

"All the time," Holly said.

Sighing, Tanna turned to find Aliata and four little faces waiting for her.

"Oh no," she said, low enough that only Holly would hear. She gestured toward the vines. "There's no point in doing all that again. But I can't just tell them to go home."

Tanna looked at their little black shining eyes, all watching her, rapt with attention. For once, they were surprisingly focused.

"I have an idea," she said. "Who wants to hear a story?"

—

So began the first of hundreds of story hours. At first, they congregated in the morning after breakfast. Later, the readings shifted to afternoon. When she had gone through her library back at Blackwood, Tanna had almost left all the children's books, especially the picture books she'd read to her nieces when they were little. But, on some impulse—honestly, it was the thought of her own future babies, that she might very well have children without ever returning—she couldn't leave any of her books behind.

Unlike human children, the little elves did not sit cross-legged on the floor in a semicircle. They sat on her lap and helped her hold the book; they clung to her arm and turned the pages; they climbed up on her back and read over her shoulder.

After a few days of this, Tanna started to look forward to it. On the third day of reading, after she sent them running to the kitchen to get their cookies from Navvee, she went out onto the side veranda to smoke a cigarette. She felt happy and content for the first time since arriving at Brynmor. She wondered if she might even be visibly glowing.

Holly stood near the front steps. Tanna started to tell her about something funny one of the yolos had said, but the words died on her lips when she saw the bag at Holly's feet.

"Where are you going?"

"Papa's coming to get me."

"Did you get a letter?"

Holly pointed to the sky above the tree line. Far in the distance, flat white pancakes of smoke rose in a column into the sky. The stack appeared to lean as it drifted with the direction of the wind.

"He's sending you smoke signals?" Tanna asked, incredulous.

"Yes." Holly sounded sad.

"How can you be sure those are from him?"

"Every tenth one is dark," Holly said, pointing again. "See?"

As if on cue, there it was, a black cloud.

"You're leaving," Tanna said. It was a statement of acceptance.

She pulled Holly into an awkward hug. She didn't have words to express how much she'd come to rely on the girl. When they'd docked at Treebridge and Holly had promised to stay with her, to go with her to the farm, she hadn't thought about the possibility of Holly's leaving.

They clung to each other, afraid to pull away because the display of affection embarrassed them both a little bit. When they parted they would have to speak. They would at least have to look at each other, and neither one of them knew how to manage that. She would not make Holly feel bad about an obligation obviously outside her control.

Tanna took the girl by the shoulders and forced her to look her in the eyes. "Thank you. For everything. You have no idea. You are welcome here anytime. Always."

"Thank you," Holly whispered. "I wish I could stay. I really do, but Papa—"

"Just promise me you'll come back," Tanna's voice broke a bit. She swallowed hard and forced herself to smile brightly. "Soon, OK?" She didn't trust herself to say much more.

Holly pressed her lips together in a line of regret and squeezed Tanna's forearm. "As soon as I can."

And there was the Graycoat on a dusty black horse, trotting up the drive out of the line of blue trees, leading a second empty mount. He stopped a hundred yards away and waited. Tanna was relieved to not have to speak to him.

"I have to go," Holly said.

"One more thing," Tanna said, catching her before she turned. "Will you keep an eye out for Buck? Maybe if you're in Treebridge, you could go by The Fairchild. I don't know, maybe you'll run into him out there somewhere." She gestured desperately toward the wide wilderness. "Tell him to come home. Or to at least send me word. Something."

"I'll tell him," Holly said, "if I see him."

She sprinted down the drive and mounted her horse, without a word of greeting from her father that Tanna could see. The Graycoat was already flicking the reins, urging his dark horse into a trot down the drive. Holly turned her roan around to follow him.

Tanna walked down onto the lawn and stood waving long after they'd disappeared.

—

That evening, after eating alone in a silence that felt like a wake, Tanna sat down at the writing desk Curtis had made for her. She ran her hands across the beautiful scrollwork that framed the bank of cubbyholes and small drawers. It looked like Virginia creeper had crawled up the back legs of the piece, its leaves and flowers frozen in petrified wood. The detail was remarkable, like all the impressive wood carvings she'd seen in Treebridge. It must be the result of magic spells.

She had written briefly to her mother once before, just a few lines to let her know she'd arrived safely. Now she penned a longer letter, describing the farm, the house, the grounds. It all sounded grand and exciting when she wrote it down. It sounded like she was happy, that all was in line for success. She mentioned the possibility of Teddy's coming to visit, maybe when he was on summer vacation from school. She planted the seeds.

Then she wrote another letter to Teddy himself, and although she wished it to have the same happiness and sense of adventure, her loneliness and desire for connection bled through. She missed Teddy and Ginger more than she could articulate. She drew a circle around a word that was splashed with water, honestly identifying the blemish as the evidence of the tears she shed.

"Come. And bring Ginger. I can't stand to think how much I'll be missing the both of you by the time you get this." She included directions to the Graycoat's warehouse down near the river.

When she had addressed her letters, she called for Still. He silently materialized in the doorway.

"Go and find my husband," she said, looking down at an envelope as she pressed her seal into the hot wax. "Tell him I want him to come home."

"I will not leave you alone here, so'onah. But I can send a runner."

"Do you even know where to send the runner?"

"I know several places to send him. It could take some time."

"Maybe you should send more than one, then. I don't care about the extra expense."

"Do you wish them to take letters to Mr. Eldridge?"

"No, it seems unnecessary for just two words."

"Two words, so'onah?"

"Come home."

19

On its southern flanks, the knoll of Brynmor sloped into pastures, eventually giving way to the rolling meadows and plains of the Cumberland Prairie that stretched to the Hawnee Hills on the southwest horizon. Wavy Creek bent east around the foot of the hill, following the boundaries of the farm for miles and drawing wildlife from every direction. Many people at Daughtry's reception party, when they heard the property she'd acquired, encouraged her to explore. Brynmor was known as one of the most scenic areas within the borders of Cumberland Colony.

She wondered why Buck couldn't stick closer to home. Then again, maybe he was out there somewhere nearby. Maybe she would glimpse him returning across the miles of flat visible terrain, far off but at least on his way. She probably would not have admitted to anyone that she was going to look for her husband. She claimed she wanted to explore the boundaries of her property, which was true. She also looked forward to wearing pants again.

She asked Ono, a Nunnahee stable boy, to saddle the chestnut mare Bronte—a man's saddle, she specified, unsure what the options might be here. She selected a rifle from Buck's rack near the hearth. He'd only left behind a few, but they were Winchesters like the ones she'd been using all her life.

She packed a sandwich, an apple, and a canteen of water. She took a pair of binoculars her father had used for what he called "bird-watching," but was usually a more mysterious and vague collection of outdoor activities.

She headed southeast along Wavy Creek until she found a clearing on a grassy slope not far from the water's edge with a stand of bamboo she could creep along. The animals could surely smell her before they could see her, but she felt less vulnerable near the plant cover.

She left her horse untethered. She'd ridden Bronte a few times and knew she would stay in one place and graze. Taking the binoculars from her saddlebag she walked on foot along the cane. She spied a herd of deer, tiptoeing through the grass, and tall pink-and-white birds stalking the creek, stork-like, maybe flamingoes or some type of heron.

It was actually disorienting to see such a vast scene so close. Tanna took the binoculars away from her face to get her bearings with a naked eye.

She heard Bronte whinny in fright, and by the time she turned, the horse was already galloping away. As hopeless as it was, her first instinct was to take off after her but—

She sensed the animal's presence before she saw it.

A black cat watched her from only twenty-five or thirty yards away. A panther. It sniffed the air and glared at her.

Panicked, she froze in a half-crouch, afraid to make herself more of a target by standing up all the way. She reached slowly back with one boot to begin her retreat.

"Don't move," said a man's voice from behind her.

Tanna froze.

"If you run, she'll think you're prey for sure."

The voice sounded familiar, but she couldn't bear to take her eyes off the cat to see who it was.

"Do you have a gun?" she whispered.

"Don't whisper. Just speak in a low voice like I am." She recognized the voice now—Jackson Gallagher, the man with the wings. She knew he would have a gun.

The cat started to pad directly toward her, its head down, never breaking eye contact.

"Shoot her," she hissed.

"Let's give her just a minute. She'll lose interest once she realizes what you are."

The cat continued to close the distance between them. She was twenty feet away, fifteen ...

"My God," Tanna's voice broke. Her legs trembled from trying to suppress the urge to run.

The cat stopped ten feet away, close enough now that Tanna could see the motion of the velvety black nostrils as it lifted its head, sniffed the air one final time, and, with a haughty, dismissive shake, turned and stalked slowly over to the cane and disappeared.

Tanna's shoulders collapsed in relief.

"See?" Jackson said, sounding pleased with himself.

She turned on him. "Just how long did you intend to wait?"

"Just long enough," he said.

In the wake of the fear and the overwhelming relief, her fury evaporated. All the things she wanted to scream at him were secondary to her desire for breath.

He shouldered his rifle and stepped close, his smug expression softened with concern. He tentatively held a hand out to her, not entirely sure she wanted to take it.

She glowered at his weathered hand as the cat had considered her. His fingers were large, the thumb thick, the lines in his hands and the edges of his nails stained with dirt.

She rejected it. "I'm fine," she managed to spit between chattering teeth.

"Let's go find your horse, then," he said.

—

"I heard you were looking for a husband," Cole Mathers called out from the shade of the veranda as they approached on horseback.

"I'm looking for *my* husband," Tanna said, dismounting and handing the reins to Ono.

"Well, how about a couple of substitutes, then?" Cole said, coming down the steps and kissing her on the cheek. "What's for dinner?"

"Apparently, I am," Tanna said.

Cole frowned, looking back and forth between them.

"She had a little dance with a cat," Jackson explained.

"Are you all right?"

"Yes, I'm fine." She patted her hair self-consciously, tucking flyaway strands up into her loose bun. "But I can only imagine what I must look like right now."

Cole shrugged away the comment. "We come bearing gifts," he sang, as if to distract a small child from the tumble she'd just taken. "Look. The bottle I promised. And another bottle. And one of Jackson's books."

It worked. Tanna took up the book immediately. It was a beautiful leather tome, soft with age. She thumbed through the densely handwritten pages, which were frequently interrupted by illustrations, sketches, and maps, like an illuminated Bible or a handmade field guide.

"A British colonist named Tucker Stokes made it in the 1780s," Jackson gazed fondly at the book while he talked about it, as if they were discussing an infant, "after nearly a decade of exploration. It's one of the earliest modern attempts—in the New World, anyway—to record information about the Green. Specifically, the parts of the Seaming connected to what would eventually become the Confederate States."

"It's exquisite," Tanna said. "I will treat it carefully and get it back to you soon."

"I don't lend books," Jackson said.

"Oh." Tanna looked confused. "Well, then ..." She tried to hand it back to him.

"No," Jackson said, shaking his head. "I'm sorry. I meant, it's a gift."

Tanna's eyes widened. "I can't accept something this rare." She felt a blush beginning to crawl up her neck and face.

"I'll trade you some supper and conversation for it," Jackson said.

"Well, I can't make any promises," Tanna said. "The cook and I are just getting to know one another. It's a daily struggle. And so far, the results have been mixed."

"Sounds perfect. I'm starved," Cole said. "Do you have any cups?"

"Actually," Tanna said with a coy smile, "I have some beautiful wedding crystal I haven't even had the chance to use yet."

"So that was crystal you were dragging behind your dirigible?" Jackson said, his smug half-smile back in place.

"I brought china too," she said.

"All the comforts of home," Jackson murmured.

"The ones I could manage," Tanna said.

Cole freed the cork with his teeth.

—

"You know, we have a history in my family of these encounters with black panthers," Tanna said, returning to the dining table with a basket of bread from the kitchen and a bottle of wine from her cellar. "It's true. My father claimed to have seen one. But he readily admitted that no one believed him."

"Not even you?" Cole asked, topping off her glass as Jackson held her chair.

"Hmm," Tanna cocked her head, considering. "I honestly don't think I did. But I would have never told him that. Part of me wanted to. I definitely loved to hear the stories. Daddy would often tell us how his own mother had seen a black panther when she was a girl, at the spring near her house. She died when I was very young, so I never heard her personal account. But, supposedly, one day when she went to fetch water, it was there, lapping away, just on the other side of the creek. A large black cat, which she called a panther. I don't know that that's what it was, but that's what she thought it looked like. It's certainly what I thought I saw today. Anyway, as she approached, it stopped drinking and raised its head and just stood there, watching her."

The tone of her voice warmed to the telling. Cole leaned in, listening with the open, happy face of a child.

Jackson watched her over the rim of his glass, his eyes narrowing. "What was her name?"

"My grandmother? Belle. Now, she was worried," Tanna continued. "She was afraid she'd get into trouble if she came home without the water. She knew no one would believe her, and at best she'd have to walk all the way back out to the spring. It was a really long walk, and she didn't want to make an extra trip, especially not if her mama took a switch to her. So, she decided to creep down to the creek, as slow as she could. She and this enormous cat just stared at each other, the cat with its head down low. Daddy said the thing that always scared him most about this story was that he knew just how narrow that creek bed was. A cat the size she described could have easily jumped across the water and attacked her. She said she talked to it the whole time as she was moving closer, and it seemed to respond to the high-pitched, lilting sounds, like the nonsense you might coo to a baby. And somehow it occurred to her that she should sing, which the panther apparently liked because it sat back on its haunches and observed her with entirely relaxed interest. She dipped her bucket in the water, careful not to make any sudden movements, singing softly and sweetly the whole time. When the bucket was full, she backed away and up the trail, still singing, and the cat never moved.

"Soon after seeing the cat the first time, her younger sister caught scarlet fever and died. Belle grew up on Lookout Mountain and always lived within a few miles of the same area. She apparently saw this cat, or at least others that looked exactly like it, a handful of times over the course of her life. She claimed it always appeared before some important event— not always necessarily something tragic, just something of significance. She believed it was an animal spirit. Her mother's family were Cherokee, and although they did their best to be good Christians, they carried some of these mystical Indian beliefs with them and passed them down to their children."

Cole flashed her a teasing grin. "Wonder what significant event your big cat might portend?"

"God," Tanna said, rolling her eyes, "let's hope it's nothing tragic."

"Black cats are indigenous to the eastern United States," Jackson said, staring into his glass, rolling the stem between thumb and forefinger. "Particularly the Southeast. It's entirely possible that's what your grandmother saw. Even in the Gray, people claim to see them from time to time. They've fared better here, of course. Or maybe they just all moved here. We obviously destroy their habitat."

Cole stage-whispered, "He can always be counted on to keep the conversation light and breezy."

"Do you always avoid shooting them?" Tanna asked Jackson.

"Yes. Whenever I can."

—

Throughout the meal Jackson and Cole entertained Tanna with embarrassing tales of one another's exploits. The goal seemed to be who could humiliate the other one the most. Then, during the roast chicken, they jumped up from the table to stand shoulder to shoulder and perform songs. To pass the time on safari together, they often practiced singing harmonies. Tanna found their vocal abilities impressive. They had composed numerous original songs as well, which were usually popular tunes rewritten with suggestive, bawdy lyrics.

Tanna had to put her fork down at one point; she was giggling too hard to eat. She suspected that second bottle from which Cole kept pouring to be contributing to her fits of uncontrollable laughter.

"What is this?" she asked, sniffing at the piney liquid. "Some kind of gin?"

"It's tarwater," Cole said. "Good old straight plain tarwater."

"I'm afraid I haven't developed a tolerance for this yet."

"Lucky you," Cole said.

—

Joona came and went from the table, hunched and hurried, clearly terrified of Tanna's piercing observations. This was an examination of sorts for him, an impromptu test of the skills of waiting tables that Tanna had been trying to teach him.

Cole took pains to be compassionate and kind toward Joona, no doubt noticing his whipped posture and fearful glances. He spoke to Joona in his own tongue at some length. Jackson also seemed to know at least a few common words, *please* and *thank you*. Tanna realized she probably appeared less than gracious for not knowing. She didn't know why she hadn't thought of it before. She vowed she would make it a point to learn some of the Nunnahee language. It would, she hoped, ingratiate her to them.

—

Jackson said he suspected, after Tanna's earlier story about Belle and the black cat, that she might be something of a tale spinner.

"I've been known to make up stories right off the top of my head," Tanna bragged.

"That's somewhere in between an invitation and a dare," Jackson said. "Will you tell us one, then?"

"Yes!" Cole banged on the table, a bit drunkenly. "Tell us a story."

Tanna flushed under the attention, and with a little more encouragement accepted the challenge. "I'll *try*."

She instructed Joona to clear the dinner and to bring them some tea. It wasn't quite the same blend or flavor Giselle had served her at the Daughtrys', but it did have a similarly intoxicating and instantly refreshing effect. She was quite proud when Joona appeared with the silver service and her good china cups and saucers.

Cole complimented all her nice things.

"The Seelie will adore you," Jackson said.

"Who will?" Tanna asked, not recognizing the name.

"The big ones," Cole explained. "The pretty ones who look like us, but with eyes like cats."

"Like Still?" Tanna said. "Our man here at the house?"

"Hmm, not Still," Cole said. "The Seelie are the aristocrats among the fae. Lord Daughtry's wife, for instance. Still has taken a vow of poverty and service."

"Has he?" Tanna put her cup back on the saucer, leaned forward with interest, and lowered her voice. "Like a religious vow?"

"Something like a monk or a priest."

"How did you know that? I had no idea. I have to admit, he's an intriguing mystery to me. I wouldn't be surprised to find out he's an aristocrat. He has such a regal bearing."

"Well, there are a few possibilities regarding his origins." Cole also lowered his voice and made a show of looking over his shoulder. "Your man Still is an Alleegee, a half-breed of one kind or another. From time to time the Seelie have bastard offspring with some of the more rustic elven tribes or the Unseelie or even feral humans. They often do claim them, but they give them a different social position. You'll find them in affluent homes acting as butlers, tutors, governesses. But they're often encouraged to take vows to ensure they stay in their place."

"Indoctrinated from childhood," Jackson muttered, obviously disgusted by the thought.

"I'd love to know more about his background," Tanna said. "But I can't imagine asking him anything personal about himself like that."

"Well, whether he would tell you or not, you may not want to know. By the looks of him, he's probably the product of an affair between a member of the Seelie Court and an Unseelie lover. Scandalous, of course, but it happens all the time. Or he could be an Unseelie prince who has renounced his people on religious or political grounds."

"And the Unseelie are ..." Tanna prompted.

"Our supposed enemies," Cole said. "The ones behind the Rippers. The ones who would see us all thrown out of this world."

"I've got a lot to learn about these cultures. I'll certainly study the book you brought me."

"Well, unfortunately," Jackson said, "you may not find much in Stokes about the politics. He's more of a natural historian. Like Audubon."

"I see. I find that every bit as fascinating as the politics, if not more so," Tanna said. "But I must admit a secret."

"Oh?" Cole asked. "I'm intrigued."

"I'm very impressed with Still," Tanna whispered. "He could be standing outside the door right now for all I know. Not only does he have eyes like a cat, he has ears like a cat too. And he can move around as quietly as one. Whenever I'm around him, I feel like I'm in the presence of royalty. I don't feel quite worthy."

"Well, some people would tell you that you might not want him to know that," Cole said, a hint of something bitter behind his words.

"That sounds like something my mother would say," Tanna said. "I doubt I can keep it from him, anyway. I'm convinced he can read my mind. Or at least smell my fear. He makes me a little nervous. But I admire him, deeply, and I find myself wanting to please him."

"No offense," Cole said, "but I wonder how in the hell a rogue like Buck Eldridge ever convinced the likes of Still to work for him."

"We're supposed to be listening to a story," Jackson said. "Stop sidetracking the poor woman with all this gossip and let her spin us a real tale."

"What would you like to hear a story about?" Tanna asked. "You have to give me a topic."

"Anything?" Jackson asked.

"Absolutely anything. The more fantastic the better."

"Dragons!" Cole said with boyish enthusiasm.

"Dragons?" Tanna said, hesitantly.

"A baby dragon," Cole specified.

Jackson instinctively realized it was a premise Tanna sought—a set of parameters, an assignment. "A young dragon growing up in the old plantation South," he said, "who wants to become a member of polite society."

She nodded her acceptance of the challenge.

"When he was very young, they housed him with the slaves," Tanna began in that low, earnest tone so different from her speaking voice. She stared through the center of the table as if there were a window into the world she was observing. "His memory of his mother was dim. He had been taken from the nest only days after he had hatched. He remembered there were brothers and sisters too. They must have been taken to different locations. He was separated from them almost immediately and had never seen them again ..."

Cole and Jackson were both captivated by the shift in her person as much as the tale itself. For Tanna, storytelling was a trance. She didn't make them up so much as she allowed them to appear before her. The less she tried to control where the story went and the more she simply followed it, the better it would be. It was best, here at the end of a meal like this, still sitting at a table with half-empty water glasses, burned-down candles, reflective glittering surfaces. She often thought this must be what fortune tellers experienced when they looked into their crystal balls.

She settled into the flow. She was aware of the sound of herself speaking, but a part of her listened with the same held breath of her audience, waiting to hear what would happen next to the characters. The now-familiar exhilaration of the tarwater, and the shine in the tea, compounded the sense that she had been transported somewhere else, that something else spoke through her.

She sensed a presence looming at her back, as if the dragon of her story had entered the room and grew behind her. Several times, out of the corner of her eye, she saw the edges of tall shadows thrown against the walls. She could swear the men could see them too. At one point, Cole glanced over at Jackson and pointed past Tanna's shoulder at something beyond her, at the far end of the room. Jackson nodded quickly, but only slightly, as if he wanted to be careful they did not distract her.

The story world she wove seemed to envelop them as a physical phenomenon. The dining room itself had passed through one of those portals along the seams between the worlds. Her imagination found an opening, her voice pulled back the fabric, her mind parted the veils, and the rapt attention of her audience held the gateway in place.

About two-thirds of the way through her story, at a particularly precarious position for the hero, an event from which it seemed impossible to save him, Tanna fell quiet. She did not speak, but rose from the table, and when they leapt up, she motioned for them to follow. She went out into the main living room, to the comfortable pair of chairs on a rug before the fireplace, and waved at Joona, who lurked in the doorway anticipating her instructions.

Joona reappeared with three glasses and a tumbler of brandy on a tray, left them unfilled, and retreated in haste.

Without saying a word, and fearful of breaking Tanna's concentration, Cole shook a cigarette from a silver case and offered one to her. Jackson grabbed one for himself and then lit them all with a brass trench lighter.

Tanna took her favorite seat and pulled an afghan around her shoulders. Cole took off his jacket, laid it across the arm of the chair opposite her, and lowered himself into the leather cushions with a satisfied sigh. Jackson sat cross-legged on the floor at her feet, looking up at her like a boy, puffing out a haze of smoke. He was closest to the tray Joona had left on the coffee table. He took it upon himself to pour them all a brandy. Tanna smiled down at him and nodded her appreciation, but still she did not speak.

She stared into the empty hearth, smoking for another minute or so before finally clearing her throat and tossing her cigarette at the blackened stones. Without explanation or preamble, she picked up the story exactly where she had left off, as if having turned the page in some invisible book in front of her.

"It was in that moment," she said, her narrator's voice grown huskier from the smoke and liquor, "that Edmund gave in to his fire ..."

And she was off again. The dancing shadows reappeared at the margins of the room, and for another half hour the patterns of the story's threads emerged with jewel-like clarity, weaving themselves together with shocking prescience. When she related a particularly harrowing emotional detail, her voice caught in her throat.

The silence that followed her final turn of phrase was like a blanket of quiet pulled over the room. Tanna emerged from her trance, smiling shyly like a girl who'd been caught napping. She looked away from the men, who stared at her now, mouths hanging open, and to cover her embarrassment she reached for her glass.

Cole was the first to collect himself, tossing the butt of his cigarette into the cold fireplace and standing up to applaud. "My God, woman!" he beamed at her. "That was tremendous. Had you told that story before?"

She shook her head. "No, silly. That's the whole point of the challenge. To tell it in the moment."

"I've never in my life," Cole gushed, at a loss for words. He turned to look down at Jackson, who still sat on the floor hugging his knees, looking at the rug and smiling inwardly.

Tanna awaited his comment, self-consciously aware of how much she desired to impress him. He looked up at her suddenly, squarely in the eye, from beneath a lock of red-gold hair that fell across his forehead. He seemed about to say something. Instead, he nodded his head slowly, as if coming to some private realization that pleased him, and then he winked at her.

"There were shadow puppets almost the whole time," Cole said to Jackson. "Please tell me you witnessed those. I've never seen them like that before. Ever."

"Shadow puppets?" Tanna asked.

"It's a phenomenon in this world," Jackson said, standing up to speak. The wink and the smile were gone; his tone was serious. "Some storytellers—a very, very few, I must stress—manifest forms, figures, and scenes from their tales out of the light and shadow around them."

"I did that?" Tanna asked, looking first at Jackson, then at Cole.

"It was incredible!" Cole grabbed her by the shoulders and kissed her on both cheeks. "Incredible!"

She looked over Cole's shoulder as he caught her up in a hug. Jackson was still staring at her, mysteriously, seriously.

"It's magic," Jackson said, so quietly that Tanna had to read his lips.

"Magic?" she asked, pushing Cole away.

Jackson shrugged. "I feel comfortable calling it that."

Tanna turned the word over in her mind, wrapping her hand around her mouth to hide an idiotic smile that threatened to overtake her face and never leave.

She giggled, closed her eyes, took a deep breath, and sighed. She said to Cole, "Light me another one of those cigarettes."

—

They stayed up late, smoking and talking. The magic had passed, and at some point they'd all become a bit drunk and shiny from the tarwater and haint-infused tea.

"So, can you tell us if the rumors are true?" Cole asked.

Tanna tried not to look as taken aback as she felt.

"Is it true that Daughtry has convinced your husband to grow haint?"

Cole had no way of knowing Tanna's fear of being the subject of gossip. While it might have been an impertinent question from a stranger, she knew he asked as a friend.

"Our original intention," she said, composing herself, thinking quickly, "was to cultivate primarily medicinal plants. Coca, poppies, hemp, valerian. Maybe a little tobacco. Even a modest quantity of our own coffee and tea, if the climate allows it. The agricultural component is certainly Buck's expertise. He comes from a family with large tobacco holdings. But the primary identity of the business, especially regarding export back home, is to be a processing plant or small factory, built here on the farm at Brynmor. There would naturally need to be a small distillery and bottling capabilities—"

"Daughtry is going around bragging that he has convinced your husband to plant a thousand acres," Cole said. "And, yes, a distillery for tarwater would cut out not only the tribes but also the humans who already make the products ready for consumption."

"I understand from my overseer that Buck has shown great initiative in being the first of our kind to enter this part of the market," she felt her voice growing haughty. "Gentry said he has displayed a lot of courage in negotiating with the Nunnahee who—"

"Courage?" Jackson interrupted. "Is that what he called it?"

Tanna saw Cole and Jackson glance at one another meaningfully across the coffee table.

Cole became suddenly quiet and intent upon the bottom of his drinking glass.

Jackson leaned toward Tanna and asked her in a low, serious voice. "Did your husband discuss growing haint with you?"

"Well, the conversation was all too rushed," Tanna said. "I must admit that I was taken by surprise. And more than a little bit annoyed with the change in focus. But I was en route across the Seaming, and the opportunity required Buck to make some of these decisions without me."

Jackson looked as if he was trying and failing to suppress outrage. "Did he not warn you about the potential danger?"

"Jackson—" Cole tried to interrupt him.

"There are a lot of forces here who have a problem with this," Jackson said. "Feral, fae, human. A lot of enemies. I question the lack of concern your husband has shown in even providing you with the facts of what you're sitting in the middle of."

"Jackson," Cole tried again, "it's not going to help her to scare the hell out of her—"

Tanna held out her hand to shush Cole. "So what are you saying?" she asked Jackson. "You're telling me that Buck and Daughtry are in danger because of this enterprise? What kind of trouble are we talking about?"

"Daughtry's not in trouble at all. His ass is up at Treebridge behind magic gates and locked doors. Not to mention the protection of his wife, who just happens to be one of the most powerful fairies in polite society."

Tanna's face felt hot with shame. "Why would he just leave me here, then?"

"Well, you're not alone," Cole said, placing his hand on her wrist. "That's why we're here. We came to check in on you. We want to protect you."

"That's why you came?" Tanna felt like a fool, trying to play the lady in the great house, the country hostess presiding over a dinner party of sophistication and civility in the middle of the wilderness. They must have thought she was entirely vapid, naïve, a silly woman, concerned with decorating her house, laying a fabulous table, and telling impressive stories in front of the hearth. All while her reckless husband went around behind her back involving them in nefarious schemes and probably gambling away her fortune. She wondered if they knew of Buck's whereabouts or with whom he might have been seen. She'd really rather someone just tell her. It wasn't like she didn't know what a scoundrel Buck was.

"That's not why we're here," Cole said, with a slightly scolding tone. "We came because we knew you were out here alone, that you'd been asking for your husband, and quite frankly I was tired of waiting for that jackass to act like a man and come check on you himself. I wanted to come days ago, actually. Ask Jackson. He convinced me to give the little bastard a chance to do the right thing. But clearly he is nowhere to be found, and you deserve more attention than that."

"My intentions were entirely selfish," Jackson said in that matter-of-fact way of his. "I came because Cole convinced me you were now the only lively conversation and civilized company to be found in this colony. I trust his good judgment and your rumored love of books. And I shouldn't let this go unsaid—I am more than satisfied with all that I have found in your acquaintance."

Tanna put a hand to her heart. "Thank you," she said, trying to bear the compliment. She wanted to say more, but was afraid she might burst into tears and come across as hysterical.

When Cole and Jackson went to leave, the sky already turning pink and gray with the dawn, Jackson gave Tanna a fountain pen of gold inlaid with malachite.

"What is this?" Tanna said. The weight of it in her hand, the obvious value of it, embarrassed her.

"A tool like this belongs with a mind that can do it justice. I could never hope to employ it as you will."

"It's lovely, but it's too much. You've already given me the book. I can't accept this."

"You can," Jackson said. "You should use it to write down some of your stories."

"Yes, well, we'll see," she retreated from the embarrassment he inspired in her, back into the safe distance of sarcasm. "Once I've repaired this house, grown a forbidden crop or two, and fought off the Unseelie hoards who want to see me driven from my hill." She gave him a wry smile. "Perhaps, then, in my spare time."

"Sounds like you have the makings of an excellent memoir!" Cole interjected.

"Don't disparage your gift," Jackson said to her. "It is magic, what you can do. In both this world and the one we came from."

It irritated her that he could make her want to impress him. She felt an unbearable urge to have him go on thinking highly of her.

Jackson tipped his hat. "Thank you for the story, the meal, and the impeccable hospitality."

"See," Tanna said, "aren't you glad I hauled all my nice things across the Seaming?"

"I am," Jackson admitted, mounting his horse. He flicked the reins and headed slowly down the drive to give Cole plenty of time to catch up to him.

Cole took both her hands and smiled warmly at her. "Please tell me I can come back."

She offered him her cheek to kiss. "Absolutely. Whenever you like, as long as it's soon."

As he climbed onto his own horse, Tanna called up to him. "Cole, if you do see Buck at The Fairchild—or anywhere, for that matter—will you tell him to come home?"

"You didn't hear it from me, but I wouldn't be surprised to find out your husband's on a reconnaissance mission for Daughtry."

"A spy? Buck?" Tanna laughed. "He's the most conspicuous person in the world."

20

Buck finally returned.

Tanna had gone out for a walk down the back of Brynmor, through the furrowed terraces where the small root balls of the bushy haint plants would be stuffed into holes. She headed toward the clearing at the bottom of the hill where they planned to build the distillery.

While it was the only practical level area of the proper size, she hated that the building might obstruct the view down over the tall grasses to the larger southeastern branch of Wavy Creek. She hoped the building might at least serve as a lookout, perhaps from a second story, providing an enhanced view of the road running parallel to the water. Anyone who approached from the south could be seen from miles away, and no matter how fast they traveled, whether on horseback or by carriage, they would kick up a plume of dust that only made it easier to track them.

She shook away the thought, realizing its origins in her anxiety. Her mind constantly drifted to visions of attack.

"You don't believe in premonitions, now, do you?" she said to herself, out loud. "Surely not."

She couldn't stop wondering where Buck might be and whether or not he had gotten himself into trouble. Wanting him to return had become a constant wish, emanating from her mind like a telegraph signal, repeating over and over. She hoped Buck might perceive it and come home.

At first, she thought the movement must be her imagination, a manifestation of wishful thinking. But the image soon resolved itself into three riders on horseback, with a few stragglers walking on foot, spread out along the road behind them. She waited for more detail to coalesce, straining her eyes, chastising herself for not always bringing the binoculars with her when she was outside.

And then it was him. There he was. The way Buck sat on a horse always made an unmistakable short silhouette—he looked like a toad in a hat and a yellow scarf. *Her* yellow scarf, she realized with irritation. She'd given up on it weeks ago, after berating poor Holly for leaving it on the *Queen of Clouds*.

Buck spotted her and gave an excited wave, as if she'd come specifically to welcome him.

She hated herself for being thrilled to have him back and for wanting to *talk* to him more than she wanted to hate him.

Buck swung down from the horse with a groan and caught her up in a hug, lifting her off her feet. He stank of sweat, campfires, and horses.

"Put me down," she pouted. "I'm furious with you."

"Why?" he asked, sounding shocked and wounded.

"For leaving like that—without a word—and staying gone, you idiot!"

"Well, I've stopped being gone, so now you can stop being mad. There, it's all settled."

"Do you really believe that's how it works?"

"That's how it should be. Let the custom start with us."

"The lessons in forgiveness that you inspire in others are simply going to be legendary someday."

—

Buck talked through mouthfuls of food, while Tanna sat beside him listening and refilling his glass. He gushed compliments about Navvee's cooking.

"*Real* food," he groaned, rolling his eyes in theatrical ecstasy. "You don't even want to know some of the things I've eaten."

"I'm sure I don't," Tanna said dryly, "although I must admit to a morbid curiosity."

"You have to come out, someday, and see it all for yourself."

"I would love to do that," she said in a sincere, dreamy voice, but then the edge to her tone crept back. "Just as soon as I finish rebuilding this ramshackle structure that's supposed to be our home and see that the money we've invested in this farm becomes actual crops and products we can sell. For more money. Which is the point of our having a farm."

Buck winced apologetically. "Look, we all know you're the smart one in this operation—"

Tanna made a rude sound. "Yes, by all means, try flattery. That's what I need from you."

"—and Gentry is the … Well, I was going to say Gentry is the brute force, but I guess technically it's the genies who are providing the physical labor. Really, Gentry is the wise one, isn't he? I mean, he's the one with the actual knowledge about the crops and the land and the business of farming. You're the ... *visionary*. That's it!" Having found the proper words and warming to his metaphor, he made wide sweeping gestures with his arms. "You see the full scope of what we want to accomplish here."

"Oh, stop," Tanna said, waving a hand at him in dismissive disgust. "Don't hurt yourself trying to shovel your usual truckload of charm. I don't need to be charmed. I don't need to be made to laugh. I needed you here and you abandoned me."

Buck dropped his fork and opened his mouth, ready to continue his blather in full force.

She cut him off. "Don't interrupt me. I don't need to hear it. There was a lot to do and I got on with doing it. Without you. But there's still plenty of work, and you're here now. So if you really want any chance under heaven of making this up to me, you'll get up tomorrow and throw yourself into this."

Buck grimaced. The look of regret someone gives as an apology for bearing bad news. "Yes. Well ..."

"You just said a *yes* that sounded a lot more like a *no*."

"Oh, darlin," Buck said, turning up his drawl, "I'm afraid I can't stay."

"You can't stay?"

"Actually, *we* can't stay. I've come to check on you because I have orders to take you to Treebridge."

"Whose orders?"

"Daughtry's."

"Do you work for him now?"

"Well, it's in more of an official colony government capacity."

"My God," Tanna laughed without mirth. "They told me you were working as some kind of spy and I didn't believe them."

Buck frowned. "I'd like to know who's going around talking about things they ought not be repeating. It puts us all in danger."

"Oh, don't give me outrage over someone else's behavior as a distraction from your shiftiness. Or shiftlessness."

"Tanna, there's real trouble brewing, and all the outlying plantation owners are being ordered into Treebridge for their own safety."

"I'm not going anywhere."

"It's for your protection."

"Well, if I'm in danger here, then the farm is in danger. Our house is in danger. Our livelihood is in danger, and that's what I'm interested in protecting. Not to mention all the Nunnahee who live here are in danger as well. What about them? Are they going to be put up in rooms at The

Fairchild? Will they get to drink gin and play cards to pass the time? Or is that just for me?"

"It's for the women and children."

"Oh, so just to be clear, I'm going to be protected as a woman, not a child, right?"

"Be reasonable. You saw firsthand what happened on the road out here the day we arrived. There's more of that coming. I would never forgive myself if something happened to you."

Tanna got up from the table, paced to the door, and then came back at him. "I'm not going anywhere. Leave me a gun. I have Gentry and the male servants and a thousand spear-carrying Nunnahee warriors living under this hill. I'll ask Queen Ananjooee to send me a small force to protect the house."

Buck sighed. He tossed his napkin on his plate and lowered his voice, no longer trying to shout over her or convince her. "Look. I need to brief Daughtry. I'm leaving first thing in morning."

"Yes, of course, leave again. Go."

"I'd like for you to come with me."

"I won't."

—

She wouldn't.

Buck tried again to convince her over breakfast. They went round and round the same argument from the night before.

Looking down from his horse, he pointed his finger at her. "This threat isn't going to evaporate, Tanna. You're in danger here. I'll give you a few days to come to your senses."

—

A few days later, Tanna was in the kitchen requesting a pot of tea when she heard hooves on the gravel drive. She found it impossible to believe Buck would have come back so soon. She ran to the front veranda in time to see the back of someone dismounting a horse. She knew immediately it wasn't Buck.

"Holly."

The girl turned to face her, struggling to suppress a sheepish grin.

Tanna embraced her with a force that surprised them both and pulled back to find Holly blushing.

Joona arrived in the doorway with the tea tray, and Tanna composed herself by instructing him to fetch another cup for Holly. Tanna led Holly to the table on the veranda and asked her how it was to be back working with her father again.

"Kind of awful, as always," Holly answered in her awkward, honest way.

Tanna cringed a bit at the girl's delivery, but she didn't want to sour their meeting by lecturing her on the art of conversation. She was concerned Holly might be in trouble. "I didn't expect to see you again so soon. Are things that bad?"

Holly's face fell. She started to breathe a bit fast and loud, nervously licking her lips in anticipation of the speech she'd rehearsed on the ride to Brynmor. Holly wasn't here to get away from the Graycoat.

Tanna withdrew behind a tight expression. "Save your words," she said coldly. "They've sent you to bring me to Treebridge, I suppose."

Holly's apologetic grimace confirmed it.

"How long do we have?" Tanna asked, picking up her teacup. "When are they expecting us?"

"Mr. Eldridge said to give you a few days to pack up some things. But not any longer than that. And they're sending soldiers here to bring you back."

Tanna laughed, an offended huff.

"And he also gave me this list," Holly said, handing it over. "Supplies he needs you to send to him and Daughtry and the troops over at the front along the Seaming."

"Troops on the front?" Tanna said.

"They're having to patrol back and forth between the main crossing points now. The Rippers are attacking the haul teams. They're cutting the lines on the dirigibles."

Tanna thought back to the lines that had tethered the *Queen of Clouds* to the men on the ground. She hadn't felt insecure at the time because there were multiple cables and ropes; even if one had slipped away, the others would have held. Of course, she'd had no idea there was a conflict, that anyone might intentionally cut them ... She imagined being in one of those balloon crafts as it came completely unmoored and floated free. The thought was nauseating.

"My God," she whispered. "Daughtry is putting a stop to it, though? And Buck is helping?"

"They can protect the caravans, as long as they can stay out there. But they need supplies in order to keep the patrols going."

"I'll send them everything they need. Of course. Right away."

There was a loud hiss in the sky.

Flying machines streaked low over the house.

By the time Tanna saw them, they were beyond Brynmor and disappearing over the plains, following the Big South Road. There were two gliders, silvery-green; bulbous, rounded nosecones; double sets of static, transparent, veined wings; and long, sleek tails.

"Idettee!" The yolos shrieked, running out onto the lawn after them.

"Dragonflies," Holly translated. Seeing the worried frown on Tanna's face, she added, "They're ours."

"Not coming for us, then," Tanna said. Suddenly, her expression softened as an idea occurred to her. "Holly, when does your father want you back?"

"He doesn't. He's in the Seaming too. He's staying with his caravans. He thinks I'm in Treebridge."

Tanna smiled at her. "We're going to take the supplies to them ourselves."

Holly looked worried. "We are?"

"They need provisions, and they want me off the farm," Tanna said. "It's the perfect solution."

"I don't think that's what they had in mind when they sent me," the girl said.

Tanna shrugged nonchalantly. "Then they should have been more specific."

21

She had pictured herself on horseback, exploring the rugged scenery of the Green, guided to their destination by the distant campfires of Daughtry's company glowing like fireflies in the dusk. She saw herself triumphantly leading this wagon caravan into camp the following dawn, crowds of hungry soldiers emerging from their tents, breaking into surprised cheers as they parted to let her pass. The vision was not unlike her arrival at Brynmor, only these were her people. Their adulation would mean more. The look on Buck's face would be priceless.

This fantasy began evaporating in the heat of the first day. There was nothing here but the brown dirt road snaking away to a point in both directions through an endless sea of grass. At home in Chattanooga, preparing for her adventure, daydreaming about the Green, she'd somehow imagined a mix of high purple mountains, redwood forests, and tropical jungles. The scale of things had proven to be beyond her imagination, and so far she'd felt like an ant—drifting across a sea of treetops, and now crawling through a sea of grass.

The first night sleeping under the open sky, she felt she'd arrived at one of those moments about which she'd fantasized only a few months ago. Here, the streak of the Milky Way galaxy was breathtaking. After the stress of preparing the supply caravan in time to evade a military escort from Treebridge, she'd enjoyed a deep, dreamless sleep, and awakened to strong tea prepared in a tin pot on a campfire.

The genies who accompanied the caravan, the cattle drivers, and the men who tended to the hogs in their cage on wheels were both deferential and inclusive. They nodded to her when she joined them, sitting cross-legged in their circle, oiling their rifles. Although she didn't understand their language, she smiled when they laughed at one another's jokes. They talked to each other in her presence with an unselfconscious freedom she'd never encountered in her house servants.

On the second day, when she mounted her horse at the head of the caravan and made a big show of leading them forward, they raised their hands in a rallying salute. But that second night she tossed and turned on her bedroll, unnerved by the collective scream and roar of the night insects. She woke up stiff and cranky, with little to say. Everyone drank their tea in near silence, and resumed the march with creaking joints and barely stifled groans.

Late in the morning of the third day, Tanna was dozing on horseback. The never-ending view of tall grasses felt like a dream. She shook herself awake at midday and called out to Holly. They rode ahead of the wagon to a small hill in the road. It was little more than a swollen hump in the prairie, but in the unbroken carpet of grass it might as well have been a mountain.

The view was unchanged. There was no sign of anything much, let alone a company of soldiers.

Tanna checked her compass for the hundredth time. The tarnished brass instrument in its worn leather case had belonged to her father. She felt that by using it his spirit might watch over her. South by southeast ... The needle had a strange wiggle to it. She wasn't sure what that meant, if it mattered. Maybe her hand was just trembling. She was afraid to ask anyone.

"How will we know when we've found them?" Tanna asked.

Holly squinted into the distance, hand up to shield her brow, scanning along the horizon in a smooth, intentional sweep. "Campfires."

"What about during the day?"

"The smoke. From all the fires. A company that size will have smoke hanging over it night and day, like a small town."

"Oh," Tanna said, impressed with Holly's simple knowledge. She raised her focus to the horizon, just above the tree line, looking for smudges low in the sky. After several minutes, turning round and round in her saddle, she sighed in defeat. "I don't see anything."

"Me either," Holly said.

Tanna watched the men pause to rest beside the wagon in the only shade they had. They passed around a nearly flat skin of water. She touched her own canteen where it lay against her belly, but resisted the urge to drink. In the coming hours, she might want that last hot swallow. Badly. For now, she could wait.

She urged Bronte as close to the wagon as the mare would go. "Still," she said in a low voice, motioning for him to lean in close. "We're out of water, aren't we?"

"We are, so'onah."

"Do you have any idea how we can find more out here?" She gestured around at the empty grasslands.

He pointed to a smudge along the horizon. "Where there are trees, there will be water."

"That's miles away. It could take an entire day to reach. And I don't even know that's the direction we want to go."

"Dig?" he suggested with a shrug. The human gesture made him seem all the more alien.

Tanna looked around at the miles of flat ground, unbroken by any potential streams or low depressions. Even if it were a detour of days, they would have to explore the closest forest, no matter how far away. There was no other good option.

"Tell them to stop drinking the goddamned water," she barked. She urged Bronte off the track they had been following and waded into the tall grass, making for the faint and distant woods.

—

It took almost another two days to reach those trees.

The forest and its backdrop of mountains seemed to recede from them, as if the gods were dragging the landscape away at the same pace that they approached. If the animals died, their entire reason for making this journey was pointless. Not to mention all these human and fae would suffer because of her error. It might be days before they could get a message to someone else to send more supplies, and weeks for those to reach them, even if they could be successfully located.

In other words, they would die waiting to be rescued.

They were surely closer to Daughtry's camp than they were to home. They couldn't turn around. The thought of arriving on horseback, close to death, without the supplies ... Tanna was mortified. Her impulsive adventure had put a military objective at risk.

Succeeding was her only option.

When they stopped to camp for the night, she pulled Still and Holly aside. "If either one of you has any idea how we find our way out of this, I hope to God you'll tell me. Please, do not defer to my authority in this situation or worry about my feelings. If you think I'm making a grave mistake, tell me."

Holly looked at her with a wince of regret. "I wish I could."

"We are all lost, so'onah," said Still, unhelpfully.

—

They heard riders approaching. As the hooves pounded closer they could make out the hiss of the tall grasses parting.

"Well, hello there," the lead rider called cheerfully.

Jackson Gallagher slid off his horse. He walked over to Tanna, still on her own mount; he looked up at her with a crooked, bemused smile.

She was mortified by the sweat stains saturating the ugly man's shirt she wore. Not to mention her sudden painful awareness of the state of her hair—she could feel it waving around, standing off her head as if electrified. Nevertheless, it wasn't hard for her to put up a genuine smile—she was nearly giddy with the relief of running across anyone who could rescue them from her leadership. That it was someone she knew made her feel like some fates or angels were protecting her after all. Jackson Gallagher was a professional outdoorsman, which was exactly what they needed more than anything in the world.

She felt compelled to explain what they were doing there. Jackson had a way of demanding information with his silence. "We're taking some supplies to Buck and Daughtry at the front," she said.

"Is that right?" He leaned sideways to look past her horse, taking in the cattle, the pigs, the wagon, the genies in attendance, as if estimating their worth. He nodded to Still and touched his hat in Holly's direction.

"I'm afraid—" Tanna continued, swinging her stiff leg free of the saddle and trying to climb down. Jackson lurched toward her to steady her arm, and she thanked him shyly. Having not bathed in days, she felt self-conscious being so close to him. "I'm afraid I've gotten us completely and entirely lost."

"I see," Jackson said. Even though he had likely been in the Green for weeks and his boots were caked in a hard rind of mud, he somehow managed to look clean, glowing, and healthy. His sunburned lips curled back with his squint, revealing his shockingly white teeth. He stood with his hands on his hips, head cocked at an angle, the sun in his eyes, waiting for her to go on.

She wiped her hands on the thighs of her pants, a bit annoyed that he forced her to ask. "So, can you help us?"

"I hope so," Jackson said. "Were you planning to stop here for the night?"

"Should we?" Tanna asked.

"This is the last place you're going to find water for miles. If you want to make it across the prairie in one day, get up early in the morning and go when it's cool."

"Then we'll set up camp here." She didn't mention she had insisted they go a few more hours before stopping. She called back instructions to Still, as if it were an easy adaptation of their plans.

Jackson turned back to his companion, the tall elven warrior who had been with him the first time she encountered them in the Sea of Trees. Jackson said something low in a language she didn't recognize. The warrior came forward, leading their horses by the reins. He was as tall as most human men but unnaturally thin. Jackson dug around in a saddlebag, took something out, and patted the horse's rump. His companion led both horses over into the shade of a nearby copse of trees and began removing their saddles.

"I doubt anyone would have given you one of these," Jackson said, showing Tanna a small, rounded leather case in the center of his palm. He unsnapped the flap of a cover and slid out a heavy object that, on first glance, looked something like a brass pocket watch.

"It's beautiful," Tanna said.

"You've been using a compass."

"Of course," she said, lifting her chin. She showed him the compass in her own hand, fingers almost permanently curled around it. She'd been carrying it for hours, constantly checking it. "It was my father's."

"Well, it's the reason you're lost. You need this." When he flipped the object over, she saw the front had a convex glass lens in a brass frame. It reminded her of the end of a spyglass.

"What does it do?"

"It's called an auroculus. It was developed by human colonists who came across the Seaming from our world about three hundred years ago."

"It's ancient!" Tanna whispered.

"Well, no." He smiled sheepishly, deep crow's feet appearing at the corners of his eyes. "This one's probably only twenty-five years old. Fifty at most. I'm not sure. It belonged to ... someone I used to know."

She studied his face, but he did not meet her eyes. He had beautiful copper-colored hairs in his eyebrows. His nearly invisible lashes were faintly golden.

He stared down at the auroculus, rubbing its metal edge between his thumb and forefinger. He glanced up to find her staring at him and quickly returned to his explanation. "Anyway, the earth's magnetic field, which allows a compass to operate, doesn't behave the same in this world. This device compensates for the differences." He looked at her doubtfully, lips twisted in his crooked smile. "Do you want me to go into detail about how? The truth is, I might fail miserably if I attempt it."

Tanna shook her head. "The law of magnetic fields is probably well beyond my depth. But if you can show me where I'm supposed to go, that's all I really care about."

"Yes, absolutely," Jackson said. "Although I'm sure your capacity to understand would exceed my ability to describe it to you. It's best if we wait a few hours after nightfall before using it. Should we have some supper while we wait?"

She self-consciously smoothed her hair. "If you'll let me clean up a bit first. I'm sure I look horrendous."

"There's a tiny spring over there." Jackson jerked his head toward the trees they'd spent all afternoon trying to reach, the only things taller than shoulder-high grass for miles in all directions.

—

Holly held up a blanket to give Tanna some privacy. The ground was boggy near the spring and she had to stand ankle-deep in mud, but at least she was able to strip to the waist and run a wet rag over her face, neck, and shoulders, under her arms and breasts. She dried quickly in the cool breeze that came up across the plains after the sun went down. She had only one drab dress she hadn't worn, a garment she'd reserved for working in the garden at home, but at least it was clean.

Still had built a fire while the other men tended to the animals. They all gathered around the bright hole in the night to dine on smoked strips of meat. They were like boot leather to chew, but salty, spicy, and full of fat. The genies boiled a soup conjured up from dried bean paste and a handful of edible grasses picked near the spring. Jackson and Kanute, the elven warrior with whom he traveled, contributed a pouch of oats, dates, and some kind of berries that tasted like figs.

After the humble meal, multiple flasks of tarwater were passed around the circle. To the whisper of the oiled cloths rubbing gun metal, Tanna recounted how she and Holly had defied the orders to go to Treebridge in order to make this journey instead, and how they narrowly escaped the armed guard sent to remove them by force, while idettee streaked across the sky above Brynmor. She animated the tale with drama and suspense, delighting in the telling of it more than the living of it. She enjoyed the version of herself she became in the story.

Jackson listened with the same rapt expression she remembered from the night at the farm when she'd made up the story for him and Cole about Edmund the civilized dragon. She glanced around a few times at the firelight on the nearby trees and the long shadows across the grass. She couldn't imagine where the magical figures—the tale spinner's shadow puppets—could appear out here in the open. She wondered if figments loomed behind her as she spoke. It was satisfying that this story was not entirely fiction; this had actually happened to her.

She was as capable of adventure as Jackson Gallagher himself, and his attention proved he found it to be true.

"It sounds wonderful," Holly said, a dreamy expression on her sleepy face.

"You were *there*," Tanna said, amused.

"But it's better when you tell it," Holly said. "I'm jealous of myself in it." She trailed off in wonder at the impressive philosophy of her own thoughts.

—

After the barest explanation of where he and Kanute had been and what they had seen—all animal life, no warmongering fae—Jackson tilted his head to study the sky. He suggested it might be time to use the auroculus.

He stood up from a seated position in one fluid motion and offered a hand to Tanna.

His hand felt hot and surprisingly damp.

"It'll be best if we can get as far away from the glare of the campfire as possible," he said.

He led her to the far side of the cottonwoods growing around the spring, facing south. It was significantly darker with the firelight blocked from sight, and her eyes adjusted quickly to the change. The stars seemed to have multiplied a million times over during their brief relocation. The sky was strewn with a giant swath of silver sand and glitter. The smear stretched down from directly overhead to plummet through the horizon. It was as if they stood at the foot of a great waterfall of stars.

"It's the same Milky Way," Tanna said.

"You expected it to be different?" Jackson asked, alert to her statement.

"Did I?" she wondered aloud. "I think I actually did."

"But you've noticed the constellations aren't quite the same?"

"Aren't they?" She searched the sky for the familiar Dippers, for Orion's Belt, the Seven Sisters. "My God, they're not. How is that possible?"

"I honestly don't know," Jackson said, a defeated tone in his voice. "Sometimes, at night, I feel like this is what drags me out on safari, over and over again. It's not to hunt or to explore. It's to ponder this sky. Where are we? How is it different? Where is this sky in relation to the one we know from home?"

Tanna waited through his silent pause in hopes he would continue. She'd never heard him speak like this, expressing such contemplations. He usually only commented in the briefest way, a kind of banter that turned the burden of conversation back on the other person. This was the first time he'd ever revealed private thoughts.

"I can't figure it out," he continued, sighing. "If the view is not the same, then we can't logically—physically—be in the same place."

They stood shoulder to shoulder. She watched him stare into the night.

"Well, we're not," she said. "We've crossed into the Green."

"So is the Green just another spot on the globe? A wild, undiscovered part of the planet, as the continents of the New World once were?"

She shrugged helplessly.

"Because, if that's the case," he said, continuing with his argument, "then where would we draw it on a map? Is it squeezed in somewhere between East Tennessee and Northern Alabama? Is it a lost canyon in the Cumberland Plateau?"

"Could it be?" she asked.

"It's impossible. The sheer size of it ... I've easily explored an area the size of half the state. It's not like you walk west and come out the other side in Memphis. You keep going, *in* the Green."

"Do you think we're on another planet?"

"I honestly do not know," he repeated, emphasizing each word. He turned to face her then. She looked frightened by the size of his questions. "The natural laws of this world are similar in a lot of ways—there's a moon in the sky, the sun rises and sets, and there is the same number of hours in a day. But then, the seasons are different. The spring, summer, and fall last longer here. Winter is brief. And time itself moves more slowly in relation to the other world. You do know about that, don't you? You were warned before you came?"

"Yes. Buck told me we might be leaving everyone behind," she said, recalling the very different way in which he described the time lag in comparison to Jackson. "That we could return to find our families and friends aged. Possibly even dead and gone, depending on how long we were here."

He nodded his head. "It's probably best, if you intend to go back at all, that you go back periodically. Frequently. Or else just wait a number of years here. Maybe a decade. That's if you want to avoid confronting those you've abandoned to age."

"Do you go back?" she asked.

"Yes. I've tried to go back at least once a year, by reckoning the number of months here in the Green. It's not always an exact estimation, but it seems about every six months, five years will have passed over there. Give or take." He took a seat on the ground and she joined him. "It's disturbing, you know. You don't really think about it. Well, you think about it, you process the concept, the theory, intellectually. But it doesn't prepare you for what it feels like. To be Rip Van Winkle. Clearly not a fable after all, huh?"

"I've begun to question everything that was ever called a fairy tale," Tanna said, not wanting to interrupt his train of thought. He spoke in questions and riddles and prompts, clearly rhetorical. It was like listening to a pastor's sermon or an academic lecture. She was spellbound by the rhythm of his speech, and she didn't want to break it. He had fallen into something like a trance state, and it was pleasant for them both. She held a breath, afraid that at any moment he would snap awake and go back to his silent, watchful mode.

Jackson wrapped his arms around his knees. "I feel bad about infecting you with this obsession of pondering. I can tell that, like me, once the mystery's introduced, it'll worry the hell out of you. I suppose I selfishly hope someone with your intelligence will see something I've missed. And I'll say, 'Yes, at last. Yes, that's it!'"

"I'm afraid I'll disappoint you in that," Tanna said, but she was privately thrilled he considered her capable. It was the greatest compliment any man had ever paid her.

"Ah, well, you lessen my pain by sharing it. You'd be surprised how few people will listen to me go on about this for as long as you have." He chuckled at a thought. "It dies in polite conversation so quickly."

This was a topic on which Tanna could comment. "People don't like to think about things they don't understand. And they don't like to be reminded that there are so many things they don't understand at all. Your conversation reminds us of our powerlessness before God's creation."

He turned to her, chin on his shoulder. "Is it God's creation, then, do you think?"

"Some god. *The gods.* It exhausts me to imagine how it was created, or by whom, but I do think this world might somehow be better than the one we left."

"Well," he seemed to come back to himself, "the good news is that even though I can't grasp the cosmology of this world, and there are not the same lineages of scientific inquiry here—not yet, anyway, not so much—there are still machines that work within this different context. Some of them may be magical objects." He pulled the auroculus out of his pocket. "This is one of them."

He pointed off to the left of the Milky Way, toward the eastern horizon, opposite the fading remains of the sunset. "There's a phenomenon in this world that resembles the aurorae. It's like the shimmering curtain of the borealis you see in the north in our world, only this one is not encircling the North Pole. It's linear, and it's broken. It reminds me of low flames along a burning stick. It's very, very faint and it doesn't reach as high into the sky, but the colors are the same. Do you see it?"

"I think I can just make it out, now that you've shown me. It's lovely. But I'm not sure I would have ever noticed it on my own."

"That is the edge of this world. The Seaming. Those individual peaks or flames are magnetic disturbances created by the crossing points. The portals. The gateways. You see the large one? It's much wider than the others near it." He pointed back over their left shoulder, sighting farther north along the eastern horizon. "That's Cumberland Gorge where you came through."

The realization gripped her with a cold sensation like panic. "No," she breathed. "That's where Buck and Daughtry are? I've been leading everyone south. Now we're going in almost the exact opposite direction. We would never have arrived."

"Your compass picks up on those crossover points. It's a weak reading, but strong enough to show it as north."

"The needle jumping," she whispered. "The needle says it's pointing north, but it quivers in an odd way."

"And, in this case, it's really pointing east. But, of course, the edges of this world—the spots where it meets the other—could be in any direction, depending on where you are."

"So why do I need this?" Tanna asked, nodding at the auroculus in his hand.

Jackson offered it to her. "Put it up to your eye."

She held the heavy object between thumb and forefinger. Her fingertips easily slipped into smooth grooves or notches in the brass. She squinted her left eye and peered through the glass with her right. The colored flames of the eastern horizon intensified; became brighter, more varied in color; and reached higher into the sky.

Jackson heard her breath catch. "See how much clearer it is? How much taller it stretches?"

"Yes," she said, her voice low as she watched the dance of light. "It's beautiful."

"Well, it's relatively flat here. But if we were someplace more mountainous, or in a valley where the horizon were blocked, you'd never see the colors with the naked eye, even on a good night. But with the auroculus you can see it reaching all the way to the heavens."

"It's almost as bright as a fire."

He waited while she wondered at the phenomenon, reluctant to interrupt her. "What time of day were you using the compass?"

"I know," she said, angry with herself. "I sound like an idiot woman who doesn't know what direction the sun rises in the sky. I do. Of course I do."

"But if you're relying on a compass—and why shouldn't you be able to trust a compass?—it's telling you the edge of the Seaming is north, and so you keep plotting a course to the right of that, which you think is east, but is actually taking you due south."

"I've been essentially traveling parallel to the Seaming this whole time." She put her face in her hands. "We never would have reached it. In my defense, I was checking in the middle of the day, when we most wanted shelter from the heat and sun. And then of course at night, when we stop, I've spent some time contemplating and plotting and worrying ..." She trailed off with an exasperated groan under her breath. "The more lost I felt, the more I clung to wherever the needle pointed."

Jackson was kind enough not to explain the obvious to her any further.

She shook off her frustration and straightened her shoulders, looking him in the eye. "So, how do we find Buck and Daughtry once we're at the Seaming?"

"Well, you'll need to go back north a bit. And at night at least you can see where the largest crossing point is. You don't want to go beyond that. But there's another phenomenon to guide you. Storms. Lightning will point the way to the nearest crossing. There are weather disturbances wherever there are gateways held open between this world and the other. The warmer air here meets up with the cooler air streaming through, especially when it's winter in the Gray and any other season here. The air temperatures rarely match. It may take a little scouting once you're close, but at that point, the smoke from their campfires should give them away during the day."

"Thank you for this," Tanna said. She tried to hand the auroculus back to him.

"No, you have to keep it," Jackson said.

"I can't keep this. You said it's an antique."

"Then you can borrow it. Give it back to me next time I come to your house for dinner."

—

When Tanna awoke the next morning, Jackson and Kanute were gone.

22

At first, it appeared as a dark disturbance along the horizon. Little more than a smudge trailing dust, wisps of smoke. There was a faint rhythmic clatter, a loud clamor that carried over the plains.

Tanna knew it was absurd, but for a moment she wondered if it might not be a train.

"It's a hoard," Still said.

Tanna jerked her head around, waiting for him to say more.

"The Unseelie," Holly explained.

"Stay here," Still said. He held out his arm, motioning for everyone behind them to come to a halt. He never took his eyes off the approaching hoard, his brows creased together in a stern frown.

As the hoard moved across the grass, it came close to their caravan.

The Unseelie resembled a parade of metals and dark colors—flashes of blue-black, silver, and scarlet. It was hard to make distinctions among their steeds, their carriages and rickshaws, those who jogged alongside the riders, the jagged forest of spears and pennants. Tanna imagined a rolling jumble of broken umbrellas, the iridescent feathers of ravens, and the horny beaks of crows. The noise was unnerving—a clanging of brass bells, the deep beating of skin drums, and a maddening din of pipes and flutes.

"They will ignore us," Still pronounced.

None of the hoard seemed to be paying any attention to Tanna and her entourage, although the caravan was clearly visible from miles in all directions. She held her breath when a few fast riders broke away from the band on small two-legged steeds that looked something like a cross between a horse and an ostrich. They rode on ahead and then circled back around to the rear of the hoard.

Without slowing down or even so much as turning their heads, the hoard continued past them, moving west by northwest. They were soon once again a clanging smudge, dwindling into the distance.

Tanna exhaled. "Well, at least they're not going anywhere near where we want to go. But where do you think they're headed?"

"The colony," Still said.

—

When they stopped for the night, the porters went into the nearby brush and returned dragging thorn tree branches. Some of the crisscrossing thorns were as long as sword blades. They arranged the branches in a circle to form a natural fence around the shallow, muddy trickle of a stream. They herded the cattle into the interior, where there was also a bit of clover on which they could graze. They also parked the pig cart within and dumped buckets of scraps between the wooden bars.

"Why are they doing this now?" Tanna asked Still. "They haven't enclosed the animals at any other point in the journey."

"There were no thorns until now," Still said. "The cats prefer to sleep and hunt close to the trees, where they can climb up and observe movement across the grasslands."

Remembering the panther she'd encountered at home, Tanna crossed her arms and rubbed her shoulders against an unlikely chill. She wondered if she would prefer to know she was in danger beforehand or if it might not be a blessing to keep discovering her peril after the fact.

With her back toward the last dying streaks of purple chasing the setting sun, she walked away from the fire so she could look for the aurora dancing in the east. She studied the horizon through the auroculus. Her course was true. Just to the northeast of their current position, the blue-green flame was tall and wide, like the lights from an enormous city seen from a distance. Although the grasslands had not yet given way to the Sea of Trees, the crossover channel in the Seaming couldn't be more than twenty miles away. They expected to find Daughtry's camp several miles south of it.

The trooping Unseelie hoard they had seen earlier that day was long gone. Still assured her it was unlikely they would be attacked by black-feathered demons in the night and speared to death where they slept on the ground. However, it might be another story where the panthers were concerned.

"Another day," Holly said, joining her. "Two at the most."

"We don't know their exact location or how close to the crossing they may be," Tanna said. "We just might make it tomorrow. But we should leave as early as possible, just in case."

They made their way back toward the comforting sight of the campfire.

—

It seemed like only minutes after she'd closed her eyes, Tanna awoke in the dark to the sound of the cattle lowing, snorting, and stamping their hooves. She had never heard them make these small nervous cries before. Holly was already awake beside her, shoving her feet into boots. As Tanna followed her out of the tent, they heard a shout from one of the genies and then the pigs started to scream.

"Cats!" Holly yelled, disappearing toward the shadows around the makeshift corral.

Tanna ran to the wagon where the extra rifles were stored.

As her hands scrambled through the side trunks, under her breath she chanted, "No no no no no." As if a prayer might at least slow time.

She had only just brought this livestock back from the brink of certain dehydration and death. That had been her fault. And with Jackson's help, she had corrected it. She thanked whatever fates had sent him across her path. But now she cursed the gods—no particular names or faces, she just roared her frustration at them all.

It wasn't fair. The animals were only a day's march from their destination.

She heard shots. Someone else had a gun. She gave up the futile search for her rifle, silently vowing to never sleep without one beside her again. She grabbed a torch from the embers of the campfire and waved it into full blaze as she ran toward the man-made hedge of thorn.

She could see the branches shuddering. The cattle were flailing against the thorns on the inside. All the animals were screaming. It was Still repeatedly firing his rifle into the air. A pair of genies struggled to pull back a section of the thorn branches.

As soon as she saw an opening appear, Tanna pushed her way through. One of her pant legs caught on a thorn. She pushed the torch in ahead of her, flailing it around. She felt claws on her shoulder as she freed her leg. But no, it was the thorns ripping the shirt from her upper arms. She was vaguely aware of the cloth falling away from her chest, gathering at her elbows and around her waist.

Inside the corral, the cattle were cowering near the pig cart to her left. In front of her a brown-and-white Hereford had fallen on her side. She struggled to rise on her own, crying out with a bleating sound that sent cold panic through Tanna's chest. Tanna moved forward, thinking to help drag the poor creature up with her bare hands, when she saw the lights of two golden eyes staring at her from the shadow cast by the cow's belly.

She raised the torch above her head and saw the flattened ears. Beneath the din of animals crying, human shouts, and gunshots, she felt the vibration of the cat's growl.

The panther glared at her with hatred, unwilling to give up its prey.

An immense feeling of offense overtook her. It was rage, fueled by possessiveness and protection. Tanna could not abide the idea that this predator believed it had a right to take something of hers.

As the cat hunkered down in a crouch, preparing to lunge at her, Tanna roared. A full-throated, wordless scream tore from her throat and she shoved the burning torch at the panther's face.

It flattened itself on the ground beside the dying cow. In that moment, when Tanna saw the cat's will falter, she climbed over the cow and drove the beast toward the wall of thorns behind it.

They faced off, like gladiators circling one another in the arena. She saw the ghostly twin lights of other sets of eyes, waiting on the far side of the thorn branch wall. They knew their sister was in trouble. They looked for a way in.

If even one of them chose to leap inside the corral ...

Tanna's rage gave way to an instant of blind panic, and in a last desperate thrust of her torch, she ran toward the panther, intent upon getting close enough to set it on fire.

She smelled its whiskers singe. Its growl turned into a cry of pain.

Looking as sullen as a house cat doused with a bucket of water, the defeated panther slunk away to the right, crouched, and leapt back over the thorn wall.

Tanna saw other torches through the branches as the genies drove the remaining cats away into the night.

Still had stopped firing. She looked up to see his calm face gazing down at her, which confused her. She realized she was lying on the ground with her head in his lap. It felt like her back was on fire. Still lifted her and carried her away from the cow on the ground, her breath coming in rapid, ragged pants.

Tanna murmured, "No no no no no" into Still's shoulder, until she heard the single shot ring out. All was quiet then, except for her sobs and the sound of Still's feet whispering through the grass.

—

The cuts on her back and shoulders burned, but thankfully the thorns had only scratched her. The wounds were by no means shallow, but they weren't the deep puncture wounds they could have been, had she been caught from the wrong angle.

Tanna's shirt lay around her waist in a skirt of tattered scraps. Still placed a copper pan of heated water on the grass floor inside the tent, looking away discreetly while Holly went to find some clean towels and a blanket for Tanna to cover herself.

Still worked gently and methodically across her back, extracting splinters with a sewing needle dipped in tarwater. He soaked away the clotted blood with warm wet cloths, then coated the scratches in a muddy paste that cooled the skin as it dried.

She felt ashamed for him to see her undressed. She tried to resist, suggesting Holly could tend to her, but he stoically ignored her protestations.

Holly squatted on her heels in front of her, obviously wanting to be a comfort or a distraction but not knowing how to start the proper conversation. The girl kept reliving the event, asking Tanna questions she couldn't seem to answer. It upset her how little she remembered.

Still stopped his ministrations, and Tanna saw Holly shrink from his glare.

The girl was silent for a long time, looking from Tanna to Still and back to Tanna again. "It was your shadows, you know," Holly finally said.

Tanna frowned.

"Your shadows," she repeated. "The tale spinner shadows. The ones you said rear up behind you when you tell stories."

Tanna remembered roaring at the cat, the rage ripping through her throat, the look of fear that crossed its face.

"It looked like huge flames were rising up behind you," Holly went on, "tall as a house. They were black at the center and the edges were bright gold. That's what ran it off."

"I thought the flames from the torch scared it away," Tanna whispered.

"It was your flames, so'onah," Still said, agreeing with Holly. "Your magic."

—

Daughtry's camp looked like a tent city on a hill. Still spotted it on the horizon when they were ten miles away. He pointed out the wispy tendrils of campfire smoke that were a giveaway, but you had to track along the ground in the opposite direction the wind was moving.

The relief of finding them made Tanna more emotional than she would have predicted. The anxiety she had sustained for the past three days—the entire last week—welled up in her eyes. She wasn't prepared to cry in front of anyone—not her own people, and least of all a camp full of soldiers.

Daughtry's men hadn't done anything to disguise their presence. They were set up out in the open on a flat plain of rolling grass. Behind their camp was a thin barrier of woods at the foot of a line of lavender mountains.

When Tanna's party topped the last knoll about a mile from the first tents, they could hear and smell Daughtry's forces. There were the ring and cheer of a game of horseshoes and the unmistakable, tantalizing scent of pork fat frying. Tanna avoided looking at the three pigs that had traveled all this way with them in the small caged cart.

In her exhausted state, the reality of all the danger, violence, and death she had presided over finally hit her hard. But the euphoria of getting through allowed her to sit tall in the saddle those last few yards as men stopped their incessant oiling of guns to stand and gawk at her. She had imagined they might cheer, but the camp grew quiet as a church. There was only the whisper of tent canvas raking the grass, the silk of pennant standards snapping in the substantial wind, and the creak and rumble of the wagon wheels.

She rode straight toward the center of the camp, where there was an enormous tent large enough to house a circus. Still had stopped the wagons well before the first ring of tents, but Holly was close behind her. There was a brief flutter of nervousness in her chest as she realized the sea of faces looking up at them was entirely composed of young men. None of them had likely seen a woman in weeks, if not months, and most of them looked to be in some state of intoxication. Many of them were likely thinking they could die before they made it home to some sweetheart.

She had brought a sixteen-year-old girl into a camp full of soldiers.

Tanna was only slightly fearful for her own safety, but she was a married woman whose husband was an officer in this company. She turned around in her saddle; Holly was looking straight ahead at her.

Tanna sent her a telepathic inquiry.

Holly's lips twisted in a small, sheepish smile, and she shrugged as if to say she would be fine. She was used to being out in the wilderness with her father's men.

Tanna saw Daughtry's silver hair and whiskers emerge from the flap of the largest tent; he had clearly been called to come out and see who approached.

His slack, bewildered face cracked in a smile.

"Lord Daughtry," Tanna said, savoring the scene. "I've brought you some supplies."

Daughtry shook his head, amused, impressed. "Eldridge!" he shouted at the top of his lungs, his voice echoing around the hills. He turned to a nearby aide-de-camp and said in a normal volume. "Somebody better go warn Bucky his wife is here."

—

Buck stumbled into the clearing in a tank undershirt, his pants unbuttoned, one foot only half-stuffed into a boot, suspenders trailing down his legs.

Tanna saw a flash of horrified recognition cross his face. There was the smallest instance of a frown before he remembered himself and covered it with a smile.

"Tanna!" he cried, his showman's mask back in place. He grabbed her by the shoulders and pressed his cheek to hers. "Never in a million years ... What are you doing here?"

"You sent word you needed a few things, so we decided to bring them to you ourselves."

"What a wonderful surprise!" Buck said for the benefit of their observers. But then he took Tanna by the elbow and steered her along several rows of identical canvas tents. "Let's go into my private quarters, shall we?" A few of the men cackled and catcalled as Buck threw open the flap to what must be his personal tent.

The high sun made a golden glow of the tent fabric; it was bright and warm inside. Tanna saw a mess of blankets on the ground. Buck looked around nervously and moved a canteen off a small folding chair, motioning for her to sit. Tanna saw him discreetly palm what looked like a small clay pipe and slip it into his pocket.

"Were you sleeping?" she asked.

"Sit down," he said cheerfully, as if he hadn't heard her question.

"I've been sitting on a horse for days," Tanna said.

"Would you like to lie down, then?" Buck asked, squatting and hastily trying to straighten his bedding, spreading the heavy top blanket to cover a tangled sheet and two greasy flat pillows.

"Actually, you could offer me something to drink—"

"God! Yes, of course," Buck said, thrusting the canteen at her. "Forgive me."

She tilted her head back to swallow and could not help but moan a little at how cool and refreshing this water tasted after the hot skins she'd been drinking out of the past few days. When she brought the canteen down, she found Buck on his haunches in the middle of the tent.

He was glaring up at her now. He looked disgusted. "What are you doing here?" he hissed.

"I told you. We got word that you were desperate for supplies—"

"You're supposed to be under protection in Treebridge." He sounded frustrated.

"Yes, yes," Tanna muttered, exasperated. "This was just a better option. For me. For everyone."

"You could have been killed." He stood and paced in front of the tent flap. "You still could be killed."

"Well, the risk was far superior to your plans for me."

"It wasn't *my* plan for you, Tanna." He planted his feet and clenched his fists. "It was Daughtry's orders."

She stalked across his bed, pleased at the boot prints she was leaving. As she brought her face close to his, he cringed a bit in spite of himself. "We did not come all this way—emigrate to another world—so that I could take orders, Buck. I thought our plan was to ensure our freedom from that kind of thing."

"You can't just ignore the orders of respected government leaders, Tanna. Especially not in times of war."

"Men telling women what to do," she smiled meanly. "It seems to be the cornerstone of government everywhere."

Buck shook his head, moved to the center of the tent, lifted his blanket, and began to slap the dirty prints from the cloth. "These are the front lines, Tanna. In a dangerous conflict that has been going on since long before our time."

"And it's our home now," she said with passion. "You're defending it. Why wouldn't I? I'm the one who's financially invested."

He let that particular barb pass, as he always did.

"This is no place for you," he finally said. But he said it softly, with compassion, with what could have passed for genuine worry in his eyes.

"You want me to leave, then? Now?" Tanna asked, incredulous. "Could we at least eat and rest our horses? We can use our own provisions. You know, the ones I procured with my money, brought all this way, and even defended with my own bare hands."

They stared at each other across the tense silence.

"Will that be too much of an imposition for you?" she demanded.

The tent flap was thrown open by a young shirtless man, already in mid-sentence talking to Buck. He almost ran into Tanna, now standing near the opening.

"Oh! I'm so sorry," the boy said, pulling up short, glancing between Tanna and Buck. "I had no idea you had company. I beg your pardon, ma'am."

"Charlie, this is my wife," Buck said, raising his eyebrows. "Tanna, this is Corporal Charles Fairchild. He's Daughtry's nephew and my personal aide-de-camp."

The boy didn't look much older than her brother Teddy. "Charmed," Tanna said, crossing her arms.

Charlie straightened and smiled. "An honor to meet you, ma'am," he stuttered.

"Tanna has just brought us provisions," Buck said, as if proud of his own accomplishment.

"I saw the wagons. The pigs, the cattle. We're really grateful, I can assure you that!" Charlie said. He stood there for a moment, as if trying to think of something else to say. He smiled sheepishly at Tanna, then turned toward Buck. "Um, I need to ask you—"

"I'm sorry," Tanna interrupted. "Do you want me to leave? I can step out—"

"No! No, ma'am. I just needed to get ..." He stepped across the bed and whispered something to Buck. Buck flushed, stood, and guided the boy out of the tent.

Tanna heard their low murmured voices conferring together. She dropped onto the camp chair so that she could see them through a gap at the tent's door.

Buck was reaching into his pocket and retrieving the pipe. Charlie took it from him quickly and asked something else in a whisper.

"Jesus!" Buck cursed. "Just a second ..."

He came back into the tent, grabbed a small leather pouch near his pillow, smiled at Tanna, and handed it out the tent to Charlie.

The boy disappeared. Buck busied himself again with straightening up, not meeting Tanna's eyes.

23

Holly had declined an invitation to dine with Tanna and Buck at Daughtry's table. She said she felt "stared at" and she wanted to go to the outskirts of the camp and find Still.

"Go straight to Still and stay with him," Tanna said. "Promise me you won't go wandering around here on your own."

"I don't want to be anywhere near these men," Holly said defensively.

Tanna stood watching her walk away until she was little more than a faint silhouette against the sunset.

Buck tugged her wrist. "Let's go."

—

There were half a dozen young men sitting together watching Buck and Tanna as they made their way between the rows of crude benches and tables. One of them openly glared, and another one smirked. Someone murmured something and several of them laughed. It certainly felt like they were all laughing at her.

Daughtry presided over a long table covered by white cloths beneath a cream-colored canvas canopy. Up close, the tablecloths were stained with wine and grease, but, after the snickers and sneers, she felt conspicuously grand to be seated there among the officers. Many of the soldiers sat cross-legged on the grass or squatted on camp stools, balancing their pewter mugs and saucers on their knees, eating with their fingers. Tanna questioned the wisdom of the leaders segregating themselves from their men with chipped china plates, real silverware, and wine glasses. It didn't seem like it would inspire camaraderie. She suspected some of the stares were not envy but judgment.

Daughtry made a fatherly speech about how he expected everyone to modify their usual behavior to accommodate the presence of a lady. Tanna was mortified by his focusing such attention on her, but she responded outwardly with as much grace as she could, considering her appearance. Her wild, dirty hair, hurriedly combed with her fingers; her sunburned face; the relatively clean shirt she had borrowed from Buck. She rolled the sleeve cuffs up to her elbows and kept self-consciously checking to make sure the too-large neck wasn't drooping down to reveal her chest.

Even with Daughtry's admonishment against rudeness, there had been a lot of bourbon before the wine at dinner. The men were soon speaking all at once, shouting over one another, trying to outdo their companions with off-color remarks. Waves of explosive, boisterous laughter rolled up and down the table.

Tanna was so relieved to have found them that it was easy to embrace their energy. It didn't hurt that there was proportionately more drink consumed than food. It would still be a few days before the animals she had brought them could be butchered and the supplies incorporated into their meal rotation. It briefly crossed her mind that this meat could very well be the cow that'd fallen to the panther, despite her efforts. The wounds on her back burned with the memory and she put down her fork, her appetite suddenly gone.

She heard her name mentioned, bringing her out of her private thoughts. Someone mentioned the dire circumstances from which Tanna had rescued them all.

"To Mrs. Eldridge," Daughtry cried, glass held aloft, fluid sloshing down his arm. Tanna noticed the liquid in his glass was clear, but considering his red face and loud, sloppy speech, there was little chance he was drinking plain water.

The stone carafe of tarwater reached their end of the table a few minutes later. Buck poured her a thimbleful in a glass jar. The unmistakable gin-like fumes with its overlay of rotting flower petals made Tanna's nose run and her eyes tear up. With the tiniest sip came the now-familiar flush of warmth spreading down her throat and up across her scalp. It became even easier to laugh at the men's jokes and to forget about the eyes she could feel watching her from beyond the dining tent.

Daughtry made a big fuss about moving Tanna to the seat at his right, shoving his aide-de-camp off his stool and motioning for her to come join him.

Buck stayed behind, oddly quiet, watching her as Daughtry pulled her by the hand and deposited her on the stool like a big doll.

Daughtry squeezed her knee lecherously beneath the tablecloth. Tanna uncrossed and recrossed her legs, angling them away from him.

"What exactly is your mission here, Lord Daughtry?" Tanna asked, seeking to distract his hands with conversation. "Or is that information you're even allowed to share with me?"

"No, old girl, it's no secret, really." He wiped his large white mustache with a grimy handkerchief. "Our presence is intended to be an obvious and visible show of force. We provide daily patrols to accompany the dirigible haul teams on their last leg through the Seaming. We rendezvous with them as they emerge from the crossing storms. No doubt you were accompanied thusly when you arrived?"

"Actually, I wasn't at all aware of it on my voyage," Tanna admitted. "Were the incidents occurring that long ago?"

He chuckled bitterly. "They've been happening forever, old girl!"

"I was under the impression the explosions along the road from Treebridge were rare, a new development. Unheard of until recently."

"Oh, you're right about that. The twiggy little bastards have become increasingly bold, coming so far into the colony. That's only been in recent months. We've never seen that type of escalation. It's always been confined toward the deep, wild center of the Green, where few of us go anyway. The dirigible crossings have long been harassed. But it's gone from one in five to nearly every vessel now witnessing some kind of disturbance."

She grimaced. "I had no idea. I'm actually glad no one told me; I would never have gotten on that airship. It was frightening enough as it was."

Daughtry patted her arm. "It's mostly intimidation. Not so much real danger as a lot of scary bangs and flashes. Their arms are more like a loud magic show than actual effective weaponry."

"So they want us to stop traveling to and from home?"

"The Rippers want us *gone*." His face reddened with anger. "And they want the crossings closed forever."

"Are they mostly elves?" she asked innocently.

"Oh, no. There's every kind of race and creature on both sides of this conflict. Our worst enemies are the feral humans who side with them." He turned and spat over his shoulder.

"There are *humans* fighting for this Ripper cause?"

"Oh, yes." He nodded emphatically. "That's who we're out here confronting."

She was incredulous. "Why would other humans want the crossings closed?"

"Some of the feral were born here and have been here for generations. They've never seen our Gray world and they don't want to. I can't say that I blame them. We don't much want to see it either, do we? Why else would we be here? But, they still believe we're ruining this world." He sighed. "To complicate things further, there are plenty of fae who desire our commerce and friendship. Most of my wife's people, of course, the Seelie Court. We've had treaties with them for hundreds of years. They built Treebridge. They worked on those tunnels and promenades for centuries, and at some point, they petrified it all with a kind of magic spell. Some say they gave the Tree to us as a gift so that our kinds would have a place to mingle. In the 1820s, a man named Joseph Randall Stuckey negotiated the removal of some of the less friendly inhabitants."

She failed to hide her disgust. "They *removed* them. Like we did with the Indians?"

Daughtry held up his hands in a defensive gesture. "Well, now, I like to think there was less bloodshed and inhumanity. We gave some of them jobs, you know. Those who wanted them. My wife's people were particularly taken with the style of service found in the old French aristocracy and the English landed gentry. They borrowed from that culture, just as we did in the Old South. You can see the relics of it."

She agreed with him that it was certainly evident. It was as if some ideals of plantation life had continued to thrive here. It had been preserved, unscathed by the decimation of Union armies and Reconstruction as it had been in the Gray. It was ironic, really—she had emigrated in hopes of getting away from the suffocating attempts of her mother's society to hang on to the past and resurrect their former glory.

"I must admit," Tanna said, "I was surprised to see so many hoopskirts still alive in current fashion. I'm afraid your wife is one of those women who makes me feel entirely underdressed and out of style, not to mention shaped like a boy. You must never tell her you entertained me at your table wearing a man's shirt, or I will never forgive you."

"Dear old girl," he smiled kindly, laying his bony, big-knuckled hand over hers, "between you and me, the ladies here are frightening in their vanity. The trifling details that consume them are beyond me. But I will tell you this—don't you worry about comparing yourself to them. I believe they're all a little bit afraid of you."

"Me?" Surprised, Tanna set her glass down a little too hard. "Why would they be afraid of me?"

"Because you're independent and fearless, old girl. The fairy women of the Seelie Court, encouraged by the plantation owners' wives who worship them, piss themselves over every misplaced bow and choice of gown color. Not to mention the power struggles they can invest in an arched eyebrow, a misplaced glance, or a lingering stare. The fairy aristocracy live too long, have too much wealth, and they don't have enough of anything useful to do. I was only too happy to come risk my life at war, just to escape the tedium." He toasted the sentiment and buried his face in his cup.

Tanna found herself liking him more than any potential social equal she had met in the Green, except, of course, Cole Mathers.

"So, will we win?" she asked.

"Win what?" Daughtry looked up, bewildered, his mustache dripping wet with drink.

"I want you to drive these terrorists back, and free the traffic coming and going from home." She held his gaze with a fierce gleam in her eye. "Unlike fairy women and rich men's wives, I came here to start a business. And in order to do that, I need the dirigibles crossing free and clear."

He turned suddenly sober and a little sad. "Well, old girl. It's not a thing that can be done the way you want. Not once and for all, anyway. We'll always be gaining a little ground, losing a little more. We can certainly hope to stay and maintain much of what we have. But if I had to, I'd put my money on the Rippers in the end. This world is theirs, they outnumber us in the millions, and they aren't ever going to stop trying to get rid of us. But don't you go repeating that too loudly."

Tanna looked stricken.

"It's like the Wild West, you know." Daughtry smiled. "That's what we love about it, and that's how it will stay. The genies will never let us fully have their country as the Indians did. It's not that they're smarter, they're just more feral." His eyes went a bit mad when he said it, lost in a vision or a memory. "It's not the worst thing to lose to—that wildness. The very thing we covet here—the wildness and the wilderness—we ruin by loving it. Because to us that means trying to hold it. Mark it, divide it up, contain it, and tell everybody we own it. It can't be owned."

"It almost sounds like you're on the Rippers' side," she said gently.

He shook his head. "God knows I'm not on their side. But I do understand it."

—

As they left the dining tent, Tanna asked Buck to help her find Holly.

"She'll be fine," Buck said, tugging on her hand. "Let's just go back to my tent and have another drink. You can find her in the morning."

"I'd hate for you to go five minutes without a drink," Tanna said, rolling her eyes. "Go back to your tent, then. I'll go find her myself."

"You don't need to be walking around here on your own, Tanna."

"And yet you don't think Holly could be in danger?"

"She's not like you."

"What's that mean? How is she, then?"

"She's ... *feral.* Surely you've spent enough time with her to know that. If any one of these men touches her she'll turn into a cat in a sack. And if she likes him, she can certainly hold her own."

Tanna jerked her hand away. "Yes, I have gotten to know her quite well. I know for a fact that she still has her ... *virtue.* And she's scared of men. She's a child, Buck, she's sixteen years old."

"Age is different here."

"Well, my friendship and my loyalty are not. If it were one of my nieces sleeping on the grass in a camp full of soldiers, you don't think I'd feel anxious and want to check on her?"

He sighed and motioned for her to lead the way.

—

Tanna walked toward the edge of the camp, where Still had stopped the wagon when they arrived. She didn't see any of her genies. They heard voices, laughing, cheering. They came upon a ring of men, all concentrated on some activity at the center. There was something cruel and jeering about their tone. Tanna felt a sense of dread similar to two nights before, when she'd been wakened by the frightened cattle.

She stalked up to try to peer over the soldiers' shoulders. She couldn't see what was going on, and she began to panic. She pushed her way in between two men, elbowing them aside roughly. The musk of their sweat-stained shirts choked her.

Just as she'd feared, Holly was there at the center of the circle with a soldier. He was crouching; she was bent over; both of their faces were intent. A handful of men held torches aloft, lighting the ground around them. With an elaborate flourish, Holly tossed something in the dirt. Dice. There was a heartbeat of silence as everyone surged forward to see how they had landed.

The circle erupted in cheers and boos. Holly stood up, grinning. She'd obviously won. Several observers jostled her as they shoved her opponent. Tanna watched Holly's grin evaporate. Her face went slack and she turned quickly, taking a swipe at one of the soldiers. He ducked, laughed at her, and made as if he were going to grab her backside. Holly looked furious as she faced off against the man, fists in ready position. Her arms flailed wildly from the side as she came at him again. This time, someone caught her arms from behind and held her elbows behind her back.

Now the girl's expression shifted to fear.

Tanna screamed her name and surged forward. She glanced around for Buck, but he was behind her and couldn't see what was going on.

"They're attacking her!" Tanna screamed at him, dragging him by the sleeve as she lurched into the circle of torchlight.

"Let her go!" Tanna barked. She walked right up to the man who held Holly and tore his fingers off the girl's arms. "Get ... your ... hands ... *off of her!*" she roared.

The man froze, hands up in surrender. The soldier who had initially grabbed Holly melted back into the crowd.

Buck stepped forward to join Tanna and Holly. "What the hell is going on here?" he yelled.

Apparently, his rank dissolved the remaining tension. The men looked down sheepishly and started to back away.

Buck ordered them to their tents, and with some muttering and grumbling, the crowd finally dissipated.

"Are you OK?" Tanna asked Holly.

"I'm fine," Holly said, sullenly. "We were just playing craps."

"Really?" Tanna glared at her. "It looked to me like they were done playing."

"I was winning," Holly whispered.

Tanna looked at Buck for support.

He pursed his lips. "I've got to go take care of something. You remember where my tent is, right?" He walked off without waiting for her to answer.

"Where is Still?" Tanna asked Holly. "Still!"

He materialized out of the darkness. "So'onah."

"Do not let her out of your sight again," Tanna said, pulling him aside. "Wherever she puts her sleeping roll down, you lie beside her. Watch over her as she sleeps. Take turns with the porters. I want someone awake and guarding her every moment we are here."

24

Buck was outside his tent, speaking to one of the young men she had noticed watching them at dinner earlier. The boy couldn't have been much older than Holly. He stood with his arms folded across his body, shoulders slumped. Buck leaned in close to him, murmuring in low, fervent tones, clearly trying to convince him of something.

The boy sighed, straightened, and held out his hand. Buck gave him a small object and he shoved it into his pocket.

Buck turned to see Tanna walking up and jerked away from the boy. "We'll speak about this tomorrow, private," he said loudly.

The boy rolled his eyes. His gaze wandered down to Tanna's dirt-covered boots, then lingered significantly on her pants. He looked her in the eyes, smirked, and vanished into the shadows between the tents.

Buck held the door flap open for her.

"Who was that boy?" She emphasized the word *boy* more than she had intended.

"Ashford?" Buck flapped his hand dismissively. "Something's always going on with Trey Ashford." He resumed his frantic straightening of the tent, stuffing his underclothes in a canvas bag, emptying ashtrays into a tin cup.

She eyed the bedroll, but chose to perch on the camp chair again.

"What about the other one?" she asked.

"Who?" Buck looked up, red-faced from bending and squatting and crab-walking around the tent.

She irritably sighed. "The boy from earlier. Fairchild, wasn't it? Like the club."

"Charlie," Buck said. "Yes, he's my aide-de-camp. He keeps me in line. He's proven quite useful. I can't function without him."

He carried an armload of trash and dirty dishes to the door flap and dumped them in a clattering heap just outside the tent. He stood for a few moments with his head out.

"What are you doing?" she asked. "Why don't you come away from the door? Come sit over here. Don't you want to talk to me?"

"Of course, absolutely." Buck dropped to the bedroll and crossed his legs, looking up at her with one of his best smiles. "It's great to see you. I'm actually glad you're here."

"Actually?" Tanna coolly raised her eyebrows.

"Well," he spluttered, "I admit, you certainly did take me by surprise, showing up like that." He fumbled in his shirt pocket. "How about a cigarette? You want one? Where's my lighter ..."

He started crawling around the tent again, opening tins, digging through a leather saddlebag. "Did you hear somebody?" He frowned intently at a shadow that fell across the tent wall. "Is somebody out there?"

"I didn't hear anyone," Tanna said, folding her arms. She sighed once more with exasperation when he got up and went back to the door, sticking his head out of the flap again.

"Just a second," he called over his shoulder, and abruptly disappeared.

"Buck—"

She saw his shadow walking around the tent. He came back in, stumbling a bit. He took a crooked cigarette from his lips, realized it was broken, and made a noise of disgust. "You wanted one too, right?" he asked.

"Are you drunk?" she blurted out.

"I'm fine," he said.

She wanted to ask about the tarwater, but she hadn't seen him in weeks, and there were more important things on her mind. She didn't know how to start the conversation she wanted to have, so she blurted it out. "I know you might not want to be with me, physically. Not just purely from desire, anyway. It's honestly not my only motivation, either. But we are married. I probably shouldn't have to ask. But ... I'm asking." She held her breath.

Buck frowned. The exaggerated facial expression would have been comical under different circumstances. "Just to be clear ... What are you asking, exactly?"

"I'm asking you to give me a child. If you're going to be gone, if I'm going to run the farm by myself, I'm fine with that. But I want a child of my own."

"You're asking me to sleep with you?"

"We never consummated. Do you think you can ... manage it?"

He smiled at her. She saw his entire body go slack. He softened, seemed to melt a little bit. "Of course." He got up on his knees, reached out, and touched her cheek kindly.

She detected pity in the gesture. Her face flushed with shame. He stood and kissed her on the mouth, softly but deliberately. He made a faint humming sound.

She rarely thought about Ford when she looked at him. To strangers, they appeared almost identical—some people thought they were twins—but to her, they had always been very different human beings. It had only been more recently, confronted with this romantic potential, that she compared Buck to his brother.

Ford had a way of breathing in her face when he was on top of her, yet never kissing her. Buck's passion surprised her. Not that he had it within him, but that he could find it for her.

He swallowed a slug of tarwater and handed her the flask.

"It makes it better," he said, wagging his eyebrows suggestively. "You'll like it."

It felt strange to kiss him. She caught herself analyzing it, thinking about it. She chided herself to release the thoughts, to melt into him, to open. She kept reminding herself it was perfectly allowed; before God and men, he was the one person who was meant to have her in this way.

His mouth tasted sour—wine, whiskey, the faint, wilted taint of tarwater. When he exhaled, the flavor shifted to wet cigarettes. It wasn't overpowering, disgusting, or impossible to bear. It was just that with Ford, or other men she had kissed, she wanted them beyond their sweat or blemishes on their cheeks or a hair on the neck missed shaving—none of that had ever been enough to distract in the way she experienced with Buck now.

To escape the kisses, to find a moment in which to collect herself so she could reorient her thoughts, she hid her face in his neck. His sweat had a sweet, boyish quality to it, like freshly cut grass. It reminded her of picking up Teddy when he'd fallen out of the tree swing and sprained his ankle last year. She had carried him to the house, aware of the proximity to his body, uncomfortable with the manly way he smelled, so different from all the times she'd snuggled him as a child.

And to think of that now, in this moment, while Buck forced his hands past the waistband of her pants and cupped her buttocks ...

She just had to manage it this one time.

If Buck could manage it, given his predilections for the pouting boys lurking outside the tent smoking his haint, jealous of her, waiting for her to give them back her husband. If he could find a way to perform this act for her, even out of pity or charity or the love of a friend, then she would bear it.

She tried to think of Cole Mathers. Instead she kept seeing flashes of

Jackson Gallagher's white teeth shining in his sun-browned face. And that too was a disturbance. She wanted to be alone to ponder those visions.

She pulled away from Buck to free her feet from the pants hobbling her ankles. She bent over, then stood upright quickly, feeling the rush of the tarwater, a swimming euphoria flushing her chest and face. She sighed and unbuttoned her blouse.

Buck hopped about the tent, cursing, boots trapped in his pants. He grabbed her shoulder to steady himself, unaware of her wounds from the thorns. She had planned to tell him the story tonight, when they were alone together. For now, she told him to lie back, pushed him down, grabbed one boot with both hands, tugged it off, then freed the other from his pant leg.

She straddled him on the blanket, where he was ridiculously struggling out of his shirt while lying down. She was naked except for the fine strips of cloth glued to her back and shoulders with the medicinal mud. He looked up at her, chuckling, red-faced with effort and drunkenness. He grabbed her by the shoulders and tried to flip her onto her back.

She cried out in pain.

"What? What?" he asked, panicked.

"My back," she muttered.

"What's wrong?"

"I'll tell you later." She waved it away, not wanting to halt the momentum. She was afraid conversation would be the end of this chance. She didn't know if she could stand to start over, or maybe ever do it again. She tried not to sound too annoyed. "Just be careful of my back."

"Um. Do you want to be ..." He moved away from her on the blanket to demonstrate the pose. On his knees, Buck put both hands on the blanket in front of him and looked at her over his shoulder.

She sat back on her heels for the moment, resisting the urge to cover her breasts with her hands or fold her arms across her chest.

"Like a dog?" Her voice sounded colder than she'd intended.

"Well." He looked embarrassed, but spread his hands in a shrug as if to ask, *What other option is there?*

"Fine," she sighed, lying facedown on Buck's dirty, meager pillow, unwilling to fully assume the posture just yet. Although he didn't suggest it out of malice or a wish to make her feel degraded, she could not help thinking it would probably be easier for him. How did her bare back differ from a young man's? Was this the way he did it with those boys? Had the pouty Trey Ashford or the attentive Charlie Fairchild been kneeling here in this very spot only the night before?

He lifted her hips, pulling her up on her knees, and ground himself against her while she breathed through the pillow and thought of Jackson Gallagher's white teeth.

She felt him poking against her. He found his mark and shoved in too deeply, too quickly. She wasn't remotely excited or open to him. It felt like a medical examination.

He heard her grunt and stopped. "Are you sure you want me to do this, Tanna?"

At least he had the compassion to ask.

She said "yes" into the pillow. But when he didn't continue she raised her head and nodded where he could see the gesture. "Do it quickly."

She was surprised that even though Buck was the gregarious, playful brother, while Ford was sullen and cold, Buck rutted her aggressively. He made fists around the flesh on the sides of her hips and pulled her back against him. She couldn't see his face, but from the sounds he made, she imagined his expression was angry and determined. If his eyes weren't closed tightly, then they were distant, looking through her into a vision of someone who excited him.

His shuddering finish was loud. She was mortified by his vocalizations, fearing nearby soldiers would storm the tent thinking she must be murdering him. He rolled away from her and lay on his side, chuckling.

"Sorry. I always giggle a bit just after. I can't help it."

She turned her face on the pillow where he could see her raise her eyebrows in acknowledgment, but she didn't say anything.

She lay still, afraid that if she moved too soon she might not conceive. Buck's sweat cooled on her skin and she felt some of his seed sliding down her thigh. She hoped there was enough inside her because she could not imagine enduring this again.

"I hope I've given you what you wanted," Buck said, his words slow, his voice sleep-slurred. Seconds later, he was snoring.

The lingering effects of the tarwater at least calmed her. She felt detached from the sensations in her body, observing them in her mind's eye, trying to imagine how long the sperm might take to reach their destination.

She wanted to urinate but resisted the need with all her will, counting the grass shadows along the tent wall near the ground.

—

She awoke to the incessant banging of a gong.

Buck was already up, pulling on his pants, a dark silhouette against the light fabric of the tent.

"We have to leave, Tanna. Now."

"Where are we going?"

"*You* are going home." He picked up her crumpled pile of clothes and tossed them at her. "We're striking camp. Moving to intercept the enemy."

The sense of urgency was unlike Buck. It made her feel panicked and breathless. Forgoing her modesty, she stood and struggled into her shirt and the filthy, mud-encrusted pants.

"Can't I come with you?" she asked.

"What?" He looked horrified. "Good God, no. That's out of the question. Daughtry's never going to allow that. It's not safe for you out here."

"And being sent back into the wilderness on my own is?"

He narrowed his eyes and gave her a shrewd, sideways look. "You made it here. With a small genie force of your own, I might add. I have a feeling you'll be just fine." He stepped into his boots. "You're not likely to run into anything. You're heading back in the other direction. The trouble's here, that way, farther into the Seaming."

"Is it? How can you know that for sure?" She followed him barefoot to the door of the tent. "We saw an Unseelie hoard two days ago, trooping in the direction of Treebridge."

He threw back the flap, stepped through, and turned back to face her. He put his hand on the back of her neck and pulled her into a full, wet kiss on the lips.

He smiled at her with that compassion or pity she'd seen in his eyes the night before. His voice was soft, and not unkind. "Go home, Tanna."

—

Trey leaned against a nearby tree, arms folded across his chest, watching her with a cruel smile. Charlie stood at Buck's side like an enthusiastic heeled dog, tail wagging.

"So, we're sending your wife back into the wild, Bucky?" Daughtry teased, covering the tense goodbye.

"Yes, we are," Buck said, matching the light tone. "Somebody might want to warn those Unseelie hoards we've heard about."

Daughtry chuckled and saluted Tanna with a raised fist. "Give them hell if you see them, old girl!"

"I hope to see you back in Treebridge very soon," Tanna said. "And I expect to be invited to the victory party."

"We will drink to the memory of how you saved us from starvation!" Daughtry said. "Now, away with you, before I'm forced to conscript your entire entourage."

25

She discovered the bright red sore between her legs three weeks after they returned to Brynmor. She assumed it resulted from her rough and hurried coupling with Buck. The sore wasn't painful; after a month it had gone away and she put it out of her mind. She did remain watchful for any signs that she might be pregnant. As far as she knew, the swollen lymph nodes in her groin were not consistent with conception.

A month later, she was bleeding normally. She was devastated that she'd failed to conceive, but her disappointment was soon overtaken by fever and aches. Her head pounded, her neck was stiff, and she awoke in the night with the sheets cold and wet with her sweat. She was afraid it could be influenza, maybe even malaria. When a strange red rash appeared on the palms of her hands, she broke down and showed it to Holly.

The girl shook her head. She had never seen this particular symptom on anyone before.

Fearing it had to be some exotic fairy disease, Tanna asked Still to drive her to Treebridge.

The doctor, whose unfortunate name was Paine, turned his back while she dressed after the examination. "You have syphilis," he said, far too cheerfully.

"Syphilis." Tanna repeated the word without inflection or emotion, with no proper tone of horror or mortification.

"Yes. You would have contracted it anywhere in the last few weeks to the last couple of months," he said.

"And you know that ... how?"

He chuckled. "The red spots on the palms." He raised his eyebrows knowingly. "There would have been a chancre. A red blister. In a private area you may never have noticed. It would have come and gone already."

"I was at the front," she said lamely, feeling she had to explain herself to him. "My husband is there with Daughtry's men. I took supplies out to them. I assure you there hasn't been—"

Dr. Paine interrupted her. "I'm afraid I don't have the resources to treat syphilis here in the Green. You'll have to go home for that. There's an experimental drug they're having some success with. It's called Salvarsan."

"Arsenic," Tanna said, with resignation. She studied her hands, nervously twisting her wedding ring around her finger. "And if it doesn't work, then I'll go insane?"

The doctor didn't respond; he only smiled sympathetically.

As Tanna stood up to leave, he said with some discomfort, "Your husband really needs to be told. He needs to be examined, too."

"If you can find him," Tanna said with a bitter smile, "then, by all means, let him know for me, won't you?"

—

It took nearly two more weeks of urgent daily messages sent by runners before Buck could be convinced to return home. He found her sitting on a trunk in her bedroom, smoking, in the midst of the chaos of packing, clothes all over the bed. A teacup and saucer near her feet was stuffed with cigarette butts. She seemed to glow a faint gray-green in the smoke, like a lamp in the fog.

She turned toward him, enough to let him know she knew he was there, but she didn't look at him. "It's syphilis."

He said nothing, but came into the room and tossed his hat on the bed. He crouched down in a squat in front of her, stinking of sweat and horses, and helped himself to one of her cigarettes.

They smoked together in silence.

Finally, she said, "You should go to a doctor right away."

Buck sighed, rising with a bit of a groan. She could hear the creaking in his knees. He strode to the other side of the room, frowning at the floor, trying to collect his thoughts.

He turned to her and spread his hands in an apologetic shrug. "I don't have any symptoms."

"And yet you're the one spreading it." She tossed her cigarette butt at the cup. It landed in the saucer and hissed when it touched the cold ring of coffee. "What kind of gods are we dealing with?"

—

Tanna went into a post office at Treebridge to arrange permission for Still to open and handle anything that came for her or Buck. She also sent a brief note to Blackwood letting her mother know to expect her. She had never received any replies to her letters before, so she wasn't sure if it would arrive or how much advance notice it would provide; but maybe, with luck, her showing up on the doorstep might not be a complete surprise.

She did mention she was ill, that she would be requiring long-term medical treatment superior to the care she could find in her new country. She did not go into detail about the diagnosis. She needed the time on the journey to either steel herself for that conversation or to possibly conjure a convincing story.

Her mother's concern for her was a complex thing. On the one hand, she would be preoccupied with what it might look like if it appeared Tanna had returned to Blackwood permanently. But Dorothy Black Cravens also enjoyed being right about what she considered to be Tanna's poor choices, and of course she had not approved of Buck.

As Tanna crossed the mezzanine in front of The Fairchild, she realized she was having trouble breathing fully and deeply. She had never experienced this level of shame before; it had a physical component. She fluctuated between numbness and sharp, invisible arrows of panic.

"Tanna!" a voice called out.

Some part of her recognized him, even before she looked up and saw Jackson watching her from the front of the club. There was a woman with him. He spoke something softly to her and she nodded demurely, posing in front of the beautiful doors.

Tanna wanted to keep walking. She wasn't sure that anything more than labored, shallow breath would come out if she tried to speak. She could feel her face heating up. Surely Jackson would notice her color and wonder what was wrong.

He crossed the distance between them in a few strides, beaming at her in a way she had never seen him smile before. But he drew up a bit short. Maybe he sensed something. He seemed unsure of whether to kiss her cheek or embrace her or shake her hand. She stood woodenly, unable to hold eye contact. He put his hands on his hips, obviously intending to be casual, but it only made them both feel more awkward.

"So, I heard you made it through. That you found them," he said. "I would have loved to have seen the looks on their faces."

The news weighing on her mind made her shy and distracted. She hated it, because he looked so happy to see her. His opinion of her seemed to shift with each meeting; he was always a little more interested, less aloof than he'd been the time before.

"It was ... very satisfying," she admitted with a genuine smile. "I still have your auroculus. But I'm afraid I don't have it with me."

"Keep it. I meant it to be a gift. You may need it again on another adventure."

"You look nice," Tanna said, changing the subject away from travel. She'd never seen him so well-groomed. He wore an impeccable gray suit with a perfectly knotted necktie. He was clean-shaven; his red-blond head was bare, his hair neatly parted. It still looked a little damp, or else the teeth of his comb had left tracks in the pomade.

"Thank you," he said, glancing at his pretty companion and waving. "I'm having an early dinner at the club with a friend."

The woman waved back, but when Tanna looked over at her, she turned her head away so the wide brim of her hat blocked her face.

"She's quite elegant," Tanna said.

"Would you like to meet her?" he asked.

"No, no. I really need to be going."

"Are you sure? I would like for her to meet you. I've talked about you."

She tried not to show her surprise at this admission. "I hope it was all good things."

"Of course. I mostly raved about your courage. How I had encountered you on your recent trip and was looking forward to hearing the details of how it all turned out."

"Yes, well ... I will have to tell you the story. Someday."

"Maybe I could invite myself out to Brynmor again for another supper one evening."

Tanna saw the woman impatiently shifting her weight from one foot to the other.

"That would be nice. Maybe when I get back—" She stopped herself. She had not meant to bring it up.

His eyebrows lifted in surprise. "Are you already headed off somewhere else?"

She wasn't prepared to explain where she was going. She had no idea when she might be back, if ever.

"When you get back, I mean," she stammered. "When you come back from your next safari."

He frowned at that. He looked like he was about to ask her something else, but then decided at the last second to let it go.

They said goodbye. She formally held out her hand. He took it briefly in both of his.

He looked back over his shoulder at Tanna as he held the door to the club for his companion. He smiled tightly. This time it looked like a wince.

Tanna waved and turned to walk away. She felt certain in that moment she would never see him again. She grieved the loss of some option she'd never allowed herself to identify before. She walked quickly down the promenade, concentrating on trying to breathe again.

26

Knowing she might not live to return, Tanna was watchful on the journey back to the Gray. She either sat on the couch in the dirigible's cabin, her face glued to the murky window, or she hung on to the exterior railing. The gondola of the *Summer Moon* had a deck that wrapped all around the cabin where she paced and paused, circling hundreds of times over the course of several days.

She spent hours peering through the low clouds, the mist, and the canopy of treetops for any glimpse of this world she was forced to leave too soon. She knew so much more about the way the landscape worked, the physical nature of the Seaming, the phenomena of the crossing points and their inherent storms. She kept the auroculus in her pocket where she could take it out at any time and watch the curtain of the aurorae inch closer. The flames of other crossing points stretched along the eastern horizon from north to south. The rain clouds and the lightning tended to form low in the sky, near the base of the smears of color, which only enhanced the illusion that she floated at the bottom of an enormous waterfall of shifting green light. She thought of the *Maid of the Mist* that nosed up to Niagara Falls like a toy.

She missed Holly's intermittent inquisitiveness, those bursts of challenging questions the girl liked to ask. Tanna spent a lot of time filling the silence, trying to answer her own questions, writing in a small pocket journal with the fountain pen Jackson had given her. She had a vague fear that if she didn't record everything she had learned about the Green she would lose it after the crossing. She worried that she wouldn't be allowed to retain and share details about this place, that the secret knowledge of the Green would be wiped from her memory by some magic spell that protected it.

When she and Buck had been researching and preparing to emigrate, everyone they encountered had been so evasive about the Green. She wondered if it were truly an unspoken collective protectiveness or if Buck had influenced the information that reached her, maybe choosing what he wanted her to know and blaming it on the reticence of others.

She no longer trusted him, if she ever had in the first place. But now, if she were to have anything to return to, she had to rely on him to care for her entire investment. She thought that, even if she couldn't be cured, she might still wish to return to Brynmor. If she didn't survive, none of it would matter. Buck would have it all.

A few days before they were to reach the crossing, when the thunder was constant in the near distance and close enough to rattle the glass in the windows, a fairy appeared. When Tanna opened the door, she darted inside and hovered like a hummingbird above her pillow. She gave off that faint light that some fae creatures projected, but it was faded and dim, an aura of fear and exhaustion.

Tanna approached the sleeping berth slowly and dropped to her knees so she wouldn't loom over the poor thing. "It's all right," she whispered. "You may rest here."

The fairy panicked at the sound of her speaking and looked like she might dash back out the window. She was a classic fairy straight from a children's book illustration—a wan, thin, naked pubescent girl, with tiny breasts, a gorgeous cloud of dandelion tresses, and wings that resembled a butterfly's, only in pastel colors of lavender, coral, and pink. Her head was a perfect china doll's, but her ears were pointed and tipped with fluffy, curling antennae.

The creature could not speak, not in a voice Tanna could hear. The pretty little thing had an expressive face Tanna found unusually easy to read; she wondered if she might not be picking up on some of the fairy's thoughts. Holly had told her many of the fae, especially the smaller flying races like the sylphs and the flower fairies, communicated telepathically, mind to mind.

The fairy landed on the blanket on a graceful pointed toe. Her wings shuddered into stillness, then stretched twice, revealing to Tanna the full splendor of the unique patterns before collapsing them behind her. The gesture reminded Tanna of a lady snapping closed a Chinese fan. The creature sat with her legs drawn up, her tiny arms hugging her knees, and smiled at Tanna with sleepy, heavy-lidded eyes.

"What are you doing so far into the Seaming?" Tanna cooed, as one might converse with a baby, not expecting any answers. "The storms near the crossings must make it difficult to fly."

She looked through her basket of foods for things that might appeal to the fairy. She found a little stone pot of honey and a small, pungent, tangerine-like fruit called a *misk*. The fairy flung herself at the honey and scooped it up in a handful, methodically licking it off her palm and fingers like a cat cleaning herself. Tanna was pleased to notice that her aura brightened visibly with the sustenance.

She offered her a skin of water, holding it in front of her upside down so that a perfect bead of liquid hung from the tip of the spout. The fairy cupped her hands beneath it and gently eased them into the drop. The surface tension broke with a splash down the fairy's arms, but she managed to cup a handful to sip. She repeated the action a few times until her thirst was satiated, drawing the back of her hand across her wet face like a child.

"You can stay and keep me company as long as you like," Tanna said.

The fairy rose in a pirouette, flapped her wings, twirled three times, and then rolled in a somersault across the blanket. She ended in a coquettish pose, lying on her side with her head supported in her hand, propped on one elbow.

Tanna became quickly convinced that the fairy either understood English perfectly or else she plucked the thoughts straight from Tanna's mind. She definitely responded to Tanna and projected clear emotions through dancing movements. When Tanna asked the fairy her name, she heard the distinct sound of a ringing bell.

"It's a lovely sound, but I can't imitate it," Tanna said with a sigh of regret. "Would it be all right if I just call you Belle?"

The fairy rang three times and bent low in a deep ballerina's bow.

"I like the name Belle. It was my grandmother's name. We'll add an *e* to the end, in the French spelling."

The fairy smiled, inclined her head, and closed her eyes.

Whether she imagined their communication or not, the fairy's appearance was a blessing. She provided company at a time when Tanna had never felt lonelier.

Her initial symptoms had faded, but Dr. Paine had warned her that even though the red rash would disappear from her palms, it did not mean the disease was gone. She kept balling her hands into fists and uncurling them, watching the color shift and spread under the skin. If she looked enough times and stared hard enough, she could convince herself the red spots were still there.

Her worry shifted to Belle. The fairy spent most of her time sleeping. While she walked about gracefully on her tiny legs and bare feet, she had not taken flight since she initially landed. Tanna looked up from her journal to find Belle sleeping in a deep crease in the pillow. Over the course of the next day and a half, she continued to eat smaller and smaller drops of honey and drank water less frequently. Tanna saved the only remaining piece of misk she had, but the fairy refused it.

Tanna convinced her to crawl into the neck of her blouse and huddle behind the upturned collar of her coat while she took some air, pacing slowly around the gondola. She paused at the railing and watched for breaks in the mists beneath them, but visibility was becoming increasingly difficult. They were flying straight into a towering wall of black cloud that roiled with thunder and flashes of heat lightning. The lower scudding white clouds just beneath them had become an impenetrable ocean of white fog. The glimpses of the landscape below revealed only a horizontal screen of green, like lily pads across a pond.

The Sea of Trees.

There was nothing to see anymore. Fat drops of rain mixed with small pellets of hail began to bounce off the balloon overhead with a random drumming rhythm.

Tanna could feel Belle shivering against her neck, her movements like a cold prickle of static electricity. She went inside, made a nest out of a stocking cap encircled with a scarf, and coaxed the fairy into it. Belle curled into a ball within the cap, her face pressed into her knees. Tanna tried to lie along the bench with her arm around the partial cocoon, hoping her body might generate some extra heat or that she could at least shield the drafts from the windows.

She found herself speaking in an ongoing monologue of meaningless observations, her tone low, pleasant, musical, as if she were lulling Belle to sleep. The fairy made no noise, but when Tanna peered at her to check she could see the small ribcage expanding and contracting with slow breaths.

Late in the afternoon of the second day, as the sun was going down, she felt the shuddering jerks and jolts of someone climbing the tow line. A small wiry man pulled himself over the rail with the cocky fearlessness of a line climber. He informed her that the haul team driver had decided they would not stop for the night. They predicted it would be winter in the Gray, and the storms would be worse during the day, when the air heated up. With less contrast between the air temperatures at night, the storms would be less violent.

"This is the last leg," he said. "The actual crossing. You might want to be prepared for dizziness and nausea, depending on how it affects you. Try not to go near the railing. Rain will probably keep you inside anyway. This is gonna be a rocky one. Is there anything you might need?"

Tanna assured him she was fine and promised she would be careful for the next foreseeable hours. He swung himself back over the railing and slid out of sight with a dwindling vibration, like a string plucked on a giant cello.

The rain became solid sheets of water falling off the curve of the dirigible's balloon, making an ovular silvery curtain visible from every window of the cabin. Tanna remained focused on Belle, carefully nudging a finger in close to the fairy's body to feel for any warmth. The fairy's diminutive size made it impossible to sense what must be a small amount of body heat. Besides, all the fae Tanna had ever touched tended to feel cool and dry.

There was a sudden sense of pressure in her sinuses. A headache formed behind her eyes and crept down her throat to become a mouth-watering nausea. She wondered if her anticipation of the effects made them seem worse, if maybe it would have been better to not know what to expect. The maziness was as all-consuming as it had been on her first crossing, but it didn't seem to last as long. She may have fainted. When she struggled to sit up on the sleeping berth she noticed a wan gray seam of light along the eastern horizon, and the rain that had accompanied the sound of rushing blood in her ears had ceased quite suddenly.

She was horrified to discover she had pushed the stocking cap nest into the crease between the wall and her pillow, tipping it away so that she couldn't immediately see Belle inside. She scrambled to find the top and carefully turn it upright without dumping the little body down into the folds of the blankets. With escalating dread, she peeled back the edges of the scarf to peer down at the fairy.

Belle's body now lay uncurled, like a broken marionette, still, pale, and dry as a dead leaf.

—

As dawn crept up the sky, Tanna realized she could see her breath. The temperature had dropped significantly. From her train case, she pulled a cardigan sweater, a cashmere shawl, and a scarf. She hurriedly swaddled herself in the bulky layers. Her movements were frozen and stiff as she waited for the clothing to collect her heat. With a pang of regret, but desperate for warmth, she carefully tipped the corpse of the fairy onto the pillow by dragging the scarf from beneath it. She pulled the stocking cap around her ears and rocked back and forth, shivering.

The *Summer Moon* was moving more quickly now. There was the hissing sound of needles as they grazed the tops of the pine trees along the steep sides of the gorge. They would soon reach the hideous tower and she would be required to climb down that terrifying wooden ladder.

She didn't know what she would do with it, but she could not leave the fairy's body behind. Maybe she'd have a funeral in the garden at Blackwood, in the plot where she had buried her pets as a girl. Until then, she needed something in which to carry the body. In her suitcase, she found a box of hairpins, a bit larger than she would have liked. She took the scarf back off and wound it around the body as a shroud. The silk cocoon also provided protective padding. She closed the lid over it loosely and tied a piece of string to hold the package together.

On impulse, she kissed the box with cold lips. As soon as she did it, she felt self-conscious. The fairy's death seemed like the perfect cue for her to shed a tear or two, but she couldn't remember the last time she'd been able to cry. All she felt was the ache in the muscles of her throat, strained from a long-overdue wail.

She pushed the box deep into the side pocket of her coat.

—

The climb down the tower was uneventful. The wagon ride along the rough road from North Chickamauga Creek Gorge south into the city was a slow journey in reverse. She was numb this time—the opposite of excited, hopeful, or even afraid. People died risking their lives in pursuit of greatness; failure was relatively safe and quiet.

She contemplated the naming of this world as *the Gray*. In the cold-weather months, once the rain had beaten the last of the glorious leaf color from the trees, Tennessee actually became somewhat purple—the backdrops of distant, ink-colored mountains, dun and lavender woods, moss green on the bruise-colored rocks, paper brown-gold on the vegetation that clung to its dead foliage. Even the pines and firs had a dusky-purple undertone to their evergreen. The sky was mostly a thin robin's-egg-blue.

As she scanned for the presence of the color gray, she found other man-made things. Pavement, steel, machine smoke, and steam. Gray clothes and gray hair. The distant streaks of unmelted snow sliding down the mountains were not gray. The gray sat in the silhouettes of buildings, the smokestacks along the river, the gutters, and in the rain-soaked, sun-bleached lumber. The Gray. Nobody in Treebridge spoke of this color as a destination. It existed only to mean *not here*, the place that isn't paradise.

For the most part, those who were from the Gray—those who lived their whole lives here—never knew it. What good would it do them if they did?

She hired a taxi downtown to take her up Lookout Mountain. She asked the driver the date.

"It's the fifth," he said helpfully.

"Of ... February?" she guessed.

"Yes." He drew out the word a bit. He peered at her, as if he possibly knew the reason why she didn't know the date. Still, he didn't volunteer the year. "February fifth, ma'am."

The buildings told her the amount of time she'd been away. Entire blocks of the city were unrecognizable. Brick façades blocked long-familiar views, casually permanent, as if they had always been there and certainly planned to endure. The presence of scaffolding and busy construction sites underscored the sense of change.

Yes, there it was, the realization she'd been warned about. Her mind was fumbling with what she saw and trying to extrapolate the process, the time that had elapsed. As more tall brick structures rose along the streets, she feared the number of years might be greater than she had anticipated.

She had been told approximately three to five years here for every one she'd felt passing in the Green. But that was a rough estimation that didn't necessarily obey an exact formula. Travelers between the worlds reported inexplicable periods in recorded human history when time seemed to slip more quickly, fluid and fluctuating.

She saw a newsboy on the street corner and shouted for the driver to stop. She fumbled in her purse for coins she hadn't used in ages. She took the paper, rolled in thirds, and clutched it to her chest, shut her eyes in a brief silent prayer, then snapped it open on her lap.

In the seconds it took her to scan for the information she wanted, she also learned that this world was unmistakably at war as well. Surely to God it wasn't the same war, with angry elves spilling into the public consciousness, blowing up bridges and skyscrapers.

She held back the curling corner of the paper and squinted to find the relatively small date.

1918.

She had been gone for four years.

THREE

27

Martha, the housekeeper at Blackwood, let her in the front door. She covered her face with her hands, unable to contain an outburst of emotion. She composed herself by snapping at a young maid named Ruby—whom Tanna had never seen before—to take the luggage upstairs. Martha was distressed by Tanna's appearance, declaring her "just way too brown and too thin." Fighting back tears, she disappeared into the kitchen to order Geneva to make Tanna something to eat.

When Ginger galloped down the hall and leapt on her, planting her front paws on Tanna's shoulders like a dancer, an uncontrollable sob finally escaped her throat. No one but Ginger could have heard it; it was buried under the sound of dog kisses and Tanna's murmuring her name, over and over. She dropped to her knees with her arms around the deerhound, rocking her in a humanlike embrace. At first, the tickling of Ginger's long tongue made her giggle, but the sound quickly turned into a silent wail.

She hadn't shed a single tear, from the moment of her diagnosis, through the painful conversation with Buck, the anxiety of arranging to leave her investments and her new home behind ... the long, lonely return voyage back into the Gray, or Belle's death.

The guilt she'd carried all this time for having left Ginger behind, confronted with the dog's total absolution and enthusiastic forgiveness, broke her heart at last. The heartbreak had been waiting for her here all this time, safe behind closed doors, in her mother's home. This was the only place she could be broken.

Unprepared to see Dorothy Black Cravens, she rushed upstairs to compose herself, Ginger bounding ahead to her room. Her bedroom looked untouched, with that cold, quiet stillness found in rooms no one uses. She stepped around her bags near the foot of her bed and went to the window, staring out at the familiar view of the city far below.

Back. In this room. This view again.

She had spent half her life in this spot wondering when she would get to leave it. It had reclaimed her. It was her view, after all. During her girlhood, before she married, it was the sight she saw every day. Until she finally went out into the view itself and beyond it, in search of her true life. This room was her home. This view of the world was the one she knew best. This was the part of life that lasted—either its core, or possibly its bookends. The beginning and the end. The middle was the part that was supposed to matter most, and it may have been the briefest part of all.

She couldn't help but think she might die here. Then she worried it was a premonition. It infuriated her to be so maudlin, so typical, this sad woman growing old in an upstairs room of her mother's house. It was her worst nightmare come true after all, the spinsterhood she had risked her life and her fortune to escape.

Everything she had run toward, the components of the life she willfully tried to create for herself, were the very things that forced her back here. It seemed too cruel a lesson for what she had attempted. She hadn't pursued fame or wealth or vanity; she was being punished for a basic sense of pride, of all things. She had reached for a tiny handful of common human desires and had her hand slapped by the gods. It was an overreaction. She had only reached for work, for purpose, for meaningfulness. She couldn't believe this much shame was a fair retribution for reaching.

—

She pretended to nap on top of the coverlet with Ginger at her side. She felt a small draft when the bedroom door was quietly opened. Someone coming to check on her. Ginger raised her head and looked at whomever it was, but Tanna kept her eyes closed. Martha had no doubt told her mother she was here. But if her mother had bothered to come upstairs to seek her out, she would have charged into the room and wakened her, already in the middle of an interrogation.

It was likely that Martha, or maybe Geneva, had sent Ruby to see if she was up yet.

The afternoon light was dying. The northeast side of the mountain was already in shadow. Her stomach rumbled. She would have to go down soon. There was no way she could last until breakfast in the morning. She dreaded speaking to her mother. For all her contemplation on the journey home she really hadn't rehearsed a satisfactory explanation for why she was here. Every time she tried, she pushed the thoughts away, feeling that the truth would somehow prove inevitable. She couldn't even think about lying to her mother; Dorothy Black Cravens would just know.

Surely she wouldn't guess Tanna had syphilis, of all things. There was no way that would ever enter the conversation as a possibility; yet, somehow, Tanna knew, that if her mother did not know the details or the exact diagnosis, she would still comprehend the character of the circumstances. Tanna knew she would radiate shame and failure. All it would take was a single look.

—

"Well, I wish you'd written and told us you were coming," her mother said. She barely glanced up from a large hardback of *Summer* by Edith Wharton. "We could've arranged something better for supper."

Tanna ignored the missing greeting, and, as she so often did, chose to play the script with her mother as if the warmth existed on both sides.

"It's good to see you, Mama," Tanna said. She crossed the long dining room, Ginger tailing her, unwilling to let Tanna out of her sight. Tanna attempted to hug her mother, who remained seated at the head of the table. The embrace was more like pressing her temple against her mother's dry, gray-streaked auburn bun. Dorothy's shoulders felt frail. Tanna squeezed her gently, without response, and slid into her usual place halfway down the table on her mother's right.

They always sat with a few place settings between them so they could have books, newspapers, or magazines to read while they ate. Meals were conducted in companionable silence with a minimum of speech, like sharing a table in a library with a stranger. Often, her mother would comment on something interesting she was reading, and Tanna would eagerly put her finger in her book and take this up as an opportunity for conversation. It might last through a few volleys back and forth before Dorothy grew silent and engrossed again. However, if Tanna attempted to do the same thing, her mother would only murmur something that was not quite a response, or in some cases glance up with a quick, clearly annoyed glare.

Tanna had not brought anything to the table to read. She had naïvely assumed her mother might be eager to hear all about her travels and her new home.

"Will you be here for Ash Wednesday?" Dorothy asked, primly biting into the piece of cold roast chicken on the end of her fork. "I'm planning a special dinner."

"I'm sure I will be," Tanna said, hesitant, preparing to dive into some explanation for her stay. "I may be here for a while, actually."

Dorothy looked up at her daughter, studying Tanna's face while she slowly finished chewing her last bite. "How long is *a while?*"

Tanna cleared her throat, uncomfortable under her mother's stare. She looked down at her lap, where she kept arranging and smoothing her linen napkin. "It could be a few months."

Dorothy didn't reply, giving no indication whether she approved or disapproved of the length of time. She dug something from the inside of her cheek with her tongue and nodded a few times. She asked nothing further.

"I need some ... medical treatment," Tanna stammered, intending to move forward with at least a vague reason for her stay. "Care that I couldn't get in Treebridge." She realized as she said the name it would mean nothing to her mother, who was probably still telling her friends that Tanna and Buck were living in California. "That's a large town in the colony close to our farm."

"I hope it's not the Spanish flu," Dorothy said. "I hate to think you're somewhere you can't even get to a doctor."

"There's a perfectly fine doctor there. I've seen him. He was the one who referred me back home. For a specialized treatment. Not for Spanish flu."

"Well, you should listen to your doctor's advice," Dorothy said, turning back to her book.

Tanna couldn't believe her mother didn't ask, that she wasn't even curious. But, then, if she could get away with staying here and taking care of what she needed to, without necessarily having to speak of it or explain what had happened, maybe that was best for everyone.

They continued eating in silence for several minutes. When Ruby came in to clear the plates, Tanna took advantage of the interruption in her mother's reading to ask about her brother.

"Teddy's up at Monteagle. I'm not expecting him back anytime before his spring break."

Tanna frowned. "Why in the world is he up there?"

"Well, he's in school at Saint Andrew's, Tanna," Dorothy said, as if she should know this. "If you want to send word to him that you're here, I'm sure he'll hurry home to see you. He has time on the weekends if he really wants it."

"I don't want to interrupt his studies, or his social life, for that matter,"

Tanna said, pushing back her chair. "But I am looking forward to seeing him. I'll write to him and just let him know. It's up to him."

Dorothy rose, tucking her novel under her arm. "That'll be nice," she said, and left the room.

Tanna watched her mother walk down the hall and turn into the front parlor. "Ginger," Dorothy called out without looking back. "Are you coming with me or going with Tanna?"

Ginger looked up at Tanna, her tongue lolling in adoration. Together they went back upstairs to Tanna's room.

—

Thus began a dull routine of days as Tanna waited for her appointment with Dr. Hill. She had sent a messenger to inquire the earliest she could come. They asked her to wait until the following Thursday, February fourteenth. Valentine's Day.

She didn't inform anyone from her old social set that she was in town. She was a little fearful about what the treatments might do to her. She didn't want to obligate herself to cheerful teas or outings to the theater if she were going to be incapacitated with nausea. Her mother might not care to know why Tanna was back home for a protracted amount of time, without her husband, but the gossipmongers among her friends would demand details. And if they did not get them, they would make some up.

Those first few days, she initially filled her spare time devouring recent newspapers. She was curious about this war in Europe, of all things. It was doubtful there was any connection with what was happening in the Green, but it made her wonder about the crossings in other parts of the world. Where did they open to, and were circumstances similar around those far-flung doorways into Fairyland? Was it just in "New California," the Green lands connected to North America, that the Rippers were active? Maybe the Brits, the Irish, the Scandinavians were on better terms with the fae. Their cultures had much longer histories of interaction with those beings. How was this war in Germany affecting relations with the fairies in that part of the world? Did it not influence their desire to sever connections with humanity that much more? It seemed there was a powerful argument to be made for closing all the portals in Europe and ripping apart the fabric that connected the worlds.

—

The morning on the day of her doctor's appointment, Teddy arrived.

She was standing in front of her full-length mirror, dressing for her trip into town. She felt suffocated by the corset, the tight tweed suit, the long skirt that limited the movement of her legs. She had quickly adopted the custom of wearing looser, warm-weather designs and light, breathable fabrics. She mostly preferred wearing men's pants. Holly Gray had more influence on Tanna's sensibilities than she would ever admit. The girl was like a long-lost little sister. She thought Tanna knew everything about being a lady, but Tanna had learned a lot about her freedom as a woman from Holly's innocence and practicality. What the society in this world would have judged as "ignorant" Tanna had grown to see as a refreshing perspective.

She looked over at the couch under the bay window in her bedroom. Holly had slept there the night before they had left for the Green. If she could go back in time, she would stay up all night talking to the girl and learning everything she could.

Tanna heard the front door swing open and heavy boots bound up the stairs. A man appeared in her doorway, breathless and grinning. He had already swept into the room and grabbed her up in a bear hug before she realized it was her brother. She caught herself just before she shrieked. She pushed his shoulders away from her so she could look at him.

"Teddy." She meant to exclaim his name, but it came out as little more than an exhalation. The surprise of him winded her, squeezed the breath right out of her. He had been a thirteen-year-old boy when she left, a gangly sapling of a person. He was like those big buildings that seemed to have appeared out of nowhere, solid, heavy, and permanent-looking.

He stood, blushing a bit, pleased to watch her take in all the various details of his transformation. He knew he had grown and he was proud of how much he had changed. Of course he expected her to be surprised by his appearance, to barely recognize him—after all, for him, it had been four years that she'd been away.

She was flooded with a sense of guilt and grabbed him again, this time returning the power of his embrace. "Oh, Teddy," she said into his collar. "I'm so sorry."

"Sorry about what?"

She pulled away from him, searching his face for traces of resentment. "How long it's been."

Teddy shrugged. "I wish you'd written more."

"How many of my letters did you get?"

"Two."

"Two?" Tanna whined. "I wrote you dozens of times, I swear I did. The postal service there ... It's terrible. You have to believe me. It's not like here. It takes forever, and I'm not even sure half of what I send makes it through."

"I figured something like that," Teddy said. "The letters look like they've been to hell and back." He bent down to ruffle Ginger's fur. The dog had been standing there, patiently attending their reunion.

"Thank you for taking care of her," Tanna said. "You have no idea how much I've missed her. Missed both of you."

Teddy noticed her gloves and took in her suit. "Are you going somewhere?"

"To town. To the doctor, actually."

"You're not sick, are you?" Teddy stood up, his expression concerned. "I wondered why you were here."

Tanna smiled and shook her head. "I'm not sick in the way you're thinking. I need to meet with a specialist. About a woman's issue."

"Oh," Teddy said, frowning. But then his face suddenly lit up. "Well, I could drive you. I convinced Mama to buy a Model T so I could drive back and forth to school."

She wasn't sure how much she could confide in her little brother—a boy, whether he was seventeen years old or not. But then, the warmth of his company and his youthful enthusiasm, after the weather on the journey home; after her mother's cold, disconnected reception; after Belle ...

When she shoved her hands deep in her coat pocket she felt the box with the fairy's body inside it.

More than anything, she needed to be in the company of someone who loved her like Teddy did.

"Yes. That sounds like a lot more fun than I had originally planned. We'll have lunch somewhere."

28

"What's wrong, then?" Teddy asked, barreling down the mountain in the car. "Why the doctor?"

She waved it away as if it were a trifling concern. "I'll know more after I talk to him. I'll tell you about it later. It's nothing to worry you right now," she lied. "And before you ask, it's not Spanish influenza."

Teddy was quick to move the conversation on to topics of his own choosing—motorcars, boarding school, horses, a monstrous teacher, and cruel, idiotic boys from families wealthier than theirs. She encouraged him, content to escape into the colorful details of his world. It all sounded as lively as anything in the Green. Teddy reminded her of the younger soldiers at Daughtry's camp. He was almost as old as Charlie and Trey, those young men who came and went from Buck's tent.

Teddy would graduate in the spring. When she asked him about college, he mentioned going to Sewanee in the fall, unless he enlisted.

"Teddy, no," she yelled over the sound of the engine. "You can't."

He flushed but kept his eyes on the road. "I can't just stay here and go to school while everybody else is over there. I'd never be able to show my face again."

—

As they sat on a wooden bench in the paneled waiting room of the doctor's office, Teddy pressed her about why she was sick.

"There are illnesses over there," Tanna started, looking around at the other patients. She lowered her voice and continued, barely moving her lips. "You know, when we travel to foreign countries, especially the tropics, there are all kinds of virulent things we aren't normally exposed to ..."

"Like malaria?" Teddy's lips pulled away from his teeth in a grimace. "Malaria gets a lot of colonists in Africa. You can drink quinine."

"Well, I've been exposed to something a little different ..."

A nurse appeared, calling "Eldridge" in a crisp, bored tone. It saved Tanna from having to explain further at that moment.

She tried to convince Teddy to go walk around town for a while, if he wanted, and come back for her. He insisted on waiting.

He squeezed her hand. "I'll be right here when you come out."

—

Dr. Hill ordered a Wassermann test of Tanna's blood to confirm it was indeed syphilis. But based on the referral from Dr. Paine and her description of her symptoms in the earlier stages, he suggested they proceed with treatment. As she dressed in the corner of the examination room, he explained the process to her—weekly intravenous injections of Salvarsan.

She sighed behind the changing screen. "What side effects can I expect?"

"Nausea, fevers, headaches," he droned without emotion. "All *possible*," he stressed. "There's no reason to borrow trouble in advance." He estimated six to nine weeks of treatment.

"And if it doesn't work, then I'll go insane," she said, stepping out into the room and buttoning her jacket.

"Well, not for many years," he said, with a dry smile. "If you were to present any dementia, it would be much later in life."

She stared at him hard, gritting her teeth.

"Let's focus on trying to cure you first," he said. "Some of your worries may never even come to pass."

"What are my chances?" she asked. "The odds."

He squinted an eye and bobbled his head, miming difficult calculations. "Good. About fifty-fifty."

"That's *good*?"

"The results of the newer treatments have been promising. Maybe you too will come in on the side of the positive statistics and make the odds better for the next person."

"But I might not be able to have children?"

"There's no reason to rule that out yet. Nothing's definite. Let's evaluate that at an appropriate time, later. For now, let's focus on the next step."

"Arsenic," Tanna said with glum resignation.

"Salvarsan," Dr. Hill corrected. "The medicinal name is intended to sound less upsetting."

—

It was exactly what she imagined being poisoned would feel like. She ached in her bones; she vomited until her stomach muscles were sore from contraction; her head throbbed, and her eyes sunk into bruise-colored pits. She took to wearing more kohl around her eyes to make the darkness look intentional. With no appetite and no ability to keep food down, she became thinner, pale, and ironically more fashionable-looking.

Teddy had insisted on accompanying her on subsequent trips to the doctor. She protested halfheartedly. They arranged for her treatments to be on Friday afternoons so he could drive up from school, take her, and be there for the weekend. Their mother never asked the first thing about it.

It scared him to see her so weak. He didn't press for an explanation of what was wrong, but, when she had not appeared downstairs for breakfast one Saturday morning, he came to her room to check on her. She tried her best to sit up and carry on a conversation as she normally would. She could see the questions in his eyes, but she was reticent to involve him in the full details of her story. His concern was heartbreaking, and she knew he wouldn't be satisfied with vague, partial truths, as her mother was, but it was hard for her to see her baby brother as a young man.

He eventually began to ask indirect, adult questions.

"Why didn't Buck come with you?"

She stalled. She adjusted her pillow and reached for the cup of tea he'd placed on her bedside table. She wasn't thirsty, but the honey pot and spoon gave her something to do with her hands. "Well, someone had to stay and oversee the running of the farm," she said.

"Did you," Teddy paused, clearly nervous to ask her, "leave him?"

"Why would you think that?"

"You don't talk about him. And I know you didn't marry him because you love him."

"I do love him," she insisted. "In a way."

Teddy shrugged and his fair cheeks reddened. "Everybody knows about Buck."

She looked him in the eyes then and saw a man looking back at her. The only adult in the world at that moment who truly cared about her enough to want to know the details of the life for which she had left everything. She saw the courage it took for him to ask. And so she told him the truth.

He sat on the edge of her bed, nodding his head in silence for some moments. Finally he said, "Well, you definitely should, then."

"Should what?"

"Leave him." His voice was hard and cold.

She sighed and took his hand. His fingers were long and white, like one of the Seelie, the tall fairy men who attended the Lady Glare. "It's complicated," she said softly.

"Are you going back?" he asked.

At that moment, the thought of that journey, across the Seaming, through the storm and the transition of the portal ... It was daunting, difficult to imagine she would ever feel up to it again. But there was an inevitable longing, and she realized, as defeated as she felt, as fearful that she might be trapped here in her mother's house in the Gray forever, the only future she saw for herself was there.

"My farm is called Brynmor. It's my home now. And I need to get back there. I want to, I do." She gestured at the sickbed on which they sat, at the hospital tray, the water bottle, the medicines on the bedside table. "But, all this ..."

"Then the first thing you have to do is get well," he said, in the same optimistic way their father would have said it.

—

At the beginning of her fourth week of treatment, as she was about to enter the doctor's office, someone screamed her name.

"Tanna!"

A pregnant woman in an enormous fur hat was waddling toward her on the sidewalk. The hat teetered like a living beaver clinging to the woman's head.

"When did you get back?"

She only recognized Maisie Crenshaw by her unfortunate teeth in the last moment before she was caught up in an overly perfumed embrace. The hat was an ugly copy of the one she'd admired on Tanna.

Maisie took in Tanna's appearance in an up-and-down glance. "You look like a girl in a Parisian magazine. Your eye makeup. You're so thin. I'm entirely jealous!" She cackled and rested a hand on her swollen belly.

Tanna struggled to think of the right thing to say, and a way to inquire about the father. "Congratulations. You and your husband must be thrilled."

Maisie covered her mouth with a glove. "You don't even know, do you?"

"Know?" Tanna tilted her head.

"Ford. I can't believe the news wouldn't reach you. We were married six months after you and Buck left town. June of that year." Maisie's eyes suddenly widened in revelation. "You really didn't know. We're sisters-in-law, Tanna!"

Tanna stared, blinking, completely mute.

Maisie didn't seem to notice. "And this little one is your next niece or nephew." She cuddled her belly. "I'm pretty sure it's a girl this time. I wasn't sick like this with Ford Junior. We call him Freddy."

Tanna tried to recall all the other times she'd had a conversation like this with her friends who had become new mothers, the things one was supposed to ask. "How old is he now?"

"Eighteen months. Can you believe it? Oh, you have to come over and meet him. He looks like just like an Eldridge. He's a little yellow-headed butterball with fat, pink cheeks. Everyone's always saying he looks just like his daddy, but I think he's the spitting image of Buck. Y'all don't have any yet?"

Tanna crossed her arms. "No. We've been so busy establishing our farm. Maybe, though, in the near future."

Maisie pouted with concern. "Oh, I do hope so." Her face brightened. "If you come see Freddy it'll be just like getting to see what your babies will look like." She looked over Tanna's shoulder "Well, hello there, Teddy!"

Teddy appeared at Tanna's side, catching up with her after having parked the car.

He smiled tightly at Maisie but moved to hold the door for Tanna, raising his eyebrows. "I thought you were going to be late?"

"Oh! I am. I'm so sorry ..." Tanna started to move away.

"Well, come see us! We're just in our new home up on Missionary Ridge. Your mama has the address. She sent me a gorgeous crystal punch bowl as a housewarming present."

"I'll—I'll try," Tanna stammered.

"How long are you in town?"

"I'm ... not sure yet."

"Did Buck come with you, or is it just you?"

"Just me—"

Teddy interrupted. "I'm sorry. We're already really, really late." Mercifully, he pulled his sister through the door, away from the other Mrs. Eldridge, cutting off her last question.

Once they were safely inside, Tanna whispered, "Did you know?"

"I'm sorry," Teddy said, miserably. "I had no idea you didn't."

—

As the weeks progressed and the cumulative side effects of the treatments mounted, she doubted she would ever be well enough to return to the Green. There were days she feared she'd never make it out of her room.

But a morning came in late March when her window filled with sunlight. She felt the urge to stand, and there was energy when she pulled herself out of bed. When she parted the curtains to look out, she saw that the dirty remains of the last snow had all melted, the color of the grass in the garden was electric-green, and the sky was a deeper blue. It didn't look like winter so much anymore, the gray was fading to the margins, and she wanted more than anything to go outside and see if it felt like spring.

With Ginger keeping a watchful pace beside her, Tanna walked up and down and around the terraced gardens behind Blackwood, in search of some connection with the wild place for which she longed. Her limbs were wasted from disuse; she had to stop and rest whenever she came upon a bench or a low stone wall.

The trees were still bare. The grapevine looked like a tangled, brittle skeleton that had crashed and spilled down the mountain.

The boulders, splattered with gray-green lichen and carpets of lime-green moss, drew her attention. She took off her gloves and laid her hands on their knobby rounded humps. They never felt as cold as she anticipated. She could swear there was a faint vibration emanating from deep within the mountain and through the stones. They hummed at a low frequency, an undercurrent of song.

When she closed her eyes she saw stone giants, swimming in a slow waterfall down the mountainside. The boulders were the giants' shoulders, elbows, the knobby vertebrae of their spines, the heels of their feet breaking the surface of the earth from which they emerged, like whales in the ocean. These beings moved so slowly it was imperceptible to human senses. They existed in a time that crawled, when seconds were centuries, while a breath or a blink took thousands of years to complete.

These great gnomes were the only fae entities who had so far shown themselves to her in the Gray. Once, she thought she saw a small face, hooded in a cloak of fur, watching her from the back of a squirrel, but the fairy steed twitched and disappeared into a bank of ivy before she could be sure. She took to sitting for hours in the garden with a heavy shawl around her shoulders, one blanket under her backside, another folded across her lap, staring at the surfaces of tree bark and stones, slowly raking the shadows for pairs of small black eyes. Sometimes, she felt they were watching her. They knew she was watching for them. They were masters of camouflage, but if you knew where to look and what to look for ...

"What are you *doing* out there?" Dorothy Black Cravens called. Her mother's voice held an incredulous judgmental sneer. She stood on the porch with her hands on her hips, then she pulled her shawl around her shoulders against the cold and went back in the house. Dorothy was waiting for Tanna when she came inside, sitting in the parlor off the entrance hall with a book perched on her knee.

Tanna stamped her feet, breathing into her cupped hands and then furiously rubbing them together for warmth. She sniffed loudly and resisted the urge to wipe her nose with her hands. Her face felt numb when she began to speak. "What do you mean what was I doing?" she asked, as if there had been no break in the conversation. She was unable to suppress the edge of defiance in her voice.

"Well, you've been telling me you're seriously ill," Dorothy said, with a polite control meant to infer her displeasure. "You're up and down the mountain to the doctor every week. And yet you're sitting out there in the cold. Now, is that something this doctor would approve of your doing? Do you think you're going to get well sitting outside at this time of year?"

"I can't just sit inside all day," Tanna said irritably. "The cold air helps with the ... nausea."

Dorothy frowned at her doubtfully. "Why don't you get Geneva to make you some peppermint tea, then. With a little ginger." She raised her own cup and turned back to her book.

—

That night, as she was about to drift off, an image came to her, bringing her back to full consciousness. It wasn't a vision; it was a memory. She sat straight up and swung her feet onto the cold floor, already reaching for the dressing gown draped across the footboard of the bed. She fumbled in the side table drawer for a box of matches, and lit a small oil lantern with shaking hands.

She wanted to bound up the staircase to the attic as she had when she was a girl, but the guttering flame, the steepness of the passage, and her desire not to wake anyone forced her to move like a ghost.

A dormer window in the attic let in the blue glow of the moon. Dorothy

Black Cravens had removed everything from her husband's study that reminded her of him and converted the room into a modern library filled with her novels and bright feminine upholstery. But none of Tanna's father's things had been thrown out; someone had carefully reassembled them all in this tableau in the attic. There stood his desk, surrounded by a few low glass-windowed bookcases and a filing cabinet. His favorite armchair and matching Chesterfield sofa, the leather dry, cracked, and cold, held down the corners of an old Turkish carpet that was slowly being unraveled by moths and mice.

Tanna knew for a fact her mother never came up to the attic, but she had spent hours up here as a young woman, clinging to the memories of her father, trying to recall his face. She had often touched his personal things, a hopeful spell that always seemed almost on the verge of working, of bringing him through from the other side.

There was a burgundy leather journal with her father's monogram in gold gilt lettering. It was the kind of book where the boards of the cover were bound together by string so pages could be added as the contents grew. It was there, in the lower left-hand drawer of the desk, where it had always been.

To sit in his chair and hold his journals seemed to call his spirit to her. She felt his shadow lean over her shoulder. She set the lantern on the desk blotter and carefully turned the pages. They were slightly thick with damp and age, and the edges crumbled if she pinched them too hard. Here were the familiar botanical sketches she had studied before—the naturalist ink and charcoal studies of acorns, petals, blades, and branches. It had been a hobby of his to render objects from the garden. Most of them were unfinished, and only a few had words or labels to identify them. The sight of her father's handwriting gave her the same haunted feeling it always had.

Here, about twenty pages in, was the image that had awakened her—a squirrel, sitting upright, its tail erect, staring out of the page with its bright black eyes. On the squirrel's back was a small form wearing a hooded cloak of squirrel fur. The cloak disguised it, with barely shaded contours separating it from the back of the creature on which it rode. Beneath the squirrel's forepaw one could discern a bent knee gripping the animal's side. An arm reached around in an embrace, clenching a tuft of the animal's pelt in a fist. A tiny face ringed by the fur on the edge of the cloak's hood peeked around the squirrel's shoulder, the eyes hidden in deep wrinkles, crinkled in a smile.

There was a single word scratched on the page: *REL*.

Her father had seen the same fae creature she thought she had glimpsed in the ivy. Dorothy used to complain about how he also would sit for hours in the garden. Tanna remembered her confronting him, asking him in the same annoyed voice, "What are you *doing* out there?"

She skimmed through the remaining pages, carefully scanning them for other faces. She didn't remember ever having seen others, and there wasn't another like it that she could find. There was one other curious drawing, on a smaller scrap of paper stuck between the pages—what was clearly a tortoise shell, with leather straps attached to it, one of them dangling a buckle, looking for all the world exactly like a soldier's helmet.

Had he known about the Green? Many people encountered the fae who wandered across the Seaming without ever consciously knowing of the existence of that other world. Many suspected without knowing the full truth of it, until they were allowed into the unmentionable secret society of the colonists, the group to which she now belonged.

The helmet was suspiciously specific. Had her father seen a glimpse of the Rippers' war that brewed in the other world?

She regretted that, not only might she never return, but she would certainly never be able to tell him of all she had seen. She would never be able to take him there with her.

But the emotion quickly shifted to a certainty that he would have at least been excited to know she had been to that other world. The shadow at her back seemed to lay an arm across her shoulders, a slight shift in air pressure that made the hair on the back of her neck stand up.

She felt him blessing her, urging her to heal and return to the Green.

29

April 19, 1918
Chattanooga, Tennessee

As always, Teddy accompanied her on her final Friday visit to the doctor. She had steeled herself for one last treatment. On her previous visit, they had drawn blood for the Wassermann test to confirm the success of the treatment. It was common to give one treatment beyond that point. The side effects were no longer as debilitating as they had been at the beginning, and she was prepared to endure at least one more dose of the arsenic.

She expected—she hoped—it would all be over soon. Still, she was shocked when Dr. Hill examined her briefly and then, with a nonchalant smile, pronounced her cured.

"Cured?" The word fell out of her mouth, stripped of all inflection.

"Well, the treatments have been as successful as we could've possibly hoped," he said. "Now, your body does need a chance to recover. You still need to rebuild your strength. I want to see you eating again. Red meat. I'm hopeful that with the treatments coming to an end, your appetite will return."

He rattled on with recommendations about wholesome foods and fresh air, and then he simply walked her to the door.

She almost left without asking him. "And what about my chances of having children?"

He smiled kindly and placed his hand on her elbow. "There are no guarantees. We'll just have to see."

"A miracle, then?" she asked, her mouth twisted with a rueful grin.

"You're fine, Tanna. Celebrate that. Go home, eat a wonderful meal, and be well."

—

She couldn't keep the smile off her face as she crossed the waiting room toward Teddy. She whispered the news to him and he whooped out loud, grabbing her in his arms and bouncing her up and down. The other patients gaped at their display.

"Come on," she hissed, taking his hand and steering him toward the door. "Let's get out of here."

Teddy chattered happily all the way home. It was as if he had been withholding his energy for weeks, afraid to overwhelm her, but now she could handle the full force of his exuberance. He gushed about how close he was to graduating from school.

When she asked him if he was excited to go to Sewanee in the fall, he suddenly became quiet.

"Teddy? What is it? What did I say? Are you thinking of going to college somewhere else?"

At the base of the mountain he told her he had decided to enlist.

Tanna looked out the window of the car at the early lilies blooming along the side of Ochs Highway.

"You're going back," Teddy said quietly, as if her return to the Green was an inevitable factor in his decision.

"Come with me," she said. It was impulsive, maybe even reckless to invite him, but it felt like the only adventure that might stand a chance of competing. "Come stay at my farm and see this other world."

When he didn't answer, she added, "Buck's never there when I am."

He sighed and his eyebrows knit together in a beseeching, wordless apology.

"There's a war there, too, you know," she said, desperate to convince him. "If it makes it any more appealing to you."

He shrugged but didn't answer. He never brought it up again.

—

The next day, she asked Teddy to drive her into town again before he went back to St. Andrew's School.

"Where are we going?" he asked skeptically. As far as he knew, it was a part of the city neither of them ever had reason to visit. She was giving him instructions piecemeal, following visual landmarks as best as she could recall them from the time Buck had brought her to meet the Graycoat.

"Do you see the roof of that warehouse," Tanna pointed, "the one that's streaked with rust? That's where I'm trying to go. I think you can get to it if you turn down here."

He wrangled the car through the narrow, broken streets.

"Teddy," she asked awkwardly, "do you think Ginger could be trained to relieve herself in a container of some kind?"

"How big is the container?" he asked with a dubious twist of his lips.

"Maybe a washtub?"

"Hmm. I guess it depends on how long you have to train her to do it." He studied her sideways and frowned. "Why does she have to go in a container?"

"I want to take her with me when I go back, but she'll be stuck on a dirigible."

All he heard was the last part, and he was electrified by the news. "You traveled by dirigible?"

"For days," she said, the memory clearly unpleasant, "without any access to the ground. At all."

"An *airship*?" His voice squeaked.

"Yes, an airship, Teddy," she whined. "Do you think she'll be able to do it?"

He shook his head. "I don't think you'll even be able to get her on it. She'll be terrified."

Tanna sighed. "Well, I'm not leaving her behind this time. They convinced me I couldn't take her the first trip. I should have."

"What makes you think they're gonna let you now?"

She laughed bitterly. "I don't think they will. But I have an alternative to propose."

—

"No livestock on the ship," the Graycoat mumbled without looking up. He continued to scan the long scroll of paper spilling across his cluttered desk.

"It's not like she's a *cow*," Tanna said, unable to keep the edge of irritation out of her voice. "She's a deerhound."

"Not on the ship." The Graycoat glanced up and noticed Teddy for the first time, hovering behind her. "Who's this one?"

"Fine," Tanna said, ignoring his question. "We'll walk, then."

The Graycoat looked at her as if she were no longer speaking English. "What?"

"We will walk," Tanna said, enunciating each word. "With the crew. The haul team goes through on foot. I won't ride in the dirigible this time. Ginger and I will travel on the ground with everyone else."

"Out of the question," the Graycoat said, slapping his paperwork on the desk. "It's not safe."

"Major Gray, your daughter and I traveled for ten days, on horseback, into the Seaming, to Daughtry's camp at the front. I assure you it wasn't safe."

"The haul team's eight men. You don't put a lady in that kind of company."

She arched an eyebrow. "I will have a large dog to ensure my protection, remember?"

He glowered at her. "No."

"How much?" Tanna began to pull crumpled bank notes from her purse, straightening them out on the desk in front of him. He could clearly see the face and denomination of each bill before she added another to the growing stack.

She paused briefly with a questioning glance. She heard Teddy make a small sound of protest behind her.

The Graycoat indicated with a flick of a finger that she should continue.

She placed three more bills down on the stack with intentionally noisy slaps, and then she straightened up and glared back at him, waiting.

"We leave the day after May Day," he growled, scraping the money off the desk and tucking it into his shirt pocket. "And you'll be sleeping on the ground."

—

April 30, 1918
Lookout Mountain, Tennessee

Two evenings before her planned departure, Tanna went straight to her room after supper to pack. A few hours later, Ruby rushed up the stairs to announce that there was a visitor for her.

"At this time of night?" Tanna glanced at the clock on her mantel. It was close to eleven.

"She came to the kitchen door. She's down there talking to Geneva right now. It seems like they know each other."

Tanna frowned. "She?"

"A girl," Ruby whispered, "wearing boy's clothes."

—

"What are you doing here?" Tanna was thrilled to see her, but she hurried Holly up the stairs to her room so they could speak behind closed doors. "Did your father send for you so you could accompany me again?"

"He doesn't know I'm here," Holly said, already down on the floor petting Ginger, the dog excitedly licking her face. Before Tanna could ask, she blurted out an explanation. "Listen. There are two portals here on the mountain. One right down the road a ways. If you're crossing on foot, there's no reason for you to go through the gorge. And there's no reason for you to pay Papa extra. Or even pay him at all."

Tanna sighed. "I already gave him the money."

The girl pulled a stack of bills from the inside pocket of her jacket and held it out to her.

Tanna's eyes widened. "Did you—"

"I got it back for you," Holly said, a defiant look in her eyes. "And if he hasn't noticed yet, he will real soon. He's probably gonna send somebody here after me. We need to go now. Right away."

"Now?" Tanna cried, waving a hand at the chaos of clothes and open bags covering her bed. "I've barely started packing. It's already pitch-black out."

"I know," Holly said. "But it's actually best if we leave while it's still dark. We have time. Right before dawn will be fine. Papa thinks you're planning to go on Thursday. And I doubt any of those drunks working for him could make it before noon tomorrow."

"You really think he'll send one of his—" she struggled to find the right word "—*goons* after us?"

"For that amount of money?" Holly huffed, a mirthless chuckle. "Yeah. For any amount of money, really, come to think of it."

"Why are we doing this?" Tanna asked. "Don't misunderstand me. I'm happy you're here, but why not just go through with the haul team like I'd arranged?"

"It's not safe for you to go through that way."

"But if you're with me, I won't be alone with them."

Holly shook her head. "No, I don't mean the stupid men. It's the gorge crossing that's not safe. The attacks in the Seaming have been happening a lot more since you left."

Tanna arched an eyebrow, skeptical. "And going through on foot, just the two of us ...?"

Holly gave Ginger a final scratch under the chin and stood. She came close to Tanna, her eyes shining, her voice hushed but excited. "Hardly anybody uses the other trails I'm talking about. Some animals and kids might wander onto them every now and then. They're called sunpaths or shifting paths. They just happen. They aren't permanently held open, and they have a tendency to move around. They're too small for airship caravans. Nobody who works with Papa is going to use them."

"How are we going to find our way through?" Tanna asked.

"The head of the trail doesn't change," Holly said, "and I know where it starts. We can step out your front door and be in the Seaming in an hour's walk. Two, at the most."

Tanna's eyes narrowed. "And it comes out where?"

Holly sighed, exasperated. "We'll get there. We'll figure it out."

"I don't know about this. Maybe we should just keep the plan as it is. You can take the money back to your father, tell him—"

"I can't go back to him now," Holly shouted, her vehemence surprising them both.

Tanna studied the girl's sullen expression, the way she stared at the floor. "Surely he wouldn't hurt you."

Holly glanced up, a brief flash of fear in her eyes. "I'm not ever going back to him," she said stubbornly, reaching for the clothes on the bed and beginning to roll them up tightly.

Tanna had no reason not to trust Holly Gray. There was actually no one she could think of whom she trusted more. She pressed the girl one more time to tell her if something had happened with her father, but Holly shook her head impatiently and continued frantically packing.

Tanna let the issue drop for the time being. "How much food do you think we'll need?"

"Just for the day," Holly said. "We can't take anything more than what we can carry."

"I'll go ask Geneva to make us up something."

—

They stayed up all night, but, with the anxiety of having to leave like fugitives, Tanna would never have been able to sleep anyway. Holly was ruthless in culling unnecessary items from Tanna's wardrobe. When the girl wasn't looking, Tanna stuffed the box with Belle's body into the pocket of her coat. It was near dawn by the time they finished packing.

"Should we just go now?" Tanna asked.

Holly nodded.

"Can you find this path in the dark?"

Holly hesitated, but nodded again.

"You called it a sunpath," Tanna said, challenging her with an emphasis on the word *sun.*

The girl groaned. "I told you, the trailhead doesn't move. I can find it."

Tanna sighed and pulled on the pair of pants she'd taken from Teddy's chifforobe. "Let's go home, then."

30

No one else in the house was awake when they made their way down to the kitchen. Tanna fed Ginger some leftover ham from the icebox and made a pot of coffee. Holly packed the sandwiches Geneva had left out on the counter and filled two water canteens from the kitchen pump.

Tanna doubted her mother would experience any emotion other than a mild curiosity when the servants reported her gone. But she did regret that Teddy would drive all the way home from school on the weekend and discover she had left without saying goodbye. Into the frame of the mirror on his bedroom wall, she tucked a short note of explanation, again imploring him to come stay with her at the farm instead of enlisting.

Laden with bags, Ginger on a lead, they waddled out the front door. Tanna stopped briefly, patting the lump in her coat pocket she'd never gotten around to burying in the garden. It was for the best; she would take it back to Brynmor. She looked at the dark house, wondering—again—if this were the last time she would see her mother's home. The first time she left, part of her was already longing to return. And she had. She felt like the longing itself might have cursed her.

—

She followed Holly and Ginger single-file along the nonexistent shoulder of the road, thinking they must look like a band of gypsies. Walking here could be mortally dangerous, especially around the sharp curve where it crossed over the Incline Railway. Tanna glanced up the steep, silent tracks climbing to the station at the mountain's brow. From this angle, the path of the Incline looked like a ladder. Once across the bridge and around the curve, Holly dashed across the highway to Willingham Road and then slowed her march up Shingle, allowing Tanna to catch up. This road was virtually level, with a slight grade that took them back up the mountain.

The woods were wet and hushed with fog. The boulders glowed with ghostly lichen. Yellow and white daffodils popped up beside their green blade leaves, exactly the way children drew them. She was leaving the Gray just as its pale promise of spring color returned.

After several minutes of walking, the road rose steeply and Holly turned left again, crunching up the gravel drive to Cravens House. They stopped on the grass and observed the white clapboard house in the underwater quality of the predawn light, such a humble, unimportant-looking building to be a historical landmark.

"Are you related to them?" Holly asked. "I've wondered. Since the first time I heard your maiden name."

"From what I understand, we are related," Tanna said, "but so much more distantly than the proximity of our houses would lead you to believe."

They walked across a corner of the close-cropped lawn, stopping for Ginger to run and investigate the monumental cannon. She also sniffed around the base of the stone obelisk honoring the Union infantry from New York. The soldier at its peak was a silhouette against the graying edge of dawn far across the valley, the city and the curling river visible to the north and east.

Tanna tutted softly to call Ginger back to them. "It feels a bit like we're trespassing, being here at this time."

Holly shrugged, adjusting the pack on her shoulders. "Nobody'll ever know we came this way. I hope, within the hour, we'll be gone without a trace." The girl walked toward the woods at the back of the lawn.

"You don't think anyone saw us walking here?" Tanna asked as they entered the trailhead.

Holly whipped around, frowning. "Why? Did you see somebody following us?"

"No," Tanna said, immediately regretting she had caused so much alarm. Holly was definitely afraid of her father. "I didn't mean that. Just that someone may have looked out their window and seen us going by. A neighbor or a servant. I was worrying out loud. Forget it."

"Let's just go," Holly said. She moved quickly up the northwest slope through the trees.

Even though it was darker in the woods, the path was fairly smooth and easy to walk, if a bit steep. Holly wasn't aware that Tanna was still a bit weak; she hadn't seen her during the worst weeks of her treatment. She still had a ways to go to recover her full strength, and this was the farthest she had walked in months, but her greatest challenge was reining in Ginger, who was thrilled at this unexpected adventure and wanted to investigate every new bush and stone she encountered. They crunched along for a few hundred yards until the trail split. They turned left again, west up the mountain, the Point visible now, a dark snout of rock looming above them. *Chattanooga* was Cherokee for *rock coming to a point.*

"Where does this trail cross into the Green?" Tanna asked. "How will we know?"

"There'll be signs," Holly said, cryptically.

"Such as?" Tanna asked, annoyed that she was having to prompt her like a child working school lessons.

"The usual. The weather. Lightning. Mist. This particular crossing is supposed to be marked by weird boulders or some kind of large rocks."

"Supposed to be? Which means you've never actually used it before." Tanna rolled her eyes. "You just named things that are all completely normal natural phenomena to find on a mountain in early springtime."

"There'll probably be Indian marker trees," Holly said, petulantly, "or some other signs of spells. I've been playing in the Seaming and crossing in and out since I was a little kid. Trust me, I'm not going to miss it."

—

Holly was convinced they would find the crossing just before Sunset Rock, which was a mile and a half away. She estimated a forty-five-minute walk, an hour at most, as long as they kept moving. But five minutes up the trail they came upon a set of boulders to their left, one of them as large and flat as a table, and Tanna convinced her to stop.

She hadn't had a chance to catch her breath since the anxiety of packing in a hurry and the excitement of stealing away from Blackwood. At this point, they were already deep in the woods and could see anyone coming up the trail behind them. It made more sense to have a little something to eat and drink before the remainder of the hike. Any rough terrain they might encounter would be ahead of them.

Tanna produced the thermos of coffee she had made before they left the house, still remarkably warm. They munched on cold ham sandwiches in silence, breaking off chunks and feeding them to Ginger.

"So what do I need to know about this magical path?" Tanna asked. "How will we identify it?"

"A crossing is usually halfway along a shifting path. They sort of bleed out from the portals, like branching lightning. Sometimes it's two lines meeting; sometimes it forks in multiple directions. Of course, they don't look like that from the ground. There's something about the sunlight that gives them away. You know, when you see those perfect columns of sunshine coming through a hole in the clouds or shining down into a dark patch of woods through a break in the leaves, the dust all golden and floating through them."

"Sunbeams?" Tanna asked skeptically.

Holly smiled. "Yeah, really pretty sunbeams. The kind that look like you could reach out and cut them with a knife. The light spills through, between the worlds, like the weather does. On a gloomy winter day, there's a path lit up like summer. Or, you know, when you see the shadows of the clouds moving across the sides of a mountain and there are gaps, breaks in between the dark patches. I guess it could happen with moonlight too, come to think of it. A moonlit trail through the woods, glowing silver, when there's not even a moon in the sky to speak of. They can move around. They can shift with time and light. But they always start in the same place, and they always give themselves away."

—

They continued up the mountain at a slight incline, walking in silence for several minutes. The birds were plentiful and loud. It could have been a pleasure outing if not for the pressure of escape, of needing to cover the distance quickly without being seen.

They were soon over the hump of the northern skirt of the mountain, curving back south and trekking along the northwest flank. The trail was almost level here. The Point was constantly above them, over their left shoulders.

The rising sun was hitting the northeast face of the other side of the mountain, casting their path in blue shadow long after the sky started lightening with pinks and grays.

"What about when it's dark, like now?" Tanna asked. "The sun's barely up."

"This is even better," Holly said. "Dawn and dusk, the gloamings. That's when we can see signs of magic with our own eyes."

"What if there aren't any special sunbeams shining down?" Tanna demanded, annoyed by the girl's nonchalance. "We could walk right past it. There's got to be some other way to tell."

"You can tell by the magic," Holly bluntly insisted. "The paths between the worlds are held open by spells, and you can see them. They're usually cast by kids or by one of the fae, and they don't care about hiding their magic. If they even know how to. People are usually not very good at that. You know all those bedtime stories where somebody wanders into Fairyland or finds some door? I'll bet most of those are shifting paths."

—

Up ahead, near another jumble of giant boulders, a tree with a curiously bent branch grew in the middle of the trail. Holly stopped and studied it from twenty feet away.

"Do you think it means something?" Tanna asked. "It doesn't look like it occurred naturally."

The tree's bole was branched, but not broken, in the shape of a backward number *four*. The right angles were perfect—the horizontal branch was level; the vertical sections were straight up and down. It had no smaller branchings and no leaves until much higher. It had that inexplicable quality found in so much of the architecture in Treebridge—it seemed both constructed and grown at the same time, trained into a geometric shape that would not have likely occurred without intervention.

More than anything they'd run across on the trail, this looked like a sign.

"It makes me think we should be across fairly soon." Holly looked away from the bent tree, back behind them, at the point of Lookout Mountain. "If we're not already."

"You think it's possible we're already in the Seaming? We couldn't have just crossed through and not noticed. I haven't felt any nausea."

"Well, I don't think we've reached the actual portal yet. But we've got to be close." Holly walked over to the boulders, released her heavy pack to the ground with a groan, and leaned back against the rock. "Are we in the Seaming? Yeah. We've got to be. Here on the mountain, the Seaming actually spills much farther into the Gray. The crossing near Mowbray— where we took the *Queen of Clouds*—you have to travel much deeper up into the gorge before you reach the portal."

Tanna dropped her own pack and squatted beside Holly, giving Ginger enough lead to sniff among the crevices between the giant stones. "And you have no idea where in the Green this crossing comes out?"

"I told you I don't." Holly glanced at her, but looked away. "It should be a ways farther south than where we visited Daughtry's camp. Once we cross over, we might have to go on foot for a while before we get to something we can recognize."

Tanna saw the flash of movement first. She sat upright and craned her neck to peer back along the trail, into the woods they'd already passed.

Holly instinctively dropped into a crouch. "What?" she asked under her breath.

"There's definitely someone there," Tanna hissed. "Back along the trail behind us."

Holly crawled behind the boulder into the cleft Ginger was investigating. "Get down here," she said. "Hurry."

Tanna scrambled down beside Holly in the wet leaves, pulling Ginger in between them and holding her collar.

She shushed the dog softly and the three of them froze, barely breathing.

They heard footsteps on the trail, someone running, already bearing down on their location. Tanna felt that whoever it was must have seen them dive behind the boulder. Within seconds, he was going to simply reach out and grab them.

A man ran past their hiding place, moving so fast he was little more than a flash of color and sound on the trail—red plaid shirt, long dark hair, and a big black beard, his breath loud and labored.

Tanna and Holly stared at each other but they couldn't speak, afraid to make any noise at all.

Holly shook her head quickly, meaning, *Don't move yet.* They stayed where they were, even though they were completely visible if the man decided to turn around and come back.

"He's after me," Holly mouthed.

"Did you recognize him?" Tanna whispered.

"No, but that doesn't mean anything. Just because I've never seen him before doesn't mean Papa didn't send him. Why wouldn't he send somebody I've never seen before?"

"He could be a hunter," Tanna said, with little conviction.

"A hunter?" Holly scoffed. "Running on a trail near a part of Lookout Mountain where people live? With no rifle, no dogs, at—what—seven o'clock in the morning?"

"If he turns around and comes back, he'll run right into us," Tanna said.

"We could go off trail and continue in the same direction, but through the trees."

Tanna looked to the right of the path, where the mountain sloped away. There was a steep drop of at least twenty feet. "How are we even supposed to get down there without breaking our necks? Not to mention anyone walking down there is going to be clearly visible from the path."

Holly pointed along the left side of the trail, where the cliffs were exposed up to the brow of the mountain's edge. "We need to at least get off the trail first and find somewhere better to hide. We can go up in between the boulders. Look at all these crevices. There may even be caves up there."

The faces of the cliffs had broken away from the mountainside, creating a series of narrow mesas, towering columns of sandstone that looked like buildings, some of them five stories tall. Once they crawled up between them, they realized they could squeeze behind them too. It was a challenge to scramble over boulders the size of houses, crawl under fallen tree trunks, and inch sideways between narrow crevices in the rock, but at least they could continue along parallel to the trail, a hundred yards up the mountain.

The steep, rugged ground slowed their progress considerably. There were vents of cold air from deep within the mountain, and the beds of underwater streams leaked out and down. They clung to the branches of laurel and dragged themselves through it, hand over hand. Ginger struggled the most. Tanna reluctantly let her off her lead so she wouldn't catch and hang herself on the bushes.

Tanna discovered an alcove, a recessed block of rock the size of a barn door, with a frame of solid stone all around it, perfectly symmetrical, all its lines and edges straight. It looked like a door. Exactly like a door. Like nothing else but a door. She felt sure that uttering a magic word or tapping on the right spot would cause it to slide away and reveal a secret opening into the mountain. She insisted Holly come back and take a look.

The girl studied it carefully, tracing the stone lightly with her hands. Her expression was cautious and doubtful; eventually her shoulders fell. She turned and shook her head.

"Are you sure?" Tanna asked. "If that isn't a magic doorway, I don't know what would be."

Holly shrugged. "That's not it. There's no sign of magic around it. And I've never seen a crossing that was solid like that."

Tanna sighed, clucked her tongue for Ginger to come close, and they continued on, creeping across the backside of the rock towers.

They came to a flat outcropping of stone. Holly cautioned against going out too far in the open; she feared their being seen by the man on the trail below. Tanna would never have gone out there anywhere close to the edge; the height made her anxious. But the view to the west opened up. They could see Lookout Valley far below and the mountainous humps that formed the eastern edge of the Cumberland Plateau receding toward the horizon.

They couldn't see the trail directly beneath them; it disappeared under the feet of the rock towers. The right side of the trail now ended in a terrifying sheer drop of hundreds of feet.

Holly motioned that they should climb down closer. Trees grew between the towers, and slides of smaller boulders made a set of giant's stairs for them to pick their way down.

"Be careful not to kick any small rocks," Holly whispered.

Tanna pictured an avalanche delivering them in a heap on the trail below, with plenty of noise to announce their arrival.

They came all the way down to the trail, tiptoed out onto the packed red dirt, and peered quietly up ahead. The trail bent around a corner, another promontory of rock. The foot of the tower was broken away. From the trail, it appeared to be the mouth of a cave, but they knew from their exploration that it likely led up between and behind the towers, as opposed to deep into the mountainside.

The path and the cave mouth were lit by a perfect shaft of sunlight, like the finger of a god pointing their way. The tall stone towers were like the threshold of a giant's door, and as Holly had insisted it would be, it was open, not solid. But, from their current vantage point, they could not see into it or beyond it. Although broken by that single visible beam, the sky above was otherwise dark with a miniature storm. The clouds seemed to boil up from a deep gorge like smoke from a chimney.

Tanna felt the hairs on the back of her neck stand up. There was a thinness to the air that produced a faint, lightheaded euphoria. Crackles and sparks swam in her vision.

"I told you it would be obvious," Holly said.

Tanna felt the familiar nausea. "Will it be worse, going across slowly on foot?" she asked, swallowing hard. Her mouth had started to water.

"Nah, it'll be fine," Holly said. "I think it's worse when you're up high in the air."

"I'm ready," Tanna said, shouldering her pack and preparing to step boldly back out on the trail. She wanted it to be over quickly.

"Wait." Holly grabbed the sleeve of Tanna's shirt and yanked her back behind a stone. "He's there."

Tanna scrambled to reattach Ginger's lead and slowly peered around the rock.

The man in the red plaid had appeared in the gateway of stone. He stepped toward the rock promontory and looked back along the trail.

With a twitch of panic, Tanna ducked back out of sight.

"He's definitely waiting for us," she whispered.

—

They couldn't move. They were trapped. The boulder provided some visual cover, but if they tried to climb farther up the mountain—if they moved in any direction at all—he would spot them. Tanna kept Ginger close. She didn't tend to bark much, but there was no telling what her reaction might be to the scent of the stranger so near to their hiding place, especially considering the smell of fear that was pouring off her mistress.

The golden sunbeam disappeared, casting the entire area in blue dimness.

"Does the portal still work without the sun?" Tanna whispered.

Holly nodded. "The crossing is where it is. I think the sunlight may only be a spell that marks the way. We know where we need to cross, we just can't do it with him standing there. I'm sure he knows it too."

"So, we what? Just hope he gets tired of waiting? Gives up and leaves?"

Holly gave her a wincing smile in lieu of any practical answer.

They crouched there for half an hour, one of them periodically stealing peeks around the edge of the rock.

"He's not budging," Holly said with a gruff, frustrated sigh.

Tanna handed Ginger's leash to her. "Hold her close. Keep your other hand on the back of her head. It calms her."

Once her hands were free, she opened the flap on her pack. "I just need to find something," she said, frowning as she felt around inside a deep inner pocket.

"Do you have a gun?" Holly asked.

"No," Tanna said, her face suddenly brightening. "But I do have this." She held out her hand, the auroculus gleaming dully on her open palm. "I'm hoping it still works in the Gray?"

Holly frowned. "It's not dark out. And we know already where the portal is ..."

"Yes, yes, we know where it is," Tanna said impatiently, "but we don't necessarily know how big it is. Or how far it reaches from that point. What if it's not just in that threshold of stone where he's standing? What if it goes all the way up the mountain or something?"

Holly's eyes widened. "Crossings are usually big blobs ..."

Tanna was already holding the eyepiece of the auroculus up to her face and scanning the mountainside above the stone gateway. "It works!" she hissed.

The aurora was pale and at first nearly impossible to see, but it was there, plain as anything, once she knew where to look. A column of otherworldly light, a loose shaft beamed down from the sky above the passage, but it also extended a little ways beyond the stone gate in all directions. It wasn't a long curtain stretched along the entire horizon, as the ones she had viewed in the Green, but the shimmering skirt of light ran up the mountain above the gate for at least fifty feet. It wasn't much, but it might be enough.

If they could sneak back up the mountain and pick their way through a tumble of small boulders and climb through a patch of laurel—without being seen from below—they could step right through the portal.

"Let's just climb up and across as quietly as we can, as far as we can," Holly said. "But he's going to look up and spot us. I think it's more important for us to try to be fast than to worry about being silent. The only advantage we have is a head start. So you have to be prepared to run. And keep running once you're through."

Tanna nodded, shrugging into her pack and forcing herself to breathe deeply.

"Listen," Holly said, looking intently into her face. "It's going to be hard to keep moving when the maziness hits. The ground may change completely, too, and throw you off. So crawl on your hands and knees, if you have to. And pray there's nobody waiting for us on the other side too."

—

They didn't even make it ten feet up the scree of fist-sized rocks before a shout went up from below. It was too steep to run. Tanna tried to crawl up the rocks, every other stone shifting beneath her hands and beginning to slide behind her. Their silence was blown. At that point, an avalanche felt like it might be helpful. Holly was ahead of her and Ginger ran along beside the river of stone, so Tanna contributed as much as she could to the chaos in her wake. She scooped with her hands, throwing the stones as she released them, kicking her footholds back behind her.

The noise grew to a loud hiss all around her. Holly and Ginger were already up and moving right across the mountainside toward the laurel trees, their feet exploding through the dead leaves.

It felt like their pursuer was right on her heels. Tanna knew at any moment her foot might be grabbed, that she could be jerked back and fall flat on her face, sliding into his hands.

She almost lost her balance when she reached the top of the scree and tried to stand with her heavy pack. For a moment she was windmilling her hands; Holly was looking back to check on her, hesitating with her hand on a laurel branch.

Tanna threw herself forward and caught the ground. Looking back, she saw the man on his hands and knees but moving up beside the avalanche, faster than she had even feared.

Holly yelled. Tanna didn't know what she was saying. Ginger was barking. Stones were exploding just behind her. Was he throwing rocks at her? No, it was Holly tossing rocks down at him.

She reached the patch of laurel and Holly pushed her into the branches. She felt a painful scrape against her cheekbone. She saw spots when she opened her eyes.

Holly was still standing in front of the entrance to the trees, lobbing large stones overhead with both hands.

The man screamed and collapsed in a crouch, hugging his knee. He fell as he tried to continue up the incline and sat down hard, grimacing with pain.

Holly turned to catch up. "Go go go go go!"

As Tanna started crawling through the trees, swinging from the branches like a monkey, she saw the end of Ginger's lead slithering by and grabbed it.

She wound it around her left hand several times. She could not lose her if she became disoriented. She had no idea what effect the crossing might have on a dog.

The trees gave way to a dry streambed. Viewed from the other side, the rocks stair-stepped down to the stone gateway on the trail.

A few more steps and she would be directly above the center of the stone gate. She should be well inside the crossing's influence at any moment.

Ginger had stopped, panting, unsure of where her companions intended to go. Tanna took the opportunity to pull the lead in to arm's length so that she could take hold of Ginger's collar if necessary.

Holly was right behind her, wrenching her pack free from a broken branch, still chanting, "Go go go go go!"

The bright red plaid was much closer than it should be ...

She wanted to warn Holly, but when she tried to speak her mouth filled with saliva. She choked; her lips felt stuck together ...

The ground changed positions with the sky. She found herself on her hands and knees, blood on her knuckles, a line of drool hanging from her lip that she couldn't seem to spit away. Ginger was licking her right ear and whining pitifully.

It wasn't better on the ground than it had been the previous times in the dirigibles. This was worse. Worse still because she couldn't squeeze her eyes shut, lie down on a bunk, and wait for it to pass. She had to keep moving.

Holly was trying to yank her up beneath the arms, yelling at her to stand. She turned in Holly's embrace, climbing her by handfuls of the girl's clothes. Somehow Holly managed to stay upright, to get Tanna's arm across her shoulders, and was dragging her, half-carrying her, away from the dry streambed.

Tanna tried to stop her head from lolling; she opened one eye fearfully to look for Ginger.

The towers of rock were gone. The dim blue gloom of the morning woods had been snatched away, like a sheet that had been draped across the sky.

They were stumbling down the side of a gently sloping grassy hill in the blazing-hot autumn sunshine of another world.

31

Tanna couldn't help but keep looking back the way they'd come. Lookout Mountain was gone, and in its place was a long slope covered in tall grass with pearly white flowers on feathery stalks. A faint path led down to the cold, deep brook, full of tadpoles and small blue-gray brim. Ginger waded up to her shoulders, snapping at the fish. Holly knelt, reaching between cattails to fill her water skin.

Tanna sipped the clean water from her own canteen—yes, it tasted different here; it tasted like something more than what it was, but she couldn't put her finger on it. She closed her eyes and tilted her face toward the sun, feeling that this warmth was exactly what she required to obliterate the remaining fatigue of her lingering illness.

Her reverie kept being interrupted by the unshakable sense that when she opened her eyes and turned around, she'd see the stone towers of the trail on Lookout Mountain.

She opened her eyes and turned her head quickly, as if she might catch the illusion out, unmask the machinations of whatever spell had transported them. But there was nothing but the gentle slope, climbing toward a blue sky and a perfectly rounded hilltop. About halfway up its flank was an ancient, low stone wall, much eroded and almost invisible in the tall grass.

There was a break in the wall, a gateway about four feet wide, from which the footpath emerged. This had to be the portal they had just stumbled through only a few minutes ago. Part of her wanted to go back up the hill and investigate, to stick her hand or her foot back through and see if they disappeared before her eyes. Maybe when viewed from closer or from a particular angle, one could see through to the Gray. But then the other part of her shuddered at the thought of going back. Not as much because of a fear of the man who had chased them as from a sense of dread that she could cross again but become stuck and unable to return.

She had no rational or logical reason to think that the magic was limited, that it would only work once or twice and then stop, but then nothing about the day was rational. She had awakened in Chattanooga,

Tennessee, only a few hours ago, and by early morning she was standing in the Green. Although where, exactly, remained a question.

She wondered why the man in the plaid shirt had not followed them through. He must have been seriously injured.

There was no one for miles around. The land was flat prairie in all directions. It resembled the part of the countryside they had trekked through to reach Daughtry's camp near the Seaming.

As Holly stepped away from the water, a cloud of tiny dragonflies, which had gathered around her as she stooped, scattered like a school of airborne minnows, flashing black, blue, and silver in the sun. Surprised by the motion so close to her face, she hunched her shoulders instinctively and shielded her eyes with her arm.

"So many of them!" she grumbled.

"I like dragonflies," Tanna said, her voice sounding thick and dreamy to her own ears. The maziness of the crossing was fading into a light euphoria.

"Those aren't dragonflies," Holly said.

But before Tanna could ask what they were, the girl had already launched into trying to approximate their location.

"Maybe we should go back up the knoll here to get a better view," Holly said, squinting west across the prairie toward a bank of blue-and-purple hills.

The thought filled Tanna with dread. She whistled for Ginger to come back to her side and the dog came bounding up, stopping twice to shake the water out of her fur. "Shouldn't our position at least be relative?"

"Relative," Holly said, "but not exact."

"Then we're probably ten or twenty miles south of Daughtry's camp," Tanna reasoned. "Look at this place, it looks like the Green side of the Seaming."

"But the Seaming goes north and south in a line, parallel to the edge of the Cumberland Plateau, for who knows how many miles. Maybe hundreds."

"And if we're looking west, then those have to be the Hawnee Hills. You can see them from my kitchen garden, looking south from Brynmor."

Holly nodded agreement. "OK. So, we should head north across this prairie. I guess we should follow this stream if we can, for a water source, if we're going to walk all the way to Brynmor ... I'm not sure what we'll do for food."

"A copper roof," Tanna muttered, mostly to herself.

"What?" Holly asked, following Tanna's stare.

She pointed to the base of the closest hump of the Hawnee. "There! Do you see it? That bright reflection?"

"Yeah," Holly said. "Somebody's windows maybe, catching the sun. Looks like we could reach it in a few hours."

"Cole Mathers told me there's a copper roof on his stables. When the sun's in the right position, one can even see it from my house."

"The orchard," Holly said.

"Havenwood," Tanna whispered under her breath.

—

Unlike the slow approach to Tanna's house at Brynmor, with its elevation and its view out over the plains for miles around, this gravel drive switchbacked up into a deep hollow, with steep stone bluffs, huge trees, and giant ferns growing close on either side. The leaf canopy overhead cast the track in shade. An ever-present mist lingered close to the ground, as if the cracks and gorges in the skirts of the Hawnee were leaking dragon's breath from a secret cave.

Tanna moved more quickly than Holly, energized by the prospects of seeing Cole. Ginger struggled to match her mistress's speed, her long tongue hanging from her mouth, her breathing loud in the quiet.

"There aren't any birds," Tanna said, looking around. "Have you noticed? I haven't seen or heard a living thing."

They came around a curve to the right and saw the front of the house in the near distance. It was idyllic in a way she'd always fantasized a great house in Fairyland would be, nothing like the plain, rustic functionality of her farm or the fussy antebellum affectation of the plantations and manor houses close to Treebridge. This was much older than any of the structures she'd seen in the colony, not counting, of course, the caves, the brugh, the rough huts and tents of the Nunnahee. Its design was clearly human in origin, but ancient, and built with elvish materials. It appeared to have grown from the landscape.

The front of the house was wedged into the cleft of the hollow. The log timbers and exposed beams gave it the feeling of an enormous cabin or hunting lodge, but based on the size of its entranceway and exterior porches, much of its interior must extend back within the mountain itself. The slate roof tiles, identical and patterned at the edges and gutters, gave way to more irregularly shaped stone tiles, eventually blending into the scree, boulders, and rock ledges of a steep bluff. It was as if the house had been birthed from the mountainside, crumbling the edges of the opening as it passed through; and once the front door had cleared, the emergence had stopped. Lichen, moss, ferns, grasses, and even small sapling trees grew in abundance on the flatter parts of the roof between the gables.

A shallow stream, black with slime-covered stone steps, emerged from underneath the elevated front stairs of the house and flowed down the hollow. A large stacked-stone bridge arched over the waterway, built high to allow for the rush of water flowing down from the peaks above when it rained. Golden light filled the glass windows on either side of the front door, and a smaller green flame twinkled invitingly from a second-story window.

They came down off the bridge, trudged up the steep flight of steps to the front veranda, holding on to a natural railing of some hard vine. The stairs were slick with what was likely a permanent dank moisture. Halfway up, Tanna paused to catch her breath and shorten Ginger's lead so she wouldn't stray too far in her investigations. She turned and looked down the hollow, seeing the flash of the copper roof of the stables a few hundred yards below the house, situated where the stream left the cleft in the mountain at the edge of a grassy clearing. She saw nothing that resembled an orchard, which was how Cole had described his family's enterprise.

The front door was an enormous wooden monster, carved with the large face of the Green Man. Tiny air plants and patches of moss were sprinkled along the curves of his beard and the locks of hair curling back from his forehead. The tendril of a small vine grew into one nostril and out the other, a tiny bud near its tip on the verge of opening. His eyes were embedded with what appeared to be two single uncut sapphires, each the size of a quail's egg. His horns were faded gold gilt.

Ginger sniffed the threshold eagerly. Holly stared up at the face on the door. Beside the doorframe, Tanna saw what appeared to be a tassel carved from wood, dangling from the end of a fat, fraying hemp rope as thick as her arm. She handed Ginger's lead to Holly, and with some reticence, she pulled the cord, hearing an answering series of clanging gongs from deep within the house.

They waited a long time, two or three full minutes, listening for the sound of footsteps or the scrape of a latch from inside. Just as Tanna was considering tugging the gong a second time, the door swung silently and slowly outward with a whoosh of warm air.

Waiting in the open door was a face that could have been Still's sister—

the same amber, catlike eyes; high cheekbones; dark, polished skin; and the silvery cocoon of a silk turban. The Alleegee woman was dressed in a pale gray-green empire-waisted dress that fell to the floor in gauzy folds, grazing her bare toes. Over this she wore a short, embroidered emerald-green vest of felted wool, laced together between her breasts like a corset worn backward. A sheer bright green shawl the color of new spring leaves draped over her shoulders, sliding down to her elbows.

She closed her eyes slowly and inclined her head in acknowledgment of the visitors.

Knowing how few words Still's people were known to speak, Tanna did not wait for further prompting. "This is the home of Cole Mathers?" she asked.

The fae woman repeated the slow dip of her chin.

"Please tell him," Tanna said, "that Mrs. Eldridge and Miss Gray are here to see him."

The fairy woman backed away from the door and padded deeper into the dark hallway. Tanna, self-conscious of the loud clomping of her muddy boots, followed the hem of the servant's gown, which seemed to hover across the slate tiles with the faintest hiss, a sound like light rain.

Holly came along, gaping at the high ceilings, keeping Ginger's lead short and close. The deerhound desperately wanted to smell everything she encountered. Holly knew Tanna would not want her dog snuffling through a manor house like this, especially when they had showed up unannounced on the doorstep. Tanna resisted the urge to blatantly ogle the contents and design of Cole's home. It had to be the oldest mansion she'd ever been in. The woodwork reminded her of English Tudor. She wondered how old the colony here in the Green might be in relation to the American Colonies in the Gray.

The hallway through which they were guided had a high ceiling of cathedral-like arches, but dark and rustic, even more like a great, ordered forest. The walls were richly paneled and carved with woodland motifs— acorns, vines, leaves, bunches of berries and muscadines—as sculpturally dense as any of the walls in Treebridge. It was hard to find the edge of a repeating pattern; the designs were too perfect to be alive, but there was a small element of randomness and asymmetry that tricked the eye into perceiving movement, almost as if the leaves quivered with a subtle breeze or the observer had caught the tip of a vine just as it stretched and curled around a new anchor point.

The Alleegee woman paused at an arched doorway and asked them politely to wait. Her voice was so low Tanna did not catch her exact words, but the meaning of her body language was clear. She and Holly stood on the threshold of an enormous hall filled from floor to ceiling with bookshelves. The servant woman floated over to a low leather sofa in front of a roaring fire in a large hearth of stacked stone. She knelt down and spoke to a heap of furs and blankets, which moved and erupted into a man, struggling to sit up. The woman supported him as he stood with some difficulty.

"Tanna! Miss Gray," Cole Mathers called out. "Please, come in."

Tanna strode forward across the large room. The walk was awkwardly long. "I followed the bright flash of a copper roof, just as you described," she said, to break the echo of her boots. "It led me right here."

He smiled his handsome, lopsided smile, but as she got close enough to embrace him, it took a great deal of effort not to visibly start or gasp at his appearance. He looked like a skeleton, like the life was leaking out of him.

Cole stiffened within her careful hug. His arms and ribs felt like a basket of sticks. The smell of rotting haint flowers sweated from his pores. Even though his skin was silvery pale, she sensed his blush of embarrassment at his emaciated, much-diminished appearance.

To cover their shared discomfort, she continued her effervescent babble. "I do apologize for our showing up on your doorstep without warning. I'm sure if you knew the full circumstances that brought us here, you couldn't help but forgive us." She rolled her eyes, mocking her own martyrdom.

He smiled, but his blue eyes looked sad. "You're more than welcome in my home, Tanna. Anytime. I hope you know that."

He nodded at Holly, who was hanging back with Ginger. "Hello," the girl said.

"Oh!" Tanna said, pointing to Ginger. "I didn't even think to ask before bringing her in—"

"It's fine," Cole said, blinking slowly. He sat back down heavily, covering his weakness by calling Ginger over and ruffling her fur. "She's a beautiful dog. Deerhound?"

"Yes." Tanna beamed. "I couldn't leave her this time."

"That's right," Cole said. "I heard that you'd gone home."

"Heard from whom?" Tanna regretted the sharpness of the question.

"Your husband," Cole said, and sensing her irritation, he immediately explained. "I asked. But he didn't really offer any details. Only that you had to return on home leave." He realized the women were still standing and motioned for them to sit. "Are you well, Tanna?" He was hesitant, unsure if he should ask.

"I'm doing wonderfully well." She brightened, knowing it felt a bit false. "I got to spend time with my brother, and of course I missed my Ginger something awful, I can't tell you." She reached for the dog's face and cradled her muzzle lovingly. Out of the corner of her eye, she could see Cole watching her. She glanced over at him. "I'm quite well. Truly. You shouldn't be worried about me."

An unspoken thought—that he clearly needed to worry about himself—trailed off the end of her sentence like a stench.

He too focused on the dog sitting between them. "I must look pretty scary, huh?"

Tanna glanced at Holly, who was uncomfortably wiping her hands on the knees of her pants. The longer Tanna went without saying anything, the more unbearable the silence became.

Cole finally looked right at her, his eyebrows raised, asking her to acknowledge the truth of it.

"You look thin," Tanna said softly, her eyes compassionate. "It's not anyone's business, and you may tell me as much or as little as you choose to, I won't pry—"

"Black wing," he said matter-of-factly, putting her out of her misery. "It's a native illness. One that we unfortunately get from time to time. Although, I must say, as a feral from a family with a long local presence, I'm a bit insulted. We hardly ever succumb to black wing. It's usually you immigrants and colonists who suffer. You go running off on safaris without a clue of how dangerous this world can be ..." He trailed off, realizing he sounded rude, accusatory. "Anyway, it's a bit like malaria."

"What does the doctor say?"

He chuffed mirthlessly. "That I'm dying." Seeing the horrified look on Tanna's face he laughed in earnest. "The man's a quack, but he's cheerfully honest."

"Cole ...," Tanna said.

With a dismissive gesture, he looked away from her pitying frown. "I'm upsetting you. I am sorry about that. My manners were the first thing to go." He leaned back and softly called, "Ioma!" As he waited for the servant to appear he apologized further. "I'm afraid I won't be able to offer you the kind of hospitality you showed me and Jackson."

"Nonsense," Tanna said. "You're unwell. And we've surprised you. Completely uninvited."

"I think Ioma can at least manage to make up some spare rooms and feed you something warm, can't you, my dear?" The fairy woman had floated soundlessly across the room from wherever she'd been hovering, moved to the back of his chair, and was now tucking the blankets in around him. He spoke briefly to her in a soft, feathery language.

Tanna had the unpleasant sensation of eavesdropping on a married couple in their home.

"After the cold ham sandwiches we had this morning in the Gray, I'm sure anything you manage will be heavenly," Tanna said, directing her speech at Ioma.

Ioma nodded her head almost imperceptibly. She slipped through the arched entrance, up a broad stairway, and along a second-floor gallery. She glanced down once before disappearing around a corner, catching Tanna and Holly watching her. They both turned quickly and stared into the fire.

"Tell me more about this beautiful girl," Cole said, making kissing sounds at Ginger. The dog thoroughly sniffed his hand, licked him a few times, and then offered her paw for him to shake. He laughed in delight, and ruffled the loose skin and hair beneath her collar.

"Ginger's the reason we hiked into the Green on foot," Tanna said. She pointedly excluded her reasons for going home and picked up on the return journey. She found herself explaining, in unnecessary detail, the reasons why she had not been able to travel by dirigible and how she couldn't leave Ginger behind.

She was nervous in Cole's presence; she didn't want him to question her own illness. The treatment had taken its toll on her appearance. But she did tell him about being stalked by the Graycoat's goon. She wanted him to understand the reason for their showing up the way they had, that they needed rescuing.

Holly wasn't much help with the conversation. She was unusually quiet, even for her, near catatonic as she sat in an armchair before the fire. Cole glanced over at the girl a few times, especially when Tanna talked about the man who had followed them.

"Your father wanted to stop you that badly, huh?" Cole asked her.

Holly didn't look at him or answer, just shrugged in the petulant manner of girls her age.

"There are a few things about the Graycoat's motivation that remain a mystery," Tanna said, looking sideways at Holly.

Cole waved his hand dismissively again, telling Tanna to let her be. "So, home leave?" he asked. "Lots of people take them. I understand there can be quite a bit of homesickness for a colonist."

Tanna hesitated, uncomfortable with her half-truths.

He mistook her blush for something else. "How rude of me," he said, before she could answer. "It's none of my business why you went home. I'm sorry. I didn't mean to interrogate you."

Tanna stammered a bit, quickly settling on Teddy as an excuse for her trip. She recounted her time with her younger brother—how he'd grown from a boy into a man during the time lag of her absence, how concerned she was about his wanting to enlist. She even managed to steer the conversation briefly into the subject of the war in Europe before revisiting their escape into the Green.

"Were you aware," Tanna asked him, after she'd finished her tale, "that there's a shifting path in the Seaming, only a few miles from Blackwood, my mother's home on Lookout Mountain? It comes out within sight of your property."

"I've known about it for years," he admitted. "As long as I can remember, actually. But I don't use it. I stopped going into the Gray when I was still a kid. Once my curiosity was satisfied, I had no reason to go back there." He looked at her with a bemused expression, shaking his head. "You surprise me."

"Why?"

"Some would call you brave. Those paths are treacherous, even without being hunted by a hired goon."

"I had an excellent guide," she said, looking over at Holly, who had dozed off in the chair in the orange light of the fire.

"Just so you know," he said, "you're safe here. Even if he does track you to my door, this house is impenetrable. It's covered in a few centuries' worth of protection spells."

Ioma appeared with a tray of strong tarwater tea and honey-flavored cookies studded with chunks of walnuts. Holly awoke and moved to sit cross-legged on the floor in front of the low coffee table, munching the cookies and rudely slurping her tea. Cole accepted a cup but refused to eat anything.

Tanna saw another private look pass between him and Ioma before the fae woman left again.

"She's going to put together a more substantial supper for you," he said.

—

Before retiring, Cole told her he would instruct one of his elves to send a messenger bird to the farm at Brynmor, to let Buck or Still know she was here and to come get her.

"It may be the better part of a day before someone arrives. Until then, you're welcome to explore the house and enjoy the meadow. Let Ioma know if there's anything you need."

"Won't you come show me the grounds? Maybe it would do you good to get a breath of fresh air. It helped me tremendously with my recovery while I was home." It slipped out. She realized too late she'd introduced the very subject she didn't want to talk about.

Cole frowned. "You were ill while you were home?"

"Oh, it was just some nasty bug, I suppose." She felt the flush creep onto her cheeks.

He graciously accepted her story and didn't pry. "I've heard it's not uncommon for people to get sick when they return to the Gray. I'm afraid, though, that I'm really not up to going outside."

"I'm sorry to hear that. I was curious to see the orchard you talked about."

He waved absently into the distance. "The orchard's quite a ways up the mountain, actually. It's probably more of a hike than you'd care for. There are some nice flat walking trails through the meadow below the stables. Some stone benches along the stream there. I highly recommend you head in that direction."

Awkwardly, Tanna let the subject drop. She suggested that she and Holly could eat supper in their rooms, if Ioma did not mind bringing it up to them.

As if hearing her cue from offstage, Ioma came to help Cole out of his chair. She inclined her head toward Tanna in one of her infinitesimal bows, and then she led Cole from the room and up the stairs. Tanna couldn't help but notice how much the fae woman had to support his weight, how he walked hunched over like a man well beyond his years, how often he paused to clutch the blanket closer around his shoulders.

—

The wing of bedchambers corresponded with the steep, rocky bluff above the front wooden structure of the house, which formed one side of the triangular cleft of the hollow. The bulk of the house lay mostly underground, within the hill itself. Tanna supposed that in order for there to be a window in her bedroom, it must open between the knees of a tree. She didn't remember seeing any lights leaking out of the gables in the hill or the telltale flash of reflective glass.

Tree roots were visible on either side of the interior window casing, extending down the wall in a framework that held a substance like stucco or plaster. She wondered how someone had trained organic structures like roots to grow in such rigid, perfect formations. Ginger too was more curious than normal, sniffing every corner slowly and deliberately, carrying her tail curved low around her backside. She wasn't fearful or upset, but her canine sensibilities seemed confounded.

Tanna ran her hands along the smooth, hard roots framing the window. Unless she was more deceived than she realized, the roots had certainly grown that way, and still belonged to a living organism. She slid the edge of the drapes between her fingers. They were made of a diaphanous, silk-like material with a color somewhere between spider web, lichen, and the first fuzz of leaf growth on spring trees.

She twitched aside the fabric and peered through the glass. Night had fallen and she could only just make out a view down the hollow, blue in the moonlight, the distant stables a dark silhouette against the faintly glowing grass meadow beyond it.

Holly emerged from a door in the wall perpendicular to the window, which Tanna had assumed must be a bathroom. "Ack," she groused. "They must think I'm your servant. You should see *my* room."

"Are they attached?"

"Yeah. On the other side of this bath is a box with a narrow bunk in it."

"Oh? There's an en suite bath?" Tanna cooed, ignoring Holly's complaint. She peered around the girl at a copper tub standing in the middle of its sizable room. "But it looks like some poor house elf will have to cart buckets of hot water up here. I'm reluctant to impose further than we already have."

As if on cue, there was a soft knock at the door and Ioma entered, followed by a small, dark elven maid, both of them carrying trays that smelled of hot food and more tea. Ginger slunk away behind the bed, unnerved by her first encounter with one of the smaller races.

Ioma gestured at a low coffee table, the only surface in the room large enough on which to dine.

"That'll be fine," Tanna said, trying to sound warm. She smiled, hoping to express gratitude, but it felt like she was grimacing. The fairy woman's manner was more severe and judgmental than Still's had ever been.

As the elf laid the table with the women's meal, Ioma carried a dish of milk and a plate of what looked like pulled scraps of roasted bird stirred with raw eggs to Ginger.

"Thank you for thinking of her," Tanna said, genuinely warmed by the thoughtfulness.

She saw the faint spark in Ioma's catlike eyes, that slight, narrowing twitch of the eyelids she had come to recognize as a smile from Still. The fae woman inclined her head and flowed from the room, closing the door behind her.

Tanna pulled off her boots with a groan of pleasure and joined Holly on the floor beside the coffee table. Their faces hovered inches above bowls of lentil stew, which they both shoveled without regard to table manners, sopping up the last drops with chunks of rosemary sourdough bread.

As Tanna paused to pour the tea she asked Holly if she'd ever heard of black wing.

Holly nodded. "Lots."

"So it's common?"

"A lot of people get it. It usually comes in waves. A whole plantation will come down with it. Or even a town. I haven't heard of anybody having it lately, though."

"Is it always fatal?"

Holly shook her head while she finished chewing a bit. "No. It's worse for babies and old people. Some people come through it."

"Then Cole is being pessimistic," Tanna said. "He just needs someone by his side, aggressively tending to him, helping him fight it."

"You don't think she's helping him?" Holly asked. "Looks like she is to me."

"Who?"

"Ioma," Holly said. "They're lovers, aren't they?" She noisily slurped tarwater tea from her mug.

Tanna closed her eyes for a moment in irritation. "Lovers?"

"Cole and that Alleegee woman," Holly said, exasperated.

"She's his housekeeper," Tanna said, blowing into her own mug.

Holly shrugged. "Seem more like a married couple than you and Buck."

32

Ginger stirred at the foot of the bed in the faint gray dawn. Tanna awoke to find a small elven maid laying a fire in the hearth. She looked like the servant who had brought dinner the night before, took away the dishes when they were done with them, and returned with a pitcher of hot water. It was hard to be sure; with each particular race, the individual elves were almost indistinguishable from one another. Tanna hoped, for the small creature's sake, that she was *not* the same elf. When would she have slept?

Tanna pretended to be sleeping until she had left. Thinking she had awakened Tanna might upset her unnecessarily. Dorothy Black Cravens had always insisted that servants were more comfortable being invisible.

Tanna dressed, washed her face in the adjacent bathroom, tapped on the door to Holly's room, and called out for her to join her when she was up.

When they ventured downstairs, they found Ioma waiting for them in front of the dining room beside the main hall where they'd spoken with Cole the day before. Ioma gestured for them to enter, where they discovered a sideboard laid with plates of sticky buns and an urn of strong black tea. Tanna was relieved she could not detect the floral smell of haint or the bitter tang of tarwater.

When Tanna asked about Cole, Ioma very softly said, "Sleeping," but with that single word she conveyed that her master was still not well, needed to stay in bed, and that they should not expect to see him again so soon.

Ginger was restless to go for a walk. Tanna asked Holly to come along and explore the grounds a bit with her. "Even if they send someone to fetch us first thing this morning, Cole said they won't likely arrive before early afternoon."

They went down the front steps of the great house. Cole had suggested she explore the meadow by the stables, but she saw a path leading up the mountain. It ended at a cliff with a perfectly straight, uniform row of trees. It had to be the orchard. The fact that he didn't want her to see it only made her more curious.

Holly headed down the hill toward the meadow, but stopped when she realized Tanna was hesitating.

"Would you mind taking Ginger on down alone?" Tanna asked. "You can let her off her lead, let her just run. She's been constrained at our sides for more than a day. If she meets any horses, it's fine. She's always been good around them."

"Where are you going?" Holly asked in that blunt, slightly suspicious tone of hers.

"I want to go up, find something with more of a view out over the countryside," Tanna said, nonchalantly. "I wouldn't mind a few moments to myself."

"He didn't seem like he wanted you snooping around up there," Holly said.

"Snooping?" Tanna snapped. "Since when is strolling through an orchard considered snooping?"

Holly twisted her lips in a wry expression, but she didn't say anything further. She took Ginger's lead from Tanna and hurried down the path toward the meadow, the excited dog veritably dragging her.

—

The left-hand path up the bluff was steeper than she'd anticipated. Stairs were cut into several sections, the stone steps slick with lingering dew, sparkling in the orange morning light. The orchard's location must have been chosen for sunrises and early rays. She was winded by the time she'd reached the top, pulling herself up by the petrified grapevine rail, worn shiny and smooth from hundreds, maybe thousands, of hands.

About a third of the way up this smallest of the Hawnee Hills, the ground leveled off along the edge of a bluff that jutted out in a shelf of earth, rock, and trees. Facing the path was a high wooden fence with an elaborately carved gate. Beyond the clematis vine that curled along the fence she could see the tops of trees marching away in perfect single file.

Below, she spotted Holly walking toward the stream. The rising sun was just beginning to illuminate the tall golden weeds of the meadow. Ginger streaked across the open field, leaving behind a wake of trampled grass. Tanna smiled. It was the first time she'd felt nothing but happiness regarding Ginger since her wedding.

The gate to the orchard disappointed her and only further engaged her curiosity. She'd hiked too far up that steep hill to instantly turn around and go back. She was still weak from her last treatment. She at least needed a few moments to catch her breath. She grabbed the brass ring that obviously served as a handhold and jerked on it, never expecting the gate to swing open. Inside, dangling from a latch above her head, was a large, clunky lock, possibly also made of brass. Keeping her feet outside, she leaned her head and shoulders in to look around.

Unlike most orchards she'd seen that had multiple rows of trees arranged in a grid, or at least a double row of plants with an avenue down its center, there was only one single line of trees on her right, along the bluff. They were so close to the edge that some of them appeared to be scrambling for purchase in midair, anchored to the steep cliff with an enormous tangle of exposed roots.

The trees reminded her of a cross between magnolias and the banyans found in the low country swamps of Louisiana. The trunks were wide and squat, with powerful knees rising high above the dirt. The central boles split very close to the ground; between three feet and six feet high, they divided into oddly numbered, perfectly symmetrical branches. Each individual branch was as thick as most mature trees; they curved outward and then straight up toward the center, equidistant from one another, creating a sort of pendant-shaped cage of empty space at the center of each tree. The leaves were large, thick, shiny, and leathery like magnolias. There were no flowers or fruit, at least not at present.

In the negative space at the center of each tree was a cocoon of some kind, or maybe an enormous seedpod. Most of the pods were vaguely human-sized and -shaped, and vertically oriented. She thought of Egyptian mummies wrapped in the fabric of one of Still's or Ioma's turbans.

She was compelled to move down the path, stopping at the fourth tree. Here the pod was much taller, an elongated teardrop. It resembled a leaf curled along its axis and stood on its stem, its tip up where the tree's branches converged overhead. There were leaf veins covering the pod's sides, parallel, striated lines not unlike gills.

She stepped up and slowly reached her hand between the branches, laying her palm carefully along the pod. It was cool to the touch, hard but slightly furred like the flattest, densest felt. It seemed to faintly hum or vibrate. She snatched her hand away and rubbed out the tingling sensation.

She looked down along the line of trees, which stretched into the dozens as far as she could see before the gentle curve of the bluff turned out of sight. She could see there were other pods that were more generally globular in shape, gourd-like, green-white pumpkins. One pod was papery golden-brown in color and capped, just like an enormous upside-down acorn.

The trees and their pods all resembled giant jeweled rings—the branches were the tines of the settings; the pods were the gems.

She couldn't imagine how such fruit could ever be harvested and for what on earth—even in the Green—they could be used. Food? Hollowed out and made into large containers of some kind?

She heard a noise at the gate. Instinctively, she stepped between the fourth and fifth tree and crouched down low. She could see beneath the curve of the pod's bottom, through a gap between its smooth surface and the thick branches that held it.

A short creature rushed into the orchard and slammed the gate behind it. The dangling lock rattled noisily but still hung open. The monster seemed to be composed entirely of arms and legs. It was about three feet high, with a small bald skull like a human infant and skin the gray-brown color of tree bark like so many of the fae. Attached to its small body were squat, powerful legs and overly long, muscular arms. It looked as if it should topple over from the weight of its massive upper limbs. Its face was pinched and ugly, eyes crossed, a fat lower lip drooping and drooling.

Tanna was guilty of thinking many of the fae were ugly, but the Nunnahee, the Seelie, Still's tribe, and the house elves she was used to encountering—for all their insect-like qualities and exotic features—were nevertheless graceful, feline. They had a terrible kind of alien beauty about them, but it was still beauty. This creature was simply hideous. She wasn't sure what kind of monster she was looking at, but the word *troll* came to mind. On second thought, *goblin* also seemed like a possibility.

It shouted in her direction, a guttural squawk in no language she had ever heard. She wasn't sure if it had seen her, but the thought of having to interact with this thing, face to face, to attempt to explain her presence to it, paralyzed her with terror.

At that moment, she felt—as much as she saw—another goblin race by, so close to her hiding place the breeze of its passing stirred the small hairs framing her face.

The creatures came together between Tanna and the gate, and began a wheezing, barking conversation, their voices urgent and angry.

Carefully peering around the tree trunk to watch them, she saw they both carried unidentifiable weapons. They were shorter than rifles, but clearly guns of some manufacture. They seemed to be made of either bones or carved stones, held together by a woven net of copper wire. The rifles were tipped with quartz crystal or some uncut, milky gemstone.

They were obviously guards employed to patrol and protect this orchard. Surely they worked for Cole, but that didn't guarantee they would be friendly. Quite the opposite—they would have no idea who she was or that she was a guest of their master, and she would have no way of explaining it to them before they shot her.

These plants were too unusual not to be valuable. She was an intruder. Cole had all but warned her not to come here. She'd done it anyway. These guards would have every reason to assume she was a trespasser at best, if not a hostile enemy.

The argument the little goblins were having seemed to grow more heated. The one who'd come through the gate after Tanna struck the other in the side of the head. It turned, hunching its shoulders against another blow, and started back along the path deeper into the orchard, its superior following close on its heels, berating it along the way. Within seconds they passed Tanna's hiding place, so close she could smell a barnyard stench wafting off their bodies. She quickly and silently crept farther around the tree's trunk, clinging to the exposed roots at the bluff's edge. Looking down, she saw a drop of hundreds of feet to a tumble of broken boulders at the foot of the mountain.

The little guards moved out of her hearing, running away from the gate, down the line of trees that curved out of sight. She pulled herself up, gingerly tiptoeing around the tree. Looking up and down the path in both directions, she didn't see anyone, but she had no idea how many of them there might be. The gate was only a dozen yards away. She prayed she wouldn't meet another of their kind coming into the orchard before she could slip out.

She flew to the closed gate, expecting it to open at any moment. She yanked it back. The lock swung on its loose latch, smacking into the wood with a bang. She heard a shriek from behind her, which decayed into a series of yips and barks.

They were coming.

As she shut the gate behind her, she heard their approaching footsteps pounding the dirt on the other side.

She hurried to the stone steps, tripping and sliding down, clinging to the railing to stay upright. The worn knots and bumps were enough to burn her hands as they slipped past. She felt like her palms were being flayed. She kept bruising her tailbone, her feet skidding out from under her as she bumped and skated down the mountain to the fork in the path near the house.

She could hear the goblins shouting. When she glanced back up she could see their silhouettes scampering down after her.

She turned to the meadow where Holly had taken the dog, and cupping her hands around her mouth, she yelled Ginger's name. She could just make out Holly, a slight form by the bank of the stream, who turned at the sound of her scream. And there was Ginger, a dark gray blur, racing toward the house, sped on to supernatural speed by the distress in her mistress's voice.

The goblins were nearing the bottom of the stairs, already aiming their exotic weapons at her. Ginger ran straight past her and toward the source of danger.

Tanna panicked, realizing she'd called for her out of instinct, but knowing they wouldn't hesitate to shoot a dog. She opened her mouth to cry out, just as someone behind her bellowed, "STOP!"

They all froze at the command in Cole Mathers's voice. Tanna, Ginger, and the goblins. The monsters ceased their guttural screeching.

"Stand down," he said, barely above a whisper. The energy required by his initial roar had drained him. He bent over, supporting himself with his hands on his knees.

Ginger's hesitation allowed Tanna an opportunity to squat, get a grip on her collar, and encircle the dog protectively with her other arm.

Ginger growled low in her throat. Tanna could feel the vibration, as well as a trembling shudder of fear. She shushed the dog, whispering and cooing to her but holding her firmly. The goblins were not likely to respect the concept of animal companions with anything resembling human understanding.

She couldn't look away from them. Up close, their faces were pockmarked and greasy. One of them had the damaged drooling lip she'd noticed earlier; the other had a smear of mucus above his mouth. They stank of rotting vegetables or fruit left out too long.

Tanna stood slowly, still leaning over far enough to hold on to Ginger's collar, and began to back away. She almost stepped on Holly, who had arrived but was hanging back from the confrontation.

Cole spoke in the goblins' language, his voice stripped, straining to make the hacking consonants and the rolling purr in the back of his throat. He stared them down as best he could, bent over in exhaustion or from some internal pain. He raised his hand and pointed them back up the stairs to the orchard, the quilt draped around his shoulders starting to fall.

The goblins lowered their weapons, averted their eyes, and reluctantly turned to climb back up the path to their post.

Tanna realized Cole was wearing only a single thin garment, a nightshirt. There were badly worn felted slippers on his feet, growing visibly sodden from standing outside on the damp ground. His face was ashen, unshaved. There was a clammy sheen of sweat across his forehead.

He turned his eyes on her suddenly, glaring up through his brows, breathing with difficulty. "What were you doing up there?"

"Cole, you don't look well at all," Tanna said, noticing Ioma hovering in the doorway, watching the scene. "Let's go back inside."

He stared at her, saying nothing, until he was overtaken by a cough.

Tanna stepped toward him, gesturing helplessly, unsure of how to support him.

Ioma appeared at his side, pushing the blanket back up his shoulders, turning him around to her and pulling it tight across his chest. She spoke to him quietly in words Tanna could barely hear and certainly couldn't understand.

Cole allowed Ioma to walk him back into the house. He half-turned and motioned for Tanna to follow.

"Stay out here with Ginger for a bit," Tanna said to Holly. "Keep her on her lead and don't go far."

—

Cole's physical condition could not support the force of his anger. It was clear that his furious whispers wanted to be roars. He collapsed into his chair by the fireplace in the main hall. Tanna remained standing, a sign of passivity and humility. Ioma hovered behind him, watching Tanna without any indication of her judgment, one of those facial expressions that reminded her so much of Still.

"What were you doing up there?" Cole hissed.

"I was exploring the grounds," Tanna said, playing dumb, knowing how unconvincing she sounded but unable to think of any other way to respond. "I wanted to see your orchard."

"I specifically asked you not to go to the orchard," Cole said.

"Well. No, you did no such thing," Tanna said, haughtily. She felt he was humiliating her more than was fair. It made her unwilling to give up the argument so easily. "You said we should take a stroll down to the stables and through the meadow."

"Exactly."

"I took it as a polite suggestion," she said, raising her chin, "not a law."

He looked at her with something resembling disgust, and bit off each word, "Here the laws are mine to make."

She started to tear up. It was an unexpected reaction. She could barely choke out a response. "I can't believe how rude you're being to me."

Cole's scowl softened considerably with shame. Seeing that her hurt feelings were having more of a desired effect than directly defending herself, she went further, allowing the tears to come freely now. "After the dinner we had in my home, the way I have admired you and wanted so much to know you better—"

She realized it was true as she said it. She was painfully disappointed. She had teased Buck that she was going to marry Cole Mathers one day, when she couldn't abide Buck anymore. It really had been something she had fantasized about, up until yesterday.

She sniffled, partly furious with herself for crying. Cole wiped his cheeks with his hands, sighed loudly, and looked back over his shoulder at Ioma. The fae woman stepped forward around his chair and handed Tanna a soft white handkerchief.

"Thank you," Tanna managed to whisper.

"I apologize," Cole said, imploring her to hold his eye contact. "Sincerely. I ... I'm not myself right now."

"No, it's I who should apologize," Tanna said, gallantly straightening her spine and smiling at him and Ioma. "I showed up on your doorstep, without any invitation, or even a warning. You're in no condition to entertain. I had hoped Holly and Ginger and I might amuse ourselves outdoors for a few hours this morning, and then we could be on our way. Yes, I was snooping. I admit it. And I truly, truly apologize. I've upset you, when you're ill. I've acted like little more than a common trespasser. You are right to berate me."

Cole rolled his eyes at the word. "Tanna, I would never wish to *berate* you ..."

"What are those things?" she blurted.

He frowned. "The guards? They're goblins. They—"

She shook her head. "The *trees*. The pods in the trees. What are they?"

He snorted, a small wordless sound of unhappy surprise.

"Yes, I'm sure I'm being impertinent," Tanna said, "and nosy and the worst houseguest you've ever hosted. But after all this—I've seen them— can't you at least tell me what they are?"

His mouth hung open in shock.

She waited, arching one eyebrow, fully expecting him to acquiesce. She intended her bluntness to be disarming. Maybe even charming, once he forgave her.

But he said nothing. He closed his mouth, visibly clenched his jaw, and squeezed the carved arms of his chair. He looked angry again, as he had before her tears.

A gong echoed through the house.

Leaving Cole and Tanna staring at one another, Ioma slipped out of the room on silent feet and floated toward the front door.

Tanna expected it would be Holly and Ginger wanting to come back inside, but she heard a deep, distinctly male voice speaking to Ioma in friendly greeting and then the loud clomp of boots coming down the hall.

Jackson Gallagher stepped into the room with a wide smile on his face. But sensing the tension, his expression faded into a confused, questioning frown.

33

"What's going on here?" Jackson asked hesitantly, looking between Tanna and Cole with suspicion.

"What are you doing here?" Tanna asked, regretting the way the question sounded, the accusing emphasis on the word *you*.

Jackson laughed and held out his hands in a gesture of surrender. "I'm here to rescue you." He smirked at the surprised look on her face, and when she didn't answer he said, "You're welcome."

"What?" Tanna tilted her head, genuinely unable to process this news.

With dwindling amusement, Jackson saw that an overt explanation was required. "Cole sent a bird to Buck with a message you were lost in the Green. That you had turned up on the doorstep at his house, requiring a rescue." He spread his hands again. "Here I am."

"Yes, but ...," Tanna shook her head, still confused by some detail she felt she was missing. "Why are *you* here?" she asked.

Jackson scoffed, his eyebrows twisted in a wounded expression.

"Oh God." She pinched the bridge of her nose. "Everything I've said for the last half-hour has come out awfully rude. You have no idea how much of it you've actually missed. I'm sorry. What I meant to say was that I expected—well, not Buck, necessarily, but maybe Still."

Jackson nodded patiently. "Buck sent me. With Still."

"Why would he send you?"

"He wanted to come meet you himself—" Jackson started.

She interrupted him with a bitter laugh. "I doubt that."

"He's busy with the farm," Jackson finished.

She rolled her eyes. "I definitely don't believe that."

He ignored her, continuing his explanation. "I've been needing to come pick up some of my own equipment, stored here at Cole's. I offered to come and get you." He spread his hands helplessly, looking a little disappointed.

She wished she could take back her questions.

"I see," she said. "Again, I apologize. That was kind of you."

Jackson requested to speak with Cole in private. Tanna graciously offered to go in search of Still. She was eager to see him and to end the episode with Cole.

She said goodbye to Cole.

He did not meet her eyes. "Goodbye, Tanna," he said, staring into the fire. She heard him sigh, as if he were truly weary and relieved to be rid of her.

—

She saw Still down in the meadow, standing like a statue beside the wagon they had taken on caravan. She walked faster, her heart lifting at the sight of him. Holly was near the creek again, throwing sticks for Ginger to retrieve from the water.

"So'onah," he said, the corners of his eyes crinkling. She took this for his version of the beaming smile she felt on her face.

"Still." She hesitated at first but quickly gave in to the impulse—she grabbed his hands, taking one in each of hers. They stood like that for a few moments. She couldn't think of anything to say, but he held her gaze, and she found that smiling and holding hands with Still was a more thoughtful connection than any conversation she'd had with anyone else in months, except Teddy.

"You are well," he finally said.

"I am well," she said, treating his pronouncement like a polite question. "Thank you." She let go of his hands and shielded her eyes from the sun. "It is so good to see you, Still."

Again, the faint crinkle at the corner of his eyes.

Jackson came down to join them, looking grim, but he said nothing of his meeting with Cole. He asked Still to help him in the small barn behind the stables. They spent the next half-hour packing the wagon with wooden crates, trunks, and bundles wrapped in faded green canvas. Tanna offered to help, knowing the men would decline. She fidgeted in the seat, trying to let go of the residual fear and anger that lingered after her heart had stopped pounding. Her eyes kept returning to a swag of orange silk stretched between two trees, exactly like the one Curtis the vine trainer had slept in when he created her furniture.

"Just a couple more and we're ready to go," Jackson said, interrupting her memories.

She made a mental note to ask him later about Curtis.

Holly slipped into the barn one last time and came out with a distracted look on her face.

"Is something wrong?" Tanna asked her.

"Like what?" Holly scowled, pushing past her. She lifted Ginger into the wagon, climbed in after her, and helped Jackson check the knotted ropes holding the cargo in place.

Tanna gazed up at the house, sick with regret over this parting from Cole. She saw Ioma at a window, watching. Then a curtain fell and the fairy woman's face was gone.

—

Jackson helped Tanna onto the bench next to Still, pulled himself up beside her, and extended an arm comfortably behind her shoulders, holding the backboard with his left hand.

She was aware of the smell of him—warm hay, chamomile, a faint tang of sweat and pine sap.

"Sorry about the wagon," Jackson said, as they bumped up the dirt track that met the gravel drive. "I know it's not as comfortable as the buggy, but I needed to bring back my things."

"Will you store it all at the club in Treebridge?" Tanna asked. "Until your next safari?"

"No," Jackson said, drawing out the word in a curious way. "I'm sorry. I was thinking you would know, but then, how could you?"

"Know what?" she asked, trying to remain poised as she was repeatedly jostled into him. Her shoulder was pressed into the crescent of sweat under his arm.

"I've been staying at the farm," he said, cheerfully.

"At my farm?"

"At Brynmor, yes. At your husband's invitation, of course."

"I see." She began mentally ticking off the weeks she'd spent in the Gray. She hadn't yet confirmed how long it had been here in the Green.

"Cole and I got to know your husband a little bit when he was staying across the hall at The Fairchild. But I'd have to say we have become"— Jackson pulled a face, looking for the right word—"*chums* while you were away."

She frowned. "How long have I been gone?"

He laughed, thinking it a sarcastic remark about the men's fast friendship.

"No, really. Cole was the first person I talked to after getting back, and I was so surprised by his illness, and then ..." She waved her hand, indicating the mess she'd made of the visit.

Hearing her sincerity and distress, his smile softened. "It's still Hunter's Moon. October. I last saw you in Treebridge about two and a half weeks ago."

Her face paled and her mouth parted as she took in a deep, shaky breath.

"It can be a shock, huh?" he asked kindly. "So, what's the reckoning?"

"Excuse me?" she asked.

"The amount of time passed over there." He studied her face. "How long were you at home?"

"Twelve weeks to the day," she said in a low voice, as if it were horrible news. "Three months."

He allowed her a moment to mull it over.

Seemingly out of nowhere, Tanna said, "I hope you've been sleeping comfortably there." When Jackson looked confused, she explained further. "Since you've been staying at my house."

"Oh, yes, of course," he said, realizing she was picking right back up with their conversation. "Very comfortably. In the room with the yellow bedspread. I hope you're not unhappy about that."

"No, of course not." She batted the thought away with a gesture. "I just didn't know. But, as you said, how would I? I didn't receive any letters from Buck. It takes so long for them to make their way into the Gray, I'm sure."

"Bucky's an entertaining one, isn't he?" Jackson smiled at some memory. "Always a laugh. Able to sleep on the ground in the wild or hold court at the dinner table in a jacket and tie. We've made good use of your fine china and silver."

Tanna made a wordless, derisive sound and arched an eyebrow.

"I don't believe we've broken anything," he was quick to add. "Not a single piece to my knowledge."

At a crossroads sign announcing "West Fork," Still turned the horses onto a broad road heading northeast. Looking around at the flat, grassy landscape, Tanna asked if this was the same road that led over the Cumberland Prairie south of Brynmor.

"Not the same, so'onah," Still said, "but they come together."

She tried to sit quietly and watch the scenery roll by, but she found it uncomfortable to be so close to Jackson and not continue their conversation.

"You've been out on safari together?" she asked. "You and Buck?"

"Not as I would like. We haven't found the time yet. Your Buck is busy overseeing the farm." He laughed at another private thought. "He jokes that he's married to Gentry now. He's been truly devoted to the business of it, invoking your name and the desire to make you proud of him. I think you will be."

He didn't see it when she rolled her eyes; she was facing away from him. "So you'll be leaving on safari from Brynmor, then? I take it you used to come and go from the orchard."

"Yeah. But I haven't wanted to bother Cole lately," he said, hesitating. "For obvious reasons."

She glanced over at him, squinting into the high morning sun. He briefly met her eyes.

"He's not doing well," Jackson said. "He's been sick before, here and there, over the years. We all have. But this time ... He's just never fully recovered."

"This black wing," she asked, "is that something he's had before?"

He shook his head. "I don't know that he's ever had black wing, specifically. There are a lot of illnesses here that are similar."

Tanna tried to think of the right words to delicately make a suggestion. "Should we really be leaving him alone at a time like this? Someone needs to take care of him, take charge of his household. I could go back, as soon as I check in at the farm ..."

"No." Jackson vehemently shook his head. "Do not do that."

She was surprised by his forceful response. "Why not?"

His tone was even, low, and stern. "He wouldn't want you there."

"Because of what happened in the orchard? That was just a silly misunderstanding, surely he won't hold that against me—"

Jackson interrupted her. "I'm not talking about that. He already has someone. He has someone ... there."

Tanna nodded. "The Alleegee woman. Ioma. It does seem like there might be something between them."

He held her gaze. "She's been with him for a long time."

She began to blush under his intense stare. "I'm glad that he has her, if that's what he wants."

"He assures me it is a great love," Jackson said softly. "But one he doesn't speak about."

"Of course," she said, finally able to look away again.

The conversation lulled, and they both fell into their own thoughts. Tanna tried to think of a way to casually bring up the question of what was being cultivated under guard at the orchard, but she suspected being coy with Jackson might backfire. He had a way of seeing through social pretensions and making her feel foolish if she employed them.

She finally decided he would respond better to directness.

"What is it that he's growing?" she asked.

Jackson glanced sideways at her. "Growing?" he asked, as if he didn't understand the question. He quickly set his gaze back on the horses and the road in front of them.

She was surprised he chose to play dumb. She laughed out loud at him. "In the orchard. I saw those ... cocoons. The pods. Whatever you call them." She held up her hands before he could tell her she was overstepping again. "I know I wasn't supposed to. But now that I have, I need to know what they are."

Jackson frowned. "No, you don't need to know what they are."

"But you do." She waited for him to say more. "And you're not going to tell me?"

He sighed again, irritated this time. "It's not my place to tell you."

"Is it some kind of fairy drug? Some kind of dangerous magic?" She grasped at farfetched speculations to provoke him into defending the more mundane truth.

He pointedly ignored her.

"Well, I hope it's not contributing to his illness. Or keeping him from getting well." She sounded like her mother when she pouted.

Jackson looked over at her with a thoughtful expression, as if something had just occurred to him. He looked like he was about to speak but then stopped himself.

"What?" Tanna prompted. "What are you thinking?"

He clamped his mouth shut, a small muscle working along his jaw. "I can't talk to you about this," he said through clenched teeth. "Don't ask me again."

—

Once back on the Big South Road they encountered walls of hedgerows on either side. Archways of creeping vines opened on oak-lined drives across sprawling plantations. It was just as Tanna had seen farther north, on her first ride from Treebridge to Brynmor. She stared at the beautiful old Georgian manor houses, snatching brief glimpses of their timeless antebellum fantasy.

One of the approaching gates was blackened by fire, torn open with raw edges of burnt and broken branches, like a gaping mouth with rotting teeth. Just as she began to ask what had happened, they passed directly in front of the opening. She saw a flash of black ruins, with nothing but a chimney stack and a single leaning brick wall where the great house used to be.

She watched Jackson, trying to gauge his reaction. He was entirely unsurprised.

Another driveway approached on the left, this one an impassable charred pit almost ten feet deep. Still had to slow down and guide the horses off onto the grassy shoulder, squeezing so close to the hedges that Jackson had to lean in away from them, pressing against Tanna.

"They were attacked?" she asked.

Jackson nodded solemnly. "Hateful little bastards," he muttered.

"Those poor people. It's horrible," she said. "Our farm is miles closer to the Seaming than this, isn't it?"

"Your farm is fine," Jackson said, carefully, evenly, intending to calm her before her imagination carried her away. "But that hill of yours is actually easy to defend. And all the tribes—Seelie and Unseelie—consider it the Nunnahee's land. They wouldn't attack them, even if they wanted to attack you."

"Why these people?" she asked.

"To show that they can."

"I worried the whole time I was away. I had the most horrible dreams about the farm. About *this*"—she flung out her hand—"about this happening to us. To my tribe."

He met her eyes and spoke intently. "You're fine. And Brynmor is fine. For now."

She rounded on him, defensively. "What do you mean *for now*?"

"Well, *right now* you're not much of a desirable target," he said in a condescending tone. "But, you know, once the crop starts coming in ..."

Tanna frowned. "They want our harvest?"

He shook his head slowly, as if annoyed with her inability to grasp what he meant. "They don't want you *cultivating* the haint plants in the first place. Some of the Unseelie tribes consider it their sacred plant. Cole and I told you this."

She swallowed with difficulty and stared at him. "We've planted six hundred acres of it."

He chuckled without humor. "Yes. You have."

His bluntness worried her. "And you think this is going to anger the Unseelie?"

"The Rippers? Oh yes."

"Does Buck know about this?"

He raised his eyebrows and sighed. "I've told him my concerns."

"Was he sober?" she asked bitterly. "Did he remember the conversation?"

Jackson shrugged. "I'm not in the business of telling grown men—or women—what to do."

—

A few of the yolos came to run alongside the wagon while it was still miles south of the farm. Once they pulled off the road between the gates, they were immediately met by others. Tanna was surprised at the numbers of the Nunnahee; it seemed there were so many more than when she had first arrived at Brynmor. She watched one solitary long-legged youth race straight up through the steep grass from the gates to the crown of the hill. He would reach the house before they could complete the first circle of the low grade. A few of the older males jumped on and rode up the hill, clinging to the sides of the wagon.

By the time they pulled onto the flat top and passed through the gap in the atzeenah trees, the Nunnahee were gathering along the drive to wave and cheer, much as they had that first day. This time, she was more excited than they were. This time, she was moved by the familiar faces and the subtle expressions of joy she could now recognize. They weren't there to get a glimpse of a strange human queen; they had missed *her*. And she them.

Jackson turned to her, a look of happy surprise on his face. "They adore you!" he said. His praise had a way of embarrassing her.

She demurred with genuine humility. "They make a fuss like this over anyone coming and going."

"No," Jackson said pointedly. "They do not. You've done something to earn their affection. That's an impressive feat for any human colonist."

"Is it?" Tanna asked.

"Trust me, I've been here a long time." He smirked.

"How would I know you aren't just flattering me?"

"Have you ever known me to do that?"

Of course she had not.

Still slowed the wagon to a crawl to accommodate the crush of Nunnahee climbing up, reaching over Jackson with small brown arms like sticks, trying to briefly clasp Tanna's fingers. Jackson braced her to keep her from being dragged off her seat. Many of the women handed Tanna individual stems of *oowadaga*, a flower like the daisy or a black-eyed Susan with red petals. The bouquet grew on her lap and threatened to spill around her feet. Jackson began taking some of the surplus and carefully arranging them into a second bouquet.

Tanna gasped when she saw the front porch of the house. In the absence of her constant trimming, the vine had once again overtaken the posts. Buck had not been around when she had declared war on the landscaping; he had no motivation to continue her battles. The great topis vine was lovely, though; it had taken on a wilder shape than she would ever have chosen. She thought of the regulated net of dead twigs crawling up the winter stones of her mother's house, and she felt a sudden rush of pride. This was her vine, her home, and, granted, without the holes in the roof or windows through which it might invade the interior, what it wanted to become was more appropriate than any forced design she might have imposed.

The vine, the glaring lime-green of the lawn, the smiling faces of the Nunnahee, the flowers in her arms as Jackson helped her down from the wagon ... Everything felt like a symbol of those things for which she had grieved so vaguely, yet so painfully, during her time in the Gray. Evidence of something unnameable that, once discovered, she could never again live without.

"Keep Ginger close to you," she called out to Holly. The dog was pacing nervously, sniffing the air, scenting the strange, exotic smells of the fae. "Don't let her off her lead."

The elves stamped and chanted as Tanna climbed the front steps to the veranda. She found herself standing in front of the crowd like a speaker at a political rally. She took her time looking from face to face, aware of the associations she had with so many individuals. She had once thought they all looked the same, like nameless flocks of birds or schools of fish. Now their names came to mind, especially the children—Aliata, Wen, Eelie, Ton, and Dakka. Jackson teased her for calling them *her* tribe, as if they belonged to her; she realized what she had intended by that sentiment was that she belonged to them.

Quickly, before tears crept into her throat and broke her voice, she thanked them all for the welcome, for the flowers. She told them how much she had missed them and how glad she was to be home. Although it had been a longer time for her, it had only been a couple of weeks for all of them. She felt they somehow knew she had been in danger of not returning.

As they cheered her with their chittering vocal version of applause, she turned shyly to peer into the house. She wondered where Buck was. She would have expected him to emerge at least to investigate the commotion she was causing.

There, on the threshold, stood the changeling girl, almost unrecognizable with her wild red hair plaited close along the sides of her head and wrestled into pigtails. She wore a human dress, much too large for her, a bit threadbare, and in an old-fashioned style that reminded Tanna of daguerreotypes of her mother as a girl. She was no longer barefoot either—a large pair of unlaced men's work boots swallowed most of her legs.

Her hands were cupped and held against her chest. Tanna said hello to her in a quiet voice, as one would to a shy, stray cat that was poised to bolt. As Tanna took a step toward her, the girl carefully extended her hands to offer her something that was flitting around inside the cage of her fingers.

"What have you there?" Tanna asked. "Is it a chick?"

It was a finch owl.

"I've been keeping her for you," the girl said, her voice loud, her manner bolder than Tanna would have expected.

"Well, thank you," Tanna said, allowing the tiny, struggling ball of fluff to be deposited in her hands. "It looks like you've taken very good care of her." She cupped her hands as the girl had, and the finch owl settled onto a finger, tucking its head under a wing.

The girl lifted her chin in a haughty gesture. "I work in the house now," she announced.

Surprised, Tanna said, "Here, in my house?"

The girl nodded. "In the kitchen."

"Wonderful," Tanna said. "Are Navvee and Joona being kind to you?"

"Yes, so'onah," she nodded solemnly.

"You should learn all you can from them," Tanna said. She realized that everyone had grown quiet, listening to their exchange. She called for Aliata. "Please tell Queen Ananjooee how pleased I am that she chose to send the girl to us. What is her name?"

"Evening," Aliata said.

"Eve," the girl corrected her. She lifted her chin even higher. "I call myself Eve now."

"Then I will also call you Eve," Tanna said, suppressing a smile. "Tell me, do you know where Mr. Eldridge is?"

"Sleeping with a headache," Eve said.

Tanna turned to make eye contact with Jackson.

Chuckling softly, he lifted one eyebrow and shrugged.

—

"Tanna!" Buck rolled off the couch and stood before he was fully awake. "You're here!" He rubbed the sleep from his eyes and caught her up in an awkward embrace. She hadn't invited the contact, and the bulge of his biceps caught her right across the throat, cutting off her breath and making it impossible for her to speak. His shirt smelled sour, a tangy mix of sweat and wilting flowers. A cloud of tobacco smoke and cigarette ash surrounded him.

Tanna coughed when he released her.

"You look fantastic." He lurched over to the sideboard and poured himself a few fingers of tarwater. "All well, then, I guess. Wonderful." He swallowed the drink and held the decanter up with raised eyebrows. "One for you?"

Tanna glared at him. "That's all you're going to say?" She felt Jackson hovering just outside the door, politely giving them a private moment to reunite.

"What?" Buck asked, spreading his arms wide in a dramatic shrug. "Jackson! Come have a drink with us."

Tanna watched as he shoved the second glass at Jackson and raised his own in a toast.

"To Tanna's return!" Buck threw back the tarwater with a toss of his head.

Jackson took a small sip, looking at her apologetically over the rim of his glass.

Tanna, with no drink of her own, crossed her arms.

—

Although the evidence of Buck's ongoing house party was apparent, the crops were well-tended. Of course, Tanna assumed most of the results were the efforts of Gentry, his son Davis, and the elven workers.

Buck was tanned in the ruddy way of men with his Nordic ancestry— blond, blue-eyed, skin baked a golden-red—but it seemed so hard to imagine he had been out in the sun, digging and sweating. It was more likely he had stayed put on a horse, overseeing the overseer, manipulating

Gentry with his preternatural charm.

When she met with Gentry on the veranda before supper, he talked about being bossed around and nagged. He was none too shy in complaining about her *little husband*.

"Your little husband keeps wanting more haint, more haint, more haint." Gentry turned his hat in his hands, uncomfortable without it. She knew he was eager to put it back on his head and be gone from her presence. "I put a few dozen more bushes in the ground, here and there, just to keep him happy. But it's not like they will mature overnight. I just did what I could."

"And we're on track?" she asked. "The plants have taken to the steep terraces and the height of the hillsides, like we'd hoped?"

"They might be a tad smaller than some of the lowland farms I've worked on. But looks like they'll flower, same as any other."

Gentry's manner had a way of disguising even the happiest event as bother and worry. After months of not knowing, not even being able to find out what was happening, she felt exhilarated that the news was mostly good.

"I'm glad to be back before the harvest."

"I knew you'd be back," Gentry said with a knowing look.

"Thank you, Gentry." She would have been a fool to think rumors of her absence and her illness hadn't gotten around. The Nunnahee had greeted her with quite a suspicious level of emotion.

—

Buck rattled on about the haint plants over dinner, incessant, a manic stream of detail, facts, and figures coming out of his mouth. He seemed unable to talk about anything else, and even when Jackson tried to share some humorous anecdote Buck brought the conversation lurching back to the farm, the crops, and above all else, his speculations about their profits.

Buck was hungry for money—more so than Tanna had known him to be in the past, and most importantly, in a different way. He seemed to be working for this money. Rather than the usual maintenance of his *connections*—swindling, charming, cash-raising, glad-handing, party-going—he was problem-solving, contriving, investing. As Tanna had once wished, Buck Eldridge's ambitions had become activated.

She was privately impressed, but she couldn't get past her personal revulsion. Not to mention his behavior, his energy, seemed a bit frightening;

he was turned up so high, hot, and loud. He hadn't reallocated his time and efforts from drinking and card-playing and entertaining young men to work—even as he worked more, he somehow still managed to host a never-ending party. And he used Tanna's house, Tanna's cook and servants, her china and silver and glassware.

Now, apparently, he had also commandeered her guests as his own.

Watching him and Jackson together made her furious—their easy familiarity, their inside jokes, their references to personal experiences. She found herself more angry with Jackson than with her husband. Buck was an ingratiating fool; Jackson was capable and clever and wise—how could a man of his caliber suffer even one dinner conversation with the likes of Buck Eldridge?

She had to get away from the table.

She muttered something about choosing another bottle of wine, craving the silence of the cellar behind the kitchen. She stepped into the cold underground room with its smell of sweating stone and onions, and hung a lantern from the hook in the ceiling. She froze like a statue when she saw the empty wine racks. The casks of ale were gone too. The whiskey bottles were a glittering diamond shelf of empty glass waiting to be refilled. It looked like they had been burglarized. For a few moments, she wondered if soldiers had raided them and helped themselves. She couldn't imagine that this much reduction in stores could occur through natural consumption in two weeks. Buck must have invited the entire membership of The Fairchild over on the weekend.

She left empty-handed. And she didn't say anything about the stores when she returned to the table.

Holly watched her cross the room with wide eyes, aware that something was wrong. She sat through the meal in silence, feeding scraps to Ginger.

Buck also knew her well enough to interpret her mood. Surely he noticed she wasn't making eye contact with him, yet he was bold enough to guess why and still never think to explain himself or apologize.

"I thought you were bringing back another bottle," he said with a taunting, cheerful smile.

She shook out her napkin with an angry snap, picked up her water glass, and glared at him over the top of it.

"We'll send Still to Treebridge for provisions," Buck said dismissively, as if he had graciously solved a problem for her.

34

Tanna found herself in competition with Buck for Jackson's attention. Jackson sensed her discomfort and tried noticeably to balance his interactions. When Buck laughed over comical episodes for which Tanna hadn't been present, Jackson attempted to draw her into the conversation, recounting the stories so she could laugh along with them.

She felt herself smiling tightly, with little genuine mirth.

As much as Jackson tried to include her, Buck seemed intent on leaving her out of conversations. It was all irritating. She kept excusing herself and going to bed early, claiming she was still catching up on rest after the harrowing crossing, but she would lie in the dark for hours, listening to the rumble of chatter and laughter from the other side of the house.

Holly fell in with the men, more comfortable in their company than she'd ever seemed in Tanna's. She did spend some time with Tanna at the beginning and end of every day. They drank tea together in the early morning on the veranda before the men were up, smoking cigarettes in silence. At night, Holly would sit on the floor of her bedroom and watch Tanna get ready for bed. The girl would oil Tanna's favorite rifle for her or brush Ginger's coat while listening to Tanna unload her worries and preoccupations with the farm. But when Tanna sat down at her desk in the main hall to go over her ledgers, the men invariably decided to go hunting and would invite Holly along. The girl would look guiltily at Tanna, spectacles on her nose, hunched over a pile of invoices. She was clearly eager to go, and Tanna couldn't blame her. She was a little jealous, but she found the compassion to say, "Yes, yes, you should go with them. Take Ginger, she needs to run."

Jackson knew Tanna's skill at hosting dinner parties, the art of her conversation, her after-dinner storytelling. She was being far too quiet, clearly not herself. She'd been home for almost two weeks, more than long enough to have recovered from a walk across the Seaming, but she was running away to her room for the third evening in a row.

When she stood up from the table, Jackson rose with her and suggested she might like to take a stroll and look at the night sky before retiring.

"There's been a veritable rain of shooting stars these past few nights," Jackson said. "I've no doubt we'll catch some if we walk around outside for a bit." He looked down at Buck, who had not bothered to rise in deference to the lady of the house leaving the table. "What do you say, Bucky? Already a bit too drunk to stand?"

Buck laughed at himself good-naturedly, as he was known to do. "Yes, let alone hike around some muddy hillside in the dark." He waved them away, his eyes a little crossed. "You two go on. Have a lovely stroll," he said, faintly mocking.

Jackson took Tanna's elbow and steered her out the French doors onto the side patio and down the flagstone steps into the dark of the lawn. Once they were out of earshot, he stopped and looked up at the night.

"He's not such a bad fellow at heart," Jackson said in a low voice. "But you have to know his conversation is no match for yours." He hesitated, searching for a delicate set of words. "And I hate that yours doesn't seem to come out in his presence. So, I thought I might create some ... space for you to speak."

Tanna shook her head, a little embarrassed, much annoyed. "Buck's always been the life of the party. He does make a good drinking companion. I know this. He was my friend for years before I married him." She sighed heavily after saying it. Calling him her *friend*, in the past tense, was an unspoken admission that Buck as a husband was an entirely different story.

Jackson turned away from the sky to stare at her intently. His face was close in the dark. She could see the small glittering reflections of stars in his eyes. "Marriage changes things," he said.

—

They wandered along the path behind the kitchen toward the southern slope of Brynmor.

"I lost the auroculus," Tanna blurted. "I must have dropped it when we crossed at the towers. We were being chased, and I was trying to keep hold of Ginger's leash. I became dizzy ..."

"It helped you find your way back, then?" he asked.

"Oh yes," she gushed. "We had to find another way to cross, while avoiding the Graycoat's man. It saved me, again. It truly did."

He looked satisfied. "Good. I'm glad you had it."

"But I'm still crushed that I lost it," she confessed.

He shrugged. "I told you it wasn't an heirloom or anything. I'll find you another one."

They stopped at the fence overlooking the terraced haint plants.

"It seems like you haven't seen much," Jackson said. "This farm, Treebridge, and a lot of flat prairie."

"Treebridge is one of the most amazing things I've ever seen in my life," she said. "You forgot the Sea of Trees."

"Ah, yes," he said. "Where we first met."

Tanna smiled shyly. "I thought you were a fallen angel, you know."

He laughed. "Really?"

"You were silhouetted against the morning sun," she explained, "standing on a treetop, with enormous, bat-like wings."

"So I looked like a demon, then." There was a smile in his mock accusation.

Embarrassed, she covered her mouth with her hands. "I thought you might be. For a moment."

He caught her gaze and held it. "And what do you think now?"

She felt the heat creeping onto her face. Her voice was breathy when she spoke. "I'm not sure what you are."

White sparks scraped across the sky.

She gasped as the lights fell in slanting beams by the hundreds. The meteor shower came and went within a matter of seconds, the silent glitter making human fireworks seem garish and loud.

"There's so much out there," Jackson whispered. "I'd like to show you."

Tanna could see the last few shooting stars reflected in his eyes. Her cheeks burned. "Maybe." She swallowed, with difficulty. "Maybe after the harvest."

—

Tanna and Holly went to work in the fields, despite Gentry's grumbling for them to go back in the house before they died of exhaustion and sun exposure. They shuffled along beside the line of Nunnahee women, imitating their actions as they pruned the haint plants. Deadheading. There were a number of buds that dried up and turned black. These they removed so the plant could concentrate its energy and resources on the buds that were still thriving. At first, the elven women seemed uncomfortable, unsure if they should continue working with the so'onah in their presence. But Gentry yelled at them all to get back to it, and they were shocked to see that Tanna also obeyed him.

Buck made fun of her sunburned forehead at dinner. Jackson suggested she needed a good hat.

That night when she went to her bedroom to change, she caught sight, over her shoulder in the mirror, of a dark something crouched on her bed. Her heart skipped a beat and she felt a chill pass through her hot skin.

She turned slowly and saw it wasn't a living creature at all. It was a brown leather Stetson, identical to the hats Jackson always wore. It was a bit sweat-stained and stiff, and when she held it close to her face the darkened headband inside the rim smelled of him—that spicy chamomile smell, like clean hay with something slightly sour underneath. It wasn't unpleasant. The fact that he'd left it for her, that he had stolen into her room to place it directly on her bed ... It felt more personal, more romantic, than any gift of jewelry she'd ever received from a man.

The next morning, she met Holly on the veranda in a pair of Buck's boots with extra socks to fill out the size, Teddy's pants, one of Buck's shirts she had found stained with red wine and abandoned to the rubbish box that the elven servants often combed through for hand-me-downs or cloth rags with which to clean, and the hat.

Holly solemnly stared at the hat but didn't comment.

"What?" Tanna asked, sipping tea.

Holly pulled a face. "I didn't say nothing."

Gentry and the Nunnahee women saw Jackson Gallagher's hat coming up the path into the fields, but it was the so'onah beneath it.

"Nice hat," Gentry said with the same scowl with which he punctuated everything he uttered, compliment and insult alike.

"It was a gift," Tanna said, unable to keep from smiling.

The elven women smiled back. This morning, they did not hesitate when she set to work beside them, and when they took a meal break at midday, they shared with her and Holly tea and oat cakes from their woven baskets.

"Oh my," Tanna said, speaking through a mouthful, "these are delicious. *Ahdo*," she said, thanking them in their own language.

They beamed at her.

"Five more minutes!" Gentry thundered.

—

Tanna looked forward to breakfast every day. Buck slept off his drink until well after she and Holly went to work in the fields. Sometimes Holly was late in rising and would suck down a fast gulp of tea just before time to leave. But Jackson rose at dawn and had already been up and about, oiling his guns before coming to find her with his coffee cup. They developed a routine of meeting on the veranda and watching the rose-gray blush of morning.

He always lit a cigarette for her, without asking, and so she began to smoke more. It made her feel connected to him—the tobacco became a sacred substance they partook of together, like the Indians.

Jackson was one of those people who made everything feel elevated, ritualized, more significant than it had been before. He didn't drink to get drunk, and he didn't smoke without intention, either. He watched every curl he exhaled, as if it were a ghost, some invisible part of himself that he had birthed into form and sent to wander the earth on his behalf, or fly into the sky and beam wisdom back to him.

He made smoking seem important and magical, like the forbidden rite of a lost religion.

And so they smoked together in the mornings; made light, pleasant observations; and soon found they could even smoke in companionable silence.

For all that he desired to hear her stories, and for all that she thought him wise and mysterious, there existed between them a quiet more meaningful than heartfelt confessions or secrets of the soul.

—

Charlie, Buck's former aide-de-camp, showed up at the farm for an open-ended visit. Buck suggested they go shooting. All of them. Holly became subdued in the young officer's presence and made herself scarce, taking Ginger and one of the horses, and disappearing for hours.

Tanna went along because she enjoyed talking to Jackson about literature and music, society and big ideas. She liked the way he asked unanswerable questions of the sky on their night walks around the farm.

Whenever Buck sensed them having a serious conversation, he interrupted loudly with a joke, a shot of whiskey, or some invitation to an impromptu game. Whether it was shooting bottles off a fence with pistols, racing horses, playing a hand of cards, arm wrestling ... It was always something meant to appeal to Jackson's athleticism.

Tanna was disappointed Jackson did not reject Buck more. Everyone always liked Buck. That's who Buck was—the one guaranteed to entertain. No matter how dull the party, he could be counted on to enliven it. If the conversation turned too heavy, too political, if posturing was on the verge of argument, he could be counted on to distract, to undermine. Buck was a jester; Jackson was a prince. But all courts required a clown from time to time.

Jackson saw Tanna pouting and correctly interpreted her displeasure. He overtly apologized to her for liking Buck. "Sorry," he would mouth where only she could see, whenever he allowed himself to be dragged away from her. He did, however, always ask her along, too.

She didn't know which was worse: to tag along on the rowdy, boyish adventures Buck masterminded or to stay home alone and sulk, imagining her husband growing closer to this man that—she had begun to admit it— she wanted for herself.

She knew Jackson wasn't one of Buck's boys. He never would be. It wasn't in his nature; there was no danger of that. But she did wonder why Jackson didn't find Buck's preference for other men repulsive.

One evening, a drunken Buck fell on top of Charlie and they remained together on the floor in front of the fire, whispering to one another, their legs intertwined. Tanna rolled her eyes and looked pointedly at Jackson.

"That doesn't bother you?" she asked him.

"It doesn't bother me," Jackson said. "But I can certainly see why it would upset a man's wife."

"Most men find it disgusting," she said.

His mouth twisted in a gesture of nonchalance and dismissal. "I'm not threatened by it."

She looked more shocked than she felt. "You don't think it's ... wrong?"

"You know, someone asked me that same question about Cole and Ioma." He looked away, his expression closing. "It's not happening to me. It's not affecting me. These are other people's relationships, not mine."

She looked at Buck and Charlie without watching them, her face growing hot from Jackson's rebuff. "You're so damn modern and unconventional, aren't you?"

"I don't know what *modern* has to do with it," he said, remaining infuriatingly unemotional. "I'm simply practical. Or practically simple. I try to be, anyway."

It angered her that he, of all people, would make her feel ashamed, given the circumstances. "So you think a man should just love whomever he wants, sleep with whomever he wants?"

He nodded in eager affirmation. "Or a woman, for that matter."

She tried one of his nonchalant gestures, knowing it came off as petulant instead of confident. "So marriage doesn't mean anything?"

"People mean something to one another." He was staring at her now. "No label or law or decree can take the place of an authentic emotion."

She finally turned to look him in the eye. "Would you sleep with another man's wife?"

His face seemed too close to hers. "That depends on one thing, really."

"What?"

"Whether or not she wants to sleep with me." There was no irony or edge in his expression. Somehow, when he said it, it was simply truth.

"And what if she does?" Tanna could feel the blush burning her cheeks and throat, betraying her.

"Well, I think it's her decision. And if our desires align—" He shrugged. "Then we can get on with it."

Buck stood, dragging Charlie with him, and together they stumbled into Buck's bedroom and slammed the door.

Jackson smiled at her, kindly, with a bit of pity. "Let's go for a walk," he said.

—

Tanna found the habit of drunken shooting parties depressing. They were exactly like the social life she'd led at home, the very kind of world she and Buck had conspired to escape. She had come here for adventure, for excitement, for danger even. She was proud to have a true need to shoot a gun, to protect herself—not because some elven boys had been ordered to scare birds out of the shrubbery on the borders of her farm.

Jackson admitted to being bored by these games. He was used to guiding wealthy men with guns like Buck through the wilderness on safari—but that was his *job*. He and Tanna had walked a hundred miles around Brynmor in circles, and he was increasingly restless for his upcoming safari to begin. She suspected he had canceled an earlier trip so he could stay with her longer. But now she sensed his leaving and felt a bit panicked by the thought of being alone with Buck. Or with Buck and Charlie, God forbid. She hadn't been alone with her husband since returning to the Green; they had yet to have a private conversation that was not about the haint crop.

She almost asked Jackson to take her with him, but she was afraid he'd say no. To her horror, when he announced at breakfast he would be off in a few days, Buck asked if he and Charlie could come along.

Jackson explained he had been hired for the next two months to guide a small group of clients, a father and his three sons, deep into the Green. Jackson said his clients had invested a small fortune in the trip and he didn't think they would appreciate his bringing anyone else along.

"I do want you to come sometime though," Jackson said to Tanna on their last evening walk around the farm. They stopped in a favorite spot above the terraces, a stone bench where one could smell the uniquely perfumed breeze of the crop wafting up the hill. The cloying odor that accompanied the drug was entirely different from the flowering of the living plants.

"This world is in danger of changing," he continued. "We're changing it. It's already happening. You should see it all sooner rather than later."

"I thought you couldn't bring along companions on a client safari," Tanna teased.

"That was the truth. Not this trip. Another one. Soon. Just for you. Maybe a few weeks from now, after I get back."

She chewed her lip. "I'm not sure if we'll be done harvesting by then. I have to be present for that, as well as whatever tasks come after. I don't know how much help I can expect from Buck."

"He did seem to step up when you were away." Jackson raised his golden brows and smiled. "Maybe you should leave again."

"Just run away on safari with you?" She was surprised at herself for saying it out loud.

"It's your choice." He wasn't being playful.

—

The walk back to the house was quiet. She tried not to outwardly show her disappointment about his leaving. She searched for some light topic of conversation, but she wasn't confident how convincing she could be. The silence continued as she failed to think of anything to say. She finally gave in to the peace of simply walking beside him, knowing he would prefer this to girlish chatter anyway.

He did pause as they reached the veranda. He also clearly wanted to say something and wasn't sure how to find the words. "I'm a little concerned about your safety here."

It wasn't what she had expected him to say.

"Because of the crop? Or the plantations that have been attacked on the Big South Road?"

"Certainly all of that," he said softly, as if he didn't want to be overheard.

"But also Holly's father. Major Gray is a criminal, Tanna, and the types he employs are even worse. I've stayed around anticipating he might show up. Or at least the one who followed you."

"Let them show up here," she fumed. She was disappointed to hear the true reason he'd stayed. Her outrage against the Graycoat and the fear he inspired in his daughter made her angry, not afraid. She told Jackson as much.

"See, now that's what I'm really worried about," he said. "You in a gunfight, right here on your front veranda with some of his goons. It's not the Rippers that I worry about nearly as much as our own kind. The fae may not want us here—there are some of them that will try to run you off this land, given any opening. But not because they think they own it. They want to set the land free. But our kind? They want what you have. Men kill each other for that. For all their disruption and their terrorizing, the Rippers still manage to value life more than we do."

—

The house grew tense after Jackson left. Charlie was an annoying intruder. Buck was ridiculous. Her only possible outlets for conversation—Holly, Still, Gentry, and the elven women in the fields—were people who rarely spoke at all.

If it hadn't been for Holly and Ginger, she would have never felt so lonely in her life. It was certainly better than when Buck had left her alone on the farm soon after she arrived. Holly had a quiet flexibility that allowed her to exist in Tanna's shadow and be entirely invisible when she sensed Tanna was not paying attention to her. The very times when Tanna withdrew, when another companion would have sought to draw her out, Holly withdrew herself. She would go off on her own—Tanna really wasn't sure where she went—but she would come creeping back eventually, like a stray cat. Tanna granted Holly a lot of room for skittishness; the girl lived in constant anxiety of her father's men showing up. She considered it an inevitability. Tanna began to suspect that Holly's comings and goings were dry run escape routing. Holly hinted that she was arranging safe houses and hiding places she could retreat to at a moment's notice. She was stashing food and burying weapons. Tanna's not knowing about these hiding places was for her own protection—she wouldn't have to pretend or lie about not knowing Holly's whereabouts when the time came. And it would.

She caught herself having conversations with Jackson in her head.

She paced their old walks. She even smoked the tin of cigarettes he'd left behind, but they had lost their ritual magic and tasted stale. She left them on the hearth in the living room, knowing Charlie and Buck would find them and smoke them without regard. She hoped they choked on them.

—

A week after Jackson left, Tanna awoke to find Buck and Charlie already up and drinking coffee. Buck announced he was taking Charlie back to the front.

"They may shoot me for desertion," the boy sighed tragically. "I hope Buck can smooth things over for me."

She thought of Teddy. She wondered how much time had passed in the Gray; the war in Europe was surely over.

"But then you're coming back to the farm," she said to Buck, "after you deliver him to the camp?"

Buck winced apologetically. "There is a war on," he said. "I can't really turn Daughtry down if he begs me to stay."

"I thought this conflict was winding down," she said.

He frowned. "There are still a lot of loose ends."

She was more incredulous than angry. "We're harvesting the flowers, Buck. Now. This is our *first* harvest."

"But you have everything under control," Buck took her by the arm, drew her close, and kissed her on the cheek. "I'm no match for you. I'll only get in your way. Take care, Tanna."

She watched them leave, still too surprised for the rage she would feel later.

35

With only Tanna and Holly on the farm, they fell into a comfortable routine, though the overhanging threat of the Graycoat and his goons kept them from enjoying true peace. With her worries, the girl had grown moodier and shyer than ever, almost little more than Tanna's mute shadow. She followed her from house to field, with Ginger rounding out their trio. The physical labor left them exhausted at evening meals, catatonic over morning tea.

After supper, Tanna scribbled away at her writing desk—invoices, ledgers, letters home to Teddy he might never receive. There was still no direct word from Blackwood. She sent inquiries to The Fairchild, asking to be put in touch with new colonists or people who had just traveled from the Gray. She hounded Still to be on the lookout for newspapers from home. She was beginning to think the people of the Green had a way of willfully denying the presence of the other world almost as much as the mass delusion that protected it from the people of the Gray.

A week after the men had left, Tanna found herself holding her pen and staring at the wall, hypnotized by the sound of the mantel clock ticking. She shook herself, tossing her pen and her spectacles on the desktop with a clatter.

"Holly, I can't take this quiet anymore. You have to start talking to me. I'm afraid we're both in danger of losing the ability to speak at all."

Holly put her chin on her hands on the back of the sofa and sighed. "OK. But can we talk about anything?"

"Of course. Anything," Tanna said, defensive to the girl's tone. "Why, what do you want to talk about?"

"Nothing in particular." Holly shrugged, a sullen, childish gesture. "It's just, whenever I ask you anything you say my questions are *shocking* and *without context*."

Tanna chuckled at the fair but unflattering impersonation. "Well. I stand by the criticism. You need to learn some conversational skills. You have to learn how to prepare someone. You have a way of leaping out of the bushes and clobbering a person with deeply personal, sometimes inappropriate, demands for information."

Holly looked hopelessly miserable, her mouth gaping, unable to form a response that wouldn't constitute saying the wrong thing.

"Oh, don't panic," Tanna said in a patronizing tone. She crossed the room and sat in her armchair. "I'll make a deal with you. You may ask me anything you like, without criticism, if you will observe two conditions. You will only speak openly and without restraint if and when you're in my presence alone. And you'll allow me to make suggestions about how to improve your approach in the future, without getting your feelings hurt."

Holly feared there might be a catch she was missing, but she hesitantly agreed. "All right."

"Oh, and a third condition," Tanna said. "You will never repeat anything I confess to you to another soul. You can ask me anything, and I will always answer you frankly and truthfully. But it stays between us. Agreed?"

Holly nodded and eagerly turned to face Tanna, pulling her knees up beneath her. She was awakened by the possibilities.

Their conversations were often practical exchanges of esoteric knowledge. Tanna found Holly to be a wealth of frank information about the feral human culture in the Green. Holly believed Tanna to be an authority on all things related to the female sex.

That evening, talk meandered until Holly's relationship with her father come up. Tanna realized she might be the closest thing Holly now had to a parent, and in a rush, awareness came to her ...

"Oh, Holly," she breathed with blunt regret. "I'm so sorry."

The girl looked suspicious. "About what?"

"I haven't asked you about her. In all this time. Not since the *Queen of Clouds*. You mentioned her briefly ..."

"Who?" the girl asked, confused.

"Your mother."

There were several heartbeats of silence, that quiet into which Holly so often retreated. She didn't look at Tanna. She stared through the coffee table and played with a button on the couch, as if she hadn't heard anything.

"She was hooked on shine," Holly finally said. She cleared her throat before continuing. "From the time I was born. Or as long as I can remember. She'd take me to the dens with her so I could watch over her when she was passed out and make sure nobody robbed her or tried to ... take advantage of her. I'd sit beside her and watch the shadows beyond the curtain. If anybody stuck their head in, I'd shake her and wake her up. I'd try to, anyway. Sometimes I had to scream before she came around, but then that usually scared them away."

"How old were you?" Tanna asked.

"Three or four. Until I was maybe five. It was probably going on earlier. I just don't remember that far back.

"She'd stay in the dens for two or three days at a time. Maybe a week, if she could find the money. You know, your sense of time passing when you're a little kid ... Everything feels like forever. But it was a long time. She'd give me food and tell me not to eat it all at once, to try to save it as long as possible, and to hide it. To scream if anybody tried to take it away from me. But—" she smiled, sad and amused at the memory, "the hardest thing was needing to pee. I'd hold it for hours and hours, hoping she'd wake up and take me. There was a row of filthy water closets down the hall at the back of the den. But it was too dangerous to go by myself. There were grown men, some of them out of their minds, looking for women, for girls, for boys ... They didn't care much. All the shiny people were scary to me when I was a little kid.

"Mama would tell me, 'Just a few hours.' She called it a nap. 'Let me just take a nap and then we'll go.' Of course, when she woke up she'd be groggy and couldn't come to all the way. I'd want her to get up and start moving immediately, and she'd beg me to let her wake up more slowly. As soon as she woke up, she was grabbing around in the grubby blanket looking for the pipe she always seemed to lose. I'd help her find it, thinking we would get to leave that much sooner. And then she'd start smoking again. At first, she'd be talkative and happy and smiling, and then she'd cross a point where she changed. She stopped moving, slumped like a big doll, her voice coming out of a frozen face, talking in that exhausted way where your lips don't move, her eyes locked on something only she could see approaching through the shadows. She'd go from talking to me to talking to the spirits, and then she would get really afraid. I couldn't see what she saw, but I did sometimes think I could feel it. I felt her being afraid.

"If you're around somebody like that, all you want is for them to stop. You believe if they just stop smoking it, stop drinking it, let it wear off, then they'll be OK. They'll get better. They'll go back to being normal. But that's not what happens with somebody like my mama. When they don't have any smoke, they have this constant nagging sense they're being watched, that something or somebody is there, peeking around the corner, following them. They hear whispering, and they're always shushing you, trying to listen, to hear what's being said. They can make out somebody calling their name, but they can't hear the rest of the message. And they're convinced these messages are some kind of instructions. They're being told something important by the spirits around them, and they're desperate to know what that is so they can fix everything. They see connections in everything, ways things fit together that don't make sense, these complicated bunches of things that are going on, where everybody around them is being controlled, but also lying, pretending, saying things on purpose that may have secret coded messages in them. This big plan. When they shine, they have it all figured out. All their problems are on the verge of being solved, and they're about to become everybody's savior. I mean *everybody*—all humanity, all the living things of the earth, and the souls who've moved on to heaven. The shine lets them see angels and demons and ghosts. And the kinds of fairies that supposedly only other fae can see."

"There are fae creatures here that we don't see?" Tanna blurted out.

Holly shrugged.

"Are they hallucinations?"

Holly shrugged again.

Tanna made a sound of exasperation, but motioned for her to go on with her story.

"The only thing they think will help them is to get their hands on more shine," Holly continued. "And when it first takes them, they have moments where everything is clear. They can just barely see who it is there in the shadows. Faces emerge. They pick up snatches of conversations. Names. Words. Whole sentences sometimes. They don't always make sense by themselves, so they think if they smoke a little bit more they can make out the rest ..."

Holly shook her head bitterly. "You see how this goes. They want to do something. They need to go somewhere. They have to tell somebody something. But before they go, they need to smoke just a little bit more. 'A little more and then we'll go.' They reach a point where there's so much of it in them, they have to lie down and sleep it off. And so it goes, on and on, until they run out of money. They get thrown out of the dens if they don't buy anything. And they start wandering the streets, looking for clues that aren't there. Even when we did have a home, when Mama and Papa still lived together, she thought the place was haunted and didn't want to go back. And she was rightly afraid she'd run into him too. He didn't make any of it any better ...

"My papa's a crook. I'm afraid of him more now that I'm grown. I don't think he feels like he has to protect me anymore. But, I do want you to know, when I was a little kid, he did look out for me. He did try to keep me away from Mama when she got real bad. He'd come to the dens to get me. He'd send his boys to do it for him. They'd leave Mama there a lot of the times. It wasn't about dragging her home. He didn't want her. He told her to leave a thousand times. He beat her. He threw her out in the streets. She'd always come back around. She'd track us down. He'd take me away on hauls across the Seaming for weeks at a time. In his own way, he tried to rescue me. He hoped he could keep me away from her long enough that she'd turn up dead. And, eventually, that's exactly what happened."

Tanna tried not to overtly show pity. She knew Holly hated that. "You weren't with her when she died?" she asked, trying to sound matter-of-fact.

"No, I wasn't. And I could've saved her. We'd just come back from a crossing. We were staying down in Rainspit then, way down there at the base of the waterfall out of the gorge, which is pretty much the end of the haul line. Somebody from Treebridge was waiting for us, saying Papa had to come right away. It was an emergency. He made me stay behind while he climbed up the gorge on foot. He was gone for two days, and I sat on a rock watching the spray from the falls and looking for a sight of him coming back down the cliffs. He had gone to identify her body. Story is, they put her out of the dens, she'd been out of money for two or three days, but out of pity they tried to let her sleep it off. She apparently found some man to share his drugs with her, but they couldn't afford the cot to sleep on, so she ended up out in the streets again. She crawled up into an alley behind some barrels, probably so she wouldn't be seen from the road when she went unconscious. Well, she was lying on her back. She vomited. Choked. There was nobody watching her sleep. Nobody to turn her over real quick."

Tanna put her hand over her heart. "It was insensitive of me to allow you to work in my haint fields."

Holly smiled uncomfortably. "You couldn't have known."

"No, but I would never have asked you to help nurture a substance that took your mother from you."

She shrugged. "It's not the haint's fault. And it's certainly not your farm that took her away."

"Yes, but here it is, bringing it all back up for you, when you might have preferred to let it lie."

"I think about it sometimes. Sometimes I don't. I like working in the fields. And I like a nip of tarwater in my tea now and then, too. It's the way they do it. It's not like it is for us."

Tanna nodded. "She lost control."

"Yeah, she did. She tried. I think she probably wanted to stop, more than anything. She just couldn't do it. And I wasn't there to keep saving her."

—

Tanna wondered if Eve, the changeling girl, had a similar history. When questioned, she gave responses comparable to all children her age. She said she was five years old while holding up the proper number of fingers. She spelled her name out loud and neatly scored the letters into a dusting of flour on a tabletop in the kitchen.

When Tanna could find the time and wasn't exhausted from working long hours in the fields, she prepared meals with Navvee, attempting to teach him the cooking techniques she learned growing up in Blackwood. Her mother's sisters were bakers, renowned for their cakes and pies, and they loved to discuss the particulars of their innovations at length. She wished she'd paid more attention to Geneva when she had helped her, but she'd usually hung around in the kitchen talking while the servants worked. Geneva had always listened to her girlish concerns with endless patience—from every petty argument with a girl at school to complaints about her mother. They shared a solidarity in an ongoing war of wills against the inimitable Dorothy Black Cravens.

Navvee employed Eve like a scullery maid. The little thing had been assigned a surprising number of duties, and she worked with serious intent. She was tall for a human child her age, which put her at the same height as Navvee, Joona, and many of the elves. But her presence among them was jarring—the startling white of her skin and the mop of tangled copper curls.

"You always have straw in your hair," Tanna muttered, picking at the crown of the girl's head. Eve ignored her, rolling dough with a pin. "They must sleep on beds of straw at the brugh," Tanna said to Navvee, "no?"

Navvee, looking terrified, as he always did when Tanna asked him questions, threw up his hands in a helpless gesture. "She doesn't sleep in the brugh."

"What?" Tanna barked, making Navvee flinch. Eve stopped and turned to listen to the conversation.

"Doesn't one of you walk her back to the brugh each evening?" Tanna asked. When Navvee shrugged, she turned to the girl. "Does Aliata come and walk you home?"

Eve shook her head and went back to her biscuit dough.

Tanna eyed the flattened nest of relatively clean hay in the corner of the kitchen house, where Ginger was now napping between the burlap bags of oats. "Do you sleep here?"

Eve looked up at her, green eyes solemn and suspicious. She reluctantly nodded her head.

Tanna swiveled to glare at Navvee. His shoulders were hunched now in a permanent shrug.

"Why didn't anyone think it was important enough to mention that a child has been sleeping in a dirty straw nest in the corner of my kitchen?"

Navvee spluttered, unable to get a word out before he fled to the cellar to retrieve some onions.

—

Tanna insisted Holly let the girl share her room. "Changeling or not, this is a human child."

Holly sulked. "I can sleep on the sofa."

"No, you will not. We'll get another small bed for the room. But just for tonight, she can sleep beside you. It's a big bed. Lots of girls your age sleep with their sisters."

"She's not my *sister*." Holly almost spat the word.

Tanna stared at her in silence until the girl surrendered with a sigh.

—

Later that night, Tanna peeked into the room to check on them. Holly was asleep on her side, curled as close to one edge of the bed as she could get without falling off. But there was no sign of Eve. With a cold rush of concern, Tanna stepped into the room and walked toward the open window.

Ginger lifted her head from the nest of blankets on the rug beside the bed, tongue lolling over the red curls lying against her. Tanna backed out of the room without disturbing her. If Eve had been sleeping on floors as long as Tanna feared, a mattress and pillow might feel foreign and even uncomfortable to her. But the sight of this child, sleeping with a dog on the floor, in her house, broke her heart.

—

In the morning, as they walked to the fields after their tea, Tanna asked Holly if she'd seen where Eve had been sleeping. Holly shrugged and looked down at the trail, recognizing from her tone that an answer was not required. Tanna was working herself up to a speech about some fresh outrage over which she had been stewing.

"When this harvest is all over, I want that girl to learn to read," Tanna said, her chin lifted in an air of formal proclamation. "I want all the elven children, and Davis Gentry too, to come here to the house for school. They all need to learn to speak and read properly. What kind of future can they have otherwise?"

"Are you going to teach them?" Holly asked mildly.

Tanna pursed her lips at the slight emphasis on the word *you*. "I could. I considered becoming a teacher at one point. It was about the only career anybody ever allowed me to consider." Her shoulders sagged with resignation. "But no. I don't want to teach them myself. I can't. I don't have the time to devote to it. I might read to them or tell them stories once in a while. I was wondering if I could find a tutor in Treebridge or a nanny from one of the plantation families who might be willing to come here. I'm going to place an advertisement."

"Queen Ananjooee is not going to want the yolos to learn to read English." Holly knew the blunt statement would be taken as a challenge, but these kinds of conversations were exercises for Tanna. More than anything, she needed to debate and argue with someone.

"Why wouldn't she?" Tanna asked, her voice becoming shrill.

"Well, she still pretends not to speak English herself, even though I'd bet good money she could if she had to."

Tanna huffed. "Oh, she can at least understand what we're saying. I'm sure of that."

"You know you're going to have to ask her permission," Holly said with genuine regret.

"Again?" Tanna groaned. "Fine. She's their leader. I respect that. Mothers want their children to have it easier than they did. Ananjooee is the mother of all the Nunnahee. I'm sure she wants only a bright future for the children of her tribe. I will appeal to her maternal concern, as well as her authority. Surely she has to appreciate the gift of learning I'm offering to provide her people."

Holly smiled weakly. They had reached the fields and the end of the debate. Tanna had made up her mind.

—

The plan was to sell their first small crop in bulk to others who could distill it, refine it, and turn it into medicine and spirits. Then, they would take some of those profits, combine it with a part of Tanna's remaining dowry, and invest in building a factory and a distillery of their own. At that point they would also begin introducing a variety of medicinal plants and herbs, as dictated by the products they chose to make.

Before Tanna arrived in the Green, Buck had decided—without her permission or input—to plant their entire farm with enormous quantities of haint. Far more than they'd originally intended for their first season. He'd spent nearly all the money Tanna had given him on this one crop, this one experimental planting. They hadn't even known yet if haint could be grown in terraced beds on land as steep as Brynmor.

It was the proverbial basket with all the eggs in it. Tanna didn't need business experience to recognize this decision as less than wise, but of course she had a hidden quantity of money about which Buck knew nothing. Her impulse to secretly withhold half her dowry had been a strong intuition. So she could afford to give in to Buck's logic—simplify their actions; scale everything up in quantity. He swore it was a more straightforward plan. Haint was an easy plant to grow. Indigenous. Practically a weed. Gentry had been hired specifically because of his experience with farming haint in large quantities.

What Buck had failed to tell Tanna, but which she learned directly from Gentry much after the fact, was that growing a hillside in this terraced formation had been Gentry's creative adaptation, an experiment at Buck's insistence.

The Nunnahee did have a history with the plant, but they had traditionally been consumers—they distilled it, used it medicinally, made beverages from it, cooked with it. The Nunnahee were experts at using it; they had only a little bit of experience cultivating it in kitchen gardens. These small plots were typically in low-lying areas close to water sources and not necessarily near the hill dwellings and caves they used as their communal centers. The Nunnahee were almost as new to all this as Tanna.

Thankfully, the plants survived the growing season and flowered. The buds swelled into heavy, shiny, teardrop-shaped pods that opened overnight. The flowers were made up of white petals and nubby, yellow-domed centers. They resembled giant daisies, especially in color and composition, but their petals drooped down and away, hanging straight toward the ground more like echinacea, purple coneflowers. They reminded Tanna of women with tall, pointy heads; the petals were their lank wet hair hiding their faces.

The flowers had to be plucked by hand, pinched off one by one, and thrown over the shoulder into a basket. Children and males and the elderly, who normally did not work in the fields, were all conscripted to harvest the flowers. Tanna wondered bitterly if Buck would have pitched in alongside them, had he been here. She chuckled at the thought of him wearing a woven basket on his back, his balding pink head covered with one of those cloths the elves wore out in the sun. No, he would've watched from horseback. At least Gentry, even though an overseer, switched gears from grunting orders to supporting the workers in the field. He still scowled while he did so, but he maintained water stations, coordinated periodic meals throughout the day, orchestrated breaks, and insisted that everyone rest.

"You too," he said gruffly to Tanna.

"I'm not even tired yet," she said cheerfully.

"You will be. Gotta pace yourself. There's days of this yet to come. Your husband planted over six hundred acres of haint weed." By his tone, he clearly blamed Buck.

"Yes, and I don't expect he's going to come riding off the Big South Road at the last minute and grab a basket to help us," Tanna said.

"No," Gentry fumed, "and damn him."

Tanna raised her eyebrows in agreement.

—

Gentry was right. After thirty-six hours, even with frequent break periods and one six-hour sleep—which she took right there under the stars near the edge of the atzeenah trees—Tanna couldn't fathom that they were only a third of the way through the fields. None of the elves complained or showed any sign of stopping—she secretly feared they would all rise up in mutinous exhaustion at any moment, announce they were going home, and abandon her, Holly, Gentry, and Davis to finish on their own. She couldn't imagine they didn't feel at least half as tired as she did, and if so, they would all begin to slow down, making the subsequent remaining days stretch on, exponentially slower and slower until they crawled to a stop.

Gentry insisted the flowers would begin to wither and rot on their stalks on the fifth or sixth day, which was something they couldn't allow to happen. Once the petals turned brown at the edges, they were almost useless. The substance that made the flowers valuable for smoking or drinking lived in the wet white pulp of the petals. The tar that gave tarwater its name was a resin that oozed from the raised yellow center. Once the centers began to dry out, the flowers would only render a low-level poison with no known marketable or medicinal applications.

Timing was everything.

It was a race to make the most of this limited window. Tanna kept trying to remind herself of the financial reward of the harvest. Yes, it was a week of agony, but for a growing season's worth of assets that would materially support herself, the farm, and hundreds of these workers for, potentially, a few years.

This goal energized her. It drew her on, and her example brought the tribe along with her. That is, until midway through the harvest, when, during a break, she asked Gentry about the tallies he had made so far. Given the numbers of what was bagged and counted and weighed, she wondered what could be projected for the total once they were done.

Gentry stared at her, reluctant to speak. "I knew the yield was gonna be under. But it's worse that I thought."

"Under?" A cold numbness spread through her. It was the same sensation she'd experienced when the doctor had said the word *syphilis*. "What do you mean?"

"These plants have about half the surviving flowers of any I've ever seen before. You can tell just by looking across the fields. Looks like they've already been partially harvested, in some random way."

"The plants usually have more flowers than this?" The fear crept up her neck and clamped behind her jaw.

"Oh yeah," Gentry said, unmoved. "Twice as many. Maybe three times. Did seem like we were having to deadhead a lot. I didn't realize it was that much."

Tanna resisted the urge to grab him by the shoulders. "So this is half of what we should be getting?"

"Barely half. I hope it's half. Some of the profit may depend on potency. But of course, rumors of a particular strain, a farm's reputation, build over time. We don't have any reputation at this point. Even if this is the strongest stuff anybody's ever cultivated, we won't know it before we sell it."

"Do you think it could be," she grimaced, barely daring to hope, "stronger?"

Gentry shrugged. "There was some prediction that the higher elevation might yield fewer flowers, but with more concentration of resin. The theory was that the plants' essence wouldn't be as spread out and diluted through a bunch of blooms, or even lost in a lot of excess deadheading."

She was momentarily stunned by the way his usually gruff vocabulary would sometimes blossom with his knowledge of the flowers. She suspected that he was nowhere near as ignorant as he allowed people to think.

"The monks at Old Rath Abbey grow at a higher elevation than was originally believed possible." She found a spark of remaining hope. "Did this prove to be true with their crops? Are their flowers more potent?"

"They are. And our plants are the direct descendants of theirs. But, hold on now," Gentry raised his hands. "They *are* grown at a high elevation, but on a flat plateau with a stream dammed into a pond. Their fields are kinda like cattails around the shallows of an artificial lake up in the clouds. But nobody's grown on terraces like this, down the side of a dry hill."

"Dry? It rains here all the time," she argued, unwilling to give in to Gentry's defeatist outlook. "There were almost daily monsoons for weeks."

"Well, let's hope. Frankly, the rains are the only thing saving us at all, and that's not water we can control."

Tanna braced herself before she asked the final question. "What can we hope for—the best case—once this is all done?"

Gentry chewed his lip, looking out across the army of elves working the fields. Finally, he shrugged. "Half the projected yield. Tops."

She closed her eyes and sighed. "That's barely going to allow us to build the factory. The distillery is probably completely out of the question. Maybe at least a simple warehouse could be constructed out of these profits, no?"

"My advice is to take whatever little bit you have to work with and next time invest in irrigation."

"Irrigation? On a hill this size? The only dependable water source is all the way down there." She gestured helplessly at the sparkling silver ribbon of Wavy Creek at the bottom of her property.

"There are probably some springs coming up somewhere. Surely, with all these caves ... What else would've made them? The brownies ought to know. Their Queen might even allow us to build something from inside."

Tanna's head dropped back as if she were beseeching the gods. "Please, nothing more that depends on bowing and scraping in front of that queen. She may be terrifying to look at, but she's even more exhausting."

"Well, the bottom line is this. Every little one of these terraces is a potential long, skinny pond. If we can't dam the water or pump it out or pipe it through the brugh, then we at least have to catch the rains. And hope they keep coming."

"For now, don't say anything about this to anyone else. At least until we're done here."

—

And so she had to finish another day and night of grueling, backbreaking work, knowing that the best of their efforts would never come close to the minimum. It was disheartening, to say the least. She lay awake on the ground that night on her rough bedroll, cursing Buck and trying to think of solutions. She wished Jackson were there. He would have insights no one else could come close to providing. By the morning's first light she was also mad at him for his absence. She was possibly even more angry with Jackson than she was with Buck. She expected it of Buck. Jackson had spoiled her, showing up to save her more than once when she needed rescue. She had come to depend on his independent wisdom.

She thought of the lost auroculus. She wished she could look through it, scan the plants, and see in what direction she was meant to go. But, for all its magic, it was only a kind of physical compass, not a tool of divination.

36

After her fifth angry letter to the camp at the front in the Seaming, each one increasingly terse—the last one threatened that she would ride out, track down Daughtry's company again, and drag him back if she had to—Buck sent a reply that he was coming home.

He arrived at Brynmor alone.

"Where's Charlie?" Tanna had expected them both to return. She couldn't help but feel concerned something may have happened to the boy.

"Daughtry's bringing his men back from the front for Armistice. We're all technically on leave."

"My God, is it over?"

Buck's mouth twisted with a doubtful smirk. "The war at home—well, in Europe—has been over for a while."

"I heard," she said. Still had finally managed to bring a Nashville newspaper back from Treebridge, but that couldn't satisfy her need for word about Teddy. "But I'm not sure I see how that would affect the conflict here."

"It doesn't," Buck said, annoyed. "Daughtry and the rest of the colonists want to pretend the Allies winning the war at home somehow constitutes a win for them here. As if the Rippers were just the fairy horde in league with the Huns. Either way, right or wrong, over or not ... It's an excuse to have a big parade and throw a party."

—

The Eldridges were invited to a barbecue at Daughtry's following a Victory Day parade. Tanna planned to go in hopes of discussing her crops and making connections with potential buyers. Gentry had essentially told her that salesmanship was the only part of the equation she could still impact—and that was, thankfully, something at which she might even excel.

She didn't have to shame Buck into working for her. As soon as she mentioned her intentions, he begged her to let him in on it. He was only too happy to buy himself back into her good graces.

"Of course you have every right to despise me for not being here to help with the harvest," he said, his eyes woeful, his head tilted to the side from the weight of regret.

"Yes, I do," she said with a sweet smile. "But just so you understand, what I mostly despise you for is investing all my money without consulting me first."

He ignored her and plowed ahead with his pitch. "We need to make this half-sized harvest seem like it's worth twice the money. Shaking hands and drinking and bending ears. Now, you know a party is the one thing I'm good at."

She couldn't argue—glad-handing and manipulating people were his greatest skills. He was possibly a better salesman than anyone she'd ever encountered in her life. He was admittedly much better at it than she would ever be. And that, after all, was one of the reasons she'd chosen to marry him, in spite of all his less worthy characteristics.

"I promise you," he said, hands clasped together in a prayerful position like a little boy, "I can make it all up to you."

"All of what?"

"All of it."

She rolled her eyes and pursed her lips. "Your tie's crooked."

—

While driving to the festivities in Treebridge, they strategized a plan.

Given the Benedictine monks' reputation for growing smaller, more potent haint at Old Rath Abbey, Buck insisted they could easily start a rumor that their experiment as the first farm to produce the plants at a higher elevation *and* on terraced land had intensified the flowers' potency still further.

"How can we prove that?" Tanna asked. "We can't. For all we know the exact opposite could be true."

"We don't have to prove it." Buck looked at her sideways with a big, smug grin. "We just need everybody to believe it long enough for us to sell what we have."

"But once a few people get their hands on it and try it, if it's weak, then word will spread—and we won't be able to give the rest away. And that could be most of what we have. Which could wind up being half of nothing."

Buck shrugged nonchalantly. "So we won't let that happen. We'll keep this amazing, potent harvest under guard, night and day. Reluctant to do anything more than whisper about it. And then, after we've had time to let the word spread around a bit, we auction it. We'll incite a little bidding war. We'll sell it all at once. By the time it works its way through the market and into various products, the source may become diluted with other crops anyway."

Tanna shook her head tightly. "The truth is going to get out. People are going to come after us with pikes and pitchforks. That's exactly why we immigrated here. To get away from the mob that's inevitably going to murder you."

His tone turned patronizing. "That's not going to happen. How about this. We sell it all into the Gray. To the people who are paying us to come into the Green and send it back to them so they don't have to make that perilous journey. Wasn't that essentially our proposition from the beginning? Our customers are not shiny feral riffraff rolling around in dirty blankets on the floors of den houses. They're distributors back home in Tennessee, Kentucky, Georgia."

She turned sideways to confront him more vehemently. "How are we going to sell back home in Tennessee? Are you planning to go back there? Because I'm not ever going back there again if I can help it."

"No. Not us." He shook his head as if she were a silly child. "Ford, Tanna. My brother. He's our answer. And our shield."

"You'd let your own brother take the wrath of all the people conned into buying a weak product with an artificially inflated price? You'd sacrifice him to cover for our lies and mistakes?"

"Wouldn't you?" he muttered. "I thought you hated the bastard."

She crossed her arms and turned away to stare at the view passing outside the buggy. After a moment's consideration she said, "I'm not entirely sure Ford wouldn't kill you over this. He's been wanting to for years."

Buck chuckled. "Yes, and as you see, I'm still here. You let me handle Ford. You just start spreading the rumor. Work it into conversation subtly. Pretend you're real reluctant to talk about it. Like you're sitting on something exciting you're dying to tell, but you've promised me you won't. Tell them your husband will kill you if he finds out. Say you *think*. Say you're *hoping*. Be forthcoming that you're getting ahead of yourself, that you shouldn't be making predictions. The best lies are mostly true."

"Is this the secret tactic you've been using all these years?" she said under her breath.

He ignored the insult. "I'll go behind you, work my way through the crowd, and pick up the details with a few choice people—the right contacts to reach Ford."

"If you want me to drop hints only with certain people, then you'll need to tell me who."

He dismissed her concerns with a quick shake of the head. "No, we can't be that obvious. It'll be better if a few people I talk to happen to have only heard a whiff of the rumor, not necessarily from you, but from somebody you've spoken to. Give it all a little air of Chinese whispers." He looked away from the road, his expression softening. "Let me do this for you. For us. I owe you."

Tanna stared into the gate of a passing plantation. "You are nowhere close to being flush with me," she muttered.

—

A mile before the Big South Road ran onto the spine of Treebridge, there were so many people and elves in the street they couldn't pass. They had to abandon the buggy to a servant in Daughtry's livery and go ahead on foot. Tanna cursed the dancing slippers she'd worn and the hem of the gown she had to keep clear of the ground.

The atmosphere was a happy, drunken chaos. It was impossible to tell where the supposed parade began or ended. They were forced onto the boards of the sidewalk as Daughtry's company marched past in a loose, sloppy knot. Many of the men were dragged off into the crowd and could be seen kissing women they probably didn't even know. Charlie spotted them and came over briefly to shout something close to Buck's ear that she couldn't make out. The boy did wave at her sweetly and mouthed hello, and then he allowed the throng to carry him farther down the street.

"What did he say?" Tanna asked, straining to be heard over the noise of the crowd.

Buck pulled a face and waved it away. "Nothing. Let's get out of this madness and go to Daughtry's," he shouted.

—

When Tanna saw the Lady Glare holding court on Daughtry's terrace, she was glad she'd worn her ridiculous shimmering gown. With the slanting afternoon sunshine and the colored banks of clouds in the west, the fairy lady was luminous. Her shawl fluttered around her shoulders like the flashing silver undersides of leaves in a breeze. The material seemed to generate light of its own that sparked and twinkled in the lady's hair.

Tanna dropped the fistful of fabric she'd been carrying while she walked in the streets, hoping it would cover her ruined silk shoes. Her carefully styled coiffure felt like tree bark against her cheeks.

Upon arriving, they had to stand in a receiving line to speak with the lady. Buck abandoned her to hold their place, with the promise he would return bearing drinks for them both. But of course Tanna found herself alone in the face of Glare's alien beauty. The fae woman's golden eyes were unnerving and predatory. Her slow, gliding movements and relative stillness made Tanna feel all the more anxious the lady could strike unexpectedly. Feeling like a bird with a broken wing, Tanna curtsied awkwardly, murmured her thanks for the invitation, and fled the fairy's gaze as soon as she could.

She found her own glass of champagne from a passing waiter. She didn't expect Buck to return or seek her out anytime soon. They had always tended to separate after arriving at a party. This went back years before they were married. They arrived, divided, and made their individual conquests. On lucky occasions, Tanna found Buck in time to see he was safely returned wherever he needed to be. But she had also learned to allow for the opposite to be true, to not worry, and to not be disappointed or personally insulted when, at the end of the night, Buck was nowhere to be found. He usually discovered a way into some kind of trouble, in places where Tanna had no desire to follow.

As Buck had coached her, she did her best to subtly work the rumor of their potent harvest into conversation.

She found herself speaking to Rose Vaughn, the spinster daughter of one of the wealthiest plantation owners in the area and the only black family living in the colony of which Tanna knew. It was rumored that unmarried, thirty-year-old Rose ran her family business with carefully crafted letters, her father's wax seal, and her own iron will while the ancient patriarch sat on the veranda in a wheeled chair, drooling and unaware of his surroundings. Her mother had died when she was a child, and her only brother had been killed in a Ripper attack years ago.

Tanna mentioned she would like to find someone to teach her little elves to read.

"I think that's very admirable," Rose said, awkwardly holding a dripping pork rib between her thumb and forefinger, unsure of how to nibble it in public. "I know of a young missionary who might be perfect for the job."

The tarwater-spiked champagne and Rose's undivided attention inspired Tanna's self-importance. "I want my Nunnahee to have a future in the blended culture that's growing here. If that is to be the mark I can make on this world as a human woman, to honor the seaming of these two civilizations—"

Tanna was grabbed by the shoulder and spun around to face an intoxicated brute of a man, his whiskers awry and bristling on his red face. She tried to regain her dignity by dusting the droplets of spilled drink from the front of her gown, waiting for some ingratiating drunken apology. She smelled the sour rot of tarwater on his breath as he shoved his face even closer to hers.

She leaned back instinctively in response to the invasion of personal space just as he began to roar at her. "*Your* Nunnahee. *Your* genies. *Your* fucking goddamned brownies. You oughta hear yourself, talking like you think you're a fairy queen. You want to raise 'em up? Let 'em think they're like us? Shit. They never will be, no matter how hard you try. You raise them outside their station, they'll just face more disappointment and lack. No wonder they hate us."

He grabbed both her wrists in his paws. She tried to jerk free, shaking a warm slosh of champagne down her own arm. She was more furious than frightened, too angry to form coherent words. The man's thumbs were grinding the small bones of her hands together. She involuntarily cried out in pain and shock, and released her glass, which shattered on the floor.

It all happened within seconds. The musicians stopped playing, the horns winding down like they had been suddenly strangled. Two servants were assisting another man to pull the drunkard off Tanna.

Rose shouted the assailant's offenses in a loud, trembling voice so everyone assembled would know what had just happened.

Tanna followed the men as they dragged her attacker across the dance floor. She had found her breath, and now her words were threatening to erupt from her throat. She had just raised her fists to begin pummeling the man's back when she was suddenly embraced from behind. Her arms were pinned to her sides. She was lifted off her feet enough that her toes skimmed the floor as she was hauled back through the crowd.

Whoever it was deposited her on the dance floor with a jolt and released her. She couldn't fathom who would be so bold as to put his hands on her and physically restrain her, moving her about the room like an oversized doll. She felt doubly humiliated, ready to make this man the new target for her rage.

In the moment it took for her to regain her balance, someone cried out for the band to play on. She spun around to see who had seized her. She almost didn't recognize Jackson without his sweaty Stetson, his reddish hair dark and slick with pomade. Instead of his dusty khaki vest and mud-encrusted boots he wore an immaculate dark gray suit and a silk tie. He forced her hands into the starting position for a dance.

"Do me the honor, Mrs. Eldridge," he said, his expression serious. He steered her deeper into the crowd on the dance floor, holding her tight, despite how she squirmed and muttered through her clenched teeth for him to let her go.

She frantically scanned the room, looking for the man who had accosted her, but they had obviously removed him from the premises. "That bastard—" she spluttered, but could think of no clear words to further convey her emotions.

"—is gone," Jackson finished for her. "And now you are dancing with me. Isn't this better?"

She struggled again to free herself from the box step he was trying to move her through.

"Look at me," he said softly. And when she wouldn't, he shook her and repeated it as a gruff command. "Look. At. Me."

She froze in shock at the sight of his pale gray-green eyes so close to hers, probing her thoughts, diagnosing her.

"I see you," she said, barely more than a breath, as if she had only just accepted he was not an apparition.

"I'm here," he said in a gentler tone. His eyes softened and she relaxed into his arms, allowing him to lead her.

"You're dancing," she whispered, incredulous.

He couldn't help but chuckle at that. "I've finally managed to shock you."

"I'm just surprised. You said you couldn't." A bit of anger crept back into her tone, an old grievance. She was still in a state of mind to fight someone.

"Ah, now. I never said I *couldn't*," Jackson corrected her. "I said I didn't *care* much for dancing."

"But you're good at it," she said, glancing at his feet, as if for some visual verification that it was indeed his body carrying hers around the room.

"That doesn't mean I can't despise it if I don't want to," he said with a brittle smile.

"No one despises a thing and is skilled at it at the same time."

"That is most certainly not true. I can think of hundreds of examples."

"Name one," she challenged him, narrowing her eyes.

He gently snorted. "Shut up and enjoy this. It may never happen again."

"Very well," she said. "I will."

She only managed a few bars of music before her carefully composed expression melted with renewed fury. "That idiot! His position didn't even make sense. What was he accusing me of? Am I treating the poor elves like slaves or elevating brownie trash? Which is it?"

Jackson stopped dancing but ignored her question. "I need a fresh drink. You want one?"

It was the first time he had ever taken her by the hand in public. As he pulled her through the crowd, she was conscious of how possessive the action was. In a setting such as this, she knew they appeared to be a couple. Together. She saw a few critical sneers, from women in particular. She raised her chin and kept her eyes focused on the back of Jackson's head, suppressing the urge to grin like a fool.

Outside the ballroom, he stopped to take a pair of glasses from a passing tray. She reluctantly released his hand and wandered over to the spot on the veranda where the wall of the house made a corner with the waist-high stone railing overlooking the gorge. There was the tall birdcage of elaborate matchstick twigs filled with roosting finch owls. The tarwater in the champagne had started to affect her; she saw lights and tiny hovering forms in the air.

"This is the exact spot where I met Cole Mathers, the first night after I arrived," she said, turning to make sure he had followed her. Of course he had. "I had met you earlier that same day."

"I remember," he said, handing her a fresh glass.

"I thought you were standing on top of the trees."

"I was," he said, moving closer to her and taking a cigarette case from his jacket pocket. "I like to stand in the tops of trees whenever I can. It's not something you get to do every day."

He lit two cigarettes and offered one to her, as had become their habit when he was staying on the farm.

"How is Cole?" she asked. She had no expectations of good news.

His tight-lipped smile was mirthless. He looked at his cigarette and shook his head.

She exhaled smoke with a sigh. "How bad is it?"

"He's not long for this world."

"You don't think I should go see him?"

"No." He shook his head deliberately. "He definitely would not be in a frame of mind to receive visitors. I don't think Ioma would even let you in the door."

"We parted so abruptly, after such an ugly, unresolved incident." She winced from the pain of thinking about it. "I still regret it so much."

"You apologized." Jackson shrugged. "No real harm was done."

"I just want to see him smile at me again."

"That's what *you* need. It's not what he needs right now. Who knows if he even remembers your little trespassing incident? I highly doubt he's thinking about it."

"Couldn't I at least write him a letter? Would he get it? Could she read it to him?"

"If you can write the letter for yourself and can let him go without the expectation of a reply, then by all means, write it. It might give you some peace."

—

Buck had disappeared. Jackson looked around the veranda and the outside gardens while Tanna peeked in a few of the inside rooms where guests tended to congregate—the solarium, the billiards room, the conversation alcoves. She stopped at knocking on guest bedroom doors. She and Buck had made arrangements beforehand. If they were separated, they would wait for one another at the Daughtrys' carriage house from two to three a.m. and drive back to Brynmor together.

It was half-past midnight.

Jackson suggested they go for a walk around the city to kill a little time before he escorted her to the rendezvous point. She was reminded again of the night she met Cole, how he had walked her back to The Fairchild.

"Did I ever tell you I was cursed?" Tanna asked. "It's true. The day I arrived. Less than an hour after I stepped off the dirigible."

She recounted the story of the Alleegee barkeep in the members lounge at The Fairchild as they wandered through one of Treebridge's large interior promenades. It was strangely quiet. The energy of the street party had burned loud and long, but the festivities had started early, and by this hour the revelers were probably all sleeping off their drink.

"When I think about some of the things that have happened to me here, not to mention the size of my harvest, it does make me wonder about that curse." She realized she was thinking out loud, carelessly so.

"But I hear your crop is remarkably potent." Jackson was looking at her sideways.

"And where did you hear that?" she asked, trying to make the question playful.

He shrugged with his hands in his pockets. "Different people talking about it, here and there."

There was an awkward heartbeat of silence as she tried to think of a way to change the subject.

"What do you make of all this, anyway?" she asked, gesturing at the trash in the street, the few drunken stragglers still out and about. Strangers made the hand sign of V for *victory* when they passed each other.

"I don't think it has anything much to do with the conflict going on here in the Seaming. I think Daughtry and his gang want to conflate the two wars, as if they can borrow the sheen of military victory for themselves. It's entirely political and frankly ridiculous. And it won't mean a damned thing to the creatures they truly need to affect."

"You don't think it might at least intimidate the Unseelie? Make the Rippers question our superior military abilities?"

Jackson gave a gruff, cheerless laugh. "This conflict over the Seaming has been going on for centuries. It's only growing as the population of human immigrants increases. The colony's military capabilities are virtually irrelevant here. This is a holy conflict for the Rippers. The fae fight with magic. They believe that true victory will be a magical victory."

Her expression betrayed her dread. "What exactly would a magical victory for the Rippers look like?"

"The crossings in the Seaming closed forever. No traffic between this world and the Gray. No more portals leaking humanity's poison into this paradise." His tone and expression were grim. "We were thrown out of Eden, and it was left to them. We were never meant to be allowed back in."

They took one of the tunnels up to the spine of Treebridge. The amber glow of the lights embedded in the curved vault overhead leeched all color from their skin and hair.

"I want to ask you something," Tanna said. "I hope it won't sound rude, but—how have you managed to stay out of this war?"

He was quick to answer. "I've never taken sides. No one can accuse me of advancing either cause. I'm on the side of the Green. Of the land itself. My cause is simply to be here, to be a part of this world."

"Then you're a defender of the Seaming, of keeping the gateways open to humans who love the Green?" She felt him bristle as she said it, but she hated the way he silenced her when they debated. If she disagreed with him, he ended their conversations with arrogant proclamations. This time, she felt her position was sound. "Seems like one could argue that you share the position of the colonists."

"I don't believe in *colonizing* this world." He made it sound disgusting. "Yes, I want the option to be here. But I'm not interested in exporting cash crops back to the States. I'm certainly not interested in defending the men who make money from those endeavors. I'm not exactly worried about whether or not their little Old South plantation society crumbles."

Tanna felt her face heat up as if she had been struck. "I had no idea how you truly felt about me and my business."

"It's not about you," he said defensively. "It was my opinion long before you came and purchased Brynmor."

"You stayed at Brynmor for weeks," she said. "You never told me you felt this way."

"You never asked," he said in that emotionless, blunt manner he employed in lieu of shouting.

She was always the most easily wounded by his simplest comments. "So, you don't support me, then. You don't think I have a right to farm Brynmor."

He sighed and stared straight ahead. "It's complicated."

"I paid for that land." She jumped when her voice echoed in the tunnel.

"Does that make it yours? The Nunnahee have lived on your farm for centuries. Possibly millennia. If it belongs to anyone, how is it not theirs? Did you even buy it from them?"

"I pay my elves good wages. I share my land with them. I don't interfere with the workings of the brugh. And I stick my neck out to defend them from the ignorance and bigotry of other colonists."

"But you *are* a colonist, Tanna. You paid another white human American for land that was taken from the Nunnahee. Annexed. It's just like what we did to the Indians for the last few hundred years. Plant your flag. Put the little brown people to work. And if any of them get in your way, shoot them."

She struggled not to cry in front of him. "That isn't fair."

They emerged onto the road along the top of Treebridge. The wind of the gorge passing over the Tree was powerful enough to blow them over. They braced themselves on the sidewalk in a flood of moonlight.

"You're only offended because you feel guilty," Jackson said.

His voice was cold and his eyes were lost in pits of dark shadow. She wondered who this stranger was, standing here in a nice suit, pretending to be the man who'd walked miles with her around her property, looking at the night sky.

She shook her head in wonder. "You're a pious, pompous ... *ass*."

—

As she stalked away, she heard Jackson feebly calling her name. His tone sounded more like he was annoyed with her than conciliatory, and it only made her walk faster. She sped right past Daughtry's carriage house, where she was supposed to meet Buck, but it wasn't far enough away from Jackson. She kept going. She was angry enough to walk to Brynmor on foot, even if it took her all night and most of the next day.

A half-hour later, still marching in those ruined slippers along the shoulder of the Big South Road, she heard the sound of approaching hooves and a driver reining in horses. Buck must have showed up at the carriage house soon after she had left. Jackson had probably still been standing there. It infuriated her to think they had spoken and that Jackson had sent her husband after her.

Buck smiled at her drunkenly, swaying on the buggy seat. He didn't even attempt to get down and help her up. She grabbed the rail with one hand, clutched the hem of her gown in the other fist, and climbed aboard. Too late, eyes crossed with inebriation, he offered a hand to her. She batted it away.

She settled herself with a huff and looked straight ahead. She could feel Buck staring at her.

"What's wrong with you?" he asked.

"Drive," she said, her voice low with ice and suppressed rage.

"What did I do?" Buck whined like a petulant child.

"Just drive."

She felt a lump in her seat, and thinking she had sat on the bulk of her dress material, she dug beneath her thigh to free it.

Her hand came away with a woman's brassiere.

She held it out in front of her, pinched between two fingers. It was gaudy with cream lace and tiny pink satin bows.

"Someone has left her underthings in our buggy," she said.

Buck said nothing. Even when she turned to look at him, he didn't answer. He was intently focused on the road, but the tops of his ears were bright red.

"Having become familiar with the sight of Charlie's dirty clothes all over my house, I seriously doubt this belongs to him. Or any of your other boys." She forced a laugh and shook her head as if amused at this final mark on a terrible evening. Deep down, she felt a little breathless. It would have disturbed her far less to find she was sitting on Charlie's underthings—on any man's underthings, really. The thought of Buck here in the buggy, late at night, intoxicated, driving around with a woman he'd met at the party ...

She found herself profoundly ill-equipped and unprepared to navigate the events of the last hour of her life.

Buck didn't speak at all the entire two-hour drive along the dark road. All the plantations had an abandoned look at this hour. Their owners had no doubt attended one of the many balls in Treebridge and were staying in their second homes in town.

They finally turned off at the familiar stone gate. It seemed to take forever to climb the spiral around Brynmor. As they broke through the atzeenah trees at the top on the last straight leg of the drive, Buck was finally ready to tell the story he must have been rehearsing in his head this whole time. "Look, Tanna—" he began.

"No," she said softly.

"I just want you to know that this is separate from—"

"No," she repeated. "I don't want to hear it. I don't need to hear anything you have to say."

"If you'll just let me—"

"I want you to leave. Immediately. You have a room at the club. Or maybe you can ask one of your lovers to take you in. I don't really care. I want you gone. Sleep a while first. Take some time when you wake up to gather your things so that you won't need to come back anytime soon. I plan to sleep late, and I'll have breakfast in my room. I would rather not run into you tomorrow morning. Please, be gone from my house before I lay eyes on you again."

Still was there at the side of the buggy with a box step and a lantern. She steadied herself on his arm and climbed down more gracefully than she would have imagined herself capable. "Thank you, Still," she said, looking him in the eyes. There was just a glimmer more expression than he normally offered, a slight narrowing of the eyes. An unspoken conversation passed between them. She nodded her head almost imperceptibly to let him know she was all right, that she had everything under control.

Buck was calling her name in exasperation as she walked up the steps onto the veranda. It was not unlike the annoyed tone with which Jackson had tried to call her back.

She ignored him too.

37

Holly said the circular symbol burned into the posts of the new warehouse was definitely the Rippers' mark.

Tanna had ordered the dried haint plants to be stuffed in burlap sacks and stored in the foundation of the new structure. It was little more than an abandoned construction site, but the completed foundation, laid out in four-foot brick walls, made an enormous box on the ground, twenty-five by seventy-five feet. The harvest was additionally protected from the elements by canvas tarps stretched across the plane of the future warehouse floor.

She had not seen nor heard from Buck, but she reluctantly continued implementing the plan they had devised together. She would sit on the harvest as long as she could, as rumor of a potent new Brynmor variety worked its way through the haint market. She hoped a bidding war between brokers and distilleries would inflate the price enough to offset her relatively small quantity.

The site of the warehouse was a vulnerability. They had chosen a level hump of ground on the back southeastern slope of the hill near the Big South Road. One day, wagons would be able to go around Brynmor and reach the warehouse by its own drive. A future distillery could also be placed in the same vicinity, with close access to the east branch of the Wavy Creek. This would keep the bulk of their working enterprise on the backside of the property, behind the hill at the base of the southern terraces and beneath the house.

It was an ambitious, expensive plan, currently stalled awaiting the sale of the first harvest.

Tanna looked down at the brown sack lumps stuffed in the foundation of the warehouse like an ugly old mattress. She wondered how many of the elves would even be able to conceive how much money those lumps represented. It was a treasure, wrapped in cloth, lying on the ground a quarter mile from the house. But there was nowhere else to keep it all.

And she had to entrust it to her elves.

She ordered the warehouse site to be guarded day and night in rotating shifts. From the fields and the kitchen garden path, she saw the silhouettes of the Nunnahee youth, "warriors" in their culture, posturing with spears, stalking back and forth across the foundation wall between the skeletal framing timbers.

It all looked incredibly fragile to her. Time and time again she realized she was holding her breath. She had to remember to breathe.

Now, she stood on the site while Holly pointed out the blackened lines on the wood and compared them to similar signs she had seen along the Seaming. Ginger enthusiastically snuffled the walls, clearly finding something that excited her but unable to communicate the details of her canine investigation.

The young Nunnahee who were employed as guards stood in a line in front of her, silently awaiting her judgment. Still translated her words for them, but she needed no assistance in understanding their shaking heads and softly spoken, vehement denials.

"They say they never fell asleep, so'onah," Still said. "They never left their post. They say the marks appeared by magic."

"Magic," Gentry grumbled. "It's more likely a prank is what it is. Somebody wanting it to look like it was Rippers. Why would they stop at a few singed posts when there's all this to destroy? Doesn't their magic usually blow things up?"

Tanna ran her hand along the marked post. "They didn't really even damage the wood. Is this the only one?"

"There're four down here," Holly said, pointing. "One where each wall's gonna go. And then a few at the main gate to the fields, on both sides of the post."

"Going into the terraces from down here?" Tanna asked.

Holly shook her head. "No. Up at the top, right behind the kitchen. The path from the garden to the first level of terraces."

Tanna frowned. "That's way too close to the house. Whoever did it obviously meant to be intimidating. But Gentry's right about one thing. Why would they stop at this minor vandalism when the remainder of our entire harvest is lying right here in front of them? You counted the sacks?"

"It's all here," Gentry said.

Tanna sighed. "Then the message seems to be *We could have taken it all if we wanted to.* So why wait? How do they expect us to respond?" She turned to Still. "Is this some complexity of tribal politics? Am I supposed to placate them with some ritual act of submission?"

"You can't give in to these bullies," Gentry growled.

"Oh, I have no intention of giving in to them," Tanna said. "I'm just thinking out loud. I wonder what they think *giving in* is supposed to be. That I stop building the warehouse?"

"But then what about the gate to the fields?" Holly asked.

"That I abandon the entire enterprise of growing this crop? I know it offends some of the fae. What exactly do they hope to bully us into doing?"

Gentry spat in the dirt and pointed at the elves. "It's some of these little brownies right here playing a trick on you."

Tanna turned to glare at him. "I don't like the term *brownies*, Carl. I don't want you calling any of our Nunnahee that."

He crossed his arms and stared back.

"I trust them," Tanna said, slowly making eye contact with each one of the elves as Still translated. "From now on, two guards at all times, around the clock. Are we clear?"

They all nodded gravely.

Gentry sighed loudly behind her.

—

Just before Christmas, letters began arriving from First National Bank in Nashville, one of the financial institutions that kept a secret office in Treebridge. Buck had taken out loans against the farm about which she had not known. This was in addition to the mortgage granted him by the Chattanooga Savings Bank, papers she had discovered in her desk not long after arriving back in the Green. But of course, at the time, with Charlie, Jackson, and Holly all staying as guests, Buck was able to avoid the kind of detailed arguments that Tanna wanted to have about their finances.

She kept the dwindling secret remainder of her dowry in a hollow leather box cleverly disguised as a copy of Milton's *Paradise Lost*. She counted the bills again, as she often did when she was alone. She knew the exact amount, but handling the bills had become a kind of financial prayer ritual, like saying the rosary. She peeled away a few of the precious, large-denomination notes and slid them into her purse.

She didn't want Buck in the house for any reason. She sent a short, nonthreatening letter to him announcing her intentions to meet with a Mr. Sterling at the First National Bank office in Treebridge. She told him the day and time, how she intended to do the talking in renegotiating the terms of the loan, but that she anticipated it might be a good opportunity for Buck to obtain some cash if he could use it. She knew he needed money. She could feel him out there wringing his hands, wondering how long he had to stay banished before he could reasonably approach her for an allowance.

She also knew that without the enticement of a payout, Buck would never show his face, especially with a person to whom he owed money in the same room. The realist in her worried that, as a wife, she would require at least Buck's presence, if not his signature, to get what she needed.

—

Leaving Ginger and Eve in Holly's care for the day, she asked Still to drive her to Treebridge and wait for her while she took care of some business. He gave her a faint frown when she climbed onto the bench beside him, but she wanted to talk through her money troubles and the strategy she hoped to employ. She had no idea how much understanding of human money Still commanded, but he usually surprised her by continuing to be the wisest person she knew. If nothing else, with no personal will to have his own opinions expressed, he was always a good listener.

After an hour of driving past plantation gates she had expressed all her worries, and now she waited expectantly for Still's response.

"Has Mr. Eldridge sold your haint flowers to his brother?" he asked.

"I don't even know. Messages take so long to get back and forth across the Seaming. I have no idea if Ford has received word yet or if the deal Buck proposed is even a possibility."

"Your best hope is for Mr. Eldridge to cheat his own brother?" She felt her cheeks heat up as the accusation hung in the air between them. Everything Still said sounded a bit like a judgment.

"I wonder if you'd say that if you knew Ford Eldridge," Tanna muttered.

Still looked over at her. She met his eyes with full vulnerability, her brow anxiously furrowed.

"That is a dirty cloak to ask hope to wear," he said.

—

Tanna was shown into an office by a pert human woman and left sitting alone before the desk, waiting for the bank manager to appear. She smoothed her skirt against her legs and patted her fashionable cloche hat. She turned at the squeak of the doorknob, stretching a winning smile across her face.

Buck bustled into the room, well-dressed in a navy suit but looking hurried. He smelled strongly of cedar aftershave, with fresh pomade in his wet hair. He was breathing hard, his cheeks bright red.

"I thought I was going to be late," he mumbled. He pressed his temple against hers and made a loud kissing noise before she could think to resist the gesture. He plopped into the chair beside her, crossed his legs, and smiled. "How are you, my dear?"

Her smile had fallen. She stared at him with a slightly arched eyebrow. "Have you heard anything from Ford?"

"Have you?" he asked, looking hopeful and excited. "Did a letter come for me at the house?"

"No. The only letters I've received for you are the threats I have right here," she said, patting her purse. She lowered her voice and leaned close to him. "The only haint brokers I've spoken to practically laughed in my face when I quoted the price you suggested."

"Let them stew on it a while," Buck said, waving his hand in his characteristic, seemingly unworried and dismissive manner. "The rumor of the superior potency of our crop is out there, working its way through the local market. Just give them a little time. Stand firm, I say."

"Gentry says they aren't bluffing. The market is flooded with supply this season. In the last few years, several other plantations around Treebridge have introduced haint crops. We're not the only ones, yet here we are asking twice the going rate when the price has fallen to half."

"But the potency," Buck insisted, holding up a finger as if she were a child, "don't forget that."

"The potency is a lie," she whispered through clenched teeth. "We'll be lucky if we don't have to pay someone to haul our crop away for us."

"I still have faith," Buck said.

"Because you're an idiot," Tanna spat. She turned away from him and faced the bank manager's desk, trying to breathe deeply and compose herself.

The bank manager burst through the door, apologizing for making them wait. Buck stood and shook hands with him warmly.

"Mrs. Eldridge," he said, softly pinching the ends of her fingers. "Hal Sterling. Pleased to meet you."

He sat behind his desk, leaned back in his chair, and spent the next several minutes gossiping with Buck about their mutual acquaintances and talk of a future hunting excursion.

It was as if Tanna weren't in the room.

She dug the notice letters from her purse, unfolded them, stood, and placed them in front of Sterling with a snap. He jumped as if she were an apparition that had suddenly appeared in his office. He took up the stack of papers with a bewildered expression, plucked a pair of spectacles from his breast pocket, and made a show of reading through the letters.

He nervously and briefly glanced at Tanna and then looked up at Buck. "Do you wish to make a payment ...?"

Buck gaped like a fish and gestured helplessly at Tanna.

"As I have only just been made aware of these debts," Tanna said, "I would love to hear your suggestions on how the payment schedule may be extended."

Buck quietly studied his nails.

"Oh!" Sterling cried, covering his discomfort with feigned surprise. "Well, I'm not entirely familiar with the details of your loan, offhand. So many of these letters are prepared by my clerks, you see. My secretary sets a stack before me each afternoon and orders me to sign them before she'll let me leave for the day." He winked at Buck. "My wife employs a similar tactic at home with the checkbook."

"We just sign what the ladies tell us to and don't ask questions," Buck said, chuckling.

Tanna glared at him until he fell quiet. "I'm afraid there has been a simple oversight in communications with my husband regarding our ledgers."

"I see," Sterling said, squirming in his seat. "I'm sure we can come to some amended agreement. Did you have specific new terms in mind?" He looked to Buck briefly but slid his gaze back to Tanna.

"I do," she said. "Here's what I'd like to propose."

—

Buck held the door for Tanna as they exited the bank manager's office. Once out in the hall, he gave a low whistle.

"Bravo, my dear," he whispered, elbowing her playfully. "You had the poor little man sweating. He was pulling out his handkerchief as we left. You were fantastic!"

"I don't know what good it's going to do us in the end," Tanna muttered, annoyed. "I bought us some time, but it will run out."

"We'll sell before then," Buck said.

"Oh yes. We will definitely sell before then because I'm going back to the brokers and telling them I will accept the same market value they're offering all the other farmers."

"But you're throwing away our only chance to make enough to go forward!" Buck's voice rose in a rare tone of true frustration.

"I can't believe you actually have the gall to be angry with me," she hissed. "And to be clear, *we're* not moving forward. *I'm* moving forward. And having rumors out there that I lied about the quality of my crop is hardly setting up foundations for future business relationships."

"You're not going to last the year with the amount of money you're talking about."

"It's not your concern anymore." She held out the bank notes she'd allotted for him.

He stared at the money, smiling and slowly shaking his head as if insulted by the gesture.

"Take it." She bit off the words, shoving the money beneath his nose.

He snatched it out of her hand. She was sure he had some difficulty resisting the urge to count it on the spot. She turned to leave.

"Hey." Buck grabbed her upper arm. "That harvest doesn't even cover the loans we just renegotiated. You do realize that, don't you? They can take our entire farm."

She jerked her arm away from him. "It's not *our* farm," she said. "It has always been *my* farm."

—

Tanna had promised to meet Rose Vaughn for lunch at a café called The Purple Garden, a tiny balcony clinging to the western side of the Tree, with small carved tables nestled between potted Japanese maples and a renowned view of the Chickamauga Gorge at sunset.

They were chatting pleasantly over coffee toward the end of their meal when Buck appeared, escorting a woman. Tanna recognized her as Cookie Blevins. Cookie was shorter than Buck, lending him a favorable illusion of height. She wore an oversized turban of dark peacock-blue with a ridiculously large feather that gave the impression her head was being consumed by an enormous sapphire cherry with the stem attached. Her oversized cape enclosed her in a split pea pod of quilted silk. She was such a small person that all her clothes seemed to be in the process of swallowing her. Tanna couldn't help but recall the elaborate saccharine ribbons on the brassiere she'd found in the buggy after the Armistice party. Cookie was a woman whose style choices smothered her on every level.

The maître d' led the couple across the balcony to an empty table not far from Tanna and Rose, close enough to see that Cookie Blevins's face was painted like a stage performer. Cookie wasn't at all naturally beautiful. Tanna wasn't sure whether this thrilled her or offended her by association.

Buck held a chair out for Cookie so she would be sitting with her back to Tanna. He leaned over to speak something softly in her ear.

"He's coming over to our table," Tanna whispered. "I enjoyed our lunch. Please forgive my quick exit."

Rose murmured her understanding before politely greeting Buck.

"Ms. Vaughn. Tanna." Buck's normally quick smile seemed a bit forced and frozen.

"Twice in one day," Tanna said. "What have I done to deserve this?" She drained her last sip of coffee and stood, too quickly for Buck to assist her with his showy chivalry. "But I do appreciate your gracious decision not to introduce us."

Buck glanced uncomfortably at Cookie, who was trying to look over her shoulder without seeming to do so, her face locked in a self-conscious pout of nonchalance.

"I thought it rude not to at least come over and say hello," Buck explained helplessly.

"How thoughtful of you, Buck," Tanna said, mocking him. "It's never too late to improve oneself."

With an air kiss near Rose's cheek, Tanna turned and stalked from the room, purposefully sweeping by Cookie without seeing her.

Tanna was moving so quickly she almost ran into a young man hovering on the interior promenade in front of the café. His familiar voice stopped her.

"I guess you've heard he's with that woman now," Charlie Fairchild said.

"Charlie," she said. "How are you?" Caught by surprise, it was the only thing she could think to say.

He was visibly agitated, shifting his weight from one foot to the other. "He's planning on marrying her, you know."

"Why are you here?" she asked, her tone more weary than cold. "Are you following them?"

He glared past her. "At least with me, you could have stayed married to him."

Tanna laughed, a single, short bark of sarcasm. "Do you think being married to him is an advantage?"

He frowned at her. "If it's not, then why do you continue?"

She had no intentions of engaging him, but she did pity him.

"Charlie, don't you have parents somewhere wondering where you are?" She hoped her sincere concern for him was evident. "Go home."

38

The schoolhouse was little more than an open-air version of one of the Nunnahee's typical aboveground huts. It had a dirt floor with no walls and slender, still-living sapling posts planted at the corners, supporting a topis vine that made a roof of broad, leather-hard green leaves and yellow flowers. The only real expense, other than the salary of the missionary she'd hired to teach, was the slate blackboard standing on its stout wooden legs.

Tanna passed the school on her way to and from the fields each day. It was built along the kitchen garden path, near the gate to the terraces, and connected to the trail winding across the knoll from the Nunnahee village and the brugh beyond the blue trees.

Holly had been right about her needing Queen Ananjooee's blessing. Still had accompanied her on another formal reception in the dim cave. The elven queen had ranted and stomped around, circling Tanna in her predatory fashion. She felt certain this time her request would be denied. Still spoke at length to the queen, surely beyond translating Tanna's words. The queen kept holding her hand at an invisible point above the floor, about the height of Tanna's knee. She was sure Still was negotiating the best-possible outcome on her behalf in this battle of wills.

Eventually, they were bowing and scraping as the queen's light descended back into her inner lair. Once outside in the sunshine, Still informed Tanna that the knee-high measurement meant no Nunnahee children taller than that could attend the school. So only the yolos, the littlest of the elves, were allowed to attend, the ones not old enough to work the fields or serve their queen. But this was what Tanna had wanted all along.

One afternoon, as she walked up through the terraces from a meeting with Gentry down at the warehouse construction site, she heard the strains of a melody. She walked closer to the schoolhouse, thinking she had caught the singsong rhyming lessons of Mr. Palmer, the young missionary. He couldn't restrain himself from leading them in children's hymns, though he assured Tanna it was in the service of teaching them to read. He was a fresh-faced, naïve do-gooder from Sand Mountain, Georgia, who had only been in the Green for a year and had spent all his time tutoring Rose Vaughn's niece at her family plantation.

He was a teetotaler when it came to alcohol or tarwater. He'd probably never seen half the fairies in his midst, other than the elves who worked the farms. He slept in a nearby tent, didn't ask for much salary, and was at least enthusiastic about his work.

Tanna crept close without interrupting. Eve's orange head was a bright spot in a small crowd of yolos and their various animal familiars. Winged things circled the air above the schoolroom; birds roosted in the branches of the roof. A pretty lavender creature called a velvet swam through the tall grass with its undulating, ferret-like movements.

The yolos were chanting the letters of the alphabet as Mr. Palmer pointed to the characters scratched on the blackboard. It was nothing like the music she thought she'd heard ...

Then, there it was again. This time, the unmistakable call of a clarinet carried over the lawn from the house. A mournful, familiar melody. One she'd often heard Jackson humming to himself.

She turned and hurried toward the house, following the sound.

The music had a strange tinny quality, as if a tiny orchestra were playing inside the hollow of a tree. She was running by the time she reached the side veranda, where the sound of the music originated. There she found a form slumped in one of the rattan deck chairs.

Jackson had fallen asleep beside an impressive Victrola with *The Portrait of a Lady* open across his chest. The music attracted winged fairies who swooped through the shafts of sunlight above the aucuba bushes. A swarm of sylphs shifted back and forth across the wooden porch railing, like a swaying figure composed of tiny moths dancing along to the tune.

The record on the Victrola came to its end and began to click repetitively. Tanna tiptoed over to it, lifted the needle, and used her hand to stop the disc from spinning. Mozart's *Concerto for Clarinet and Orchestra in A*. The intrusive quiet, combined with her presence, shattered the fluttering, tornado-shaped funnel of the swarm. The sylphs scattered, disappearing into the trees.

She glanced over to see if the sudden silence had wakened Jackson, but he was still lightly snoring. She dragged a matching chair over close to him and sat down upon it, taking the moment to study his face in a way she'd never had the opportunity to before. It was clear from the deep brownish-red of the skin on his forehead and the white tone of the hair on his arms that he had just returned from weeks in the wilderness. His boots were caked with their usual hide of mud. There was a faint reek of sweat when a breeze came through the veranda.

He finally stirred. Barely opening his eyes, he looked at her, and then closed them again, shifting position in the chair. "That's an apology," he murmured.

She tried to remember the details of the argument they'd had on Victory Day, before she'd stormed off on foot along the road. "The gramophone? It's lovely."

"Hmm," he nodded, still not fully opening his eyes. "We're taking it on safari."

—

Tanna ordered Joona to fill a bath for Jackson in the guest bedroom while she worked in the kitchen alongside Navvee to throw together a supper worthy of their reunion. She screamed Holly's name out the kitchen door until the girl finally appeared, with Ginger in tow. Tanna asked her to fetch Eve from the schoolhouse when Mr. Palmer finished his lesson.

"Navvee will have some dinner for both of you, but I want you to eat it in your room. I have an unexpected dinner guest."

"Who is it?" Holly asked in her usual blunt way.

Tanna rolled her eyes at the girl's lack of tact, but didn't want to waste the time and energy on an etiquette lecture. "It's Jackson."

Holly's face lit up. "I want to see Jackson."

"I'm sure he'll be spending the night," Tanna said.

"I really need to tell him something," Holly whined.

"Well, you can talk to him tomorrow. Tonight, just keep Eve occupied."

Holly left, sulking, her shoulders rounded.

Tanna was setting the table when Jackson emerged in a fresh shirt, looking boyish, his red hair dark and bristly with damp, his skin shiny and scrubbed.

"My boots are a disaster," he apologized, pointing down at his bare feet.

She smiled and waved away any concerns about his appearance. But she realized with some horror she was sweating like a field hand, wearing a stained kitchen apron, and the hasty twist she'd employed to get her hair off her neck was coming apart in a fair impression of Medusa herself.

She told him to help himself to a whiskey and dashed to her room to change. She wondered for half a second if she should change into a dress, but she knew it would seem false. She opted for a clean pair of riding pants, but changed her workman's shirt for a more feminine white linen blouse. She groaned in frustration when she caught a glimpse of herself in the looking glass.

She found Jackson pacing the dining room, sipping whiskey and smoking. She could tell by the set of his shoulders and his restless movement that he was uncomfortable.

"I hope it's OK, my showing up unannounced like this," he said. "I was coming up the Big South Road, and going right by ..." He trailed off.

"Of course you stopped," Tanna said brightly. "I'm happy you did."

"I realize I made an arrangement with Buck. At the time, I was trying to stay away from the orchard as much as possible to avoid disturbing Cole. At least, not sleeping there in the house. Buck had invited me to bring some things here before I left on safari. Of course, that was right when you returned. It had all been discussed and decided when you were away in Chattanooga. I'd certainly anticipated returning here to Brynmor at some point. But when I came back into Treebridge for Victory Day, it made more sense to just stay in my room at the club." He paused, looking a bit tortured. She had never known him to apologize or struggle this much to explain himself. "Of course, then you and I argued. Now, Buck's not even here. So I suppose I should give you the opportunity to, you know, rescind his offer of hospitality. You're not obligated to honor his invitation to me."

Tanna grabbed a glass and the whiskey bottle off the sideboard and poured herself a drink. "You mean, kick you out?" she asked.

"If you feel my showing up like this or my being here is ... inappropriate."

She was genuinely surprised he would suggest it. "Is it inappropriate?"

He shrugged helplessly, his spiky damp hair lending him a comical aspect. "I honestly don't have the ability to apply conventional standards to anything anymore."

"What standards do you use?"

He gave her a lopsided smile. "My own."

"Maybe it's time I tried *your* standards," she said, attempting again to lighten the conversation.

"No." The word was too blunt; it sank the mood in the room. He frowned as if it pained him and shook his head. "I don't ever want to encourage you to use anyone else's standards, including mine. But I do believe you should discover your own."

His unwillingness to back out of the heavy, philosophical nature of his statements, or his inability to recognize the social cue of her playful, bantering tone, left her standing speechless and uncomfortable in the middle of the room.

She took a large swallow and stared at the brown liquor in her glass. "I'm not sure what my own rules are anymore. Or what they should be, now that I've asked Buck to leave."

"*Rules*," he muttered, looking away from her.

She chuckled. "God, you hate that word, don't you?"

He rolled his eyes but declined to comment.

"How about another word, then?" Tanna said, matching his serious tone at last. "Why don't we call them ... boundaries?"

He nodded, considering it an improvement, at least. "What about just ... wisdom? Or discernment? Personal desire."

She raised her eyebrows. "That's two words."

"Fine." Jackson looked her in the eyes. He held her gaze now, until she felt her cheeks grow warm. "But what happens if you replace the word *rules* with *desires*?"

Tanna allowed the question to linger in the air. What were her desires now? She smirked as if her silence were intentional, but she really couldn't think of any way to answer him. She was also a little afraid her voice might break if she tried to speak.

Fortunately, at that moment, Joona came bumbling in with a tray, and she quickly found some words to critique his clumsy service.

Ravenous from weeks out in the Green, Jackson sat down and consumed everything Joona put in front of him in silence. Tanna watched him eat.

—

Jackson stayed on at Brynmor. He never formally asked and she never formally invited him, but one night became another, and soon it was approaching a week.

With Buck and Charlie no longer in the house, they had taken to extending their after-dinner smokes on the veranda and their walks around the farm. But it was winter now, so they settled down in front of the fire for hours with whiskey or tarwater and cigarettes.

Occasionally Holly drifted through. At times, she seemed to want to say something, but when Tanna would prompt her to speak, she became shy, shook her head, and soon after disappeared when they weren't paying attention. The girl was company when Tanna required it, but her greatest quality was her independence. Compared to every other woman with whom Tanna had been friends, this was atypical. It took her some time to trust that Holly's silence and her retreats into her room did not constitute sulking. Her disappearances were not a response to having been offended in any way.

Jackson was like this too—unflappable and free of the usual social anxieties.

It was difficult for Tanna to release her impulse to worry. It was like sharing her home with a couple of cats. In many ways, it cost nothing. And the benefits, although different from the norm, were plentiful and mostly positive. She was far from being able to emulate either of them, but after some consideration she concluded they were both superior to her in some way. They were comfortable in their own bodies. They did not need to become some other versions of themselves. Neither Holly nor Jackson seemed to worry much at all. They certainly didn't feel the need to share their thoughts if they did.

When Tanna was in a good mood and all felt right in her world, it was a delightful, peaceful energy around her. But when she required a target for her frustrations, an ear for her grievances, or even a sparring partner—she and Buck enjoyed a mutual love of arguing—she felt thwarted by her guests' aloofness and disconnection.

Jackson spread maps out on the floor in front of the fireplace. Tanna had never known him to be as talkative as he was when planning an expedition. She planted herself in her chair with her drink and her cigarette case close at hand, dragged some mending out of her sewing basket, and listened to him think out loud. He rattled on a bit about locations, weather patterns, alternate routes ... Although a few of the place names were familiar to her, she had never been to any of them. That was the point of this safari—for Jackson to expose her to the interior of this wild world. To date, she had only skirted along the civilized margins of Cumberland Colony, barely even twenty-five miles from the Seaming, and certainly nowhere close to the heart of the Green.

"You haven't seen anything but that damned sea of grass you got lost in," Jackson teased her. "And you can see most of that out your kitchen window."

"Not true," she protested. "I've also crossed the Sea of Trees. Twice, I'll have you know."

"Ugh," he groaned. "The monotony."

"And you're forgetting the soldiers camp," Tanna continued. "A gamey, drunken dinner on wine-stained tablecloths with a few hundred unwashed men. It was quite an adventure."

"Seriously," he said, his brow creased in earnest. "You need to see some of this world. Before we change any more of it. Or before we're thrown out of it."

"The Garden of Eden all over again," she said.

He seemed to have suddenly remembered something. "You know, Eden is part of the origin myth of the feral humans who claim to have always been here. At least, they can't trace back to a time when their ancestors weren't here. They call themselves the Kin. Have you heard this before?"

She dropped the stocking she was darning into her lap and pulled her feet up into the chair, settling in for one of Jackson's *lectures*, as she liked to think of them.

"The Kin—the feral humans, the ones who go way back—claim to be the direct descendants of the men and women who never left Eden."

"What about Adam and Eve?"

"Well, yes—see, Adam and Eve are the ancestors of the Gray world. But there were others in Paradise who never left. There were also descendants of Adam and Eve who went back into Eden, back into this world, just as we have. These migrations have been happening for millennia. For as long as there have been men on this earth, some of us have always been present in the Green."

Warming to his subject, he shifted around from kneeling in front of the map to be seated on the floor, elbows locked around his knees, looking up at her. Just as he had, she remembered, that first evening when he and Cole had come for dinner.

"There are supposedly humans living so deep in the interior of the Green they've never encountered anyone from our Gray world. There may be whole communities of them for whom we are more myth than the fairies have ever been to us. There may be mortal men and women, our human Kin, living in this world with absolutely no inkling there is any other. They've never seen trains, telegraphs, or motorcars."

"Like isolated tribes in the Amazon. Or in parts of Africa. It sounds very likely to me," Tanna said. "Is that where all the blacks and Indians went?"

He gaped at her.

"Well, they certainly aren't here," she explained. "I've seen every color of face since I arrived here. More than a few of them aren't even human. But other than Rose Vaughn's family, no blacks, and for all that the fae resemble them sometimes, not a single Indian. I mean, surely the Seaming crosses the Trail of Tears and the Underground Railroad. Some of them must have found freedom here. Don't you think?"

"Thousands of them," Jackson said quietly. "But the last place they'd want to be is anywhere near all these plantations. More than a few of the Cherokee, too, in the years leading up to the Removal. I'm sure their settlements are nowhere near the Seaming. But I'm talking about the people who came before them, who live even farther away from our world and this colony." His eyes sparkled and his voice decayed into a whisper with the sheer intensity of feeling the thought inspired. "I want to go find them," he said.

"What—now? Next week?" Tanna asked. "You and I, when we go on our safari? I thought you just wanted to take me a little ways in, not recruit me on some Lewis and Clark expedition."

Jackson shrugged. "Why not?" His tone became defiant, losing all effervescence.

"Well, because I'm running a farm here," she said. "One that is not doing that well, I'll remind you."

"Which is why you need to come away now. Get some perspective."

She stood suddenly and flung her sewing into the basket. She lighted a cigarette and paced in front of the hearth. "Most of my perspective is currently engaged with spending every remaining penny of my inheritance finishing this warehouse, going forward with the distillery, and putting another haint crop in the ground this spring. I'm essentially gambling away my entire fortune on the next growing season. The first time didn't work out so well. You could say, odds are that this is a terrible bet."

"I know," he said, calmly, recognizing one of her descents into anxious preoccupation with her work.

She stopped walking back and forth to loom over him. "I can't just leave and go on some journey with no timetable, no end in sight. Who would make decisions? What about Eve?"

"Holly will look after Eve. Remember, that girl lived in a cave with several hundred elves before you adopted her. She'll be fine. As far as the farm goes, you have an overseer. Doesn't Gentry manage all this for you anyway?"

"He doesn't make the big decisions. He certainly doesn't hold the purse strings. I would never trust him with a blank check." She pressed her palm to her forehead. "I wish I could give all my authority to Still."

He grunted. "I'm afraid no one's going to accept that."

"I know. You don't have to tell me. I can't even talk about it without wanting to scream. It's ridiculous. Still is the smartest person in this entire colony. If it were up to me, he would be the governor of Treebridge, living in a mansion next door to Daughtry."

"Well, your word is law here at Brynmor, at least. Give Gentry a budget before we leave, enough to operate on, and tell him if and when it runs out, he has to go to Still."

"Gentry? Answering to an Alleegee?" She made a rude noise. "He practically chokes trying not to call them *brownies* in front of me."

"Do you fear for Still, if you leave him here to handle Gentry alone?"

"Fear for Still?" She chuckled. "Never. I wish he could come with us. But if I'm not here, Still definitely has to be. And Holly has to stay behind with Eve and Ginger."

"Sounds like a perfect arrangement."

She sighed. "I do want to go away with you. More than you may know."

"Good. Then it's all settled."

She laughed, took a last drag of her cigarette, and tossed the butt at the cold grate. "It's hardly *all* settled. But—" She turned her head to blow smoke away from him as she crouched down on the floor beside him. She scanned the maps over his shoulder. "If we do go out—on just a short trip, mind you, maybe a week—where would we go?"

Jackson's eyes lit up above a mischievous grin. The twinkle was back.

FOUR

39

Jackson wanted to take her west into wilder territory, away from the Seaming, which ran north to south along the eastern edge of the colony. On the north side of Chickamauga Gorge, on the other end of Treebridge where she'd never been, and then to the west, beyond the boundaries of the colony, were the rumored settlements of feral humans and wilder tribes of fae. But that was a long journey, one with a duration he couldn't estimate. He decided it would be best to take her into the part of the country where he took his paying clients on safari. There were lush forests and wild rivers, large populations of wildlife to observe. This was all to the south and west, beyond the Hawnee Hills.

"We'll stop at Cole's," Jackson said at breakfast. "There's something we have to pick up at the orchard."

"We won't disturb him?" Tanna asked. "I don't want to give him another reason to be mad at me." She was secretly hopeful she might have a chance to apologize again, to make peace with Cole.

"We don't even have to go up to the house," he said. "What I need is in the barn, down by the stables."

Holly was in the dining room, half-asleep, blowing on her cup of tea. She started. Tanna saw her look up sharply and stare at Jackson. She looked like she was waiting to say something.

"What is it?" Tanna asked her.

"Nothing," Holly mumbled, shaking her head.

When Jackson excused himself to go load the buggy with their luggage, rifles, and a few baskets of picnic food, Holly bolted after him.

Tanna followed at a discreet distance. She saw Holly overtake Jackson in the drive. She heard the girl ask him something about the orchard. They spoke for a few minutes, their heads close together. Holly stood with her back to Tanna, but she could see Jackson's face. He listened intently, frowning but nodding his head in encouragement. The quick exchange was concluded with no smile or handshake, no indication of what the content might have been.

—

Still, Holly, Eve, and Ginger stood in front of the veranda steps, the girls waving goodbye as the buggy set off down the drive. Jackson smiled and mumbled something Tanna didn't catch.

"What?"

"I said, you have the perfect little family there," he repeated.

Tanna smiled back, but with a quizzical expression. She turned to look over her shoulder. For an instant they were framed by the buggy's back window, but then Holly released Ginger's lead, Eve chased the dog, and Still disappeared into the house.

—

They drove for a few hours along the Big South Road, the sun climbing off on their left, turning the prairie grasses gold.

Tanna sighed loudly, closing her eyes to better feel the light on her face.

"You look awfully content," Jackson observed.

She squinted at him. "This is the first time I've been on an excursion into the Green that wasn't prompted by duress. I'm not running from colony soldiers or the Graycoat's goons."

They drove for several miles in companionable silence. Conscious of the long amount of time they would be alone together, Tanna kept her impulse to chatter in check. Thoughts of the farm, and its swirl of concerns, tried to move in like clouds and eclipse the beauty of the scenery, but she chose to mentally bat them aside. She had left it all miles behind. Her last decision for the next week or so had already been made. Even if she thought of something she should have done, an order she could have given, a decision that would change everything, it was too late. It would all have to wait. And she vowed to let it.

Soon after turning onto the West Fork, the road that led southwest to the Hawnee Hills, Jackson pulled the buggy off near a copse of red cedar where they could relieve themselves and stretch their legs.

"Do you want to eat something," he asked, "or do you want to keep going?"

"It's too soon to stop for long," she assured him. "I don't feel like we've gone far enough away from home yet."

They continued on, Jackson now discussing their timeline for the day.

He hoped to stop briefly at the orchard in the early afternoon, then make it up and over the Hawkeye Pass through the Hawnees by sundown.

"What was it Holly wanted to talk to you about so desperately?" Tanna rolled it casually into the conversation after Jackson had mentioned the girl's name in another context. "The moment you arrived, she said she had to tell you something."

He didn't answer, only stared at the road ahead. He finally shrugged, twisting his lips in a gesture of exaggerated nonchalance. "She thinks she may have left something at the orchard the day I came for you. She asked me to look for it."

"Why wouldn't she just tell me that?"

"She put something in the barn when we were loading up the equipment I had stored there. Remember? Anyway, she thinks she must have set it down among my things."

"Well, this sounds awfully mysterious."

"Yes, well, it may seem that way to you." A muscle clenched along his jaw. "But she asked me to handle it for her. In confidence."

"Well, surely you can tell me what it is."

"No, I surely can't," he snapped. "That breaks the very definition of *in confidence*."

A moody silence emerged between them. After a few uncomfortable minutes, Tanna softly apologized. "I didn't mean to make you angry."

Jackson still said nothing, but he urged the horse a little faster.

—

They left the West Fork and drove a few miles up the approach to the orchard before turning off on the access road to the stables. Tanna sat in the buggy gazing up at the imposing front door of Cole Mathers's house. She scanned the windows and the dormers embedded in the hillside, thinking she might spot Ioma's face watching from behind a curtain. But there were no signs of activity.

Some droning summer insects hidden in the grass of the pasture whined away at a surprisingly loud volume.

"Are you getting out?" Jackson asked, coming around the side of the buggy carrying the Victrola. "We're leaving your horse and buggy here."

"To go on foot?" She couldn't imagine it, not with the amount of provisions they had to carry.

"No," he said, exasperated. "We're riding a couple of my horses. They're stabled here. Don't worry, your horse will be cared for until we get back. We'll park your buggy in the barn."

Tanna frowned, pointing at the Victrola he carried. "Did you plan on stuffing that into a saddlebag?"

He laughed. The tension of the conversation about Holly and the last few hours on the road seemed to have finally evaporated.

"I have something to show you." There it was again, that twinkling in his eye.

—

The last thing Tanna had expected to see was another dirigible.

When Jackson opened the doors to the barn behind the stables, she had no idea what she was supposed to be looking at. Her eye went first to the recognizable orange hammock she'd seen on her last visit here. She was on the verge of asking Jackson about Curtis the vine trainer when her vision settled on the huge balloon. This dirigible was significantly smaller than either of the airships on which she had traveled—it was barely a third the size of a hot air balloon, not much larger than a wagon, really. It was almost perfectly round, incredibly smooth, seamless ... and chartreuse.

The balloon was the color of a new leaf, somewhere between pale silver and bright yellow-green. Instead of a basket dangling from ropes or the canoe-shaped pallet of the cargo balloon attached to the Queen of Clouds, this vessel had a cluster of five smaller, pillow-like shapes at its base. They were a subdued brown color and of a tougher substance, the panels of a woody shell that had broken open with the fruit of the balloon at some earlier stage of growth, but had curled to form hollow compartments.

"The pods," she whispered. "Growing in the orchard. This is one of them."

"It is," he said, matter-of-factly. "One of the first to be harvested. I used it on my last safari."

Tanna's face contorted in confusion. "How?"

"We're not riding in it," Jackson said. He set the Victrola on the ground, took his canvas duffle bag from the buggy, and walked across the barn to beneath the dirigible. With his free hand he grabbed hold of what Tanna had thought at first to be a trailing rope. On closer look, she realized it was one of a half-dozen living vines, dark-green in color, with large leathery leaves and curling tendrils like a beanstalk. "It carries our things."

He tugged one of the vines gently and the entire dirigible sank smoothly and soundlessly toward the ground. He stroked the edge of a woody shell and its tip began to uncurl away from the base of the pod, revealing a compartment stuffed with bundles of canvas and the jutting ends of wooden poles.

"The tents," he said, pointing, looking over his shoulder at her with a grin.

She watched dumbfounded as he stroked open the other curled husk compartments and slid one of her suitcases and a picnic basket carefully inside.

"You do have to be careful not to hurt it," he explained. "It's alive."

"Alive?" she repeated, horrified.

"As much as any other plant." When he saw the look on her face he planted his hands on his hips and rolled his eyes at her. "It's not a monster. It's just a big vegetable. Like a pumpkin or a gourd out in your kitchen garden." He seemed to consider his words. "Well, a highly magical, spell-encrusted pumpkin," he conceded.

"Cinderella's carriage," Tanna breathed. She stepped up close to it and stroked its smooth hide. It was taut as a melon, cool to the touch but slightly furry. "Won't it scare away the wildlife we want to see?"

"More than a horse-drawn wagon would? You know, that team of oxen you took into the Seaming announced your arrival for days in advance. That's how we found you."

Of course she hadn't possessed that self-awareness at the time. She'd blundered into the Green, a half a breath away from her next life-changing decision at any given moment, with no idea what she was doing or where she was. To her, those woods and that ocean of grass had been the middle of nowhere, with no one else around. Even now, the thought that anyone had been watching made her shudder.

With the gentlest of tugs, Jackson coaxed the dirigible from the barn. He coiled one of the trailing vines around his wrist, but Tanna impulsively lurched forward as the balloon scraped softly past the top of the door. She expected it to launch into the sky, dragging Jackson with it. But it continued to hover, the storage compartments at its base approximately four feet above the ground, the perfect height for Jackson to load their things.

He talked about the craft's origins as he transferred the last of their cargo from the buggy. "It's virtually silent," he said. "It can move over any terrain at varying altitudes. It can carry almost as much as a wagon, definitely more than the boot of a buggy. And it doesn't require any beasts to drag it around."

"We're just going to drag it behind us, like a child's balloon at the fair?" She looked up at it. She couldn't shake the feeling the craft knew they were talking about it. "How are you able to hold on to it with just that one vine or rope or whatever it is?"

"Oh, I'm not holding it in place. It responds to my wishes." Jackson smiled at the shock in her face. "My thoughts. It does help if I'm touching it. But these vines are also a bit like tentacles—"

At that word, she grimaced squeamishly and hunched her shoulders. It immediately took on the aspect of a vegetable octopus, floating in the air.

"Stop acting like it's a monster!" he admonished her. "She's a beauty."

"It's a *she*?" Tanna was horrified further.

He rolled his eyes. "Only in the way all vessels and ships are referred to as *she*'s." He spread a pair of the tentacles between his hands. It was hard to tell whether the wispy spiral tendrils and the leaves were moving because of his manipulations, if they were trembling in a breeze, or if they were animated by some other force. "These tentacles—OK, we'll call them vines—can anchor the vessel, pull it through the forest canopy, lift and lower small objects. Like roots, they can absorb nutrients and water. And, most fascinating of all, if we touch them, we can communicate with the vessel." He held one of the vines out toward her. "Try it."

She stepped closer but hesitated. "Is it a spell?"

He winced apologetically. "It's definitely fairy magic. But I don't know if the power is inherent in the creature itself or if it's enchanted. There's certainly been a bit of everything thrown at it."

She stroked the vine with a fingertip. It was cool to the touch. It reminded her of a kudzu vine, heavy and faintly furred with silver hairs. "Will it obey my wishes too? Or only your commands?"

"Well, it knows me. I've been tending to it since it was grafted onto the tree that nurtured it to maturity. But we believe it will get to know you, over time, as an animal might."

"We?" Tanna asked. "You and Cole?"

He nodded slightly and blinked once slowly. The gesture reminded her of an Alleegee.

"You've been helping him grow these things in the orchard." She wanted him to admit to it.

He ignored her prompts and carried on speaking as if the conversation had already gone in another direction. "We'll keep her at a low altitude. Just high enough to skim over the treetops. It's a newer way of doing things, but if it works as we hope, then I can employ them when taking paying clients out on excursions or scenic walkabouts."

"Oh, I see. This is a test run for a new kind of safari. Trips for the wealthy men coming in to colonize the Green, the ones whose new boots are still stiff from the store shelves back home in the Gray."

"Yes. Or possibly to help carry the rich colonial ladies who can't walk around their plantations without growing faint," he said in a mocking tone.

"I work in my own fields, you know," Tanna said archly. "I don't need to be dragged about on a floating fairy litter."

"Oh, I know you don't," Jackson said.

—

They left the orchard without going up to the main house. At one point, Ioma did come out on the front porch and stood for some time watching them. Jackson waved to her, walked part of the way up the path, and then stopped to stand with his hands on his hips. They stayed like that for a few minutes, staring at one another. He soon turned around and walked back to Tanna, frowning. Ioma slipped back inside.

"What was that?" she asked.

Jackson shook his head and sighed. "Cole's not doing well today."

"How do you know that?" She wondered if she might have missed some kind of hand signals.

He ignored her question. "We won't go up. He doesn't need to be disturbed."

—

"We have to call it—her—something," Tanna said, turning around in her saddle to peer at the eerie bright green balloon floating along behind them. "You know how I am about naming things."

"What do you think we should call her, then?" Jackson asked.

She hesitated only a heartbeat before answering. "*Jewel*. When I first saw those things growing in the orchard, they reminded me of precious gems; the forks of the trees were like the tines of a ring setting."

"So like *Jewel of the Treetops* or *Jewel in the Sky* ..."

"No." She cut him off, shaking her head. "I don't think these creatures should be named like boats or airships. They're different. If they're alive and aware, then it's more like naming a horse or a dog."

"OK," he said. "I concur with that logic. Just *Jewel*, then."

"Just *Jewel*."

—

They reached the top of the Hawkeye Pass in the last golden hour before sunset. Close to the road, the flattened shoulder of land had been cleared of brush and stones. It was obviously a popular place for travelers to stop. The grass was trampled and the earth was packed. There were blackened stones ringing a handful of cold fire pits.

Jackson dismounted and led his horse past the campsites, up a slight grassy rise to the south. Tanna climbed down with some difficulty, her muscles already stiff from having not ridden so much lately. They waded a few hundred yards up a slope through waist-high yellow grass. Ahead of her, Jackson stopped on what appeared to be a bluff overlooking the southeastern flanks of the Hawnees. When she caught up with him, she saw it wasn't a sharp drop at all, but another deep saddle between the lower peaks, this one unspoiled by roads or traffic.

It fell away in a gentle curving slope all the way to the Cumberland Prairie below. There was a small level shelf of land about halfway down, with a skeleton of an enormous dead thorn tree.

"This is one of my favorite spots in the world," Jackson told her as they made their way down. "You'll be glad to know I named it. Dead Tree Hill."

The flat piece of ground was big enough for the horses to graze beside a small campfire and one of the tents. Jackson insisted on putting the tent up for Tanna while she gathered firewood beneath the gnarled tree. He sent *Jewel* to hover behind the tree so she would be somewhat camouflaged from the road below.

They finished their tasks in time to witness the western sky behind the hills bruised with plum-colored clouds. They turned their backs on a dirty gold sunset to gaze upon the way they'd come. Jackson traced the line of the West Fork from the Big South Road. The orchard was just out of sight to their right, tucked up in the skirts of the southernmost hill of the Hawnees.

"There's a trail from here all the way to the north gate of the orchard. I usually don't even come here by the road. I often hike up here from Cole's instead of staying in one of those morbid guest rooms of his."

"Morbid?" Tanna was surprised by the description. "Cole's house is wondrous."

"It's something about its being under the hill. Those visible tree roots framing the windows. I feel a bit cold and smothered at the same time. I don't like sleeping in caves. So I come up here."

She put a few pieces of bread with chunks of cheese and bacon on a flat stone near the fire so they could toast and melt. "Have you brought anyone else here before?" she asked.

"No." He seemed surprised by his own word, as if only just realizing it himself. "Well, Cole, of course. And Kanute."

"Your fairy servant?" she asked.

Jackson started shaking with silent laughter.

"What?" she demanded.

"My *fairy servant*," he mimicked her, shaking his head. "You just have a way of putting things sometimes that sounds like it came straight out of a Victorian novel."

"He's fae. He's your servant," Tanna protested, but she smiled, playing a part for him. "It's an entirely accurate description, isn't it?"

"No," he said, forcefully. "It most certainly is not."

"Then what do you call him?"

"My *friend*." Jackson sounded angry and faintly disgusted with her.

"Of course," she whispered. "I didn't mean to sound insensitive."

He let the moment pass in favor of one of his self-reflective tangents, an extension of the epic ongoing conversation they had been having about the night sky. This moment was another continuation of their after-dinner walks around the farm and their shared cigarettes on the veranda. The fire had died down a bit and the lights of the first stars were appearing straight in front of them, over the great southern Sea of Grass.

"I'm sure there is some scientific principle that would explain it," Jackson said, without introduction.

"Explain what?" she asked.

"I can't say that I know what makes it so, but I swear you can see farther into space when you look at the night sky here in the Green. And the deeper you go into this world, away from the Seaming, the more detailed that streak of dense, galactic starlight becomes. There are more shooting stars. And I've even seen a comet." He paused for a moment, then rolled on his side to look her in the eyes. "I've also seen mysterious, slow-moving craft, winking at intervals with artificial light. They putter along, in far too straight a line but too fast to be a planet. I would say they might be dirigibles, but they're clearly at a height our balloons could never reach. The chariots of angels."

The chariots of angels. The way he said it sent a shudder down her back. Jackson Gallagher was hardly a person to believe in angels. She pulled her shawl tight around her shoulders and fearfully scanned for airships with blinking electric lights.

He had moved on with his lecture. He lay down flat, one arm bent behind his head, sighting along his outstretched arm some other kinds of twinkles in the ether. Tanna eased down onto the grass with her head near his. Sound was muffled with her ears close to the ground. She tried to look at features of the sky as he pointed them out to her.

"It's better without the tents," he said. "You know, when I went out with Kanute we never used them."

"Where is he, by the way?" she asked, afraid of saying the wrong thing and making him mad again. "I thought he always accompanied you on safari."

"He used to. He's dead." Jackson said it so matter-of-factly; he could only be speaking about a friend who had died as if he were trying to suppress the pain.

She knew expressing pity or sorrow would make him uncomfortable, so she tried to match his tone. "There was something about him. Something fierce. If I hadn't known you were friends with him, I'd say he must have been Unseelie."

"No. You are right. He was Unseelie. Half, anyway. His father was. His mother, believe it or not, was a house elf, so he was raised among the plantations. When she died, we went to find the other side of his family."

"You went with him?"

"Indeed, I accompanied him on that journey. To discover his Unseelie self. They are like no one else, you know. They're even less like the other tribes than you imagine. We will never civilize them. Or tame them. Or educate them. We won't. We think it's inevitable, an eventuality that they will go along with our ways and become like us. It's not. They cannot process our concepts of right and wrong. The fae in general do not embrace the duality we live by. Good and evil. Light and dark. Seelie and Unseelie. *We* call them that. It's not a concept they apply to themselves or each other. If you put them in one of our prisons, they spontaneously die."

"Why?" The anguish in her voice surprised her.

"They live only in the present. They have no concept of the future. They can't understand that one day they might be let out. For them, in the moment, they're irrevocably *caged*. And that's worse than death to them. For them, the present moment is the same as the infinite. Now is forever. And so, their confinement is an eternal torture, a damnation that, in their perception, might as well be permanent. And so they will themselves to die."

She sighed loudly, a wordless expression of her empathy.

"They are the ones that don't care about us," he continued. "They really do not identify with us at all. They have little compassion for anyone who's not their kind. They only care about one another and the land itself. This Green world is an extension of their bodies, of their society. And anything that threatens it is a plague upon nature."

She felt a need to pull him back from the darkness of his words. "Did Kanute tell you all that? Around a campfire like this, at night, looking at the stars?"

"No," Jackson said. "We didn't really talk."

"Ever?" She was incredulous.

"Never."

They both fell silent, listening to the shifting embers of the fire and the distant screams of night creatures in the trees.

After a few minutes, he rolled over, stood, and stretched. "It's an early day tomorrow. You should get some sleep." He offered her his hand.

"Oh." She stirred, clutched her shawl in one fist, and allowed him to pull her to her feet. They stood for a moment, close together, still holding on to one another in an awkwardly prolonged handshake. "What happens tomorrow?"

"I have no idea," he said, all seriousness. Then his mouth crumpled with a small smirk. He playfully bounced her hand in his a few times and then let it go.

He gave her a small lamp, and she backed away from the warmth of the fire to the single tent he had set up for her privacy. She watched him through a crack where the flaps met. He sat on the ground with his back to her, poking the fire with a stick. She undressed and blew out the lantern. When she peeked at him again, he was stretched out, sleeping on the ground in the same spot he'd occupied that night and likely so many others.

40

Jackson was right. It all changed on the other side of the Hawnee Hills. Tanna would have called the Doheenagee Forest a *jungle*. It resembled what she imagined the Amazon must look like. The plants grew on the oversized scale she had encountered in other parts of the Green. The trees, the flowers, the ferns—even the blades of grass—made one think of a time when dinosaurs roamed the earth.

The forest grew around the Yooway, a river that was five times as wide as the creek that curved around the foot of Brynmor. Jackson said the water was relatively shallow but fast, with stretches of rapids crashing against the boulders. They forded the waters at a shoal of smooth lavender stones the size and shape of flattened eggs. They slid out of their saddles so the horses could more easily pick their way among the small rocks. Tanna hefted one in her hand.

"Amethysts," Jackson said.

She gasped. "Where did they all come from?"

"I have no idea," he said, his eyes sparkling.

She wondered if she should put some of the amethysts in her pockets or in one of her saddlebags. Maybe there was room in one of *Jewel*'s compartments. Or, then again, it might be too heavy. She turned to look at the giant yellow-green balloon drifting silently behind them. Its tentacles pulsed and writhed, reaching into the water.

"Look, she's drinking!" Tanna yelled.

Jackson stopped to watch, his hands on his hips, a wide, white-toothed grin splitting his tanned face. He marveled, shaking his head slowly.

Animals, birds, and creatures of every kind were drawn to the waters. There were species Tanna would never have imagined seeing with her own eyes, yet here they were, living just two days' journey from her own home. A mother bear fished in the deep rushing currents as her two cubs scampered about on the rocks. A forest of blue heron lined the shallows on the far bank. A cyclone funnel of hawks spiraled high in the air above them. It wasn't so much the types of animals but the sheer numbers in which they appeared. Clouds of black birds took off from the treetops, nearly darkening the entire sky. Thousands of butterflies covered a fallen tree, sipping moisture from the spongy moss, barely flexing their upright wings.

She caught Jackson staring at her, watching her reactions as she took in each new sight.

They skirted the edge of the Doheenagee to make it easier for *Jewel* to follow them. They spent most of the day crossing a meadow carpeted with blue and purple wildflowers. Tanna kept waiting for it to end, for the color to give way to plain grass or for them to reach the wood's edge along the horizon that constantly receded from them.

The land began to gently rise into a perfect knoll covered in emerald-green clover. Jackson called a halt, and they dismounted for a picnic in *Jewel*'s shade. He wound a trailing vine around his fist and gently tugged. The little blimp silently sank until her storage compartments were five feet from the ground.

"I love this thing!" he said, petting open one of the husks.

He employed the tentacles to help him carefully remove the Victrola and lower it to the ground, then he went rooting around for the records.

"Let's play them some human music," he said.

"Play it for whom?" Tanna asked.

"For the fairies of the wild," he said with a manic smile.

He told her the knoll in front of them was a brugh. He pointed out a few shadowy depressions a third of the way from the top of the hill.

"Entrances to the caves and halls within," he whispered, as if those who dwelled inside might be listening.

"Are they Nunnahee?"

"Nah," he shook his head. "From the size of the doorways, I'd say they're a significantly smaller race. Hill-dwellers, yes. But not the same humanoid elves living around your farm. We won't know for sure until we coax them out."

Tanna's nose wrinkled with worry. "How are you going to do that?"

"With Mozart!" he said.

They left the Victrola on the slope of the knoll, close to two of the cave entrances. They walked the horses and *Jewel* far across the meadow to a nearby copse of trees and then crept back to the brugh with a record and spool of twine. Jackson cranked the Victrola and set the record spinning, but attached the thin line of rope to the arm of the player. They were able to lie down in the clover, nearly invisible, and start the music from fifty feet away.

The elves that tentatively emerged were tiny and gray, half the size of the Nunnahee, barely twenty inches high if they stood upright. They remained in a rounded squatting position. When they walked, they swung on their long arms like crutches, the tops of their hands planted on the ground, similar to the way many primates move. They didn't wear clothing or jewelry or cover their hair with colored mud like the elves Tanna had grown used to seeing around the colony. But they were bolder and more curious. They chatted to one another loudly and enthusiastically scampered closer to the Victrola. Some of the smallest individuals turned cartwheels, while the older creatures stood in circles and swayed to the strains of the music. Their eyes became slits. They were hypnotized, mesmerized, transported.

"Look at that!" Jackson could barely contain his excitement. "They may have seen some people here and there, from a distance, but they've probably never heard our language or seen one of our machines up close. I certainly doubt they've heard human music before. And here we are, after all these centuries, playing them Mozart. Just think of it!"

Tanna laughed. His delight was infectious. With his face so close to hers in the bright sunshine, she realized for the first time his green eyes were flecked with gold.

He said, "I think we just did something amazing, you and I."

Before she could respond, the music ended in a loud ripping sound as one of the rambunctious young elves reached out and grabbed the spinning disc. He shrieked and somersaulted backward, careening through the crowd that had formed to watch him. Protective of his records to a fault, Jackson jumped up and ran toward them, waving his arms and yelling, sending the whole tribe screaming and disappearing back into the caves.

—

They found a game trail leading away from the Yooway River through the densest part of the forest. It was wide enough to allow them to ride side by side astride their horses, with plenty of overhead clearance for *Jewel* to follow. The craft's tentacles explored the ground and the branches of nearby trees, daintily unfurling and tapping like a blind man feeling his way with a stick. It must have driven all the wildlife into hiding. They encountered only a few brave squirrels and large flocks of birds seen from a distance.

Even the insects had gone quiet for miles around them in every direction.

"So, I have an opportunity to get more business," Jackson said.

"Doing what?" Tanna asked.

"This. Taking people on guided trips."

"No more hunting dragons?" she asked.

"Hunting dragons?" he repeated, amused.

"Well, you had an enormous pair of wings the first time I saw you," she said defensively.

"You're serious." He stared at her as if she were insane.

"What did I say?" she demanded. "They were dragon's wings, weren't they? Or was Cole just playing a joke on me?"

"No, no. They were definitely dragon's wings. But I didn't *kill* the dragon. I never said that. I found them."

She felt her face and neck beginning to flush. "You never talked about it. I never asked."

Realizing she was embarrassed, he tried to lighten his tone. "Did you really think that's how I made my living? That I'm a professional dragon slayer?"

"Well, there were the wings, and the other trophies in your rooms at the club. And you were always talking about going on safari," she explained earnestly. "I just assumed that meant big game hunting, killing lions and ... all that."

Jackson grinned at her, his eyes crinkling at the corners. "You have a very high opinion of me. You make me sound like a hero in an epic. Have you ever seen a real dragon?"

"Other than the one in the story I told you?" Her eyes narrowed playfully. "No."

"Well, they look like alligators," he said in a flat, disappointed tone. "Big, mean, ugly gators. And they don't breathe fire. They run as terrifyingly fast as any other alligator and they've got those huge wings, but they don't even use them. I've never seen one fly before. I don't know if there are still any around that *can* fly." He paused to take a swig of water from his canteen. "And, by the way, the only treasure to speak of is what you might get for selling a pair of their wings to some rich bastard who wants to hang them above the mantel in his den. But I would never kill one just for that. A lot of people do. Too many, if you ask me. The day before I met you, I happened to run across one that had only just died. There was no reason to let the wings go to waste. But to tell you the truth, cutting them free of the body sickened me. It was harder than you might think."

"Are there any around here?" There was no way she could ask the question without sounding fearful.

"Nah," Jackson shook his head. "No reason to worry. Like I said, they're hunted way too much. It was unusual to find one, living or dead, so close to the colony."

They rode in silence for a few minutes.

"*Dragon slayer,*" he muttered under his breath and chuckled.

"Well ...," she shrugged helplessly. "So, tell me more about this new venture of yours."

"I met a gold prospector at The Fairchild who just brought his daughters into the Green. They only joined him a few months ago, after their mother died of Spanish flu. They're fifteen and seventeen. They've grown up in Birmingham society, and I doubt they've ever been camping overnight. Should be an interesting trip. I'll be gone either a whole month or an hour and a half."

"You should take Holly."

"Should I?" He sounded genuinely surprised by the suggestion, but curious. "Why?"

"Well, she's been a great comfort to me, on more than one journey. And she's the same age as your client's daughters. She sets an example, I think. Of a new type of girl. The type of girl one needs to be able to survive here in this world. She's used to being on expeditions, back and forth across the Seaming with the Graycoat. And, of course, she's terrified he's going to come for her, make her go back with him, or at least demand the money she took. I would gladly give it to him, if it would make him go away and leave her alone. But I think she may be hiding something else from him. And from me." She paused and looked at Jackson pointedly, waiting for him to comment on whatever Holly had confided in him.

He didn't meet her eyes.

"But, between you and me," she continued, "I'm more worried she's going to become bored to death hiding out on my farm."

"Isn't she old enough to decide for herself whether she stays or goes?"

"I would certainly say so. But the Graycoat has shown up at my house before, and she went with him. There's no explaining the hold he has over her." She sighed. "Anyway, I wouldn't mind seeing her off on safari. Especially with you and a couple of girls her own age. It could be good for her. It could be good for the success of your trip, too. There are probably lots of other women who would like to see the wilderness."

He stared at her thoughtfully. "I will ask her, then, when we get back. See if she might like to come along."

—

They heard the flying machine coming long before they saw it, like a hiss of wind across tall grass, and then a buzzing sound like a nest of hornets. No sooner had the bright, light-green spot appeared on the horizon than it was streaking directly over them. It was an elongated glider with wings, like a giant dragonfly skimming over the woods. It skipped across the forest canopy like a stone thrown across a lake, only the contact with the treetops seemed to fling it farther and faster along its trajectory.

Jackson slid off his horse and ran after it, as if he could follow. He stood for several moments staring in the direction it had vanished, his mouth hanging open with wonder.

"Could you tell what it's made of?" he asked, when she and the horses caught up with him.

"Some kind of paper or cloth?" she guessed. "Like the dirigibles?"

He shook his head. "Guess again."

"Oh!" She remembered the bright green color. "It's alive. Like *Jewel*."

"Yes." He nodded his head emphatically, pacing in a circle. He seemed ready to burst out of his skin. "It's essentially an enormous curled leaf. It was grown in that shape, slowly molded and trained into that form. Entirely organic."

"You've seen one before," she said. "Somewhere." Surely he could tell her everything now—about *Jewel*, the orchard, the other things Cole might be growing ...

He only beamed his too-white smile, shading his eyes and staring at the sky.

When he didn't volunteer any other information, she cast about for some question to keep the conversation going. "I wonder where he'll land?"

"The point is to not land at all. Did you see him skim the treetops? He rides the canopy of the woods wherever he can, like a boat on choppy water. The contact generates energy and speed. Then, he launches out into the wide open spaces and glides." His shoulders fell, as if all the energy and excitement coursing through him had shot away into the ether with the flying machine. "God," he whispered, "I have got to fly one."

41

The game trail cut through the horseshoe of dense forest and met the Yooway as it curved back around and ran north. Over millennia, the river had carved its way down through layers of dark slate, leaving shelves on either bank reaching toward one another fifty feet above the water's surface. They continued walking their horses for miles along this perfectly flat stretch of rock, smoother and more durable than any paved road back in the Gray. They chose to make their camp on a carpet of spongy moss cluttered with butterflies.

Jackson caught four small bluegill at a bend in the river where the water curling back around in a slow eddy had eroded a deep, shallow bay. They roasted the fish over a low orange fire on spits whittled from cattail stalks. Later that evening, beneath a moonless purple sky, they drank chamomile tea from tin cups spiked with tarwater from Jackson's silver flask.

She gazed out at the relentlessly glittering waters, barely visible in the starlight. "This is how I imagined it would be out West," she said.

"You've never been out West?" he asked, an expression of mock torment on his face as he dug around in an open saddlebag.

"No, but my father went to the Grand Canyon when he was a young man, before he married my mother. He loved to tell me stories about it."

With a triumphant, wordless cry and a flourish, he pulled out his tin of haint flowers and tobacco, and set to rolling cigarettes on his knee. "Are you close to him?"

"He died." Tanna paused, prepared to tell the same rehearsed story she'd told a thousand times, the version of events that her mother and her aunts approved. But something cracked open, and an exhilarating breath of spontaneity slipped inside her. It filled her lungs, and when she exhaled, the old story leaked away as a sigh into the air. She saw it meet the smoke above the fire and shoot up into the night. On the verge of breathlessness, the truth came out. "He killed himself when I was ten years old."

Jackson didn't say anything, but he froze with the cigarette paper at his lips. He slowly blinked at her a few times and swiped the cigarette across the tip of his tongue.

She saw no judgment in his eyes, nor a ravenous curiosity for particulars. She cleared her throat and adjusted the shawl around her shoulders. "You know, he knew about the Green. He believed in fairies. He'd seen them. When I was back ... at home last year, I found drawings in his diaries. I remembered having seen them when I was a little girl."

She watched him roll a second cigarette. He glanced up once, signaling for her to go on. "Apparently, he saw one of the same creatures in our garden that I saw. Something riding around on the back of a squirrel." She gazed inwardly for a moment, then shook away the memory. "Anyway, he also discovered a helmet made out of a tortoise shell. A gruesome, Unseelie thing, in my limited frame of reference. This wasn't the kind of sighting you usually hear about people having in their gardens—sylphs or flower fairies. I don't know; I suppose one could argue that he *envisioned* it. But still, of all things, a soldier's helmet? I doubt he could have known about the Seaming, the conflict here. But I can't help but wonder if the helmet belonged to a Ripper."

"Why would you think that?" He lit both cigarettes and handed one to her.

She thanked him and inhaled deeply. "Well, why would armored fae be found in the Gray, barely five miles from at least one known crossing point? How many others were there, hiding out, lurking in the vines? I see these flashes in my mind's eye of hundreds of them, scooting through the leaves unseen, like vermin."

Jackson exhaled a cloud of blue-white smoke, frowning, hesitant. "You think it had something to do with his death?"

It made her anxious the way he alternated between intently studying her face when she was speaking and then not looking at her at all when he finally spoke. "Looking back on it? Maybe." She shrugged. "I don't know. I never really could fathom why he killed himself. I've never been able to resolve it. The lack of answers—the inability to even ask questions—was maddening for me. For a long time. Eventually, I just had to accept it as part of what happens to those who are left behind when someone takes his own life."

Jackson leaned forward and tipped the flask into her cup again.

"My mother was so ashamed of him," she continued, shaking her head with regret. "She'd find him squatting in the garden or staring at a crack in the stone walls for hours. I saw him too, from my window, still as a statue, mesmerized by something in the flowerbeds. She'd yell at him to come inside. And later I'd hear them arguing behind closed doors. Mostly, she berated him about what people would think if they saw him. That worried me too. I didn't even know what it was exactly that people might think of him—think of us—but, at that time, there was a particularly nasty group of girls at school whose parents all socialized with mine. I had this vague, selfish fear that I would somehow receive even worse attention because of his odd behavior. It hurts my heart to admit that now."

Her story trailed off as she took another sip of tea and another drag off the cigarette. She made a face at the sour aftertaste of wilting flowers. She looked off to the right, past the fire, at the edges of the pool of light it cast. There, in the underbrush, where the shadows started ... faces. Hundreds of them, only inches above the ground. The more she watched, the more she could see them, dancing close. Some shyly peeked at her, openly awestruck, while others made mischievous, taunting faces. As quickly as their features materialized, they darted back into the dark.

Jackson heard her gasp and followed her line of sight. "See them?" he whispered.

"Yes," she breathed, barely audible.

"I wonder if they've seen the likes of us before?" he muttered, but then he turned back to her and waited patiently for her to go on.

She couldn't quite tear her gaze from her fairy audience, and she spoke in lowered tones, as if to keep from frightening them away. "If he was seeing the kinds of things I think he was, if he had glimpses of this world or its inhabitants ... and if he was talking about it, making claims to other people ... He would have been ostracized, at best. He may have been persecuted. I don't know." She looked at Jackson, helplessly shaking her head. "When I think about how isolated he may have felt because of what he saw ... He had a little evidence, the sketches he made, but it was an incomplete truth. And now, here I am, sitting in the middle of this world, and it's a reality. Not only would he have felt vindicated, but he simply would have loved it here. If he'd known—if he'd truly known this was a possibility... He would have brought me here. He would have been one of those men taking his daughter on safari in the Green. He would have loved this." She smiled at Jackson, but there was a small break in her voice. "And I think he would have liked you, too."

He nodded once, acknowledging the compliment.

She swallowed, her voice thick with suppressed tears. "I think I fight to make the farm work so I can stay—so I can be here—for him as well as for me."

"What was his name?" Jackson asked.

Her voice wavered, but she got it out. "Kenneth Theodore Cravens."
Jackson raised his cup in a toast. "To Kenneth."

—

They continued west along the Yooway River. The shelf of rock on the southern edge dropped away to reveal a grassy plain stretching to the horizon. They continued along the northern bank, where the rock eventually dipped down to the water's edge in a perfectly smooth pavement. It was pleasant to take off their shoes and walk for long stretches, cooling their feet in the shallow water. Farther up the bank to their right, the thick carpets of moss continued to provide the perfect place to set up camp each night.

The landscape to the north of the river was a nearly impenetrable forest. They foraged in the cool shade, but there were no good trails for the horses and certainly no clearance for *Jewel*. For now, it was easier to travel along beside the water, but Jackson started scanning for a place that was shallow enough for them to ford. They wanted to explore the meadows to the south, where they saw large herds of animals.

It was early afternoon on their third day along the Yooway when they finally found the perfect spot. The smooth rock bank flattened and disappeared beneath the waters. The river seemed to overflow its bed, spreading out over twice its width, but the water was barely six inches deep here. Jackson suggested they rest for the remainder of the day and cross the river in the morning.

After they set up camp, he spent a few hours fishing for their supper. She collected firewood and groomed the horses. Her own scalp itched from days without washing her hair, and the longer strands were becoming more and more tangled. She'd let it go, tucking it into a loose bun and stuffing it under Jackson's old Stetson. Now, she couldn't even get a comb through it. She impatiently tugged until the ivory handle broke off, leaving the teeth embedded in a knot of her hair. It was right at the base of her skull. Jackson found her in front of the tent, cursing, trying to awkwardly reach the back of her head. She had the pocketknife ready and was about to start sawing.

"Whoa whoa whoa!" he yelled. "Hold on there just a minute."

He hung the string of fish on the branch of a nearby tree and sprinted back to her.

"I don't think we're quite that desperate," he said, taking the knife from her.

"I can't even—" she gestured angrily at her head, too frustrated and near tears to speak.

"Let me look," he said softly, as if calming a horse.

He pulled up a camp stool behind her and made her sit between his knees and lean her head forward. She complied, studying his wet bare feet planted to either side of hers. His feet were calloused and ghostly pale, but his toes were long and daintily shaped, with well-groomed nails. She'd never seen feet on a man she thought were *pretty*. Buck and Ford both had similar meaty slabs with fat, stubby toes. Teddy's nails were always broken and dirty from running around barefoot.

"How do you feel about a bob?" Jackson asked.

Tanna's shoulders slumped and she sighed tragically. "Give me the knife," she demanded.

"Wait just a minute," he said. "Do you trust me?"

She twisted her head to look at him sideways. "Trust you to what?"

He told her to stay put, dashed over to the saddlebags, and returned with a small leather kit. He opened it to reveal a pair of scissors, a straight razor, a file, and a sharpening stone. "May I?" he asked.

She immediately started instructing him on what to do, feeling for the broken comb in her hair.

He shushed her, but she ignored him.

"I have something I need to tell you," he said in an ominous voice.

She stopped talking at once.

"There's something you need to know about me, about my past."

She couldn't see his face, but she turned her head slightly, encouraging him to go on.

"My father was a barber at a company mining town in Kentucky. My mother was a lady's maid for the women of the family who owned the mine. She dressed all their hair and they were envied by every girl in the county."

It was the last thing on earth she would have expected him to say. "Is that true?" she asked. "Or are you just telling me a story so I'll let you cut my hair?"

"It's true. And, yes, I am telling you so you'll let me cut your hair."

She hesitated. He tugged gently on the comb and she winced.

"Will you trust me?" he asked again.

She groaned. "Yes."

"A stylish bob it is, then."

—

While he snipped gently behind her, he told her stories about the barbershop. How much he loved the smells of aftershave and pomade. How proud they all were of his mother's position in the big house on the hill. The Davenports. When his father died when Jackson was fourteen, the Davenports sent him to boarding school and later paid his way through college. His mother and younger sister both worked for them and live in that big house to this day.

"How did he die?" Tanna asked, staring at the huge wet coils of her hair drying on the tops of his pretty feet. Her shoulders were resting against his thighs. She could smell the river water and sweat in the dirty canvas of his pants.

"Mine explosion," he said, brushing hair off the base of her neck with his fingertips. "Half the buildings in town disappeared in a crater."

He stood suddenly and stepped back to examine his work from a distance. He commanded her to stand also. She was conscious of his body so close against her back. "Just one little thing ..." She felt his breath on her cheek as he made one more small snip.

Then he was in front of her, studying her without seeing her. His focus shifted from his work to her watching him. His intent expression opened into a smile. He winked.

"Let me see," she said, reaching for the kit and the small mirror she'd seen there.

"No no no," he said, looking hurt. "I'm not finished."

He made her sit and wait while he went to pick rosemary from a bush he'd spotted. He took the mirror with him so she couldn't peek. She sat groaning with impatience as he heated water, steeped a tea of rosemary sprigs, and then waited for it to cool. He instructed her to lean back with her shoulders on the camp stool, her head hanging almost upside down. He held the back of her skull with one hand and balanced a tin cup of the brew above her forehead, tilting it carefully. She felt her neck muscles straining, and she squinted in anticipation of having the liquid poured into her eyes.

"Would you relax?" he scolded her. "I've got your head. Just relax into my hand."

She closed her eyes more gently and concentrated on letting go.

She flinched as the water spread around her face, streamed along her temples, ran through the roots of her hair. The warmth was heavenly; the smell and tingling sensation of the herbs was divine; and, with a sigh, she felt the muscles in her face go slack.

She opened her eyes to find him watching her with a grin on his face.

He toweled her hair roughly and then insisted on arranging the locks for several minutes. He even licked his fingers and used his own spit to set a particular curl in place near her ear.

"Give me that mirror," she said between clenched teeth. She snatched it from him and studied her reflection. She looked carefully, from every angle, plucking at a strand here and there. She was quiet for some moments.

He kept saying "Well?" but she couldn't answer because she was terrified of crying in front of him.

"It's lovely," she finally managed to say. "I like it."

He beamed at her.

She smiled back shyly, unable to hold his gaze.

—

The shyness from the intimacy of the haircutting lingered into the evening, becoming an awkward quiet between them. Tanna compulsively stroked the back of her neck, marveling at the disappearance of her hair. Even though she liked the result, she felt naked and self-conscious about her appearance. She wanted to hide in the tent and look at herself in the mirror in private.

More than once she caught him staring at her. To cover it, he lurched into narrating his actions, explaining in too much detail how to properly prepare the fish and bank the embers in the fire pit. He realized he'd been speaking for several minutes, and when he finally glanced her way, she was studying him with a bemused expression. His voice trailed away to nothing in the middle of a sentence.

They stared at one another.

"I'm absolutely sick of eating fish," he said.

She chuckled.

They stared at one another a few moments more.

She broke the silence. "Do you ever worry about dying?"

The question came out of nowhere, but he didn't hesitate to answer. "I worry more about getting old," he said.

"I had syphilis." She held his gaze, calm on the exterior, but her heart pounded as she waited for him to react.

He didn't look away, but his expression was blank, unreadable.

"That's why I went home," she explained.

"I know," he said. No guilt, no pity. She had always suspected Buck must have told him.

She exhaled with a shuddering sigh. "Well, the doctor said I'm cured. I should have a normal life now. And I shouldn't go insane. Not from that, anyway."

He acknowledged her attempt at humor with a small, rueful smile.

"But I can't have children," she said.

He nodded as if something had just occurred to him.

"What?" she asked. It sounded more defensive than she wished.

"The school," he said. "Eve. Even Holly to some degree, I think."

"Yes, the school," she admitted, acknowledging the truth of it out loud. "All the little ones who rely on me. The school, the farm. That's really all I am now."

"No, it's not," he said.

42

The next morning, they took the rifles, picked across the river on the flat stones at its most shallow stretch, and headed south onto the plains. They left the horses hobbled near the camp and *Jewel* bobbing gently above it. Most of the wildlife came and went from the river, so they wouldn't need to go far to find game.

The land was a maze of scrubby pine trees surrounded by tall yellow grass with wide game trails between them. One could only see several yards around the next bend in the trail. They frightened a small herd of animals grazing on the tips of the grass. When the creatures bolted and ran, they looked like small, short-necked ostriches with all their plumage plucked; but when they all settled down again, they revealed themselves to be two-legged horses. They were three feet tall, with short, glossy brown coats; black, flowing manes; and oversized hooves.

"Abelope," Jackson said.

"Tell me we're not hunting them," Tanna said, looking stricken.

"No, no," he assured her. "They're tiny and lean as hell. Nothing to eat. I'm hoping for some large hares or pheasants. We could maybe handle a small deer. But we'd only be able to carry part of it back to camp."

They reached a copse of trees and grass that was surrounded by bones. Old bones, bleached by the sun, spreading across the entire trail like a cobblestone pavement. Jackson stopped her with a hand gesture and pointed silently to a dark, moist spot on the ground. A perfect print pressed into a circular patty of dung.

She instantly recognized the rounded toes of a cat's paw. A cat's paw larger than a man's hand.

He held his finger to his lips in a gesture of silence, moving forward with exaggerated slowness, carrying his rifle across his body in a low-slung, ready position. They heard grunts and soft snorts coming from the next clearing.

They were almost right in front of them before they realized it.

Two black panthers, sharing the carcass of a large deer.

Deep in the bliss of gorging themselves, the cats had not noticed them yet.

"Back up," Jackson mouthed without making a sound. "Easy."

Tanna obeyed, creeping backward as slowly as she could, even as every cell in her body wanted to turn and flee. She knew if she did so, the cats would run her down within seconds.

She couldn't look away from the tops of their shiny black heads, fearing at any moment their eyes would glance up and lock on to hers.

They cleared a stand of grass that blocked their line of sight to the cats. She was able to inhale a little deeper, but was unsure what to do next.

"Be ready to fire," Jackson whispered, sliding two cartridges out of the bandolier across his chest. He turned and began to finally walk forward again, moving more quickly but still as light on his feet as possible. Turning their backs on the cats was an unnerving sensation, even at this distance and with the screen of grass.

Tanna raised the rifle to her shoulder and mimicked Jackson's movements.

The growl behind her was pitched so low she felt its vibration more than she heard it. She turned to find the panther staring at her, already padding slowly toward her. The cat held her gaze with an unblinking stare.

She was paralyzed, some part of her mind screaming. The panther came straight on, creating the illusion of a head floating above padding front feet. It took a moment too long to consciously realize how fast the cat was moving and how close it already was.

The panther closed the last twenty-five feet with a sudden loping gate.

She fired, only seconds before it sank low to prepare for a long final leap.

The cat went down in a somersault ten feet in front of her.

She heard a scream of rage from the other cat.

She jerked around to fire again, but Jackson had already taken aim.

From Tanna's angle, the cat was moving toward him too fast. It was already leaping when he pulled the trigger. He dove sideways as the animal landed hard in the spot where he had been standing only seconds before.

"Reload!" he barked, sighting along the rifle and pivoting in a circle.

She panicked, realizing he was anticipating more of them. Her hands trembled as she fumbled to load another cartridge.

By the time she was prepared to fire again, Jackson was slowly lowering his weapon, relaxing his hunched shoulders, and standing up straight again.

He took a deep, exaggerated breath and stared at the ground. Assured that the two puddles of black fur were no longer moving, he turned to her.

"Are you OK?" he asked.

She nodded her head.

He frowned and moved toward her, with a strange expression on his face. He whipped the kerchief from around his neck and pressed it against her lower lip. He pulled it away and showed her the bright red spot on the cloth. Her lip stung where she'd bitten it, and she tasted blood.

—

Unfortunately, dinner was fried fish. Again. Their rifle shots had scared away all the birds for miles. But, in the aftermath of the encounter with the panthers, Tanna had no appetite. She felt faintly euphoric, with a craving to smoke more than usual. She had the tobacco tin at her feet and was rolling the cigarettes herself.

"I'm getting good at it," she said, holding up the perfect cylinder of white paper.

Jackson poured them each some straight tarwater, not bothering with tea. He raised his tin cup above his head in a toast. "I'm really glad you came," he said.

"Cheers," she said softly, hoping he couldn't see her blush in the firelight.

A sliver of new moon was high in the sky, and the air above the river was full of sylphs. Clouds of tiny, winged air fairies, trooping along in their hovering cyclone formation.

"The first time I ever saw fairies it was exactly like that," Tanna said, inclining her head in the direction of the sight.

Jackson turned to watch the slow tornado of silver wings.

"Moonlit sylphs, dancing at the bottom of a garden," Tanna said in a wistful voice.

"That sounds like the beginning of a story," he said. "You know, I've been waiting for the right opportunity to hear a story on this trip."

She raised her eyebrows, inviting him to go on. He already knew the rules of the game.

His eyes focused on something in the air above her head as he searched for the first sentence. "There was a young girl growing up on Lookout Mountain," he intoned in a storybook voice, "who got lost one day on an unfamiliar path in the woods."

"It was a fork off the trail above Cravens House," Tanna said, "a trail she'd never explored before." One of the most effective ways to channel these stories was to pick them up and continue out loud, without pausing, trusting she would find the words hanging in her mind's eye half a second before they came out of her mouth. "It climbed up around the steepest part of the mountain, beneath Point Park. She couldn't resist the urge to see where it might lead. It was a mystery to her. A mystery she had to solve ..."

He was staring at her. His eye contact was often intense, but this was almost disconcerting. She licked her lips and shaped them to form another word, but she couldn't continue. Her breath caught in her throat.

She dropped her eyes, but she stood. The perfect unlit cigarette rolled from her lap onto the ground. She stooped to pick it up, steadying herself by putting her hand on his shoulder. Unable to meet his eyes, she squeezed gently, then turned and walked to her tent.

She assumed he would follow. God, she hoped he would understand he was meant to follow. She stepped inside but left the flap door hanging loose and open. His shadow fell across the canvas. She felt him there, just outside. She thought she could hear his throat working as he swallowed. With her back to him, she began to unbutton her blouse, and when she heard him pull aside the heavy fabric, she turned to face him

"I'd like to do that," he said.

His hands trembled. He grunted under his breath as his thick fingers struggled with the tiny buttons. He gave a small cry of triumph as the last one came free, and they both chuckled.

She quickly unbuttoned his shirt. She reached inside the sweaty fabric, sliding her hands across the wiry hair on his chest, up and around his shoulders, pushing the shirt off. It draped across his back, hung at his elbows. She allowed her fingers to trail down his biceps and pull the sleeves down his arms. His forearms and wrists were shockingly furred. She had grazed them accidentally from time to time, and she had always wanted to stroke them more boldly. The hair was as springy as copper-colored moss. She caught each of his wrists in the loose rings made by her thumbs and forefingers. He let her weigh his hands with her own for a few moments, and then, finally, he bent his face close to hers.

She felt his breath soft on her mouth, his lips barely grazing hers, and he pulled away, remembering that she had bitten her lip.

"Will that hurt?" he asked.

"No," she said, the word barely more than a sigh.

It did hurt, a little. His lips were rough. The tip of his tongue caused the wound to sting, but their mouths opened with the urgency of the kiss.

The warmth and moisture of their tongues melted their sun-chapped lips.

She had taken off her brassiere when she bathed before dinner. He reached inside her open blouse to gently cup her breasts in his palms. His thumbs found her nipples and gently pressed them into the areolae, purposefully withholding the sensation of friction.

She shoved her hands past the waistband of his pants, briefly grasping his buttocks before withdrawing from the kiss. He held his breath as she unbuckled his belt, the weight of the leather causing his pants to drop to his ankles.

He bent over double, trying to free his boots from the cuff of his pants.

"Lie back," she insisted, pushing him down on her cot. He watched her on raised elbows as she twisted off his boots. They were both aware of the smell from his damp socks. Self-consciously, he tried to yank them away from her, but she held on to his ankle and peeled the sock off one foot, then repeated the motion on the other. She held his naked foot against her, his heel against the top of her thigh, his toes beneath her breast. She massaged his foot, wrapping her arms around it, embracing it against her.

He stretched his hands toward her, gesturing with his fingers for her to come into his arms. She unbuttoned her own pants as he watched, but hesitated before sliding them off. He twisted sideways, reaching for the lantern, and turned it down until it was a low orange tongue of light. She stepped free of her pants and crawled onto the bed, placing one knee between his thighs. The cot creaked and she hovered above him uncertainly, hoping for one moment that the narrow bed could sustain their combined weight.

He pulled her down on top of him for that blissful first full contact. For several minutes, the sensation stretched along the length of their bodies, silky, dry, and cool, elongating their combined energy, braiding their legs. As their bellies pressed together, the heat built between them, drawing the sweat to the surface.

She braced her arms, her hands in the damp fur of his armpits, her breasts swinging just far enough above him that his chest hair tickled her nipples. He squeezed the back of her neck, his fingertips scraping furrows through the short hair along the back of her skull, pressing almost painfully against her scalp.

She stayed on top, facing him, his hips arching up to meet her. She could only see two faint, winking reflections of light in his eyes, but it was enough to know that he looked up at her the whole time.

—

She lay awake beside him, balanced along the edge of the narrow cot, his arm barely keeping her from rolling off onto the ground. He stirred, and realizing she must be uncomfortable, turned on his side to make more room for her. He faced her, smiling softly in the predawn light.

"I keep thinking," she whispered, "about the panthers. If I lost you, what would I do out here alone?"

"You'd find your way," he said.

—

The following day, without discussion, they took down the tent, packed up the camp, and began their journey home. They rode side by side on horseback, wherever the shelf of rock along the river was wide enough to allow it. They kept a more comfortable silence between them now, but she found it harder to resist looking at him, studying his profile. And now she didn't feel the need to look away when he caught her watching him. He glanced over from time to time and smiled, warmly enough. But it wasn't a noticeably different expression.

"I need to know how to think about all this," she said.

"Why?" he asked.

She didn't answer, reluctant to voice all that came to mind.

—

Ioma stood on the front steps of Cole's house, the fringed edges of her lichen-green shawl dusting the steps like the trailing tips of willow branches.

Tanna watched Jackson dismount and stare up at the Alleegee woman. He gave Tanna a hand and helped her out of the saddle.

"We should go up," he said. "We can see him for a few minutes before we leave."

—

The sight of Cole devastated her. He was a wraith, swaddled in blankets in his chair by the fire. He smiled at them, his eyes glittering with whatever energy was still available to him.

Jackson performed for his friend, radiating charm and mischievous humor, stalking up and down the room, jumping up on the hearth to bring life to the story of their travels. He never once acknowledged Cole's condition or appearance in any way, he didn't ask about his health, and he never allowed his brow to furrow with concern.

Although she wanted to fall on her knees beside the chair, take Cole's hand, and beg forgiveness for the argument they'd had before their last parting, her instinct was to follow Jackson's lead. She acted as if nothing were wrong, as if it were a night of storytelling by the fire, just like her fondest memories. She wasn't sure where her wits were coming from, but she managed to match Jackson's humor with her usual quick conversation. Cole watched her with a bemused, lopsided grin.

Ioma stood nearby, just behind Cole's chair, saying nothing but watching the entire time. There were shadows of exhaustion under the fae woman's eyes. It was hard not to read her impassive expression as either judgment or even contempt. Cole asked her to take Jackson to the cellar to retrieve some special bottles he was sending away with them as gifts.

Once they were alone, Cole tilted his head and fixed Tanna with a sly smile.

"He loves to give gifts, you know," he said. "But don't be disappointed when he forgets your birthday or goes on safari over Christmas. He'll come back. He may never mention your anniversary, but the days in between will be more with him than with anyone you've known before."

"More?" Tanna asked.

"He'll love and respect you more than anyone else is capable of," Cole explained. "It'll be the kind of friendship few can promise, but the kind of love that may defy your desire for naming things. The very thing you will most want to find a word for, the word for what he means to you— or, actually, the word for what you mean to him—just might elude you forever."

Tanna met his ominous words with feigned nonchalance. "I'm aware that Jackson Gallagher may be the dangerous adventure I came here for."

His brows came together in genuine concern, and the effort of the change in expression seemed to pain him. "You know, when the old mapmakers reached the edge of what they knew, they wrote, 'Beyond this point, there be dragons.'"

—

Cole's prediction came true.

Back home at Brynmor, their comfortable routines expanded. The barriers that had once existed between them evaporated—her marriage to Buck, and the walls of the guest bedroom to which Jackson used to retire. Constant companionship replaced the old polite partings at the end of evenings. Their after-dinner walks now ended in Tanna's bed, where they undressed each other and laid together in a cycle of physical exploration, dozing, and talking.

Her memories of Ford were like recalling a terrible illness that she'd barely survived. Unbuttoned pants, skirts around her waist, the way Ford lay flat and heavy on top of her, rutting and grunting. He rolled off her without speaking and went to sleep, or pretended to in order to avoid speaking to her. Afterward, Ford had subtly punished her for days with less patience and barely contained temper. He never struck her, but he addressed her through clenched teeth as if his rage were only moments away from exploding from him.

Buck, drunk and intoxicated with shine, had barely managed to use her from behind, while no doubt closing his eyes and conjuring up the image of a boy half her age.

The way Jackson looked at her unnerved her. He demanded to always see her face when he was inside her, telling her to leave the light burning or to pull back the drapes so he could see her by moonlight. Sometimes while they were kissing she opened her eyes to find him watching her. Even in the dark, she could detect the reflections of faint light in his eyes when he blinked.

Jackson faced her. He looked at her, and he listened without speaking. He saw her and he stayed.

The household never questioned his presence. The girls—Eve, Holly, Ginger—all adored him. The servants and the yolos treated him as a benevolent master. Navvee prepared special dishes he knew Jackson liked. Joona waited on them at meals with a grin he couldn't suppress. It annoyed Tanna that Jackson so instantly commanded the affection and respect for which she had had to fight.

Holly had to steer Eve away from Tanna's bedroom door when necessary. Mr. Palmer couldn't help but stare righteous daggers at Tanna when she walked past the schoolhouse. The elven women tittered and pointed when they saw the couple wandering the fields.

ERIC SLADE

All that attention felt far away, heard through bedroom walls, glimpsed in passing. It reminded Tanna of slow dancing with Jackson in a ballroom, the crowds parting to let them sweep by. She remained focused on his face, so close to hers, always watching.

She wondered every day what her life would have been like if she'd been married to him these past years, instead of chasing the name of Eldridge.

—

"I've been thinking," he said one evening after dinner. They were in the living room listening to the Victrola and the downpour of rain outside.

She looked up from the button she was sewing onto one of his shirts. He was pacing in front of the hearth.

"With all the new safari work," he continued, "and these guided tours, I barely have time to go into town, let alone stay there. I have little use for the room at The Fairchild anymore. Cole has no need to share it as we did in the past. And it's unlikely that Buck's going to be dropping by here." He was clearly struggling to ask something. She set the sewing down in her lap and shifted in her chair, settling in to give him her full attention. "I don't know that I would be any good at it. I don't know that I can make it mean what you might want it to mean ... But how would you feel if I kept a few of my personal things—the things from my room in Treebridge—here at the farm with you?"

Tanna hid the sensation of joy that flashed through her. "You would come and go from my house?"

"Yes. And from Cole's barn, of course, as I require equipment. I would launch my safaris from the orchard, but, in between my travels, I would spend the breaks here." He paused, watching her face intently. "If that's what you want."

Her pulse raced. She released a breath she didn't realize she'd been holding.

"'When the gods want to punish us, they answer our prayers,'" she muttered.

There was nothing he could say in response to that. He thought he saw signs of her mind beginning to whir. He didn't want to indulge her in self-flagellation or in analysis of *what it all meant*, so he changed the subject. He said the only other thing he needed to tell her that could rival what he had just changed between them.

"Cole is dying."

She crossed her arms. "How do you know?"

"Ioma sent a message."

She put her hands on the arms of her chair, feeling the need to leap up, but she sagged back at the last moment. "Are you sure he doesn't need us to go to him?"

"She's with him," Jackson said pointedly.

"Then at least we know he will be loved," Tanna said, "all the way to the end."

43

They buried him in the Mathers family plot in the churchyard of Old Rath Abbey.

Tanna looked up from the bowed heads, her attention drifting from the priest's words. She saw Ioma watching from outside the gate, clothed in the silvery-white color of ashes that the Alleegee wore in observance of mourning. Her face was as stony as ever, but there was the smallest hint of anger in her eyes, the tiniest furrow in her brow.

Tanna wondered if the rage was for them, the mortal colonists who assumed control of Cole's final passage from this world without even allowing her to stand beside the grave.

Jackson said the fae despised the way humans tried to preserve the bodies of the deceased in boxes and stone crypts. Christian notions of resurrection conflicted with their perception of the cycle of life. The fae were particularly concerned with the return of bodies. They had diverse rituals for the spirit, depending on the race and tribe, but when it came to the mortal vessel, the fae agreed about its disposal—it should preferably be buried in fertile soil, without a container or obstruction of any kind; or, the body should be left in the wilderness, where carrion birds and animals could take it apart. The body must be given back to nature and transformed by natural laws.

Cremation was an exception in the circumstance of humans disposing of the body of a fae. Tanna remembered the elf they had shot and burned in the Crenshaws' fields the day she decided to come here with Buck. The fae insisted humans should always burn a fairy corpse beyond recognition or use. Tanna wondered what *use* they might have for fairy corpses.

Tanna hoped Ioma didn't care about customs, that, after all the years of loving Cole, she simply mourned. In that nearly imperceptible frown, Tanna saw only a wife's grief. The grief of a widow. She decided she would speak to Ioma, as she would to any wife at her husband's wake.

When she walked toward the churchyard fence, Holly followed. The girl looked incongruous in the dark man's suit she had borrowed from Jackson's wardrobe. "Where's Jackson? Isn't it strange for him not to be here, of all people?"

Tanna stopped and peered around at the horizon. "Oh, I think he's off with Cole. In some private wild spot they both loved. Somewhere they live together in spirit. And you and I both know that's not in a churchyard."

She turned to continue on toward Ioma, but the fairy woman was gone.

—

During the days that Jackson was at home with her at Brynmor, they never spoke of anything ordinary. She didn't think out loud about her troubles with the farm—whether her next crop were going to do better or possibly fail again, if the refinery were going to be built in time, if she would ever be able to pay off the bank notes ... They had given her extensions with a smile and well wishes, but the paperwork they sent to her lawyers included ominous language and hefty interest.

Jackson talked about his work less than he ever had, even though he was often right there, in the living room, with his maps spread on the coffee table or across the empty space on the rug in front of the fire. He muttered to himself and puttered about making lists, writing letters, and sending the yolos here and there on errands or with messages. But he didn't discuss any of it with her.

He seemed to withhold the one thing Tanna expected him to bring home, the one topic that should have bubbled up in outrage, breaking through their companionable silences—what was happening to the Green. The escalation of the violence was reaching well beyond the Seaming, throughout the plantations of the colony, and deeper into the interior. He had to witness it every time he went out. She saw him plotting courses around the areas he knew best, looking for alternate mountain passes and ways to skirt around the wide open plains. Now he was always creeping under the cover of forest canopies, fording streams quickly, and never camping near them as they had on their safari.

She feared the reality of what was happening out there, but she cherished the sense that they were far away from it, apart. It felt like they had stolen a reprieve. Here, after dinner, with snifters of tarwater, brandy, or cups of coffee and their haint cigarettes, there were no outstanding debts; there was no fear for the safety of hunting clients who failed to acknowledge they were being hunted back.

And sometimes there were stories. The ones she made up.

By evening, she was tired of business. Poring over the account ledgers would do nothing to make the rain fall or the crops grow or the haint flowers miraculously multiply. She had taken to jotting down notes for stories, and then, when he made himself comfortable at her feet, like a child, she read to him. He spread cushions across the floor like a couch in front of the fire. She pulled her feet up under her in her favorite chair, or sometimes she moved down close to him, sitting cross-legged on a pillow like Scheherazade herself. And Jackson listened, clear-eyed, as she read him a long tale she had been working on, from beginning to end.

—

One afternoon, Tanna came in from a walk over to the schoolhouse, where it was her habit to read books out loud to the children. Jackson asked her why she didn't tell them her original stories, but she had wanted them to associate stories with books so they might someday seek them out on their own. Finally, at his encouragement, she began to tell them some of the tales she'd been scribbling in the evenings, slipping them in among the usual myths and fairy tales. Now, she tried out her newest stories first with the children, and if they were well-received, then she told them to Jackson.

She found him pacing in front of the hearth, studying an oversized scrolling document. A lit cigarette burned forgotten in the stand ashtray next to her chair. Hearing her enter, he rolled the paper up and tapped it against his open palm. Without looking at her, he opened his mouth to speak, but then he hesitated.

"What is it?" she asked, suddenly fearing bad news.

"Cole's property. These are the official papers." Jackson finally met her eyes. "He left everything to me."

"Oh," she said, relieved, but unsure of his mood. "Well, it seems like you must have expected that."

"I did." He went for his cigarette in the ashtray, but finding it burned down, he stubbed it out. "We discussed everything before he died."

"I hadn't thought of it before. But knowing it now, I can't say that I'm surprised. Whom else did he leave behind?" Of course, she meant that Cole had no family or heirs.

Jackson took the question literally. "Well, there's Ioma. And a handful of other servants who've lived at the orchard their entire lives. I know the place seemed deserted when you and Holly stopped over there, but there's actually a good-sized little village of souls that keep that place running. The house, the groves, the stables. The various enterprises on the property.

There's a whole brugh, deep in the mountain behind the kitchens and under the cellars." He stared out the window, looking southwest and tapping the scroll against his hand again. "I'll need to go see to a few things."

"Of course." She tried to cover the disappointment in her voice, even though he'd told her that her attempts at nonchalance were unconvincing. "How long do you think you'll be gone?"

"A week. Maybe two." He was infuriatingly practical. No mention of regrets, no acknowledgment that their private world—their honeymoon—was coming to an end.

She nodded, as if they were discussing a grocery list and he was only driving down to the market. She couldn't ask him not to go. She waited another couple of breaths, hoping in vain he would ask her to come with him. But the natural moment for that to occur had already passed. The pause was becoming awkwardly long and she needed to say something.

"I know I may be wasting my breath," she said. "But will you please send me word of how things are going? When you might return?"

His eyes narrowed and his brow creased. He was clearly confused by her tone. "I'll be back," he said.

"I know." She sighed. "I'll be here."

—

An airship.

Tanna knew something was unusual about this one. It streaked almost silently over her head, much closer to the ground than the one they'd seen on safari. She could hear the faint sound of wind along its body, like a whistling through thin branches.

She was out on the top terrace of haint plants closest to the kitchen garden. As the craft passed directly over the house, it dipped sideways and then righted itself quickly, tipping its wings as if in greeting. It dove down the back side of Brynmor, perfectly following the slope much closer than it needed to. Whoever it was intended to put her down in the flat field past the warehouse, alongside the Big South Road.

Feeling another urgent prickle of intuition, Tanna set off running to meet it.

It was shaped like a rolled wedge, like a giant leaf turned in on itself along the strong vein of its central axis. As the pilot brought the skinny craft in low and fast over the field, skimming the tops of the tall grasses, the sides of the ship unfurled, snapped apart like the casing around a beetle's wings; and silvery-green sails emerged and caught the air like short, rigid parachutes, slowing the vehicle with remarkable speed. It skipped and slid across the ground with a loud hiss and came to rest, humming and faintly vibrating.

As she ran, she saw a hand reach out and give a jaunty wave. She knew somehow by the twist of the wrist that it was Jackson. He was nestled in a cradle at the back of a cocoon, grinning like a bug behind goggles, his hair hidden beneath a close-fitting leather aviator's cap.

"Where did you get this?" she asked, running her hands across the crisp yet faintly velvety hull.

"She's part of my inheritance."

"Cole grew this?"

"Along with a dozen others. They're called *boughrunners*." He handed her a pair of goggles. "You'll be happy to know I already named this one. *Gypsy*. Get in."

She took the goggles and pulled herself up, as she might climb onto a horse. She swung her legs over the side and into the passenger compartment in front of him. She hesitated before she sat, twisting around to look down at him. "When did you learn to fly?" she demanded.

He flashed a manic grin. "Yesterday!"

With a tremor of anticipation and a surprising lack of reticence, she clambered into the front seat and strapped the belts across her chest and lap just as the craft began to move.

With only a light blustery wind left over from rainstorms that morning, the craft picked up an impossible amount of speed across the flat field. A slippery paper rasp came from the belly of the hull's contact with the grass. *Gypsy* rose to the tips of the stalks, parting the grasses and then skimming over them, bouncing like a boat across swells of water. Jackson steered the aircraft due west, crossing the width of the pastures below Brynmor at their narrowest point and arrowing toward the edge of Bryn Wood. She involuntarily braced for their crash into the trunks of several trees, but *Gypsy*'s nose bucked upward like a rearing horse. There was a moment of silence as the whispering contact with the grasses ceased, and they leapt the remaining twenty yards to skate across the treetops, again crashing over the swells of leaves as they had the grasses only moments before.

The canopy of the woods stretched in three directions as far as she could see over the nose and sides of the boughrunner, a great lake of fluttering green. They sailed across it, faster than anything she'd ever ridden, faster than a Model T barreling down a paved road or a train across a plain.

Wing-like sails were flattening along the craft but not entirely closing around it, and they were beginning to lift away from the trees now. She felt the last shuddering vibration, a few skipping kisses with leaves, and then an eerie hush of nothing but wind, as they were now climbing the sky.

The dirigibles had never felt like true flight. At best they had offered the sensation of floating, but also being dragged, bumping along, never disconnected from the earth. This was the freedom and the euphoria of winged things. Gypsy's wings were connected to Tanna's body and her soul. The vibration traveled from the ship into her trembling limbs. Her heart rode high and forward in her chest, as if she had been gripped and pulled through the clouds by her heartstrings, bringing the boughrunner with her.

Jackson steered them in a slow curve toward the southwest, where the Hawnee Hills rose above the forest. She looked ahead for the flashing copper roof of Cole's stables. They flew directly over the road at the Hawkeye Pass, the way they had traveled on safari, but they were close to the level of the clouds and could have easily cleared even the highest peaks. Mist from the rains tore away from the mountains in shredded veils. It reminded her of the Appalachians back home in the Gray, and the phenomena for which they were called the Smoky Mountains.

She grew braver and more comfortable, leaning her face out into the stream of wind, as far out as the straps of the safety belts would allow. She had to strain to look over the sides and straight down, but her soul craved the sight, the miniaturized living map of the familiar places where they had puttered and crawled, walked and ridden. Now, it was laid out for her as if she were a goddess, the benevolent creator or overseer of this world.

Jackson followed the course of their previous excursion, the miles and days of traveling on horseback disappearing beneath them in minutes. He found the Yooway River, a silver ribbon far below, and shadowed its snaking curves. There was the first bend with the mossy banks of butterflies. He dipped low, sending a cloud of the colorful creatures up into the air, trailing in their wake. He dropped down through the clouds so they could skim closer, maybe only a hundred feet above the shelves of smooth rocks where they had camped. She cried out over a site she recognized, their cold fire pit a black circle in the green, as if a giant cigarette had been put out there.

When the Yooway widened and flattened out, where its shoals met the southern plains, the final campsite on their safari, Jackson flew so low she braced for a spray of water. The river was covered from bank to bank with a flock of thousands of pink flamingoes. They all took flight in a single shimmering mass, a slight delay from one edge of the flock to the other, like a huge piece of silk lifting off the river.

Jackson surprised her by banking right and climbing again. They flew on, north by northwest, beyond the land with which she was familiar. They had to be past the boundaries of the colony, flying over the places even Jackson might not have been on safari.

They were level with the clouds now, the ground too far beneath to even see. She sat back in her seat and looked straight forward and up, the sunshine in her eyes. Completely overcome with emotion, she was thankful the wind whistled loud enough to cover the sound of her sobbing.

She reached up and back, her fingers open for Jackson's hand. She felt his leather glove close around her fingertips and squeeze.

This was like nothing she had ever experienced. This was a glimpse of the world through the eyes of a god. She wanted to extend it, to suspend herself within it, with him. This was his perfect state of grace. She felt it in their clasped hands. He said to her, *This. This.* And she knew what he meant. She wept softly, specifically for the alternate life they had somehow missed. An existence together as flying things, as mated swans, as sylphs who drifted together and never came down, as angels, patrolling the lower levels of heaven.

—

"Is this where you were the day of Cole's funeral?" she asked.

He nodded.

They were sitting on a blanket on Dead Tree Hill, overlooking *Gypsy* parked on the Cumberland Prairie below. Jackson had landed her with surprising precision, and they had hiked straight up through the grass instead of taking the West Fork Road over the Hawkeye Pass as they had on safari.

"I don't think he was at that churchyard," she said. "I think he was here with you."

He smiled, the setting sun burnishing his brows and lashes and the whisker stubble on his jaw.

"Bury me here," he said.

"OK," she said. "If I outlive you."

Seeing her troubled expression, he stumbled toward one of his natural history lectures. "That tree," he said, gesturing toward the gnarled and ancient form. "It's been broken by storms and gravity, hollowed out by disease and animals, but it's still richly alive with other living things. There are creatures—even some tribes of the fae—that never set foot on the ground."

Her face lit up with a private remembrance.

"Why are you smiling?" he asked.

"It just made me think of you, standing in the treetops with your wings. Part fallen angel, part cowboy, part dragon hunter."

"That tree—this whole hill, really—is a great place for hunters."

"It'd be a nice level lookout for the panthers," she said, gazing out at the prairie. "Not that I would want to find them here."

"It's covered in finch owls," he said, staring over her shoulder at the tree.

"Is it?" She twisted around, peering carefully at the vines carpeting the dead branches. There were little dry gray-and-brown leaves, visible against the black bark, fluttering in a breeze. She gasped. "I thought they were foliage! It's covered in them."

"I don't think I've ever seen a parliament of finch owls that large."

"Not even on safari?" she asked.

"No. And it surprises me to find them so close to a main road."

"We're not in danger from them, are we?"

"No matter how large their populations get, roosting together, they still always hunt in smaller groups. You'd think that several hundred might descend on us and tear us apart like piranha. They could. If they wanted to, they could absolutely kill a human being. Or any large mammal, really. For some reason, they don't."

Tanna grimaced. "Why did you have to tell me that? I didn't even notice them. Now, it's a little hard to enjoy sitting out here in the open like this."

"You're right, it is a great lookout for the big cats," he continued. "You often see the panthers and the finch owls living close to each other. As predators, they like certain spots for the same reasons."

"It seems like even the cats would be afraid of a thousand finch owls hovering over them."

"I've often wondered that." He frowned. "I guess they don't prefer the taste of big cats or people."

"I think it would be better for you to bury *me* here," Tanna said. "That way, I know you'd come visit me often."

"OK. I will," he said. "If I outlive you."

44

They were sitting in their favorite chairs on the side veranda when a new shiny, unrecognizable buggy pulled up the drive. Buck jumped out and stepped right into the middle of their afternoon coffee. He took off his hat and self-consciously smoothed his yellow cornsilk hair across his thinning crown. He nodded curtly. "Jackson."

"Buck," Jackson said, slightly amused by his friend's uncharacteristically formal manner.

"Can I speak with you in private, Tanna?" Buck asked.

"Of course," she said, throwing a glance at Jackson before leading Buck to her desk in the living room. "Please tell me you're not here for money, Buck, because I don't have any."

"That's not why I'm here," he said, putting his hat on a chair. "I've been thinking you might be wanting a divorce."

She looked at him sharply. She searched his face for any trace of humor, but found him entirely serious. Realizing what was happening, she sighed. "I can read your mind, you know. Why, out of all the people in the world, is it you whose mind I can read as clearly as a glass book?"

He smiled sheepishly.

"Who is it, then? Someone with money. Cookie, I presume?"

He grimaced in a self-deprecating way, but he did not correct her.

"And you've managed to convince this poor woman to marry you?" She gave a bitter chuckle and shook her head at him. "What wonderful timing for you, Buck. One has to wonder what she's getting out of it." She leaned back against the desk and crossed her arms. "She's certainly buying more than she bargained for, I'm sure. I should probably refuse you, for her sake, out of a sense of sisterly protection." She paused, but he met her derision with a steady gaze. "Were you never afraid of ... giving it to her?"

They both knew the disease of which she spoke.

Buck crossed his own arms, mirroring her defensive posture. The question had certainly angered him a little, but he maintained his cool position. "Our relationship is more ..."—he pretended to search for the perfect word—"*spiritual* in nature. It's more intellectual."

"Intellectual?" Tanna made a rude noise. "It challenges my conscience to release you to her, it truly does ... But then I've never attempted to protect anyone else from your corruption, so why should I start with the woman who's stolen my husband?" She waited for a response, and not getting any, she finally threw up her hands. "Well, I guess I'm supposed to accuse you of something. You know, for the petition in court. They ask for a reason for divorce. I'm afraid if I list the real reasons why I deserve to be parted from you they may decide to just throw you in prison, for the good of the entire colony."

He smiled. "I could always accuse you," he said sweetly, inclining his head toward Jackson out on the veranda. "Another man, living here with my wife ..." He raised his eyebrows suggestively.

"You wouldn't dare," she said wearily, letting her lack of concern show. He was only an annoyance to her at this point, and she wanted to make sure he knew it.

"No, of course not." He waved away the thought. "I feel the least I can do is let you be the one to slap me across the face in public." He reached into the inside breast pocket of his jacket and brought out a scroll of crisp new papers. "I went ahead and had the first round of papers drawn up. In case you agreed. To move things along."

She took them from him, slipped off the ribbon, and flattened the document on her desk with an empty whiskey tumbler and a full ashtray.

"The reason you're divorcing me is on the second page," he said, pointing. "Some legal terminology for my gambling and starting debts in your name without your knowledge. About how I generally ran through your fortune." He shrugged, believably humbled. "I figured at least it's true, and it's something that can be backed up by any number of institutions."

"Is all that even enough of an official crime to grant me a divorce, in the eyes of the law?"

"I've been assured it will be. And I won't contest it."

She moved the ashtray and turned to the signature line. "How long is this supposed to take?"

"Oh, maybe a month or two. They handle these things pretty quickly in the colony court. Especially when you know the right people." He winked at her and, with a flourish, produced a fountain pen.

Tanna angrily snatched it from him. "That's my father's pen." She signed the papers where he indicated and let them snap back into a sloppy roll. "Bless her heart," she muttered, shoving the pages at him. "I'll be as happy for you as I can, Buck."

He chuckled good-naturedly, straightened up the scroll, and kissed her on the cheek. "Thank you for this, Tanna. Truly. Thank you for everything."

"How do you manage it?" she asked, her voice softened with emotion. "After everything, to somehow still keep me as a friend?"

"I've always been your friend," he said. "I started out that way."

He turned and strode back through the house, going out the side veranda, even though it wasn't the most direct route. She assumed he wanted an excuse to speak to Jackson, so she hung back inside the door, eavesdropping.

"You know, Jackson," she heard Buck say, "you could have asked."

There was a pause.

"I did ask," Jackson said. "She said yes."

—

Tanna returned to her chair and lit a cigarette. She sat silently smoking, watching Jackson read. Finally she said, "When you go away on safari, are you ever with someone else?"

Moving only his eyes, he glanced away from his book. "If I wanted to spend time with someone else, I'd stay here with you. Or take you with me." His gaze shifted back to the page.

She watched his eyes dart back and forth, tracking the lines of type. He showed no signs of engaging her.

She held her breath, knowing it was an interruption, a forced conversation. "Do you ever feel lonely?" she finally exhaled.

"Sure," he said quietly, not looking up from the book. "Sometimes."

"Do you ever wonder if I'm lonely?" She regretted the stress on the word I as soon as she heard it come out of her mouth.

His eyes stopped moving. "It's not something I dwell on."

"Do you even think about me at all when you're away?" She knew the sulky tone would anger him, but she couldn't stop herself.

"All the time," he said, his tone purposefully even and tight.

"But not enough to come back." She said it under her breath, looking away. She crossed her arms and her legs, and bounced her foot.

With a frustrated sigh, he snapped his book shut. "I do come back. All the time." He studied her stubborn profile. "You want to tell me what this is about?"

She trailed a hand through the air in a breezy, nonchalant gesture, but she still didn't look at him. "It seems I'll be available again soon."

"Available?" The expressionless repeating of words was a sign of his profound annoyance.

"Buck has asked me for a divorce," she said, spilling the words, as if he had been pressing the news from her. "He's found another woman who's willing to marry him. One who still has money. Unlike me." She rolled her eyes in self-deprecation. When she spoke again, it was almost a whisper: "I just thought we might do that someday."

She inspected the buttons down the front of her blouse, but her foot bounced so furiously it was a blur.

He shifted to face her then, leaning toward her as far as the arm of his chair would allow. "How would getting married change anything between us for the better?" She recognized one of his attacks—he combined challenging questions with careful enunciation and a total lack of expression.

She couldn't withhold her petulance. It erupted from her in a strident wail. "I would have someone of my own!"

"No, you wouldn't," he said. "You already have everything you've ever wanted. The big house, the business, the children, the position." He was imploring her now. "You have the love too. I know for sure you have the love."

She refused to hear him. Her chair legs squeaked against the tile as she leapt up and started pacing in front of him. "Don't you *ever* want to marry?" She stopped to tower over him. "Anyone?"

He shrugged, incredulous. "Why would *you* want to marry again?"

"Why wouldn't I?" She crossed her arms, hugging herself tightly.

He gestured angrily in Buck's wake. "Well, there's one sorry example."

"That was an arrangement. We didn't marry for love."

"Can you name even one couple you admire who married for love?"

"Yes. Of course I can. Many," she said, a little too quickly, raising her chin. When she paused he raised his eyebrows for her to elaborate. "The Crawfords," she stammered.

A hateful bark of laughter escaped him. "Hal Crawford told that poor woman he was going on ahead into the Green to scout out their homestead, but, unlike your Bucky, he never bothered to mention the time lag to her before he left. He was gone for over three years!"

"Oh, please," Tanna huffed, flapping a hand at him in disgust. "That's a cocktail party story. A myth."

"I've heard him tell it myself!" He stood now too, his face red, reclaiming the advantage of height. "Whether it's true or not, the fact that he tells it at all, while laughing his ass off, speaks volumes."

He stomped inside, went to the sideboard in the dining room, and poured himself a finger of tarwater. She followed him, but he didn't offer her a drink.

"People who are in love get married," she said, lowering her voice to a calm, reasonable tone. "It's not revolutionary. There are animals and fae that mate for life."

"Geese," he tossed out over his shoulder, as if it were ridiculous. With his back to her, he drained his glass and remained facing the wall.

"And velvets," she offered pathetically. But when he started acting like a boy, she knew she had at least a chance to regain the moral high ground. "You use the fae for your own arguments, all the time. But now you don't want me to use them for mine."

He set the glass carefully down and turned to face her. He looked tired. "I would mate for life," he said, his eyes earnest and sad. "It just needs to be one day at a time."

Melting a little, she sighed. They stood there looking at one another, allowing the conversation to cool.

"You know, I just want someone to ask me," she finally said. Her voice was barely more than a whisper, stricken with a defeated honesty. "Just once. That's all."

He cleared his throat. "Buck didn't ask you?"

"No. I proposed to him." She chuckled at the memory bitterly, embarrassed. "It was more like a bribe."

Jackson was compassionately silent.

"If I promise to say no," she said, a bit of the girlish whine returning to her voice, "will you at least ask me someday?"

"Hmm. That feels like a setup," he said with levity, trying to drag the conversation back into the sunlight.

She wasn't ready to stop basking in her shadows. "When you go away, though ... You don't always go on safari, do you?"

He cocked his head and looked at her, his disappointment evident. He didn't answer, refusing to wander into the trap she was trying to lay.

"You just want to be away," she said, answering for him, her cheeks slack with martyrdom.

He gave in to her poking and lost the will to remain quiet. "It's not about you, you know. It has nothing to do with you. And it's certainly not meant to hurt you."

"Well, it does," she pouted.

He made fists but managed to swallow his rage. He opened and flexed both hands, but couldn't resist jabbing a single finger at her. "I am with you—when I am with you—because I *choose* to be with you. I don't want to live according to someone else's idea of how we're supposed to live. So don't ask me to do that. I don't want to find out one day that I'm at the end of someone else's life."

Her face reddened. She had pushed him, and she knew it.

"I'm willing to pay a high price for my life," he continued, his voice growing softer with deeper anger. "To live my life the way I want to. And yes, sometimes that means I might feel lonely. I'm willing to feel lonely. I'm willing to pay that price. I'm even willing to die alone, if it comes down to it. And I think that's entirely fair."

"That's not *fair*," she spat. "You expect me to pay for it as well."

"No, you have a choice, Tanna. I leave your choices up to you. But it doesn't seem you're willing to do the same thing for me. I won't be closer to you, I won't love any more—I will never *belong* to you—because of a piece of paper."

—

For the next few days, the only way they could exist in the house together was to pretend the conversation had never happened. She feebly tried to bear the grief of it by chattering about her other troubles. She attempted to make Jackson her ally again by confiding in him.

"I can't afford to pay Gentry much longer. I told him he and Davis could stay in the cabin as long as they needed to, until he decides what his next move might be. I hope that's fair. It's all I can offer him. I'm sure he wants to kill me," she muttered, shoving the sewing needle through a button.

Jackson didn't answer. He was on his knees before the hearth, his face inches away from a map spread across the floor. He grunted, acknowledging that she was speaking to him, but he wasn't listening.

"I'm sorry," she sighed. "I'm sure you don't want to hear me whine about the farm."

Something in her tone broke through to him. He glanced up, but his eyes were drawn to her task. He frowned. "What are you doing?"

She looked bewildered. "I'm mending your shirt."

"You don't have to do that."

"Don't be silly. I want to do it." She smiled at him, biting through the thread.

"Don't."

There it was—that thing she thought she'd been burying under handfuls of steady, everyday prattle—his contempt for the concept of belonging to her.

She made a show of dropping the shirt, the needle, and the spool of thread into the basket beside her chair.

"I'm planning a trip to Dawolee Gadusee," he continued, as if her sewing had been an interruption. "North of Chickamauga Gorge. I'll probably go ahead and leave in the morning."

"You just got back," she protested.

He ignored her. He folded up the map and plucked his pencils off of the rug, tidying up as if he planned to walk right out of the room and into the Green within the next few minutes.

He stood, stretching out his limbs, looming over her. "Holly has asked me if she can come along on this one."

Tanna shook her head. "Poor thing. Once a week, she decides she wants to bolt. She thinks the Graycoat is going to show up any moment, but surely he already would have if he were going to. She sees how you manage to keep moving. I'm sure that's appealing to her."

She could sense he wanted to comment, but he was hesitating for some reason.

"I almost told her she couldn't come." He rolled the pencils between his fingers, looking at his hands. "I didn't think you'd like both of us leaving. Together. And leaving you here alone."

"Well, you're right," Tanna stood to face him. "I wouldn't like that at all."

He finally made eye contact with her. "But there's no real reason for me to tell her she can't come."

She snorted in disgust. "Yes, there is. This isn't a client trip, is it? There are no women or girls for her to wrangle for you. It would just be the two of you. Unchaperoned. It's not proper."

"*Proper*?" He frowned as if worried about her sanity. "Me and Holly Gray?"

"Well, it certainly wouldn't look proper to other people," she said, her eyebrows raised. Her chin in the air, she stepped away from him and stomped around the room, ostensibly tidying up, unnecessarily clattering cold cups and saucers.

Jackson winced at a crash of silverware. "Thank you," he said sarcastically, spreading his hands.

Before leaving the room, she looked over her shoulder. "For what?"

"For confirming how ridiculous it would be for me to tell her she can't come, based on how it might look to some vague, random somebodies. Or what they might think. Or say. Or whom they might judge."

Tanna came back into the room, fuming, her hands awkwardly clutching dishes. "It's me that would be judged. And Holly too. She wears pants and speaks gruffly and she's braver than most grown men, but don't think she's exempt from these things." She wished she hadn't picked up so many dishes; she couldn't hold them much longer. "Just blame it on me, then. Tell her I can't bear to be alone. Tell her there will be a better trip coming up later."

His eyes screwed up as if he could not comprehend what she was saying. "Why would I do that?"

"Do it for me," she said flatly, and, thinking to end the matter there, she turned toward the kitchen.

"What's next?" he asked, his voice a strained whisper. "What else will I be required to do for you to prove whatever it is that you want me to prove?"

She looked around for somewhere to set down the cups and saucers before she dropped them. Spotting the sewing basket with Jackson's half-mended shirt, she strode across the room and threw the dishes in with a crash of breaking china. "You think your philosophies, your freedom, are more important than mine." Her voice was shrill. "I'm not allowed to voice my will."

He pointed his pencils at her. "I've never tried to limit your freedom or thwart your will. I've never requested specific declarations from you. I've never demanded you take any actions just for my benefit. Never. You're allowed to think and do and say anything you want with me. I've supported you in becoming any version of yourself you want to be."

She laughed hysterically. "As long as it doesn't include needing you. Or wanting a future with you." She made as if to pull out handfuls of her own hair, but then she shook her fists at him. "You support my freedom only in terms of my *independence*. I'm not free to want you. I'm not free to *need* you. I'm not free to expect anything from you. Really, I'm just free to leave."

Wanting to deescalate the violence of the conversation, he sighed. He shook his head at her in pity. "You don't need me."

"I do." Her voice broke.

"No, you don't," he said in his most practical tone. "If I die, are you going to die? You don't *need* me. You're confusing what you need with what you want. You always have."

"If you had it your way, there wouldn't be any love in this world at all."
She'd gone too far already; it didn't matter if she cried in front of him.

"Yes, there would be. The kind you don't have to prove to anyone.
Especially to the person you love." He finally tossed his map and his pencils
down on the desk in resignation. "What is it you're really afraid of? Do you
honestly think I'm going to try to go to bed with Holly?"

"No," she mumbled petulantly.

"Then this is a ridiculous argument!" he finally shouted, beyond
frustration.

"If it's so ridiculous, then why are you fighting so hard to win it? Why
can't you just let me have this one?"

"At this point, it just sounds like you want to be right, Tanna. At any
price. You just want to win. You don't care what it costs."

She moved closer to him, imploring him. "There are some things worth
having that come at a high price, and I want to be one of them."

He looked at her but said nothing, his expression like stone.

Seeing that he wasn't going to give in, she straightened into her
haughtiest pose. She went over to her desk, scraped up his pencils and his
map, and held them out to him. "If you're going to value me, if I'm going
to continue giving myself to you, if we are going to belong to each other ...
There are some things I just won't allow."

He scowled at her. "*Allow? Belong?* Do you hear yourself?" He snatched
the pencils and the map from her and shook them at her. "Do you have any
idea what it does to me when you use that kind of language?"

She smiled in grim triumph. "You know, I used to think you didn't
really want anything, you didn't need anything. But I was wrong. You want
to have it all."

Her accusation hung in the air like a struck bell.

He shook his head at her, as if in sheer wonder. "You know, Tanna,
you do have it all. Absolutely everything on your list. You already have it.
It may not have come exactly as you ordered it, so you ignore most of it.
Or, you know, maybe you really can't see it, which is truly heartbreaking.
You've never even acknowledged your best friend in the world."

"Who? You?"

He made a soft sound of disgust and walked toward the door. "I'm
leaving in the morning," he said, so softly she could barely hear him over
the blood in her ears. "And I'm going to tell Holly she can come along if she
wants to."

"Then be sure you take all your things when you go," Tanna said, "so you won't have any reason to come back."

He left, his shoulders slumped with weariness and resignation.

45

A soft whisper awakened her.

"So'onah."

There was an urgent tugging on the sleeve of her nightgown.

The awareness crept in. She had never heard the word *so'onah* in her bed ...

Someone was pulling back the covers, exposing her, tearing away the last shreds of dreamless oblivion.

She finally roused to see the faint outline of a dark face emerging from the shadows. An elven face, transformed into a sinister mask by red light.

Red light.

"So'onah," Joona said, "they are coming."

"Who's coming?" She was already dragging herself out of bed, reaching for the curtains, parting them to look out the window.

She was looking on hell itself.

The entire southern sky was alight with an enormous fire. Down the hill, to the left.

"The warehouse," she whispered. "Oh God, no."

She stepped into her work boots and reached for the robe thrown over the footboard of the bed. She tripped over the trailing sash, her laces skittering on the floorboards. She stumbled into the hall screaming for Eve, for Still.

"Run get Gentry!" she yelled at the cluster of terrified faces lurking in her hallway. They scattered in front of her, flattening themselves against the walls. They let her pass and take the lead, then fell in behind her.

She paused at the back door long enough to tuck the laces into her boots. She couldn't stop to tie them properly. She lurched through the kitchen garden, straight through the rows of plants, tripping over the uneven furrows, kicking through the vines that caught her feet. The gate opposite was the most direct shortcut to the southern fields and buildings at the southeast bottom of the hill.

As she ran toward the red wall of light and smoke, the edge of the darkness broke and re-formed with the shadows of small people, running with her to the scene or on some panicked errand or possible fleeing to safety in the other direction.

She slowed to a walk, trying to comprehend which structure exactly was burning. The flames were too big. The refinery was still far from completion; it wasn't that large ...

"No," she moaned, realizing it was both buildings—the warehouse and the refinery.

Gentry's tall silhouette stood out against the chaos. She yelled something to him, but the hot, roaring wind swallowed her voice. She could barely hear herself. She reached out to grab Gentry's arm, but pulled back her hand in shock. He was too hot to touch, slick with sweat.

An alarm bell was clanging now.

Gentry ignored her, bellowing orders to the elves. He was trying to get them to form a bucket line. Some of them dashed at once to do his bidding; others seemed too frightened to comprehend what they were meant to do. Davis tried to show them.

Eventually, a small army carrying buckets and bowls formed a ragged line down to the nearby creek.

Tanna waited in agony for the first vessels of water to make it up the hill. It seemed to be taking forever. The shadows of the structures within the fire were already little more than wavering twigs.

Matchsticks.

She goaded the little people with wordless cries of urgency. And then she choked, unable to yell anymore or even speak. The air was becoming too hot to breathe.

One little bucket of water. A second pathetic little splash ...

The remaining timbers in both buildings simultaneously shivered and fell like black trees, collapsing into pillowy skirts of sparks.

"Let it go," she managed to croak to Gentry, trying to pull him back.

She waved the yolos away from the flames, pointing them up the hill where it was unimaginably cool and dark. She didn't want anyone getting hurt. The fires were too large and beyond their efforts to affect.

She staggered away, walking backward, unable to stop watching. She couldn't turn away from the sight. Her farm was dying. She needed to hold its hand and look it in the eyes as it left this world.

Someone took her hand. She looked down, saw Eve, and dropped to her knees to hug the girl from behind. She leaned her chin on the bony little shoulder. Eve was stoic and silent, but Tanna still whispered cooing noises, as one might to quiet a crying baby. Some of the other yolos were there, hanging on to her, creating a small huddle of children around her.

They all watched the blaze together.

"All gone," Tanna murmured in a lullaby voice.

The children grounded her grief. They dictated a way for her to behave. Her actions in that moment became a performance of sorts, speaking the words and the level of emotion she felt a child could bear. It was her tale spinner's voice.

She turned around to find that hundreds of Nunnahee had gathered behind her, their faces stony with subtle traces of pain, all of them looking at her. They weren't watching the fire anymore; they were watching *her* watch the fire. She imagined for a moment what it might be like to wail and fall on the ground, to be dragged away by stronger hands.

She chuckled to herself at the image.

A part of her consciousness hung back and slightly above the scene, as if it were a child riding on her shoulders. Maybe it was the burning haint in the smoke. People talked about being *in shock* all the time. It's such a common phrase, a cliché, really. *I was in shock.* Shocked. This was what that was. It wasn't poise or breeding or etiquette or faith that supported her movements and her words—she was numb. Thankfully anesthetized, cushioned from the reality that had just crashed around her.

She stood like that, watching the fire burn down for what must have been hours. At some point, Still's profile appeared at her side.

"You know, the gods are supposed to give us a really good crop next time," she said. "I was clear with them about that. But I can't remember if any of my prayers specified what was supposed to happen with the buildings ... They're like evil genies in lamps, the gods. You have to be very careful how you word your wishes. I think I forgot to pray for the buildings."

—

In the morning, examination of the charred, smoking site revealed faintly glowing petal shapes. Giant shapes, like daisies, like haint flowers themselves. They were clearly blast imprints. There were eight of them, at the corner of each main post of both the buildings.

It was obvious that these were explosions.

"Are we even safe sleeping in our houses?" Tanna asked Gentry and Still. "What if they come back? What will they take down next? I want all the elves to return to the brugh. No exceptions. They can't stay in their village anymore. No aboveground structures. Is that understood? Make them understand this is for their safety. Possibly their survival. I'm responsible for them. But I don't know how to protect them from this."

—

This time, the bank manager requested that Tanna's lawyer be present when they met. She turned heads as she walked down the interior promenade of Treebridge. By now, everyone knew her as the survivor of the tragic fire—a bold, cruel act of war—bombs set by Ripper agents. They were calling it "The Brynmor Attack." The other plantation owners were scouring their property for the Ripper's mark, as rumors spread about the signs found on Tanna's warehouse months ago.

She walked with her eyes cast down to avoid the gauntlet of pity she would have to endure. She knew she reeked of smoke. After ten days, everything at Brynmor still stank like an ashtray. Even though she'd bathed and washed her hair twice a day, the clean clothes in her wardrobe had a faint campfire smell, more detectable once she arrived in Treebridge. Thankfully, she had not been burned and the soot marks on her cheeks had been easily wiped away. A part of her was glad that what she suffered was intangible to witnesses. She didn't want pity, but she would happily accept mercy from the bank.

Mr. Sterling was flanked by a company lawyer and his pert assistant, who had the grace to meet Tanna's eyes and nod just as she would at any other meeting. To Tanna, the woman's respect was true compassion.

Sterling looked stricken. "We have been pressed to be very clear with you today ...," he started. He spread his hands helplessly, not wanting to say it.

Even though she knew what they were here to discuss, she felt a small flutter of panic. "Of course," she said. "Go on."

The lawyer interjected with a soft-spoken speech, read from a page of crisp, official stationery, about the foreclosure of her property and all assets related to the farm and the house at Brynmor.

She waited patiently for him to finish speaking, and then she asked, "How much time do we have?"

Sterling talked around his answer, trying to soften the number with apologies, platitudes, and regrets.

"How long?" she repeated.

His lips twisted with a rueful smile. "Sixty days."

She said nothing, making the silence all the more uncomfortable by taking the time to slowly hold the gaze of everyone present for a few seconds in turn.

She ended with Sterling, who sat directly in front of her across the table. He winced. "I am sorry if we appear in any way to be unyielding or unsupportive. There is a board that we answer to, and that entity's requirements can feel unsympathetic, I know."

Tanna nodded at him. "You have a business to run."

He laid his arms on the table between them, reaching toward her as if he might take her hands in his. "Would it be unprofessional of me, Mrs. Eldridge, to confess how much I've rooted for you? How badly I wish to see you succeed here."

Her hands remained clasped in her lap. "That's very kind of you," she said. In truth, she found his kindness humiliating. The attempt at compassion, delivered by the executioner ... It was unbearable. She was afraid if she didn't shake hands quickly and get out of the building ... She wouldn't shatter into tears, necessarily, but she might begin to scream right there in his office.

She hated to justify his pity.

The lawyer rattled through the details, that the papers would be sent to her own representative by the close of business day, et cetera, et cetera, while Sterling smiled at her as if he were consoling her.

It was the kind of smile with which one hopes to comfort the dying.

—

The return journey to Brynmor seemed to take longer than any other in her memory. The sun was low in the western sky, burnishing the Hawnee Hills. The golden light, the rocking motion of the buggy, and of course Still's silent companionship all conspired to set her dozing in her seat.

The relaxation was the result of relief. She felt guilty that she felt so relieved, but the anxiety of surviving was over. How long had she been hanging on? Now they had declared her bankrupt, were foreclosing on her land, and had given her a date by which she must leave. She could surrender. She could finally let it all go.

When they turned at the stone pillars marking the gate to Brynmor and started up the drive, she was thankful the knoll hid the blackened carnage on its southern side. Here, approaching from the north, the whole of the hill was a silhouette against the rosy afternoon sky, the crown of atzeenah trees backlit like a halo. This big hill had come more and more to resemble her hopes and dreams, and in this moment, the first time seeing it as no longer legally hers, she was struck by pangs of unacceptable grief.

She could imagine Jackson's philosophical arguments, but how could Brynmor ever not be hers? How could it not belong to her? She knew all these songs of it, all these stories. She would be haunted for the rest of her life by lullabies and clapping games, the voices of the yolos chanting its name.

She wondered if they would make up games someday in which her name appeared. Would the Nunnahee sing of a time when she was so'onah? Would the children from her school scratch her name into the trunk of a tree? Did they even know her name?

By the time they reached the top of the hill and the last stretch of the drive, she had worked herself up for a cry. The house was in shadows, the western sky beyond it bruised by the sunset. She willed the tears to come, not caring that Still would witness it. She had only a few moments to let it out before facing anyone inside.

But the tears stalled. Her throat ached with her need for a wailing cry.

There was a crowd at the end of her veranda, a formal line of elven warriors, their spears like a forest of bare saplings in winter.

"What's happening?" Tanna asked, forgetting her grief. "Why are they standing there?"

"The queen has come to call," Still said.

—

She'd never even seen the queen outside the gloom of the brugh, and here she was, seated on her side veranda. Even though Ananjooee was significantly taller than the rest of her people, her relatively small frame made a throne of Jackson's favorite wicker chair.

Here, in the light of day, the queen's presence reminded her of the Lady Glare and other members of the *Sidhe*. Even if Ananjooee was considered a common hill-dwelling elf, she emanated the same ethereal qualities as the grandest of the Seelie women—the fluid mannerisms, the illumination. The ribbons on her clothing trailed the boards like grass beneath the surface of a creek. The light found her, sparkling on her skin, delineating the angles of her bones.

She was different at this meeting. Her trilling speech was faster; she sounded less commanding and more anxious. She was pleading this time, speaking more directly to Still and only glancing over at Tanna periodically. She watched Tanna's face with an expectant intensity, eager to have her response, her silvery-brown forehead crinkled with concern above the black holes of her eyes.

Tanna realized the queen was frightened.

Still rose from a deep bow before Ananjooee and turned to translate.

It was a stream of fears—her people in imminent danger of another attack by the Rippers; the curse laid on the Nunnahee by the Unseelie for farming their sacred plant in collusion with the *yoonaygah*, an ugly term for the white man; and for the loss of their brugh, once Tanna was made to leave and could no longer protect them.

Tanna immediately launched into apologies. Before she could articulate a promise to do everything in her power to protect them, the queen climbed off the wicker chair, her attendants rushing to her aid. She stood before Tanna, the height of her headdress making her nearly as tall. She had to look up to the human woman, but the intangible weight of her presence and the intensity of her eye contact made Tanna feel physically small, weak, and plain.

Ananjooee motioned for the younger attendants to step closer, youths who were much older than yolos, close to adulthood, but whose black, uncolored hair still marked them as adolescents. Only adults stained their bangs with red mud. When Tanna had first come here, they all looked the same to her, diminutive naked people in loincloths, but now she could recognize many of the symbols of their social positions within the tribe.

The queen used her hands to indicate a particular height, as she had originally defined the age of the children allowed to work for Tanna or attend her school. Now she changed the height of her hands, once to indicate a slightly older child and then again to match the height of the youths that stood awkwardly between her and Tanna.

Ananjooee gripped the upper arms of one young female and pushed her toward Tanna, offering her out to the so'onah, the vocal command desperate. She commanded the other children to fall in line behind the first. Tanna knew almost none of the words, but the meaning of the gesture required no translation. *Take her. Take them.*

Alarmed, Tanna looked to Still.

"The queen wishes you to educate all the Nunnahee children, not just the yolos. She wants you to teach them all to read, quickly, before they are sent out into the world."

Tanna shook her head helplessly. She couldn't resist stepping closer toward Ananjooee. She would have touched her in that moment if she could have, to console her, but the attendants bristled, blocking her from touching their queen.

Tanna took the hands of the first girl who'd been presented to her, holding them in a prayerful position. "Yes, yes, of course, everyone is welcome to learn." She pumped the girl's hands up and down to emphasize the sincerity of her speech. "Make her understand, Still," she sighed, "that I intend to do everything in my power to ensure that her people will be allowed to stay here. And if I fail at that, I will find a home for them where they can all stay together. I will not rest until I do. I swear it."

As if responding to a telepathic command, the entire crowd of elves turned as one and began to file out onto the lawn. Without saying goodbye or acknowledging Tanna any further at all, the queen exited abruptly, floating between the corridor of warriors and spears that flanked her.

Tanna watched them depart, melting into the early evening shadows of the lawn, disappearing into the hedges and the tall ferns. She turned to Still, ready to convince him of her guilt and grief, but found him holding out a soft green handkerchief.

It was only then she realized she was openly weeping, and had been for some minutes.

46

She spent two days in bed. She rose only to use the bathroom and to drink more tea, ordering Joona to make it stiff with tarwater, even though it tasted horrible. She found a tin of haint-laced tobacco Jackson had kept in the table on his side of the bed, his little rolling machine and papers beside it. He'd often absentmindedly turned out a surplus of cigarettes while they lay in bed talking or while she paced around the room, sharing her inner world with him.

Now, she smoked until her mouth tasted like the charred remains of the warehouse and the distillery at the bottom of her hill.

Navvee stubbornly sent plates of food to her room, which she insisted Joona eat so they wouldn't go to waste. Eve came bounding in a few times a day, jumped on the bed, and told her gossip about the battles of wills in which she was engaged with various elven children. Tanna managed to smile and chuckle at her stories, but when the tale spinner shadows started to whirl on the walls behind the girl—it did register that Eve conjured them too—she sent her from the room so she could nap.

On the third day after the foreclosure and the queen's visit, it started to drizzle. It was the first real rain that had come since the fire. There were still tendrils of smoke and embers buried at the bottom of the ashes if you stirred them. She wondered if the raindrops were making hissing noises, and finally, of all things, that mystery was the one that roused her enough to go out and walk the farm.

She took her time getting to the bottom of the hill where the scars of the burned buildings lay like a violent wound. She kept her head turned so she couldn't see it, walking the trails between the terraces as she had when Buck had first left her alone on the farm. She could squint and remember the way it was before, but now the haint plants made the farm feel like a lush vineyard in an Italian painting. She looked back at the house, where the flowering topis vine had been coaxed away from the windows and allowed to engulf the lower edges of the roof. With the black slate tiles of the pointed gable sticking up, it all looked like gaudy yellow feathers on the brim on some kind of witch's hat. But it had also become softer and prettier, charming, like a house in a storybook.

She heard that story in her head—"Once upon a time, there was a lady who had a farm in Fairyland, on top of a great big hill ..." She had the urge to return to her bedroom, where she would sip tarwater and smoke late into the night, her lantern throwing tale spinner shadows on the walls as she scribbled down her story with Jackson's beautiful pen.

All the stories. She wanted to write and write and perhaps never speak again until she was done.

She wondered where he was, thinking surely Holly would want to return to her the minute she heard ... But she couldn't be sure he would come with her.

—

Gentry must have seen her walking the property.

She was sitting at her desk in the living room, listlessly sorting through the mail that had accumulated while she was ... resting. She opened the personal letters and set them aside without reading them, still accidentally catching snatches of the regrets and the concerns. She averted her eyes and straightened the other pile of official letters without opening those.

Gentry saved her, really. She was grateful when his hulking shadow appeared in the doorway. He was shocked by the cheerful way she called out his name. His first name—"Carl!" She never called him that.

He must have thought her drunk, especially when she offered him a drink. She waved him into the room. He took exactly one step inside but remained standing by the door, his hat in his hands, nervously looking at his boots.

She noticed the leather was wet. "Don't worry about tracking up the floor, just come in," she said, with an impatient gesture. "Come in."

As he came tentatively closer, she got a better look at him in the lamplight. His hair was wet too, neatly plastered against his skull, the comb tracks still fresh. She could smell the pomade. His shirt was a deep indigo blue, one she'd never seen him wear before. He looked like a farmer on his way to church on Sunday.

He declined the drink and cleared his throat. "I'm wanting to talk to you about my wages. I've been working to get home, you see. Back to Alabama."

"Oh." She frowned. "I didn't realize you wanted to go back to the Gray." But even as she said it, she thought of his barely contained hatred for the "brownies," and his grumbling work ethic suddenly had an entirely new context.

"If you can't pay me," he stammered, "I need to know. I want to get my boy back to the real world, before he's too grown. That's how they become feral, you know. Good Christian people having kids here that never know anything else. They don't learn nothing about how to act in the real world, and then they can't go back when you want them to. Davis's mama wouldn't want me letting him grow up to be some uncouth wild child, some heathen changeling."

"I understand your concerns about Davis," she said, interrupting him before he got too wound up in one of his close-minded sermons. She had heard him use the word *changeling* before to disparage Eve and Holly, but she chose to overlook it now. "Of course you can have your wages. I'll personally give them to you. In U.S. dollars, how's that? It sounds like you might need the cash right away."

He looked surprised, not only that she'd agreed so quickly to pay him, but that she had real money on hand.

She needed to retrieve the book where she kept the bank notes hidden, and she couldn't have him standing there watching. Unable to avoid it, she had to ask him if he would mind waiting for her on the side veranda. He was quick to scurry out of the room, either a little bit offended or, she hoped, only uncomfortable.

She gestured vaguely to indicate she needed privacy. She followed him halfway down the hall, apologizing multiple times. "Are you sure you won't take a drink?"

He scowled and shook his head.

"I'll only be a minute."

She raced back to *Paradise Lost*, counted out the notes on her desk, made a quick mark in the back of her ledger, and returned the book to its shelf. She'd never liked Gentry much, but she felt responsible for him and guilty to have failed him. But she had an idea for him—she had meant to speak to Jackson about it the night they fought. She had started to tell him about how she was afraid she'd have to let Gentry go, but that was the moment he'd seen her mending his shirt.

Gentry counted the bills in front of her. She stood, arms crossed, awaiting his judgment. He grunted in approval and retrieved his hat from the wicker chair.

"Gentry," she said, stopping him before he dove into the night. "I wish Mr. Gallagher were here so I could talk to him on your behalf." She paused awkwardly, afraid to say too much. "As you probably know, Cole Mathers left him the orchard at the foot of the Hawnees ..." She trailed off. She wasn't recommending anything specific; it was just a possibility.

Gentry frowned at her curiously, but she definitely had his attention.

"I don't know what or when—and it's not my place, understand that—but if I were you, I believe I'd talk to Jackson about a position working for him. I can't imagine being gone as often as he is that he doesn't need someone to oversee the lands around the orchard."

Gentry's expression softened. "What would I be doing? What kind of crops?"

"I don't know, exactly," she admitted. "There's a fae woman—an Alleegee like Still—who runs the household, and as far as I know, Jackson has promised she can stay on." She spread her hands in a helpless gesture. "It's just a thought. A notion. But if he returns before we have to leave Brynmor—we have weeks until that happens—I will certainly broach the subject with him on your behalf. If you'd like for me to."

Gentry nodded.

"I wanted to mention it to you, just in case. If we're parted for some reason before I can speak to Jackson, find him. Ask him yourself. After I'm gone."

"Mighty obliged," he mumbled. He put on his hat with both hands, tipped the brim to her, and disappeared into the rising scream of cicadas.

—

The following two weeks were hectic with frantic requests to call in person on various plantation owners. She'd never been received in most of these grand houses. She'd waited more than a year for her reputation and social etiquette to drive invitations that never came. Now, here she was, showing up on their doorsteps a bankrupt, divorced woman, the target of Unseelie religious heresy and the victim of Ripper terrorism. They let her in, partly out of a sensationalist greed for details about her tragedy, partly in fear that she might know something they needed to protect their own properties.

Once seated in their fine parlors, with cups of tea on their knees, more than a few of them were openly contemptuous of her mission when they heard it. Much to the horror of his wife, Leland Matheny asked her to leave the premises immediately the moment she mentioned returning lands to the Nunnahee. The other landowners were less overt but still transparent in their distaste for the subject of the rights of the indigenous fae.

"Genies don't believe in owning land anyway" was the defense she heard again and again.

It took several attempts before she could find anyone who would at least give her advice about whom to contact. Rose Vaughn was miraculously able to make her poor, demented father understand Tanna's immediate need to relocate her elves. And with his letters of inquiry, forged by Rose herself, Tanna obtained meetings in a blur of stuffy offices in Treebridge. Still drove her into town almost every other day to speak with someone who was supposed to be an "official."

By now, rumor of her crusade had spread among the upper class. She had become numb to the open stares she received when she walked the promenades of Treebridge. She heard the murmurs when she passed. She was a curiosity, infamous. Her celebrity was a cruel irony in the face of what she had hoped to become here.

—

She finally landed in the office of a Mr. Featherton, who had promised to meet with her as a personal favor to Daughtry. Having no higher contact within colony society than Daughtry, she hounded the old man every step of the way, keeping him abreast of all her bureaucratic encounters. She'd written several terse, scathing reports regarding the intelligence of quite a few of Daughtry's colleagues. They were all eager to find a way to placate this relentless woman.

Featherton sat with his back to an impressive window overlooking the gorge. Tanna was distracted throughout the meeting by an approaching airship that was clearly somehow propelled by its own means.

"I'm afraid there's no particular plot of land that size within the colony's borders." He steepled his hands on the desk between them, tapping his fingertips together thoughtfully. "Not on which we would put a group of indigenous people, that is."

"No, of course not *indigenous* people," she said sarcastically. "Since it's already their land."

"The indigenous fae do not believe in the concept of land ownership," he said, as if the fairies had created the system all by themselves and the white landowners had been forced to adapt to their customs. "According to colony law, these lands belong to the United States of America. I'm afraid to tell you, what you want is pretty much impossible."

"Yes, it always is," Tanna said with an ugly smile. She sighed, exasperated. "So, who do I talk to next?"

"I'm afraid you've run all the way up the chain," he said, tilting his head to the side.

"Really? *You're* at the top of the chain of command?" She knew she'd offended him, but she no longer cared.

"Well, I'm only the top of the surveying committee," he said, blushing. "But you're already close to Daughtry, from what I understand. There's really no authority above his."

"What about the governor?" she asked. "I've heard there's someone coming in, to be over Daughtry. Right at the top. A general or a governor. I'm not sure which it is."

"That is true," he said. "He's both actually—a general who has been appointed our governor. Due to the particular need for military leadership at this time. But he hasn't even arrived yet."

"But he'll be here very soon," she said, pinning him with a hard smile. "I believe there's a reception planned just three days from now. I'm still worthy of being invited to things, aren't I?"

With his shoulders sagging a little in defeat, Mr. Featherton, the final bureaucrat on the list, invited her personally, on the spot, to meet the general and his wife.

47

The reception for the newly appointed governor of Cumberland Colony was held on the lawn at Bluff House, the oldest and largest freestanding home on the edge of the gorge. It was positioned on the flat lip of the bluff directly above the South End neighborhood of terraced mansions where Daughtry lived.

When one walked out the back door of Bluff House or came around the walkways through the side gardens, the stones of the patio appeared to terminate at a sheer drop into the gorge. It was unnerving to walk toward that void, with no railing or balustrade in sight. It was only upon nearing the edge that one realized there were broad, flat steps leading down to lower terraced levels.

A white linen tent had been set up on a patch of green grass east of the flagstones. A steel-haired middle-aged man in a military uniform stood beside Daughtry in front of an ostentatious high-backed wicker lawn chair, speaking to someone at the head of the long reception line. A small dove of a woman in a mauve dress and a large brimmed hat sat primly at his side in her own matching throne.

There were already at least twenty or thirty couples waiting in line, the men in either military dress or seersucker suits, the women all in pastel summer party dresses, hats, and gloves. With the exception of the commanding view, it all reminded Tanna of any number of barbecues she'd attended throughout her life.

She hurried down the terraced steps to take her place in line. She adjusted her plain cream linen dress, glad she'd at least chosen the straw hat she'd worn to Kentucky Downs when she was twenty-five. She had long ago stripped it of adornment and really only wanted it to block the sun. Seeing all these little women colored like Easter eggs, she felt quite chic. No doubt many of them envied the physical comfort of her choice, if not the style. She could feel the stares and actually hear some of the blatant comments about how she had come unattended. She wasn't here to socialize or maintain her fragile standing; her mission simplified her actions and her concerns. She had only come with one intention—to grovel in front of this government official in a last effort to make the cause of her Nunnahee known to someone with the power to help them.

No one in her immediate vicinity spoke to her, although she nodded to faces she recognized and mouthed a few polite hellos, as she would in any similar circumstance. It no longer mattered whether she was pitied or reviled or laughed at. She waved away a waiter with a glass of champagne. She already felt surprisingly giddy and reckless. She had nothing left to lose. There was a part of her that regretted she hadn't always been allowed to feel this way.

Daughtry was introducing the couples to the general, laughing and joking with each in his typical loud and tipsy fashion, no doubt to everyone's mortification.

Her time came soon enough. To his credit, Daughtry cried, "Old girl!" and embraced her warmly, smacking her on the cheek with a big wet kiss. He remained holding on to her hand, pumping up and down in the air as he spoke. He introduced her quickly by name and regaled General Scofield with a brief recounting of the triumphant moment when Tanna had ridden into his encampment on the Seaming with supplies to save all his men from starving to death.

The general smiled, if a little coolly. His wife blinked slowly at her with an expression of blank politeness that rivaled the fae women of the Seelie Court.

General Scofield reached to take her gloveless hand. "I'm sorry to hear that we're losing you as a member of our community," he said, the smile not quite reaching his eyes. He had already dismissed her and was looking to the couple in line behind her.

Tanna panicked. She glanced at Mrs. Scofield, who had lifted her chin but was still closely watching her.

"Then you've heard about my tragedy?" Tanna asked.

The general was caught by surprise. He briefly frowned at her impertinence, but stammered to find a compassionate response.

"Yes, and I was gravely bothered by it." The receiving line had gone deathly quiet, breaths held as everyone strained to hear his response. He took the opportunity to raise the volume of his voice, and he shifted his tone to an oratory style. "My greatest hope is that under my leadership, nothing like this will ever happen again to one of our own. I am truly sorry that I could not be here sooner to assist you—"

"I'm so grateful to hear that you want to assist me," Tanna said. "You still can."

The general glanced at Daughtry, and a silent message passed between them.

"You have been told of the plight of the people who live on my land?" Tanna asked.

Flustered, the general did not meet her eyes. "I can assure you, Mrs. Eldridge, my administration will make every effort to—"

Tanna went down on her knees before him. It was clear from the chorus of gasps that the assembly was scandalized.

General Scofield was visibly disturbed. He urged her to stand up, spouting any number of useless platitudes. He sounded disgusted and angry, on the verge of ordering her out of his sight for making such a spectacle.

"Please, sir. Don't be embarrassed for me that I have to beg. I've lost everything. I'm in a position to beg, and so I'm begging you—"

"Get up, Mrs. Eldridge," he growled again, grabbing her upper arm, prepared to haul her to her feet himself if he had to. Five soldiers sprang to his aid, ready to put an end to the scene she was causing.

"No. Wait." The voice behind her was soft but resonant with authority. "Leave her alone."

Tanna looked over her shoulder. She seemed to rise above herself, to see herself from outside her body. There she knelt on the grass, in front of everyone, frail and tired, a ring of armed soldiers surrounding her, an angry old man in a uniform yanking on her arm, the knees of her stockings and the front of her dress already stained a vivid green.

An unconscious part of her mind instantly recognized the voice, but she had to see him before she could believe he was there. It was a voice she strained to hear, one she repeated over and over in her imagination. In that moment, it sounded the same as her fantasies.

"Let her speak," Jackson said.

He was fresh from safari, the leather of his Stetson dry and dusty, cracked from the sun and greasy looking at the same time. When the breeze picked up, he reeked of sweat from ten feet away. He looked like he had crawled here from a battlefield. Against the backdrop of white tents and draped bunting and swags of spring flowers, the military dress uniforms, the pale fussy sundresses of the ladies, he was a solid brown smear of dirt. Confronting all the pomp and pretension of this self-appointed aristocracy, he looked like a prince.

Everyone had frozen in a tableau at the sound of his voice.

Tanna waited for Jackson to meet her gaze. She couldn't decide if she was furious with him for having the audacity to save her, as if she wanted or needed anything from him.

He didn't look at her with love or pity or compassion. He defended her with pure respect. He inclined his head slightly, a gesture of encouragement for her to go on. She couldn't decide if it offended her that he would probably offer this same dignity to anyone.

She had no choice but to take the opportunity he had just ensured for her.

Still on her knees, making no move to stand, Tanna looked up at the general. "Do you know what it is that I'm asking for?"

Scofield sighed, exasperated. "As far as I understand it, you've made a formal petition for land for your indigenous servants. You wish to *gift* them real estate you purchased from the colony. A large property, which you have lost due to financial mismanagement by you and your former husband. A property, whether you realize it or not, that sits on a geographically significant location from a military standpoint. You wish the new government to intervene on behalf of these displaced ... *genies*. A few thousand of them, I hear."

"The land you're talking about is their land. They've lived there for hundreds, possibly thousands of years. We just took it from them—" Her voice broke with outrage. She had to clear her throat, but she didn't break eye contact with the general. "They're good workers. They know the land. They know the animals and the fairy creatures that we can't even see. They have a wisdom about this place we most certainly do not. We may never fully possess the understanding we need to thrive here in this world, but if we're to acquire the proper knowledge, it's going to come from them. My Nunnahee are educated. Many of them now read and write English. The children will all grow up with the potential to participate in this society you say you are here to defend—"

"Your petition has been received," the general interrupted, a perturbed twist to his lips. "I can assure you it will be given due process in the courts—"

"Sir," she said, her face a hard mask of stone. "I don't have time to shepherd this request through a new system of courts. I've lost everything, I'm destitute, and I'm fleeing this place against my will, chased by misfortune. I have only a matter of days before I have to leave. You must understand, I'm not asking for myself. I'm asking for them. The Nunnahee. I cannot go in good conscious without knowing that they're provided for."

He nodded impatiently. "We'll look into it. We'll do our best to speed things along, out of great deference to your efforts and your passionate plea. But please, stand up. I'm the one begging you now."

She did not move a muscle. "May I have your word, sir? As a general and a gentleman?"

He sighed again and rolled his eyes heavenward. "For God's sake, woman ...," he muttered.

Mrs. Scofield rose then and stepped forward in a single graceful motion. For a moment, Tanna feared she'd embarrassed this woman and would now pay for it with the scathing verbal ridicule that few husbands ever have the cleverness to perform.

But instead, the general's wife extended her gloved hand to Tanna. "You have *my* word," she said.

Tanna took her hand gratefully, and finally she stood. She felt a rush of relief and emotions too complex to name. Her legs were a little wobbly from kneeling too long. She stepped close to Mrs. Scofield, the brims of their hats almost touching, making a private screen in which they could exchange a few personal words. Tanna put her other free hand on top of the lady's glove. She squeezed her fingers and held her hands tight. She wished she could convey her thoughts without words, simply send her hopes and memories to this woman through her touch. She thought that maybe, on some level, by some magic, Mrs. Scofield had received her heart and responded to it.

"I hope you will be happy here," Tanna said in a quiet, remarkably steady voice. "I was. I was happier than I knew."

The general's wife scowled briefly, but it quickly melted into soft-eyed compassion. "I'm sorry I won't have a chance to get to know you," she said.

Tanna nodded. "This is a magical place. If you will let it show you what it is, instead of trying to make it what you want it to be."

"I will remember that," Mrs. Scofield said, and smiled.

Tanna bowed her head, and at last she backed away from the receiving line.

Jackson caught her by the elbow and steered her around. She allowed him to walk her back up the terrace and across the patio.

—

"We came back as soon as we heard," he said, as they crunched down the gravel drive toward the main road.

Tanna pouted, saying nothing. She wasn't quite ready to let him know how glad she was to see him.

She saw Holly pacing anxiously beside Still and her wagon outside the main gate to Bluff House. The girl ran to her, her tanned face crumpling in tears. She sobbed into Tanna's neck, unable to speak. Tanna put her hand on the back of Holly's head and rocked her, shushing her like an infant.

Jackson tactfully suggested they could catch up on the drive. He pointed with his eyes back toward the house. Tanna saw that onlookers had followed her and were watching from the side garden.

She stepped aside so Holly could jump onto the front bench next to Still, and then Jackson handed her into the back seat. He took the opportunity to look her in the eye, up close. He squinted at her, his face sunburned and freckled.

"We didn't know about the fire until about four days ago. We heard it from a band of T'looga elves, tree dwellers who migrate through the forests. We weren't sure at first, given the language barrier, what farm they were talking about. But we clearly heard *Brynmor* and we both had a bad feeling ..." He trailed off, winced, and then he just stood there, staring at her.

"Well, I suppose there's one way to get you to come home from safari." She really had meant to make light of the tense reunion, but the joke sounded bitter, even to her own ears. She changed her tone. "I've got most of your things packed."

"Where do you plan to go?" he asked.

"Home," she said, shrugging. "Back to my mother's house. Again. This time penniless. I'm bankrupt. But, of course, I need to find out what has happened to Teddy."

"Let me help you out," he said, blinking slowly. "Financially."

"As a friend?" She bit off the word, with a mocking roll of her eyes.

He held her gaze but showed no emotion.

"Have you changed your mind about keeping me, then? Now that I'm a helpless woman and all?"

He said nothing, but his expression shifted a little into sadness.

"Never mind," Tanna said dismissively, turning to face forward in her seat.

Jackson sighed and nodded to Still. "You go on home with Tanna," he said to Holly. "I'll see to the horses."

He stepped away as the wagon lurched into motion.

48

The next several days were spent preparing to get rid of almost everything Tanna owned. She hoped to sell as many of her possessions as she could in a large yard sale. She had no need for the furniture and wedding gifts she'd brought with her on the first crossing. Of course, she would be thankful for any amount of money she might raise, but she couldn't bear the thought of trying to take all that she'd acquired here back to the Gray. With the exception of personal items and mementoes, she would have nowhere to store anything at Blackwood but in her bedroom or in the attic tomb already filled with her father's things.

The day before the sale, she took a box of paper tags with strings and moved through the house as quickly as possible, pricing everything at ridiculously low amounts. A part of her protested, especially over the custom items crafted by Curtis the vine trainer, but she wanted it all to be carted away for her, to disappear in a single day if possible. Holly, Still, Joona, Davis, and Eve helped her move everything onto the lawn and the front veranda. It was bad enough that strangers would be pawing through her things, judging them, taking them away for fractions of what they were worth; she didn't want them crawling through the interior of the house too, gawking as if it were the scene of a notorious crime. She planned to be gone well before the legal deadline, but it was still her home for several more weeks.

She caught Eve pulling a hairpin box from the pocket of an overcoat. For some reason she couldn't quite articulate, she still had not buried Belle's body. She had been careful to never unwind the cloth that bound it; the small corpse had become mummified.

"Oh good, I'm so glad you found that," she said, snatching the box from the little girl before she could get the lid open. "Give it here."

Eve demanded to know what was in it.

Harried and scattered, a partial blunt truth was the first answer that came to her. "It's a secret," Tanna stammered.

She was distracted, trying to direct the chaos while answering everyone's questions about what went where and what to do about an item missing its tag ... She had stayed up late the night before, reading and rereading the papers that had arrived from the Cumberland Colony government. They had designated a "reservation" deep in the interior of the Green, northwest of Chickamauga Gorge, and were offering military escort to relocate the Nunnahee.

In addition to *relocate*, the word *removal* was used.

It chilled her.

She asked Still if he knew about the Cherokee, the wild peoples of the Gray whose lands had been stolen by the government. How they had all been forced to abandon their homes and walk hundreds of miles to unwanted lands they knew nothing about, many of them dying along the way.

"Not all of them," Still informed her. "Some of them came here and chose their own place."

Not for the first time, Tanna wondered what had become of them and the colored people who had escaped from slavery in the previous century. Jackson had wanted her to go with him on a journey to find their new territories. They might have flown there within a matter of hours. She wondered if he would think about her someday when he went there alone, and if he'd wish she were there to share it.

She shook away the daydream and continued her conversation with Still. "Well, the land that was chosen for the Indians was inferior to their home. It had nothing they were used to. Here, the beauty of the lands in the Green might not vary so much, but I'm still fearful of this solution for my elves." She laid her hand on top of his cool, dry fingers. He still looked at her in surprise when she touched him. "Please, make sure they know how hard I fought on their behalf. That I tried everything to secure them this hill that has always been their home. All the land at Brynmor—the fields, the terraces, the crops—it will stay as one estate. And it's to be auctioned off to the highest bidder." She encircled his wrist with her fingers and squeezed. "Please, Still. You're the only one who can communicate to them and make them understand. They're not going to like it. The colony simply won't allow them to keep their tribal seat in the brugh, even if they promise to stay underground. The aboveground village, the collection of huts that the farm workers and the house servants live in, the small gardens they keep. It's all part of the property, and it's all been lost. They can't resist or fight this. I don't want to see anyone hurt. They have to go peacefully now, before some brutes are sent to *escort* them. I won't be here to speak for them."

She pulled him over to her desk to look at a small map that had been included with the documents. "Take this, and see that they understand where it is they are sanctioned to go."

Still studied the paper. "This is many, many miles away."

"Yes, it is," she said. "Please tell Ananjooee how hard I tried. You know how many people I talked to, how I groveled. But this is the best that I could do for them."

"They will remember you well."

She nodded, suddenly unable to speak further.

—

Jackson's boots made a slow, clomping echo in the empty room. He found her, wearing a dress, sitting on a packing crate in the living room. An oil lantern stood on a leather trunk beside her, throwing a honey-colored glow across the bare floorboards. The makeshift table also bore a plate with the crumbs of a cold supper, a glass of whiskey, and an ashtray.

She watched him, smoking in an elegantly slumped posture.

He stood before her, hat in his hands, looking around the room as if he were evaluating it. His eyes stopped on the Victrola, precariously perched on four short stacks of books on the floor. He crooked a thumb back over his shoulder. "I walked down around the refinery and the warehouse before I came up."

She responded with a bitter chuckle, flicking her cigarette with careless disgust in the general vicinity of the ashtray. She missed by several inches.

When she looked up to meet his eyes he was frowning at her intently, but the grief and compassion she saw there shocked her, like a slap to the face. She couldn't imagine anyone articulating that expression with words.

There were no platitudes for such an occasion, but she tried to say something anyway to cover the silence. "You know, I think maybe I should've always had it like this. I kind of like it."

"I was just starting to like all your possessions," he said.

"I was just starting to like living without them."

The silence returned, hanging hard around them, reverberating off the bare wood surfaces of the empty room.

Jackson finally spoke. "You've ruined it for me, you know."

"Ruined what?" she asked, startled, instantly defensive.

"Being alone," he said.

She held her breath, waiting to think of a response before she tried to exhale, but she couldn't think of anything to say in that moment. Her sigh bled out in a slow hiss.

"I'd love to come with you and see you off," he said.

"I'm obviously not going anywhere near the Graycoat this time. I'm going down to Old Rath in two days and taking the airship route straight into Cloudland Canyon."

"Perfect," he said. "Let me fly you, then."

"Don't you have to go away again?" she asked, genuinely trying not to sound accusatory or argumentative.

"I have a few things to take care of at the orchard," he said. "But I can be back here day after tomorrow."

She nodded as if considering it. "I've packed your things." She jerked her chin toward the books on the floor. "But as you can see, I'm still separating out your books."

He shrugged. "I can pick it all up when I come back. Or hire someone."

"Would you like a drink?" she asked.

He shook his head. He dropped his hat on the trunk and went over to thumb through the records leaning near the Victrola. He found what he was looking for, put the record on, and cranked the arm.

The opening strains of "Let the Rest of the World Go By," the song they had danced to at the Victory Day party, began.

He held his hand out to her. "Come dance with me."

She hesitated. It felt a bit too much like allowing him to win. But she decided to give him this one. She reached out and let him pull her up.

He led her through a slow box step, moving her down the hall toward the front door. As the muted trumpet took up the melody from the sad violins, he broke the step, took her hand, and dragged her across the veranda, down the steps, and over the drive. There in the dewy grass, under the moon, between the onlooking silhouettes of the large furniture pieces someone planned to bring a bigger wagon back to pick up in the morning, he pulled her into a close, swaying embrace.

Her face pressed against his neck; she could hear his pulse. She was sure he must have felt her inhale his clean, grassy scent.

"I've developed this little trick," she said in a low voice. "This little game I play with myself lately. When it gets so bad, and I think I can't go on ... I try to make it even worse. I make myself think about our camp on the mossy rock shelf above the Yooway River. And I think about Cole. And that first time you took me flying in *Gypsy*. I think about how good it all was. How much I had that I could never own. And when I'm sure I just can't stand it anymore, that I can't last one more minute, I make it through another heartbeat. I take one more breath … and then I know I can stand anything."

They had stopped moving. She pulled away to look at his face in the moonlight.

"You were right, you know? *My* Nunnahee. *My* haint plants. *My* things. None of this was ever mine. Even the farm never really belonged to me."

"But you definitely belonged to it," he said.

When the song ended, they held hands and walked the paths the way they had after dinner so many times. Neither of them spoke until they were back on the side veranda, awkwardly standing where their favorite wicker chairs used to be.

"It's not too late for you to offer to keep me," she said.

"Listen. I want you to know how much I regret that I can't raise the cash to cover your losses, purchase this farm, rebuild it all for you." The words spilled out quickly, and he looked pained as he said them. He had obviously been thinking about it, struggling with it all. "I inherited Cole's physical property, yes. The orchard and its surrounding lands are mine. But I guess I'm what you wealthy estate owners call *house poor*, right? I'm sorry."

She held up her hands defensively. "I wasn't talking about saving the farm. With or without money, I don't think I have the will for it anymore. I'm resolved to let it all go."

"I may not have money, but Cole's house is mine," he said in a reasonable tone. "I can invite anyone to stay there that I want."

"Isn't Ioma still there?" she asked.

"Well, yes. Where would she go? I told her she could stay there as long as she needs. That's the reason Cole left the place to me, so I could protect it and make sure she has a home. The colony government would never let her inherit that property."

"Will you stay there too, then? Now that you can't be here at Brynmor."

"I've always been welcome there. I've stayed there so many times over the years. I expect it can continue as I require it." He frowned. "When you said that I could keep you, did you mean you might stay there too?"

"At the orchard? No, no. I love that house—it's incredible, truly—but I think that would be inappropriate. At least awkward, don't you? The former owner's mistress and the new owner's mistress, together under one roof? No. That's not what I meant."

"You're not my *mistress*, Tanna," he said, annoyed by the terminology.

"But if I can't rebuild your farm and you're not willing to stay in my house ... I don't see how else I could possibly keep you."

"No. You don't." She laughed bitterly. "You really don't see it. But it doesn't matter. I want to be worth something. Something more. And to you, I'm not, and I never will be."

"That's not accurate," he said, a warning in his tone. "It's not true."

"It is true," she said. "According to my labels, my language, and what it is that I want."

He sighed. It was the same impasse. They were both too stubborn, too much themselves. This was what it looked like when they both won.

He kissed her on the cheek and walked down onto the lawn, disappearing into the long shadows on the grass.

49

The sound began as a low hum.

Tanna stood on the steps of the veranda watching Ginger and Still out on the lawn overseeing the men sent by Mrs. Stuckey to load the chifforobe she'd purchased onto a wagon. Tanna resisted the urge to direct them. It wasn't even hers anymore. The piece was already paid for—she hoped the sheet she'd thrown over it last night was enough to catch the dew—and she wouldn't be here to receive any complaints, should the old woman have any.

The hum became a deep buzz.

Tanna shaded her eyes and looked above her at the vine covering the porch overhang. Earlier in the summer, the yellow trumpet flowers were thick with large indigenous honeybees the size of finch owls. But there were no flowers left, and no bees. She walked down onto the lawn, looking back at the house, scanning along the eaves. She even peered into the nearby atzeenah trees for a hornets' nest, but she didn't see one.

The buzz became a loud drone.

She shivered with the repulsive notion that the walls of the house itself might be full of bees. Surely she would have noticed before now if there were enough creatures of any kind to make *this* much noise.

Joona and Holly both came out of the house, looking up at the sky.

"What's that sound?" the girl asked.

Tanna saw that the moving men were standing by their truck, mouths hanging open, also staring at the sky over the house. Still was looking south, but he had knelt down to wrap his arms around Ginger.

Together, Tanna and Joona walked backward out onto the lawn so they could see beyond the roof. Navvee was watching from the kitchen garden. Eve and the yolos had stopped their game near the schoolhouse.

The whole southern sky over the plains along the Big South Road roiled with black clouds. A storm front stretched from horizon to horizon. Tanna had never seen anything like it. The darkness advanced quickly, like a sheet being pulled over the light. As she watched, the edges of the cloud seemed to disintegrate and re-form. In an instant she thought *smoke*, but discarded the description. That wasn't what she was witnessing.

Flocks. The glittering shifts and mass turns of an enormous flock of birds, like every starling in the world flying together.

"Eve!" she yelled.

The droning buzz of the swarm was so loud now there was little chance the girl could hear anyone calling her name. Tanna instinctively moved toward the children, who were gaping without a care, and Holly moved to follow.

"Get the dog!" Tanna yelled. "Take her back inside with you."

Tanna picked up Dakka, the smallest elven girl, and motioned for Eve and the others to follow her back to the house.

The sky dimmed to a murky twilight, and a wind preceded the storm of flying things. When Tanna glanced up again, she could make out larger shapes within the swarm. The long, silvery dragonfly spears of boughrunners were breaking away, streaking overhead with an ominous hiss.

Tanna met the moving men, hesitating in front of the veranda steps, uncertain about going into the house uninvited. "Get in, get in," she waved them inside, pushing the yolos through the front door.

She lingered with Still, waiting and watching. The roof blocked the mass of the approaching swarm.

"Unseelie hoards?" she yelled.

Still nodded. "All of them," he said.

He pushed her inside and shut the door. They ran to the back of the house, where everyone was staring out the windows. From here the view of the sky was entirely black.

It sounded like the first heavy drops of rain in a summer thunderstorm. A few gunshots. A patter in quick succession. Then rattling leaves giving way to a waterfall rush.

These drops were creatures. Landing on branches, skittering across the grass, and taking off again so quickly it looked like they were appearing and disappearing in the blink of an eye.

Some were birds, some insects. Others resembled tiny monkeys, four inches long, covered in velvety gray fur, with eyes like vermin. Most numerous of all were small creatures with skin like dead autumn leaves, wings like wasps, and human faces.

Something struck the window, hard enough to rattle the glass in its frame. Another landed more carefully on the sill and peered in at them. It laughed, a cackle like the squeaking of bats, and took flight.

Ginger barked and whined, Holly trying in vain to soothe her.

They all moved away from the windows and huddled in the center of the room. One of the moving men prayed in a quavering voice. Tanna kept looking up at the ceiling, hearing the rustle and patter as thousands of small things crawled over the house.

The squeaking, the scratching, the incessant hum, all against the roaring drone ... The din must have lasted for at least fifteen minutes. And then it ended, as quickly as it had begun.

Silence and sunlight returned to the windows.

Tanna looked around the crowd of shocked faces in her empty house.

They tentatively moved apart and went outside to investigate.

—

It was early afternoon when word reached Brynmor that Treebridge had been attacked.

Reports were little more than rumors, a few lines scribbled in haste, carried out to the closest plantations by messengers and birds, and then spread farther by word of mouth. Explosions, fires, bombs dropped from the air on the South End. Destruction in three areas along the Tree's span.

Tanna posted a few of the older yolos at the gate to ask anyone traveling away from town for more details. But, by early evening, there had been no additional news.

Seated on the floor, Tanna, Holly, and Eve tried to eat bowls of tomato soup off the packing trunk in the living room. Shaken by the day's events, none of them had much of an appetite. Tanna kept picturing the great city breaking to pieces and tumbling into the gorge. Holly kept naming people they knew—starting with Jackson—and wondering out loud what might have happened to them, until Tanna snapped at her and told her to stop. Eve was singularly worried about Jackson, wanting to know if he had been flying when the hoards came.

Tanna assured her he had gone to the orchard, which was nowhere near Treebridge. She couldn't imagine departing the Green tomorrow, with everything that was happening. But she hoped he would still show up as promised.

—

After dinner they all walked the long drive down to the front gates. Tanna didn't want to let the girls out of her sight. The thought had occurred to her that there might be refugees fleeing the city. She wondered why the yolos had not yet reported seeing anyone on the Big South Road. She was worried they might have encountered some trouble, and she couldn't rest until she had personally checked on them.

Wen and Eelie weren't alone. They had gotten up a game of *pakka* right there in the road, with teams of Nunnahee children playing. Many of their parents were ostensibly watching the game, but Tanna caught the elders craning their necks and peering down the darkening road toward Treebridge. They were eager for the same news as she.

Eve ran among the children and Holly wandered down the road with Ginger on her lead. Tanna called out to them not to go far. She found some of the women with whom she'd picked flowers in the fields and sat on the grass near them. Wooden cups of perfumed, fermented drinks were passed around. Tanna accepted hers graciously and pretended to sip, although the fumes alone made her eyes water. Bone pipes of haint and tobacco came her way, along with clouds of smoke; and having forgotten her cigarettes at the house, she was happy to take a few puffs. Some of the elves began to beat drums and the others sang, and they all swayed and rocked to a chanting, never-ending song.

As the stars rose, Tanna thought about how she'd never gone among her elves after dark. She'd never joined them in their village or attended their festivals, even though on her late walks around the farm, she often saw the wavering light of dancers around campfires and heard these low, incessant drums. But then, they had never invited her, and she would never have presumed upon their private spaces.

Now, she looked around and thought how fortunate it was that on one of her last nights at Brynmor, she had stumbled into this spontaneous gathering. She joined in timidly on the song's refrains. The music had a mournful, spiritual quality. But it often felt that way to her ears; even the ecstatic tempos gave the impression of voodoo, of magic spells being cast. She did wonder if they might be praying for Treebridge now, or singing about tragedy, but she didn't want to interrupt anyone to ask.

—

She must have dozed, lulled by the rhythm. She jerked upright to find the elves had gone silent. Many of them were standing and staring down the road. Tanna rose, towering over them, able to see the wobbly lantern lights approaching like drunken fireflies. The elves retreated from the road to allow the walkers to pass.

It was a straggling herd of people—a few humans, but mostly elven fae—exhausted, carrying their possessions in packs on their backs. Tanna caught the eye of a man dressed in the livery of a great South End house and called out to him. He stopped and waited as she pushed her way through the crowd to reach him.

She peppered him with questions, several variations of requests for news.

He told her the bluff-side neighborhoods at the South End were gone. The first bombs started avalanches, which sheered the vertical mansions from the face of the cliffs and sent them into the gorge. This group of people lived in Woodall House, only a few blocks away from the bluff above Daughtry's mansion. Their master owned a hunting lodge near the Hawnee Hills to which they were all retreating. He had sent this group of servants ahead, and the family would be following with their attendants by carriage once they had packed more of their things.

"Does anyone know if Daughtry is OK?" Tanna asked.

The man wearily shook his head. "A lot of people along the road have asked about him. There's a lot of speculation, but nobody knows."

"But there are ...," Tanna hesitated, unsure how to word the question, "a lot of people dead or wounded?"

His red eyes grew round and wild. "There must be hundreds dead, if not thousands."

"But the Tree itself is still intact?" she asked. "Still spanning the gorge?"

He nodded, but seemed lost to an interior vision or memory. "It's a wonder. But yes, it's still there." He pointed weakly at the backs of his people, their lanterns stretched along the curve as the road went around the great hill. "I have to go."

—

The Big South Road became a slow river of people fleeing Treebridge. Even the horses had to pick their way carefully among so many small bodies. Carriages and wagons had to wait every other mile for those on foot to move aside and let them pass.

Of those who stopped to speak with her, few could tell her much more than what she had already heard. Most only described the ominous din of the approaching hoards—which those at Brynmor had experienced themselves—and the booms of the explosions and rumbles like earthquakes. These were not witnesses or the ones who might have dove into the fray to rescue others or even gone seeking information. These were the people who were far enough away from the Tree itself to leave at all, the first waves of those who were safely beyond the chaos.

In the coming hours and days there would be walking wounded, those who had escaped the real horror. Tanna had disturbing visions of desperate souls who, instead of peacefully wandering past Brynmor, would climb the hill in search of shelter or food. The colony itself was a war zone now. Not only might the Rippers who had burned her buildings to the ground attack again, but she'd grown up hearing gruesome tales from her elders about soldiers on both sides losing their humanity, going feral, raping, stealing, murdering people in their own homes over the smallest things.

She gathered her girls and took them back up to the house, Still carrying Eve, who was already asleep. They piled together on a mattress in the floor of Tanna's bedroom. Still lay on the far side of the room near the door on the hard floor with only a small blanket rolled up for a pillow. The lack of drapes on the windows unnerved her. A few rifles remained in the house after the sale, leaning in the corner of her room. She told Holly to stay with Eve and she slipped out, taking Ginger and one of the weapons. Still silently followed, her ever-present fairy shadow.

She loaded the rifles, filled her pockets with extra shells, and walked cautiously through the empty house, reminding herself that Joona and Navvee might appear if they heard her up and about. She went outside and crept around the perimeter, walking briefly down into the garden behind the kitchen. Still motioned that he would go farther down through the fields. She nodded and stayed behind. From where she stood above the terraces she could see the Big South Road stretching onto the Cumberland Prairie. There were hundreds of slowly moving lantern lights, firefly-green and amber, flowing from the blackened, burned remains of the warehouse and the distillery toward the southern horizon and the dark silhouette of the Hawnees.

—

When she and Ginger returned to the side veranda, the dog gave a short woof and began to growl lowly in her throat. Ginger rarely made angry or frightened sounds; it was like cold water down Tanna's back.

Inside the hallway, she saw shadows of movement in the living room and heard the noises of someone blatantly going through her books. Someone who was not trying at all to be quiet. There was no way Still could have made it back from the southern fields so quickly. It had to be one of the servants, or more likely one of the girls.

Ginger disagreed. As they passed the end of the wall, the dog gave another low growl. There, in a paned patch of moonlight, kneeling in front of her books, was a man in a red plaid shirt. A lumberjack, thumbing through the hardbacks, lifting them and fanning their pages, obviously to see if anything fell out. He worked methodically, grabbing books from the piles on his right, shaking them, rustling the pages, and depositing them with loud thumps on his left.

She raised the rifle and pointed it at his back, outraged at the monstrous way he was treating her books. "Who in the hell are you?" she spat through clenched teeth.

"God!" He started, lurching to his feet, one hand clutching his chest. "I didn't think anybody was here," he said, holding a book in front of him like a small shield, as if it could stop a bullet.

"Put that down," she snarled.

He placed it carefully on a nearby stack, as if it were a loaded weapon, and lifted his hands in the air.

He was inching toward the front door, and instead of blocking him, she circled to stay as far away from him as she could. "I really thought the house was empty," he gasped, struggling to catch his breath.

She recognized him. The black beard, the red plaid shirt ... Graycoat's man, the one who had followed them when they fled along the trail on Lookout Mountain.

"You," she whispered. "You were at the towers."

"I really thought the house was empty," he repeated, sliding a few more inches toward the door. "I'm leaving, I swear."

"Wait a minute," she said, taking a step toward him, threatening, lifting the barrel of the rifle. She realized she couldn't shoot from this angle—the girls were sleeping on the other side of the wall behind him—but he didn't know that. "I want to know what you're looking for," she demanded, sounding more annoyed than scared.

He backed away from the gun, his eyes pleading. "Just some papers."

"What papers?" She glanced over, looking for the hollow book where she'd hidden the money from her yard sale. It was all the money she had left in the world. Fortunately, it was still on the bottom of one of the stacks he had yet to go through.

"Just some papers that might have been left behind when the owner moved."

Tanna scowled at him. "Why would I have left important papers behind?"

"They're not ... yours," he said, admitting he knew who she was, or at least that she was the owner. "They belong to my boss."

The thought of the Graycoat demanding anything that belonged to her and having the nerve to send a thief to rifle through her house in the night while the colony burned under Ripper attacks ... She swelled with anger, raised the barrel of her rifle, and aimed it at the intruder's face, enjoying his discomfort. "Who exactly is this boss of yours?" she bellowed, even though she knew.

Before he could respond, Holly stepped into the room with the other rifle pointed at his head. The side veranda door slammed open. They all jumped at the loud bang. Holly turned to see who was running down the hall.

Tanna saw Still's face emerge from the shadows just as her rifle was shoved toward the ceiling. She lost her balance, and, trying to hold onto the gun instead of catching herself with her hands, she sat down hard on the floor. She grunted, a shocking pain in her hip sending a white flash across her eyes.

The intruder bolted out the front door, and Holly followed.

Tanna yelled for her to stay, and Still went after them.

There were two loud rifle shots. Then a third.

Eve came down the hallway, confused, rubbing her eyes. Tanna was still on the floor, trying to massage feeling into her backside. She motioned for the girl to come to her and squeezed her tight. They clung to each other, listening.

The cicadas had gone silent. A board creaked.

Still appeared in the doorway, Holly behind him.

"What happened?" Tanna asked, expecting to hear that the intruder had been shot.

Holly and Still shared a look.

Holly shook her head. "He got away."

50

Jackson kept his promise. It was late in the afternoon, but he did show up the next day. He flew *Gypsy* directly over the house, circling twice before putting down in the empty pasture where he always landed.

Tanna walked down to meet him, eager to exchange news. "Well, the old bastard finally sent a goon after her," she said.

"Under cover of the attack?" Jackson asked, incredulous.

"Not exactly," she said, breathing hard from the climb back up the hill. "Last night. I caught him pawing through my books. *Your* books, actually. I get lost in them every time I try to separate them," she mumbled.

"What did he take?"

"Nothing. There's nothing left in the house to take. He told me he was looking for papers that belonged to his boss."

"He said that?" Jackson frowned at the ground.

"That's exactly what he said. Why?"

He didn't answer; instead he asked, "Where's Holly?"

"She's at the house. Sitting on the front porch, actually, cradling a gun and guarding the driveway." Her tone shifted. "So, what has happened? Treebridge. Tell me what you know."

He repeated the details she'd already heard—there had been five explosions, the first two hit the South End; the other three hit along the Tree's span.

"Bombs," he said, shaking his head. "That's what everyone describes. There's nothing else to call them. Dropped from the dragonfly craft."

"Then why the swarm?" Tanna asked. She told him about the black sky, the evil hum, the hideous skittering noises across the roof, the creatures that peered in the windows and laughed at them.

Jackson shrugged. "Intimidation. Terror. The Rippers think if they scare us badly enough, we'll leave on our own." He continued with details about the destruction. "The Fairchild is gone. Survivors in the nearby promenade said the blast came from inside the club, not from above. It may have been a coordinated explosion, timed to go off during the air raid."

"They want to get rid of the members," Tanna whispered, "the leaders of the colony. Daughtry?"

"Well, your theory's right on the money," he said. "The South End is gone. Entire neighborhoods on both sides of the connection points. The cliff-side terraces above and below Daughtry's mansion ..." He trailed off, shaking his head. "It's all gone. It's at the bottom of the gorge somewhere."

She covered her mouth with her hands.

"But—" Jackson stopped her when they reached the veranda. "The rumor is that Daughtry and the Lady Glare left days ago. They released their servants and sent a bunch of them away. I met one of them at a makeshift camp for the displaced elves who don't have anywhere to go. A little maid I always liked. I sent her to Ioma at the orchard. Anyway, it's believed the lady knew about the attack somehow and they slipped away. They escaped."

"Thank God," Tanna said.

"Well, yes. But it's complicated." He lowered his voice. "If it's true, it looks bad for him. Very bad. If they knew, why wouldn't they have done something to warn the rest of us instead of just saving their own skins? It smells like treason."

"What about the governor and his wife?" Tanna asked.

"Bluff House wasn't damaged."

"Come talk to Holly," she said, pulling him around to the front porch. She quickly recounted what had happened with the intruder. Holly and Jackson were both strangely quiet, although she observed them exchanging looks. "What is it?" Tanna asked Holly. "Do you know something about these papers the man said he was looking for?"

Holly looked at Jackson again.

"Tell her," he said firmly. "I haven't said a word. But you need to tell her yourself."

Holly cleared her throat. "They were drawings," she said, looking at her hands. "Some kind of blueprints. I heard Papa bragging about stealing them from somebody. And when I saw them there with the money—your money that I stole back for you—I just grabbed them. I don't know why. I wish I hadn't. I was afraid to say anything to anybody. I kept putting it off. I wasn't sure what to do with them, but I knew somebody like Papa shouldn't have those kinds of plans."

"What were the plans for?" Tanna asked calmly.

Holly looked up, her eyes smudged with fatigue and worry. "Guns," she said softly. "Some kind of magical guns."

Tanna glanced at Jackson. He nodded at Holly to continue.

The girl swallowed. "I left them at Cole's. At the orchard. When we stopped there after crossing through the towers on foot. I thought it might be the reason we were being followed, and I just wanted to get rid of them as soon as possible. Remember, we didn't know if he was dead or if he would come through after us. So I hid them. In the barn behind the stables."

"I'm going to suggest Holly go hide herself there as well," Jackson said.

Tanna frowned. "Who's to say they won't go there next? They probably know it's the first place we went that day after crossing back into the Green."

"Well, I want you all to go there," he said. "The orchard is more heavily fortified than you may realize. Cole had his own private army."

"You mean those hideous little goblins that attacked me when I was strolling the grounds?" Tanna said.

"If I remember correctly," Jackson said, challenging her haughty tone, and only partly teasing her, "you went to a part of the property you had been expressly forbidden to explore, broke through a locked gate, and went boldly snooping through the groves."

"I did not *break* into anything," Tanna said, her voice rising. "That gate was unlocked. It was just hanging open."

He ignored her. To Holly, he said, "If you stay inside the house, you'll be perfectly safe. Unfortunately, the spells that protect the outbuildings, like the barn and the stables, are significantly weaker."

"That's where she hid the damned things!" Tanna interrupted.

Jackson held up a hand, demanding her patience. "I retrieved them. When she told me about them. I hid them in the house, and even Cole didn't know where. I think it's better if I don't tell you, then you don't have to lie about it if anyone asks."

"You mean if the Graycoat and his men capture her and try to torture it out of her," Tanna said archly.

"Let's not waste our concern on something that's not going to happen," Jackson said. "Don't go snooping around the house trying to find them. You'll only wind up on Ioma's bad side. Just leave them be, and I'll deal with them when I get back."

"Back from where?" Holly asked before Tanna had a chance to.

"I've agreed to fly some reconnaissance for General Scofield. They want a simple flyover of areas that are the hardest to reach on foot. We need to see if the hoards hit anything else in the colony we haven't heard about yet."

"You always said you didn't want to get involved," Tanna argued.

"I know. But it's different now," Jackson said. "And I have *Gypsy*. Whom else can they ask?" He tapped Holly's knee. "Go get your things together. I'll fly you. It would take weeks to get to the orchard by the Big South Road right now. With all the people and horses on it, one thunderstorm and it's going to turn into a quagmire."

Holly handed the rifle to Tanna and ran into the house.

"I'm assuming your plans have been delayed," Jackson said.

Tanna gestured helplessly. "Obviously I'm not leaving today. Do we even know if airships are still departing from Old Rath Station? I can't imagine anyone in the colony just carrying on as if everything were normal."

"I can certainly take a look down there as well. It's the reason I'm doing the flyover."

Tanna waved the thought away. "Do what needs to be done. I'm ahead of schedule vacating the premises. I can stay."

"Well, you can't stay here any longer than absolutely necessary," Jackson said. "I'll go ahead and take the girls now, before we lose light. They can both fit in the front compartment together. I'll come back for you and Ginger first thing in the morning."

Tanna nodded.

"I don't like the thought of you being alone here tonight, though," he said.

She lifted the rifle and raised her eyebrows. "I'm a good shot, you know."

He smiled. "I remember."

"And I'm not alone," Tanna said. "Still is here. Joona, Navvee. I haven't seen Gentry or Davis since before the attack ... They may have already wandered away."

"I'll see you tomorrow," Jackson said.

"Until tomorrow, then," she said.

—

She sat on the floor of the living room, smoking, tossing the ashes into a cold cup of tea and leafing through the crates of Jackson's books. They were the only things left in the house other than her personal luggage. She wasn't sure if they would fit in his aircraft—if the storage compartment were large enough, if it would be too much weight—or if he'd still need to send someone after them.

She hated the thought of leaving them unattended in this empty house, one of Graycoat's goons coming to rifle through them ...

He was later than he said he'd be. By the position of the shadows, she guessed it was getting close to eleven a.m.

As she waited, she glanced through a few of her favorite titles, partly to pass the time, mostly to say goodbye to them. She'd grown fond of Jackson's books in the months they had lived in her library. She found it harder to give up his books than all her other possessions combined.

She finally heard boots in the hall, and picked up a volume of poetry she'd set aside with an envelope marking a particular page. She'd found a stanza she wanted to read aloud to him, verses about a mossy bank beside a stream in another world ... The description could have been their camp on the Yooway River.

She cleared her throat as the footsteps approached—wondered why he was walking so slowly—and began to read in her best projected voice.

After the first two opening lines, she glanced up for his reaction.

It wasn't Jackson.

"Buck." She shut the book with a snap, frowning to cover her embarrassment. "What are you doing here?"

Buck said nothing. He stood there, turning his hat in his hands as if trying to find the right words.

She sighed, remaining seated on the floor but leaning back on her arms. She braced herself for some annoying request, for him to shred whatever peace remained to her.

"I would offer you a drink," she said, nodding at the cup overflowing with cigarette butts. "But that was the last cup of tea I plan to have in this house. And I'm afraid I don't have anything stronger."

"Jackson has been killed."

She stared at him, waiting for him to take it back, to apologize for such a cruel and ill-timed joke.

"His airship crashed," he said, holding her gaze with no trace of humor.

Her expression shifted into anger—contempt directed at Buck for hurting her, for being the one to say these words out loud to her.

But then she paled. Hey eyes flashed, remembering something. "The girls ..."

"No no no." He rushed to quiet her, holding out his hand. "They weren't with him. He had already dropped them off. He was alone."

She reached for her cigarettes, her hand trembling with the match.

"It was too dark. There was no moon," Buck continued. "He probably couldn't see. He shouldn't have gone up at all. But they think he may have been shot down. They aren't sure yet. There was a fire ..." He trailed off. "It happened late last night. I left to come tell you as soon as I could, hours ago, but the roads are still full of people trying to get out of Treebridge. I had to abandon the buggy and ride on horseback." He paused again to give her a chance to say something. "But I can drive your buggy, if you like. Take you back to town. Or wherever you need to go."

Almost casually, staring at the wall as if she were trying to visualize it, she asked, "Who decided to send you?"

He shrugged. "I thought I should be the one to come."

She looked at him, the anger still there but shifting toward wonder.

"You're awfully brave," she said.

51

She brought the men out to Dead Tree Hill a few days early to dig the grave. She showed them the exact spot where she and Jackson had spread their blanket on the ground. She even laid down in the tall grass to orient the grave a few degrees off due east, facing the part of the view he loved most. She propped herself up on her elbows and declared it just right.

—

Ioma silently assisted Tanna in making all the necessary arrangements, while the pine elf Giselle took care of her girls. Jackson had found the little maid in the aftermath of the attacks on Treebridge, after the Daughtrys had fled, and sent her to Ioma for employment at the orchard.

The wake was held at the house, but the path from the north gate to Dead Tree Hill would have taken them through the forbidden groves, so they caravanned the long way round up to the Hawkeye Pass. At least they were able to take advantage of the roads for most of the trek; it was challenging enough to get an entire funeral party on foot for the remaining quarter-mile across the mountain saddle.

Tanna insisted they employ *Jewel* to lift the casket. They attached the living dirigible to the funeral wagon and pulled it up to the site. Then, she wrapped the tentacle vines around her hand and directed the creature with little more than her thoughts, allowing her to bear Jackson's body to the grave without anyone's help.

—

She stood with her back to the prairie, at the foot of the rectangular hole, noticing that the right angles seemed too perfect for this wilderness. She clutched a small book to her chest, squeezing her fingers inside to hold her place. When the crowd had all managed to pick their way through the tall golden grass and gather together like crows, Tanna pitched her voice to carry over the wind.

She read the poem she'd intended to read him the day he returned to Brynmor to pick her up and fly her to safety.

Midway through the recitation, she took a breath and glanced up at the assembled mourners. Something caught her eye. There, up on the hill, beneath the dead thorn tree, a silhouette. It was Kanute. She recognized him immediately. What other Unseelie warrior would have come to witness this event? There was no question it was him, only how he had managed the miracle.

She wondered if the ghosts of the fae could appear more easily than those of humans. Maybe it was a dark Unseelie magic that made it possible.

She pulled herself back to the duty at hand, and when she completed the poem, she paused to let the words hang in the air. She looked back up to the spot where she had seen Kanute. The apparition was gone.

"Now, take back the soul of Jackson Hamish Gallagher, whom you have shared with us," she intoned in a formal, ministerial voice. "He was not ours. He wasn't mine."

She exhaled loudly, a shuddering breath, and steeled herself. Holding the book in one hand, she awkwardly knelt beside the neat mound to take a handful of dirt with the other. Still stepped over to support her elbow when she stood. She tried to shake the dirt onto the coffin beneath her. She heard a few rattling pebbles and rasping particles hit the smooth wood. But her hand would not work properly. She couldn't unclench her fist. She couldn't let the dirt go.

She tried to inhale slowly and deliberately, but a hiccoughing breath caught in her throat. It hurt. The sob was stuck there. She clutched the fistfuls of dirt and poetry to her chest and walked away from the assembly, down the hill, toward the view that Jackson's grave would point to forever.

—

"You don't have to go back," Holly whined, repeating it for the hundredth time.

Holly, Eve, and Ginger were piled on Tanna's bed, watching her pack. It was the same guest room she stayed in at the orchard house after she returned to the Green with Holly on foot.

"I don't have any money," Tanna said, exasperated that she had to keep saying it. "And I have to find out what happened to Teddy. I have to."

"Jackson would want you to stay here. I know he would."

"Jackson and I discussed this, more than once," Tanna insisted, stuffing clothes into her train case. Still would be driving them to Old Rath in a few hours, and from there they would board the airship for Cloudland Canyon. The next bedroom she slept in would be her own at Blackwood. Lowering her voice Tanna said, "Ioma is the lady of this house. She has been for a very long time. You may not understand why, but it just wouldn't be right for me to stay on here. You'll have to trust me on this."

"Well, I'm here," Holly said. "And I'm a ... *lady*." She grimaced at the word.

On another day, it would have made Tanna laugh. "Your being here is an arrangement Jackson made with Ioma's knowledge. He brought you here himself." She studied Holly as she sulked. "You can come to Blackwood too, you know, if you want to stay with us."

Holly immediately shook her head. "I'm feral. I'd die in the Gray."

"Well, you've been back and forth more than anyone I know," Tanna said. "You can continue to do so. The crossing at the towers is only a few hours' walk from here. You can come and see us as often as you want."

Eve frowned. "Will I die in the Gray?"

Tanna shot Holly an accusing glance. "No," she said. "You most certainly will not. Of all the souls I've met in all the worlds I've been to, I'd bet you're the one who can live anywhere. Both of you have that quality, actually. You're my changeling girls."

"Why do they say it's gray there?" Eve asked. "Isn't there any green at all?"

"There are both," Tanna said. "It's not as beautiful as it is here, but the Gray has its own kind of magic. It's different—it's people magic, not fairy magic. There are wonderful machines of which you've never seen the like. Carriages that move on their own, with no need for horses." Tanna could see reflections in the child's eyes of the tale spinner shadows starting to flicker behind her.

"Can I ride in them?" Eve asked, as if it were the one part of a bargain she would seriously consider.

"Someday, you can even *drive* them yourself," Tanna said, widening her eyes. "Teddy knows how. He can teach you."

—

Carrying the bags down the stairs, Holly made her last pitch for Ginger. "She'll live longer here," the girl insisted. "She's getting old. What if the time goes by really fast and she dies before I come to Blackwood?"

"Then don't wait to come and visit," Tanna said.

They paused for a moment in the foyer to let Ioma open the door for them. Without setting down her bags, Tanna leaned close to Holly and said in a low voice, "Please understand. I can't abandon her again. I have no way of explaining it to her." They both looked at Ginger, who was happily scrambling past Eve. "You will come to Blackwood."

"And you'll come back here," Holly insisted.

Tanna couldn't resist asking her one more time. "Are you sure you're going to be OK here? I don't like leaving you on your own."

"I'll be fine," Holly said, groaning. "There are spells all over this place, just like Jackson said." The girl's tone changed, and she looked at her feet. "So, when we get outside, I'm going to put these bags by the buggy, and then I'm going to walk away really fast. I'm not going to hug and say goodbye and cry and all that. I'm just going to walk away, OK?"

The muscles in Tanna's throat ached from keeping her voice steady. "Yes, of course. It's a good trick. I've used it myself."

Holly nodded. "Don't let them follow me," she whispered. She launched herself through the front door and across the porch, passing Eve and Ginger on the steps. She placed the bags on the gravel at Still's feet and took off down the path toward the meadow and the stables.

"Holly!" Eve called out, and Ginger started barking. Tanna managed to drop her bags and grab the girl's hand, but the dog had already slipped down the stairs and was chasing after Holly.

Tanna watched helplessly as Holly turned and crouched for the dog to run into her arms. She knelt on the ground with her arms wrapped around Ginger, her hair hiding her face. It looked like she was telling the dog a secret. And then she stood and pointed for the dog to return to the house. She looked up to lock eyes with Tanna for one excruciating moment, pleading.

"Ginger!" Tanna called, praying her voice wouldn't break. "Come!"

Ginger hesitated, looking back and forth between them, visibly torn. The bond was only slightly stronger, or maybe it was just older—maybe it was Holly telling her to go that made her obey—but she reluctantly returned to her mistress.

Tanna immediately busied herself helping Still with the luggage so she wouldn't be tempted to watch Holly walk away. Once she had Ginger and Eve settled in the seat, she stole a glance toward the meadow, and the girl was mercifully gone.

Tanna put her hand on Ioma's wrist and looked into the fairy woman's eyes, trying to imitate the wordless communication of the Alleegee. As with Still, there was a faint narrowing of the eyes that conveyed something deeper than a smile or warmth or even respect. Ioma's gaze held her in full acknowledgment. She willed it to be reflected back.

Then a thought struck her, and her face must have changed because Ioma actually looked startled. "What is it?" she asked.

Tanna blinked it away. "I'm sorry. I just realized I never said goodbye to Brynmor." She looked at Still, stricken. "With everything that happened—Jackson—I rushed here. And I never went back. I didn't think to stop and look around one last time."

"It was only an empty house," Still said, taking her by the arm, lifting her and physically placing her in the buggy, compliant as a doll or a sleepwalker. "Your memories are full."

—

She would have recognized the members of The Fairchild club without the sign hanging above them, because they were all together. She had rarely been tested by encountering them individually. They were the type of men who only seemed to exist in one another's company. They were somehow all the same, like penguins or the chorus in a Greek tragedy.

Old Rath Station was little more than a collection of three huge, vaulted buildings—*hangars*, the locals called them—opening onto a central lawn with a large oak tree shading the grass and a tall, sturdy tower for boarding the dirigibles. Two of the hangars held dirigibles undergoing some type of repairs or maintenance. The third hangar was similar to a train station—it held offices, a ticket window, and a large schedule board with a map. There were rustic accommodations for waiting passengers, such as benches, picnic tables, and even a counter selling sandwiches, coffee, and lemonade.

The members of The Fairchild had taken over most of the tables that spilled out onto the lawn under the tree. Tanna recognized The Fairchild sign from the façade of the establishment in the Treebridge promenade. Someone had rescued it, much charred but miraculously intact, and placed it in the crook of a low branch above the assembled members. They were generously tipping their flasks into each other's cups, drinking and talking loudly about what was surely a dark milestone in most of their lives and fortunes.

At first she wondered what they could possibly all be doing together like this, miles from Treebridge. But then, of course, many of them were now leaving, as she was. Some returning for good. A few were staying behind to manage common interests and were only here to see off their friends and business partners. Everywhere were small huddles of travelers sharing last-minute instructions. Arranged along the benches under the hangar roof were the female counterparts of the men in the resurrected Fairchild club, rows of women and girls drinking tea off cups and saucers balanced on their knees.

Tanna dreaded interacting with either crowd. She gave Eve permission to walk Ginger on her leash along the margins of the lawn. She wandered over to take her place in line for the ticket window where she could confirm her reservation. Still joined her at the end of the long line snaking past the benches, its tail in the middle of the grass. They stood there together, between the cocktail-swilling men and their tea-drinking wives and daughters. She was aware she stood significantly closer to the tarwater. She half-hoped someone might offer her something stronger than tea.

Grant Woodall rose from a nearby table and made his way decidedly in her direction, walking with his hands clasped behind his back and an expectant, apologetic smirk on one side of his face.

"Oh God," Tanna muttered under her breath. "Is that pompous ass seriously going to come over and remind me I'm not allowed on the premises? I'm standing in a line in a public station. How do they expect to enforce such a rule with no walls? A sign in a tree is hardly a clearly defined jurisdiction."

Still half-turned, discreetly glancing to watch the man approach.

"Prepare yourself," Tanna whispered. "He may try to have me removed from the grassy lawn."

"Mrs. Eldridge," Woodall said warmly.

"Mr. Woodall," Tanna said coolly, eyebrow arched, her lips barely moving.

"We wondered if we might invite you to have a drink with us?"

"With us?" Tanna asked, a little rudely. She was taken off guard, alert for some sign it was a joke at her expense. "Whom do you mean by we?"

"Well, the members," Woodall said, sweeping an open hand toward the men at the tables. "The members of The Fairchild."

She looked over at them suspiciously. They had all gone silent, frozen in a tableau as if waiting for a photographer to take their picture. Many of them were smiling at her. A few nodded gravely. One gentleman raised his cup to her in a stately gesture.

She looked back at Woodall, searching his face.

He smiled meekly, his head inclined, looking up at her through his brows.

"All right," she said fearlessly. She felt the women's gossip go silent as every head in the hangar turned to watch her. "Maybe just one."

She asked Still to keep their place in line and allowed Woodall to escort her to a table directly beneath the tree. The men all stood as she passed, like she was a bride in the aisle. A nervous young man in a bow tie and apron asked her if she wanted her tea with or without tarwater.

"The tarwater, please," Tanna said, "and hold the tea."

"Two of those," Woodall said, nodding at the barkeep.

The men all chuckled, one drunk fool among them laughing loudly and banging on a table.

Tanna took the chipped china cup and discreetly sniffed the familiar fumes of rotting flowers. All the members were watching her with a similar expression, obviously expecting her to say something. A few words; a toast, maybe.

"To all those we've lost, in the Green and the Gray, here with us in spirit," she intoned, raising her cup.

There were murmurs of *Hear, hear.* Someone in the crowd bellowed, "Brynmor!"

She started at the name, a thickness welling up in her throat. She scanned the faces for the one who cheered her home, but unable to place him, she looked at all of them in turn, carefully holding each individual gaze.

"Thank you." She barely managed more than a whisper, but everyone was holding his breath and straining to hear. "All of you."

She walked slowly back to Still, the women behind him staring at her, and reclaimed her place in line.

"The curse is lifted," Still said.

She swallowed with difficulty, and finding herself unable to speak, she just nodded.

—

Still walked them to the base of the boarding tower.

"Tell Still goodbye," Tanna prompted Eve.

"Bye, Still!" she called without even glancing back, already following Ginger up the stairs.

Tanna shook her head and shrugged apologetically, watching them ascend toward the dirigible, not wanting to face him.

She turned quickly and grabbed both of his hands. She looked down at their interlaced fingers. As always, his hands were dry, cool, and smooth. They could no longer be alien to her, only nimble and strong and beautiful. The hands of a pianist, a priest, or a great artist.

They had rarely ever touched each other physically, other than his protectively steering her by the elbow through darkness, over a puddle, or down from a carriage. In all the months he'd been with her, she had never seen the shape of his skull beneath his turban or the room where he slept each night. She'd never asked him about his mother or if he had ever been in love. Yet, for her time in Fairyland, he had been as constant as her shadow. She was always saying his name, calling out to him, ordering him around, demanding something from him. She had awakened herself before from a bad dream with his name leaving her lips. Here in the Green, he was an extension of her person, her opinions, her will.

Still.

Looking closely into his cat's eyes, intentionally holding the gaze with true fondness and no uncomfortable desire to end the moment, she thought it was likely she would see his face on a dark ceiling someday when she drew her last breath.

"Farewell, my friend," she said.

"How will I find you where you are going?" he asked.

It was the lingering unspoken question she thought she might get away without having to answer. She hadn't even asked him where he would go after she was gone.

She sighed. "I don't think you'll ever be able to come where I'm going. It would be dangerous for you, in so many ways. I promise you, you wouldn't like it there."

"It's not important that I like it," he said. "Only that it is where you are."

She shook her head. "It would be a hell for you. I'm not even sure how long I will last. You have to trust me on this."

He did not blink, speak, or move.

"Remember when we were on our journey, trying to find the encampment of Daughtry's men?" she asked. "You'd ride on ahead and find a good campsite, and make a bright fire."

"So that you could find your way," he said, completing the shared memory.

"Well, now I need you to make a great big fire in your heart and pray that I find my way back here."

She smiled at him warmly through her tears, hoping she was projecting all the fondness for him she had and hoping he could receive all the kindness she'd ever felt from him returned tenfold. She wished more than anything that with a look, the tale spinner shadows would rise behind her and dance, sing a song of all that she should have said to him along the way and didn't.

She turned away, planting her right foot firmly on the staircase, her hand on the rail. She pulled herself up the first two steps, but then she stopped, as surely as if she'd reached the end of a tether. She was pulled around to face him one more time.

"I want to hear you say my name," she said.

"Your name, so'onah?"

"Not *so'onah*. My name. I want to hear what my name sounds like when you say it."

"You are Tanna, so'onah. Tanna Sophia." He hesitated for half a beat and added, "Cravens."

Tanna Sophia Cravens.

She had come all this way to change her name and to become someone else and to find out who that woman was. Who it could be. An Eldridge. A Mathers. A Gallagher. The only name that ever suited her was the one with which she had started. And maybe if someone had spoken it to her the way Still just had—with grace and respect and affection and a little bit of awe— she would have heard the music in it.

52

December 23, 1926
Lookout Mountain, Tennessee

On the Thursday before Christmas, a creature from another world left a package on the doorstep in the snow. Ruby, the maid at Blackwood, swore she had seen a dark-skinned child, barefoot and nearly naked, scurry across the yard and disappear into the frozen shrubs. An "Indian," she called it.

Most envelopes that crossed the Seaming showed up years later—if at all—yellowed and soft with age. Tanna had been at home a little more than three months when the parcel arrived, crisp and creamy-white. The elven runner must have followed her out of the Green within days of her leaving.

The parcel was larger than normal correspondence and addressed to her in Holly's childlike hand. Inside was a short letter from the girl about the panthers she'd seen at the grave on Dead Tree Hill—Jackson would have liked that—and after reading the first few lines about "legal documents" she put it aside for the moment to scan the trifold of larger, stiffer pages enclosed.

Jackson Gallagher had left his estate to Tanna.

Cole Mathers's property.

The orchard—that house—and all the adjoining lands were hers, referred to throughout the will as *Havenwood*.

THIS IS NOT

THE END

THE END

FREE FICTION

For announcements, book resources, free fiction by Eric Slade, and more about the world of the Seaming,

please visit

eric-slade.com

GLOSSARY

ahdo — thank you in the Nunnahee language.

abalope — diminutive, two-legged horses.

Alleegee — the half-breed Seelie/Unseelie caste to which Still and Ioma belong.

brugh — correctly pronounced like the word brew; it is an ancient Scottish word describing a fairy dwelling. It is usually translated as 'castle' or 'mansion' but really means the interior of a barrow or hollow hill.

digadusi — hills (plural).

elven — refers to actual elf entities and their physical attributes.

elvish — refers specifically to the language, architecture, crafts, cultural artifacts of elves.

fae — a collective reference to all native beings of the fairy realm, including the Children of Lilith, the fae kin of humanity.

feral — there are two different types of feral human beings living in the Green: those who have moved from the Gray and "gone native"; and those who are genetic humans but natives of the Green (from old families who have been in the Green for generations). Many of the humans found in the fae have Native American ancestry, especially the longterm Kin.

gadusi — hill.

genies — short for indigenes or indigenous beings; usually one of several elven races — often employed as servants and field hands.

The Gray — also "the Gray world." The world of contemporary mortal humanity. What we would call the "real world."

The Green — the dimension which mortal humanity (in the southeastern North America, particularly) calls Fae, Faery, Fairyland.

idetti — grasshoppers; the small magical flying vessels engineered by humans.

keeper — a type of fae creature who "shepherds" a specific species of animal. (There are keepers in the short story "Killing Fairies" a separately published prologue which can be found at eric-slade.com .

kin — the magical, fairy cousins of any animal, entity, or race of being also found in the Gray.

misk — a small, pungent citrus fruit, similar to a tangerine.

Nunnahee — elves; the tribe of hill dwellers who live at Brynmor.

oowadaga — the red daisies the Nunnahee women give Tanna; symbolically similar to long-stemmed roses.

pakka — a Nunnahee game like soccer that the yolos play.

rath — Fairy forts (also known as raths from the Irish referring to an earthen mound) are the remains of lios (ringforts), hillforts or other circular dwellings in Ireland.[1] From (possibly) late Iron Age to early Christian times, the island's occupants built circular structures with earth banks or ditches. These were sometimes topped with wooden palisades, and wooden framed buildings. As the dwellings were not durable, in many cases only vague circular marks remain in the landscape.[2] Raths and lios are found in all parts of Ireland.

tarwater — distilled spirits made from the resin of the haint plant.

Ti'waga — the people of the red maple.

T'looga — a race of migrant tree-dwelling elves.

topis — an ornamental vine that can form a roof of a broad green leathery leaves and yellow flowers.

velvet — a fairy animal found in the Green that appears to be a species of Mustelidae, such the as ermine, ferrets, minks, stoats, weasels and other mustelidae found in the Gray.

wawona — the big trees.

yolo; yolos — the littlest Nun'nahee children.

yoonaygah — disparaging term for white man.

For other resources such as maps, locations, origin of the Nunnahee language, historical background, and more, please visit the author's website:

eric-slade.com

ACKNOWLEDGMENTS

I am most indebted to my early readers, beta readers, and advance readers. Special thanks to Tina Rives Smith, Randi Chastain, and Julie Marie Jones for valuable insights. I am grateful to the following for spotting corrections: Bonnie Hack, Janet Thomasson, and Laura Dunn.

The book would not exist in its finished form without the keen eye, intelligence, grammar knowledge, and mad skills of my editor Ashley Hopkins. (Thank you Sean Phipps for the introduction!)

Special thanks to my publicist Rebecca Feldbin who watched me sigh a lot across a cafe table for months on end and urged me on. To Lacy Seale for continued anti-psychic advice and for listening to me talk about my book.

Thanks to the baristas of The Camp House for the pots of Earl Grey. (This is what I was working on, guys!) Thanks also to the alternate Sunday baristas at Brash for that one perfect pour-over per week.

Forever grateful to my parents who always believed this was what I was going to do when I grew up, and encouraged me to believe it too. Thank you Joan for staying up late to finish the book.

And last, but not least, a big tear-filled long silent hug to Seth Crews who hovered nearby for fifteen years as I built the world of the Seaming. No one on earth could have been the fairy godfather to my fictional children that you have been.

ABOUT THE AUTHOR

Eric Slade holds a degree in English from the University of Georgia and lives in Chattanooga, Tennessee.

For free fiction—as well as information about the world of the Green, the Seaming, and Havenwood—please visit:

eric-slade.com

OTHER NOVELS BY ERIC SLADE

Cloudbusting

www.ingramcontent.com/pod-product-compliance
Lightning Source LLC
Chambersburg PA
CBHW031939260626
47157CB00016B/24